PRAISE FOR *IMMORTAL LIFE*

"A rattling good yarn. . . . An engaging and cautionary tale about the direction in which Spaceship Earth is hurtling. . . . Bing's unsettling account of the future is leavened with wry humor and satire. His job is not to be a seer but rather to conjure an entertaining narrative, one that periodically lends itself to commentary on the planet's present plight."

—*USA Today*

"Stimulating, satirical, and perhaps even visionary."

—*The Wall Street Journal*

"Bing uses a light touch, biting mockery of Silicon Valley culture, and grotesque imagery to good effect."

—*Kirkus Reviews*

"Wildly entertaining."

—*Publishers Weekly*

"*Immortal Life* is one of those terrific books you'd take along if you had to escape to a desert island. Which is looking increasingly likely."

—Stephen Colbert

"The well-known, pseudonymous author Stanley Bing has written a suspenseful, sharp-eyed, and entertaining tale for our artificially intelligent times. *Immortal Life* has its finger on the pulse of a generation determined to live forever."

—Christopher Buckley, author of *The Relic Master*

"Bing has been poking fun at business for decades, and his satire of absurd gadgets, virtual life, and techno-billionaires flips all the right switches."

—*The Washington Post*

T0083970

BOOKS BY STANLEY BING

NONFICTION

NOVELS

IMMORTAL LIFE

(A SOON TO BE TRUE STORY)

STANLEY BING

Simon & Schuster Paperbacks

New York   London   Toronto   Sydney   New Delhi

Simon & Schuster Paperbacks
An Imprint of Simon & Schuster, Inc.
1230 Avenue of the Americas
New York, NY 10020

First Simon & Schuster trade paperback edition October 2018

SIMON & SCHUSTER PAPERBACKS and colophon are registered trademarks of Simon & Schuster, Inc.

For information about special discounts for bulk purchases, please contact Simon & Schuster Paperbacks Special Sales at 1-866-506-1949 or business@simonandschuster.com.

The Simon & Schuster Speakers Bureau can bring authors to your live event. For more information or to book an event, contact the Simon & Schuster Speakers Bureau at 1-866-248-3049 or visit our website at www.simonspeakers.com.

Interior design by Paul Dippolito

Manufactured in the United States of America

1   3   5   7   9   10   8   6   4   2

Library of Congress Cataloging-in-Publication Data is available.

ISBN 978-1-5011-1983-5
ISBN 978-1-5011-1984-2 (pbk)
ISBN 978-1-5011-1985-9 (ebook)

To Craig Venter, Larry Ellison, Sergey Brin and Larry Page,
Mark Zuckerberg, Marc Andreessen, Elon Musk, and all
the visionary titans of tech now exploring the possibility of
eternal life for those who can afford it.

When you talk to a human in 2035, you'll be talking to someone that's a combination of biological and nonbiological intelligence.

—*Ray Kurzweil, Google*

If emulation of particular brains is possible and affordable, and if concerns about individual identity can be met, such emulation would enable backup copies and "digital immortality."

—*Nick Bostrom, Oxford University*

I don't want to achieve immortality through my work. I want to achieve it through not dying.

—*Woody Allen*

Contents

– ONE –

1

Le Morte d'Arthur

The room was kept dark on purpose, a soft pin spot here and there, because at the age of 127, the creature that had once been Arthur Vogel couldn't stand bright light. It hurt his eyes, his skin, the tiny blisters that had formed at the top of his skull. Also, he couldn't tolerate being seen clearly by anybody but Sallie, not even by himself. Hence the absence of mirrors, the proscription against implements that had the capacity to record video.

A while back, at the age of 103 or so, Arthur had retired from public view almost entirely. There he nestled on his vast estate in the pastoral heart of the urban sprawl that stretched from Santa Barbara to San Diego: by day, on his vast outside patio soaking in the vitamin D that he believed would keep him alive forever; after sunset, retreating to his private study to feed the lizards, toads, and spiders that inhabited his massive assemblage of terrariums; and throughout, at all hours, constantly, incessantly doing business through the wireless communications implant that ran beneath the wafer-thin layer of his skull.

Yet as powerful a digital presence as he still might be, he had for some time not actually been seen by human or inhuman eyes; he who had once been the most visible mogul in his coterie of behemoths, the center of a prodigious entourage whose dissolute hijinks had become the stuff of legend, the subject of more ridiculous scandal than Emperor Tiberius in his prime. Orgies! Bottomless onslaughts of willing, wily gold diggers! More ex-wives than the sultan of Brunei! Yachts! Private islands steeped in unpardonable sins! And now—nothing. This absence led to some speculation about his whereabouts, his health overall, and his ability to manage the enormous empire that was currently valued at $63.1 trillion in global operations alone—and that didn't count the growing hydroponic farm now being built under the surface of the planet of Musk, formerly known as Mars, where he had been first to strike water back in 2034.

Physically, he was all right, as far as it went. But it couldn't go on like this for much longer. Arthur himself knew that. There were limits to the art of life extension, and he had reached them.

He began every day the same way. At three thirty in the morning, his eyes popped open as if a starting gun had gone off inside his head, and there was no more sleep after that. This was the hard time. The vast beyond beckoned to him then: the possibility that he would not exist; that this magnificent edifice he had built would have the temerity to go on without him. It was then that he was most human; the least fortified with the armature of fame and wealth and technology. It was then that he felt the terror of what most certainly lay ahead if his plan did not succeed and he did not find a permanent solution to the problem of death.

A solution was clearly called for, that was for fucking sure.

So Arthur, who had once been known to friends and enemies alike as the "Mighty Vog," faced up to the darkness that gripped his heart like a vise in the dead middle of each night and did what he had done since he was a little boy back in the lost, long-ago twentieth century: he got busy.

There was always a lot to do. First, he had to put himself together, which was no inconsiderable task. For more than a year, even Sallie had not seen him in his raw self—what he was before the application of implants, cyberware, and wetware, which were brought to bear each day upon the desiccated nugget of flesh that remained of his original body.

First came the eye, which was the beginning of all things. The eye was loaded with hardware and software that interfaced directly with all the original neurostructure that lay behind it and was the link between his brain and the rest of the intelligent objects that would be added on and expected to obey his unspoken commands. The communications hookups were already loaded into his head, of course, as they were with the superelite that had gotten tired, some twenty years before, of carrying around all those stupid smartphones and, without much trouble, given the limitless human and financial assets at their disposal, figured out a way to place all the necessary electronics into the hard bone that sat right behind the earlobe. Put the eye and the implant together, and you had a pretty fair operating platform suitable for just about any support function.

The thing about the eye, though, was that it was very, very delicate. The least little jostle of the tiny gelatinous orb brought down the whole mechanism. Since each new one took months to build, program, and field-test, this was a verifiable fucking pain in the neck for sure. Not that cost was any real issue, but he still got a little pang when he was forced to shell out more than $2.5 million for a backup that he knew would work 100 percent without fail, hopefully. The thing itself was pretty disgusting, too, he thought as he gently inserted it in its socket and heard the soft *click* that indicated it was seated correctly in position. Like tenderly placing two fingers of frog guts into your head. He would be glad when he didn't have to do it anymore. That day was coming.

The rest was a little easier. Propped by the side of his bed was the hip-and-leg assembly that made his limited mobility possible. It was very strong and supple, a welcome addition since—What was it? Six? Ten years ago?—they had pretty much written off the right side of his body completely. Fine, he said. Then he invented the fucking thing himself. Made the sketches. Called in Bob. Had the entire assembly printed—bones, muscles, veins, arteries and capillaries, the knee and all its delicate cartilage, the joints, whatever. That was no big deal; they had been able to print just about anything for years. Implementing an installation process he could accomplish by himself—now, *that* had been a real bear. That was when a guy like Bob really came in handy. Patient. Brilliant in his own way. Willing to do anything if the science of it presented a challenge to him. Very valuable guy, Bob. Key guy, really. Now more than ever. Had to watch him, though. Motherfucker could get the idea in his head that it was he who was running things.

Arthur put the $6 billion leg in place and felt the pulse kick in on the cyborg ankle. He rose to his feet and carefully walked to the door of his bedroom, which whispered open as he approached.

"Diego," he said into the murky dark that lay outside his threshold.

In a beat or two, there was a small rustling not far off and then a pleasant hum, which grew modestly in volume until its source materialized in the doorway. The object in question was a circular, Frisbee-sized platter, perhaps eight inches thick, glowing about its edges, that could be described as a cross between a nineteenth-generation Roomba and a late-century Hoverboard. It floated in midair about chest high. This was Diego, Arthur's virtual manservant. Imbued with modest AI, Diego was capable of performing many household functions: carrying messages, making simple reservations and appointments and audio/video calls, and, of course, cleaning carpets and doing some light dusting. The original human Diego, who had served Arthur for more than thirty years, had expired due to old age some years prior. Arthur, missing his amanuensis and friend, had downloaded a wide variety of messages and responses into the little android that the original Diego had been kind enough to record in advance of his demise. And so Diego, in a sense, lived on—not in his own consciousness, because he was dead—but in that of his master. It was insufficient as a source of comfort and companionship that the real Diego had provided. But it was something.

"Good morning, Diego," said Arthur to the floating Roomba. "I'm up. I know it's early. I hope I didn't disturb your slumber."

"Not at all," said Diego. "I'm always awake at this hour. Come to think of it, I'm awake at every hour."

Arthur recognized that this was not one of the prerecorded responses the nonvirtual Diego had provided to the database. It was clear that the machine was learning as it went along, adding to its trove of potential replies with new rejoinders assembled by its rudimentary artificial intelligence. This was either amusing or not, Arthur thought. With originality of thought came a host of other possibilities, not all of them congenial to servitude.

"I'll have my breakfast now," said Arthur.

"What will you have, sir?" asked Diego, hovering in the air before his face, but tilting a little bit, as a dog will do when it strikes a position of inquiry.

"I want a big fat steak," said Arthur truculently.

"I will bring you a bowl of berries and a small portion of synthetic yogurt."

"Okay, goddamn it," said Arthur. It was true that the massive T-bone in his imagination, if he ate even a small portion of its crusty, salty, fatty magnificence, would kill him: stick in his ancient craw and choke him to death. He also felt very strongly that it was more than worth dying for. Steak! God, to eat a steak! Chew it with a strong, working set of teeth and feel its delectable juices slide down his powerful, muscular gullet and into a resilient stomach that could process a tin can if such was required. But no. Those days were over. Anything more dense than a raspberry or a bowl of gruel was to him as potentially lethal as a schuss down one of the black diamond slopes he used to run with ease at Gstaad. This was no life, no life at all. He would not tolerate it one second longer than was required. Call Bob, he thought. Nail down the timetable. "And tell Sallie she can come in now," Arthur added, slipping his day teeth into his mouth.

"Thank you, sir," said Diego. "And may I say you look your best today," he added, and left. What did a compliment mean from a floating Roomba? When he was a boy, the talking elevator had made its appearance. He remembered the first time one had told him to "Have a nice day." Well-wishing mechanical entities had proliferated since then. He still didn't find them convincing, but the penalty for failure to embrace what was defined as progress was severe—not just socially but economically as well. So he had chosen to lead the parade rather than resist it. And now he would do so again.

The defeat of death was no small achievement, after all. It could be considered the crowning achievement of a life, particularly if that life were established to be of a very high quality—and without end.

There was much to do. While even the earliest birds were still huddled in their cold, dark nests at this hour on the verge of the continent, it was a bright day on the East Coast, late morning in London, and tomorrow in Mumbai and Macao. And in all these locations, there were his people, hard at work doing whatever it was they were supposed to do in pursuit of corporate profit, each of them trembling with fear at the possibility that if Arthur got it in his mind to call them, they would not be on hand to greet him with shiny noses and bushy tails. So he did what he always did to fend off the despair that comes with early wakefulness. He contacted people at every corner of the globe and frightened them to death.

Arthur didn't have to scream and yell anymore to give them a hot blast of motivation. His low, almost imperceptible rasp was enough to throw even the heartiest two-star general into anal rictus. "Are you aware, Mr. Georgikashvili, that it is almost February, and the pylons have yet to be put into place?" he would whisper to the manager of a project designed to redefine the function of the Black Sea, which was now all but empty. "I'm hoping I interpreted the launch schedule wrong, Dick," he barked very quietly at the engineer in charge of the interplanetary space station shuttle. Quiet barking was a skill one developed over time, particularly when it became a necessity. It was hard to achieve volume when the sound was being generated by artificial vocal cords, even very good ones. A final call was made to a small island off the coast of Vanuatu, in the South Seas, which he had owned since his early seventies, when his wealth had grown so extreme that it shocked even him.

How in the world could one person get so rich? He wondered about it every day. It seemed to him that his life had been an unending pageant of relatively ordinary events, each of them taking up time, but, in the end, he had been granted no time at all. Where had it all gone? For instance, back in the day (as they used to say back in the day), Arthur had attended something called Woodstock: a concert that had, at the time, embodied the chaotic hopes and ideals of his peers. Jettisoning those as soon as he reached manhood, he plunged with his customary focus into his true calling: making money. He had been in finance for about a decade, made a plump bundle, and retired by the time he was thirty-five to tinker around in a small laboratory he maintained in his garage. There he pursued dark studies, working for weeks at a time without food or sleep, delving deep into the practical applications on the leading edge of science. Synthetic viruses, for example, were then all the rage, along with other entities that bridged the gap between organic and inorganic. The gray area between life and death—that was his hobby, his obsession. At one point, he had a wife and a couple of children, but at about this time, they fell away from him, and nothing had been heard of them for many years. They were not part of the necessary database.

In the early part of the current century, Arthur had invented a tiny nanomagnetic switch based on quantum electronics that was capable of being both on and off at the same time. Nobody could think of a use for it until it was discovered to be essential in constructing the first generation of machines that could truly think in a meaningful, human sense of the term. The ability to sustain two conflicting thoughts simultaneously appeared to be a fundamental part of genuine cognition. The nanomag relay made this possible. It had yet to be supplanted by any subsequent design, and Arthur was now worth several trillion dollars—an amount that seemed large but, in truth, didn't go as far as it used to. There were at least a dozen trillionaires on the *Forbes* list, although he was the leading one. Virtually limitless resources were at his disposal. There was nothing he couldn't afford or do if he got the idea into his head. Now he had gotten it into his head to call Vanuatu.

"Hello, Eddie," he said into the air in front of his face. His utterance was picked up by the infinitely tiny wire that ran up his mandible and into the wireless pod that nestled in the mastoid bone behind his right ear. "Tell me about the sunrise," he said wistfully. Of course, Arthur could pick up a live hologram of the rising sun itself from the setup he had installed on the island, but this was better: one real, nonvirtual human being to another. There is no better sight than that which is provided by your mind's eye, properly stimulated. Eddie was surprisingly good at that.

Eddie had been born on the island when there were people there. Now there was just him—all four hundred pounds of him, usually in a sarong, because that was all that would fit him. He was accompanied by six dogs and a giant Komodo dragon that might have been one of the original residents of the place. His job was to take care of things on Vanuatu in anticipation of the day when Arthur would arrive and greet the sunset of his life. Eddie would do so until he died and then would be replaced by a new Eddie. He was fine with the solitude. He was a poet by nature and had a trove of the best weed in the world. His descriptions of the sun, the moon, the rain, the stars, were a little different every day, but, then, so was nature. He spoke to Arthur about that for a while. Arthur sat there, watching his terrariums, and listened.

After some time, there was a change in the density of the air in the room, and a very mild scent of something ineffably beautiful crept in, and Arthur knew that quietly, in the darkness, Sallie had arrived.

"Hi, Artie," she said. He turned off his head and felt her presence.

"Where the fuck have you been?" he said, not impolitely.

"Asleep," said Sallie. "Like most normal people."

She came close and sat on the bed. She was in her morning caftan, which was bright orange and very roomy. Her hair was tousled high on her head, tied into a giant exclamation point by a ribbon. Sallie appeared to be a rather youngish forty, but that could mean anything. Tall—way taller than Arthur. High cheekbones. Lovely bottom. Not a big nose for the size of her face, but not a small one, either. A little bit of a button on the end. A few freckles, if you looked close.

"I missed you, teacup," said Arthur.

"Take your medicine?" asked Sallie.

She disappeared into the massive bathroom suite that lay beyond the bedroom.

"I want you," he said quietly.

"We can have a very good time if you take all your meds," came the voice from the dark beyond.

"Fuck," said Arthur. "I hate this shit."

Sallie came back with a tray that held a variety of bottles, tubes, and poultices, and a big glass of water. She handed him a large brown pill, scored in two. "Your Denamarin Chewable for your liver." He took it. She presented another: this one small and light yellow. "Now your Renagel, for your phosphorus." He took that, too. "Eat this little water cracker," she said, offering him a pale wafer. "You're supposed to take the Renagel with a little food and water." He took it and munched on it for a few moments with an expression of mild disgust.

"It's dry," he said, with a little tang of complaint in his voice.

"I'm sorry, Snooks," said Sallie. "Put out your palm." He did so. From a weekly medication organizer, she removed a fistful of tablets and capsules. "Heart . . . kidneys . . . lungs . . . arthritis . . . vitamins," she intoned as she extracted pills from the med strip, each of its compartments embossed with an initial for its name of the week. Then she placed each into his waiting hand.

"Tumil-K," she said. "Furosemide. Vetmedin. Enacard. A half tab of spironolactone. Half tab of Rimadyl. One tab Welactin." He took each without comment but with a little bit of water. At the end, he said, "Pathetic," to nobody in particular.

"Put your head back," said Sallie. He did so. From her little tray, she selected a succession of very small plastic bottles, dispensing one drop of each into Arthur's original working eye. "Dexasporin," she said, "one drop . . . cyclosporine, one drop . . . tacrolimus once daily . . . one, two . . . and your Opticare. There."

She put away the bottles on the tray and placed the tray on the night table. "Okay, now, Artie. Roll over."

"Goddamn it," he said. "Motherfucker."

She gently lifted Arthur's bathrobe and pulled his silken jammies down a little bit, exposing one very elderly cheek. She kissed it. Then she removed a small pneumatic hypo from her caftan and expertly administered an infusion. "Stay still, Artie. Daily subcutaneous fluids. You know."

"I want you to call Bob. Call this morning. I don't want to wait anymore."

"Artie. You can't rush this. They say he won't be ready for another month, maybe two."

"Oh," said Arthur. "Right. Right." But he had stopped listening, because he had made a decision, and once you've made a decision, that's the time you stop listening. After a while, he rolled over again and looked at her. She accepted his gaze.

"You look very juicy, Buttercup," he said, feasting both his analog and cybernetic eye at her with tremendous appreciation. "You are so beautiful. I can't believe how beautiful you are."

She had put away all the paraphernalia of old age now, and she leaned over him as he lay in bed, his tiny, slightly artificial head resting lightly on the pillow. "I love you the way you are, Artie, you know that, I hope," she said, quite serious now. "All this stuff you're going to do to yourself, it's for you, honey. It's not for me."

"That's nice," said Arthur, "but you're deluded."

"It's the human condition, Artie. There's something okay about just being human, you know? Going with that flow."

"Fuck that," said Arthur. He put his arms around her and kissed her, and she kissed him back.

"Go ahead," he said. "Print one out."

"Okay."

Sallie patted the top of his mottled, shiny head. "You are one horndog," she added, moving over to the dresser, where she addressed a small printer that rested unobtrusively next to a houseplant. She made sure the readouts were appropriate, and then she pressed a button and went into the bathroom. Turned on the shower. A bit of humming.

Arthur lay back on the bed, his hands behind his head. Profits were good. His businesses enjoyed a 78 percent market share in every single space in which they operated. That was not particularly unusual. Amazon and its subsidiaries controlled 87 percent of all online retail. The global conglomerate that was once Facebook now held a 92 percent market share of all online advertising. He listened to the sound of Sallie in the shower. Gonna get laid soon, he thought. That's one thing that never gets old.

Sallie came in, still wearing her flowing caftan. "Ah, here we go," she said. She gently removed the brand-new penis from the 3-D printer and placed it on the little plate of bone-white china that rested on the night table by the side of his bed. "Now I'll leave you for a minute," she said demurely, and once again went into the bathroom, the sound of running water coming from the sink.

On the way out, she had dimmed the lights. It was nice in the room. The shades were closed but the sunlight was streaming in; it was still early! Lots of time for all the great things you could do in a day if you weren't dead. Arthur looked at the freshly created penis. It was a decent size, but not ridiculous. Quite attractive, actually. Much nicer than what had become of his original, when he considered it.

She came back in just a few minutes later, without the caftan. "You ready?" she said, smiling.

"Baby," said Arthur, snapping the new appendage into place with a soft and reassuring *click*. "I'm always ready."

2

Gene Wakes Up to Find His Mind Is Empty

He was sitting on the edge of the pond near the giant white tower when it all came rushing over him. "You're here," said a voice inside him, and he knew it was true. He was here. He liked it. Until then, he wasn't quite sure, but the little voice announcing his arrival to himself kind of settled it for him. He was here. Now all he needed to know was where he was. And who.

Enormous building blocks were strewn in clusters around the hillside in front of him. Thin asphalt roads more suitable to golf carts than to proper automobiles snaked to and fro between these rectangular piles of white stone. Here and there, a self-driving vehicle went by at a benign rate of speed, with one or two passengers inside doing nothing obvious except consulting transmissions from their inner electronics. Across a major thoroughfare from the short, squat building units stood a tower of white concrete that appeared to be the hub of the complex. What went on in there?

People went in and went out. He watched them and wanted to be them. They were nicely dressed, and many carried what at first appeared to be briefcases but upon closer examination revealed themselves to be screens with little handles jammed with electronics and data. They all had itty-bitty antennas sticking out of the tops of their heads.

He looked at the big white obelisk for a while longer. It seemed familiar somehow. Could this be the building where he lived or worked? Did he work? If so, what was his job? Shouldn't he know? This big, tall structure . . . was it a residence or an office? From the demeanor of the human and vehicular traffic going into and buzzing around it, it could be a residential tower, no doubt about it. On the other hand, why did people look so intent and purposeful upon entering it as well as leaving it, unless it was a business of some kind? Perhaps it was both?

Nobody ever got in trouble for taking the time to watch things, so he did that some more. He was still quite concerned, though. There were obvious gaps in his awareness. He seemed to know a bit about some things. Language and associations didn't fail him. He knew the names for things. But at the center of his consciousness of himself, there was something missing. Among the things that were missing was an idea of what was missing.

What time was it? The sun was relatively low in the sky, but that could mean either morning or early evening. It seemed more like morning. He decided to go with that as well.

He felt hungry. Did he have any money on him? He felt for his pockets and realized he didn't have any currency whatsoever. This gave him some additional uneasiness. How would he pay for things? He seemed to be appropriately attired in what might have been characterized as casual business wear—slacks, collared sport shirt, tasty little canvas tennis shoes. He was clean and not starving. Did he have access to funds? He certainly hoped so. Life without money is no life at all; he knew that, at least.

"Right index finger," said a little voice behind his mind. And yes, at the end of the longest finger on that hand was the chip. Ah, good. He was not without means, then. Who put it there?

He felt like he'd just woken up out of a deep nap; the kind that leaves you discombobulated for the rest of the day. But it was still morning! Did he have some kind of a night job? Why didn't he know?

15

"Can I help you with something?"

He turned in the direction of the voice, and there he was: a man in a simple one-button gray suit and a black 3-D exo-fitted Kevlar second-skin T-shirt capable of modulating itself in accordance with external conditions, as well as the mood of its owner. He was neither tall nor short, of middling weight, neither fat nor thin. His hair, which was thick, curly, completely white, and quite disordered, was cleared neatly away just above his ear to make room for the rather stylish cerebrocortical implant that was the emblem of his class and status.

Gene could tell by the way the man was looking at him that he was known to this fellow. He now paused in his attention to him for a moment, and Gene knew the mysterious stranger was listening to an incoming message. He waited for the transmission to finish. Nobody likes being required to shuttle between the analog and the digital realms too abruptly.

"Hi, Gene," the distinguished figure said at last. Then, when Gene failed to answer: "What's going on in that empty noggin of yours? Anything?"

Okay, thought Gene to himself. I do know this guy. But how?

The two just looked at each other for a little while.

How old was he? Forty? Sixty? A hundred sixty? Gene couldn't tell. If you looked very closely, there was a roughness about his skin, a touch too much sinew about his neck, and a delicate boniness about his hands that bespoke age—possibly great age. The hair was truly remarkable: a perfect, shaggy mane that would have been the pride of a teenager, except that it was completely white. There was a firmness about his midsection and upper body, though that had to have been engineered in some way. Any age, then. But healthy. Very, very healthy.

"Do I know you?" Gene asked, as politely as possible.

"Oh my," said the man. "We did it."

He sat down on the bench next to Gene and placed a gentle hand on his shoulder. Gene peered into the dignified, friendly face. It didn't look wholly unfamiliar to him. The sun was behind the face, creating a radiance above and around it. He couldn't quite grasp all the details, though. They did look comforting, at least. "We've seen each other around a little," said the man. "You're Gene, of course," he said. "I'm Bob. I work in Building Eight, over there. Remember?" He gestured to the phallic white tower.

"I do . . . ," Gene said, which was not completely true . . . although if he tried very hard . . .

"Ah, but you don't." Bob looked sad, but a little triumphant, too.

There was a short silence in which the two once again looked at each other, to no good effect. Then Bob leaned into him, not too close, but not too far, either.

"You need to come see me now, Gene." It was not a request.

"Building Eight," said Gene.

"Yep." Bob appeared to be seized by some powerful emotion that rendered speech impossible for a moment. Then: "Yep," he said again. "I'll give you a couple minutes to enjoy . . . whatever." He stood. "Take about five minutes. Then come on over. You know the way, right?" He tapped Gene on the side of the head that held his communications implant. Then he turned and moved off toward the structure he had identified as Building Eight. Every now and then, he turned as if to check something on the horizon, but Gene could tell Bob was looking at him. Eventually this began to make him nervous, and he got up, crossed the lawn, and meandered off down the path in no particular direction whatsoever.

"Top of the mornin' to you!" said a pleasant voice with a very slight Irish lilt.

It was an extremely large security bot built into a Segway: a 3-D holographic screen mounted on a mobile platform with one comically chubby wheel. These bots had been invented fifteen or so years ago in a rush of start-up enthusiasm. Their AI had yet to be completely perfected. They had no body to speak of, although the early models—essentially a TV on a rolling stalk—had been so top-heavy that teenagers had initiated a sport of tipping them over. They would lie there, complaining in a polite, robotic tone until their battery quit. Then they would be carted off.

That was not their only deficiency. In addition to their balance issues, these initial, skeletal models were extreme residents of the uncanny valley, so creepy that a simple upper body sporting a faux uniform had to be added to second-generation iterations to calm the fears of older citizens and small children. It also rendered them greater stability. They were also issued with protopersonalities, to make them less scary. For the most part, that failed, too.

In spite of this inauspicious debut, the newly improved models caught on in the security space. There were now hundreds of them around the city in the employ of one privatized police department or another, perambulating about open public sectors on their big, fat wheelbase, transmitting video to a central databank and resolving simple interactions with a certain low-level competence. Anything remotely complex got relayed to human observers back in the command hub.

"Officer O'Brien," said the bot. "That's me. And I was just wonderin' if I may be of some assistance. You look a bit lost, and I'm sure there's someplace you need to be." It waited, taking Gene in. A small amber light blinked on the brim of the electronic creature's fake police cap, which was built into his head.

"Thank you, Officer," Gene replied deferentially. "Do you happen to have the time?"

The light on the cap immediately flipped to green. This was an inquiry its intelligence was built for. "Nine-fourteen in the mornin'!" it said with pleasure. "Time to be doin' what you're supposed to be doin'!" Then it scanned Gene's face, once up, once down, with a horizontal beam that came out of the brim of its cap. There was a short silence while the machine digested this data. It was weird being scanned this way, Gene thought, without his permission.

"Nice weather," he said, just to say something.

"Likely to turn nasty later on," Officer O'Brien replied, tipping its trapezoidal head skyward, which tilted its entire body backward at an awkward angle.

"With what probability?" Gene inquired.

"Eighty-two point six percent."

"Well, then," said Gene. "See ya."

"Actually," said the bot, "my data show that you are scheduled for a meeting with Dr. Bob in Building Eight"—it whirred a little bit—"ten a.m. sharp." It started whirring again.

Of course, the thing knew everything about Gene, including his name. After a similar scan, it would probably know everything about anybody. There were a lot of names in the world and there wasn't a chip available at any supermarket checkout stand that couldn't hold them all.

"Okay," said Gene. "Well, thanks for the help, Officer O'Brien." And prepared to go on his merry way.

"Dr. Bob!" said Robocop. "That's a pretty big deal." And the little indicator monitor on the brim of its cap suddenly mutated over to amber again and then to red. Then it leaned over and planted its hologram of a face, which was now assuming a stern expression, very close to Gene's. "Don't be late," said the bot with a touch of menace. It was so close that Gene might have felt its breath, if it had any. He also noticed that the hologram of Officer O'Brien needed a shave.

Its duty done, this protector of public safety reassumed its pleasant demeanor, pivoted 180 degrees on its axis, and, with a saucy rev of the tiny Segway propulsion system, tootled down the pathway toward the next cluster of buildings.

Bob, then. Gene felt his guts tighten with a passing shadow of dread. Who was this Bob person? Why did he have to go see him? He didn't want to! What power did this guy have over him? None! Ha! The morning was bright and blue, with flecks of white at the very top of the dome. It was pretty, and he felt like a walk anyhow. So he put one foot in front of another and headed off in the opposite direction from Building Eight. Fuck 'em, he thought. I'm a free person!

"Where ya goin' there, champ?" Here it was again, the intrepid, artificial Irish cop. Whoever had programmed this thing had a sense of humor. The bot had circled back, then sped up to move alongside him, rolling along on its ridiculous propulsion system at precisely his speed. A small siren announced itself, very softly, from a sonic warning system embedded in the entity's head. After a moment or two, it repeated its question with slightly less cordiality.

"Where d'ya think you *are* goin', actually."

"I really have no idea, Officer," said Gene, and he kept moving. They're not really dangerous, he told himself. They wouldn't give a firearm to a machine with the IQ of an intelligent toaster, would they?

"You have . . . no idea?" said the officer, as if the words were disassociated concepts that did not fit together in the slightest.

"That's right," said Gene, turning to the bot and staring deeply into its receptor space. "Maybe I think it's just too nice outside to keep my appointment with this Bob fellow."

"Well. That can be ameliorated," said Officer O'Brien. It immediately began to rain, not everywhere, but right over Gene's head. A brief clap of thunder was followed by a single bolt of lightning that came dangerously close to his ear.

"Now perhaps you can keep your appointment," said the bot.

For this unique annoyance, Gene might have blamed the Stanford University physicists who had recently introduced the notion that, in order to do their jobs well, servile entities would need to incorporate simple emotions essential to decision making. Right now the machine was smirking in satisfaction at the solution it had engineered with its brand-new, state-of-the-art local environmental manipulator.

"Okay, very funny," Gene said. The rain stopped.

"Get going, pardner," O'Brien growled. But there was a twinkle in its crystal eye. "Building Eight."

Gene put his arm around O'Brien's molded shoulder. "Your shoe-lace is untied," he said.

"That gag was old a hundred years ago," it said, but it did look down at exactly the point where its feet might have been.

Gene turned and walked on until he reached Building Eight. People were streaming in and out of the enormous, arched portal. "What is this place?" he asked a comparatively friendly-looking citizen who was hurrying by.

"It's Building Eight," the man replied. Polite. Annoyed.

"Yes," Gene said. "But what *is* Building Eight?"

"Well," said the fellow slowly, as if checking an internal regulator. "It's where we're both going." Then he tore off through doors that hissed open at exactly the right moment to gain him entry.

Gene examined his alternatives. Then he went into the building.

An image exploded in his head. He had walked through the front doorway of a great cathedral sometime in the far-distant past. The light was streaming in through immensely tall stained glass windows, and there was singing in the choir high above. He felt awe and, most annoying to him, fear, mingled with a desire to obey the builder of the temple. He felt himself breathing differently. A hum surrounded him: a low purr of human activity that was both soothing and exciting. Towering, translucent elevators transported people skyward.

"Bob?" he asked a floating eyeball conveniently located in a slender kiosk marked INFORMATION that abutted one of the elevator banks.

"Excuse me for a moment," said the bright and shiny object. "You're Gene, right?"

"Who wants to know?" growled Gene. This was pissing him off.

"Well," said the glowing optical sphere, "if you are Gene, then you are cleared for entry to the elevator. If you're not Gene, you aren't."

"Okay," he said, trying to sound as belligerent as he could. "I am, in fact, that person."

"You might want to watch that attitude, pal," said the eye pod darkly. Then it brightened. "Or have it medicated out! That's available on the fourteenth floor." Was it smiling? How do you smile if all you are is an eyeball?

Gene determined to stay off the fourteenth floor if he could help it.

There was one solitary elevator provided for transportation to Bob and another advanced mechanism to summon it: a deep socket in the wall of the elevator bank intended for insertion of the supplicant's finger. He placed his digit into it, and, after a moment of thought, it lit up. A little hologram of a dodecahedron rotated within the minuscule housing in the wall while the elevator came to meet him.

Big deal, thought Gene.

The elevator came. It was a transparent room of clear polymer and spun titanium supported by a massive steel floor that floated like a leaf on the wind. Similar vehicles glided up and down throughout the spacious central atrium. "Thanks, Gene," said the room as it deposited him at the doorway to Bob's office. It was the only space on the floor. A small panel in the front door slid open, revealing a 3-D screen.

"Hiya, Gene!" said a fat, friendly face in the monitor. "We're expecting you! Please take off your shoes when you come in the house." It clicked off.

The house? thought Gene. Up here? But he left his shoes neatly in the tiny vestibule between the elevator and the front door, which now opened to reveal the fat face that had greeted him in the security screen. The face was on a head—nothing but—that was just floating there. A triumph of hovercraft tech if ever there was one, thought Gene. It started with skateboards. And now this.

"Hey there," said the head. It looked affable enough.

Gene took a peek around. He was in the foyer of a capacious New Orleans manse in the days before the great flood, when that lovely city finally disappeared beneath the waters of the Gulf for the last time. Ah, what a shame. But . . . how did he know that? Yet he did know it, and more. History of the antebellum South. Furniture that was in favor immediately after the first American Civil War. And at the same time, he actually knew nothing at all. All his knowledge had been overlaid upon a base of wet, gooshy stuff. It was frustrating.

"Bob's not quite ready at this moment," said the head in a light Southern accent. "He asked me to keep you company here in the foyer while you wait. My name is Edgar." It floated there, looking at Gene expectantly.

Gene felt some reply was required. "Hello, Edgar," he offered at last.

"The truth is," said Edgar, with an odd mix of humility and enthusiasm, "I'm trained only for vestibules and foyers. Next month I hope to graduate to waiting rooms."

"Well," said Gene. "Good luck with that." He couldn't think of much else to say. A strangely uncomfortable silence then ensued in which Edgar continued to hang in midair, grinning the way people do when they want to appear friendly but had run out of conversational topics.

This was one of the new CyberPals that the very wealthy could purchase for business and entertainment purposes. They were competent at virtually any form of communications: scheduling, greeting, and the like. Obviously, they came up short if any manual labor was required, since they had no arms and legs. It was not until the Disney unit of Alphabet entered the market, however, that something really went wrong. The Goofy head, for instance, refused to stop crashing violently into any wall that was available to it, exclaiming "Gorsh!" over and over until it incapacitated itself. The Mickey head would be quite pleasant at first but would end up wandering around the house, laughing in a strange, high-pitched giggle. They were eventually phased out and could now be found mostly at garbage dumps, still awake, blinking and muttering to themselves until, after several years, their solar power systems died.

Edgar was receiving an incoming alert. "You can go in now," he said.

"Thanks, Edgar," said Gene. Then, just to be friendly to a fellow creature, he added, "And good luck with your, you know, career progress."

"A man's reach must exceed his grasp, particularly when he has no arms," Edgar replied with exaggerated gravity. Then they both cracked up.

"Through there?" Gene inquired, pointing to a doorway beyond.

"Yeah," said Edgar. "Good luck to you, too."

This time Gene's bowels seized up for real. He felt like he was about to go onstage for a crucial performance but had neglected to learn his lines. He stood rooted to the spot.

"Go on," said Edgar, scooting over and nudging Gene with his flat plastic forehead. "You'll do okay. Bob's a nice guy."

"Really?"

"No," said Edgar. "Not really." And he laughed, a tinny, sparkly sound, and ascended to the corner of the vestibule near the front door, where he deactivated himself. The entire far wall of the room suddenly dematerialized, and Gene found himself in a brand-new, expansive living space. The man he had encountered earlier was rising to greet him from behind a desk in the far corner, a wobbly grin on his handsome face.

3

Bob the Great and Powerful

G ene couldn't move. What was he so fearful of? This mild-
looking gentleman in front of him didn't seem to offer much
of a physical challenge. What was there that bestowed such
tremendous power over him? Nothing that showed. Something, then,
that didn't show—that was invisible. Among things that we fear,
aren't those the worst? The monster under the bed? The creature in
the closet? The angry parent in the next room?

"Come on over, son," said Bob. "I won't bite you. Much."

Gene approached slowly. The room was enormous and spectacular, preternaturally quiet, with huge, towering windows of the
old-fashioned kind—not hermetically sealed plate glass—that actually opened onto the great outside world that lay beyond the pristine
tower of Building Eight. They were very high up. Gene walked to the
open window. The vista before him consisted mostly of what had to
be called suburbs. He could see many pretty houses: some for medium occupancy, many others for one or two families, and, in several
places, what were obviously gated communities sporting castles of
which the Thane of Cawdor would have been proud . . . whoever he
was . . .

There were also some very clean industrial parks with spiffy acres
of expensive vehicles parked for a variety of serious purposes, he was

sure, and what looked to be dozens of self-contained strip malls with the same configuration of small stores in each. He could make out at least ten gigantic big-box stores, too, guarded by hovercraft bristling with high-tech weaponry. Everywhere, in every direction, the same. But no, wait: there along the very distant rim of the smoky horizon to the east, the ancient bones of some ancient urban center lay smoldering, a strange green haze rising from its decaying towers, a warm, definitely analog light radiating from its old stone piles of glass and steel.

"It is mysterious, isn't it?" said a voice immediately behind him, so close that it seemed to be emanating from within his own head. "The old city."

"What is that stuff way, way out there?" Gene asked without turning around, as one would do with a friend with whom pretense was no longer an issue.

"You've seen it before, Gene. But you remember nothing about all that, do you?" the voice inquired. Gene did not reply, because no reply was necessary. It was true. He knew a lot of random junk. But he remembered nothing.

After a time, the man behind him, in a voice choked with emotion, said, "You've got nothing up there but the basic superstructure, do you, son?"

"I wish I knew what you were talking about," said Gene, turning around to face his interrogator.

"Let's sit," said Bob. "There's no reason we can't be comfortable while we get this little part over with. Then you'll be off to the next chapter of your great adventure. Would you like that?"

"Again," said Gene. "I think you have me at a disadvantage."

"I have you at a disadvantage. Jesus. It's like talking to myself." Bob returned to his default position behind the desk, reached down, and came up with a rather large Xnfiniti silver cushion about a meter wide, deflated, and held it in front of him like a child about to play a fun game with a new friend. "I like to sit on this," said Bob. "It helps my whole sacral situation. Remember?"

"The floating tuffet," Gene observed.

Bob peered at him thoughtfully. "Still some memory in evidence," he said, as if dictating to an invisible microphone, as indeed he was. He positioned the deflated cushion behind the enormous slab of steel that served as a desk, sat down on it carefully, crossed his legs, and then activated it. The thing then glowed with a very gentle white light, inflated to a full, plump ovoid, and lifted itself smoothly about a foot or so off the floor. "Ah," Bob sighed. "That's better. Age is a terrible thing, Gene. And it's the spine that goes first, you know."

Bob then sat in silence, regarding Gene with thoughtful concentration. Gene felt the sensation of Bob probing the inside of his brain with delicate, inquiring fingers, moving his various lobes this way and that, peeking underneath one and then the other. Finally he inquired, as politely as he could, "Is this supposed to be some kind of conversation? Because if it is, you're doing very well holding up your end."

"You're doing great, right?" Bob inquired abruptly.

"I guess so," said Gene. Then, after a second, he added, "Though I suppose it depends on what you mean by 'great.'"

Bob assumed the same dictational tone and spoke to nobody in particular. "The substrate of consciousness appears intact," he said, "but the long-term and short-term memory issues seem to have been resolved, and with them the problem of consciousness."

"Bob." Gene stood up. "I think I'll be going. I personally feel like this is getting me nowhere."

"Right. Right. You should." He stayed seated and fixed Gene with a steely gaze. "Just a couple more questions?"

"Go ahead." Gene sat down.

"You know who you are?"

"Well," said Gene, "I mean, sorta."

"Do you remember anything about the last couple of weeks? Friends? Activities of any kind? Stuff like that?"

"Actually, no, Bob," said Gene, who felt a bit relieved to be asked about it. "Where I live. What I do. My clothes. This chip I have on the end of my finger." He looked at it quizzically. "This thing behind my ear . . ." He touched the communications implant, which leapt into life and hummed congenially. "I have no recollection of acquiring any of these things."

"Well . . ., you have them, don't you?" said the doctor. His eyes were light blue and slightly watery. "I mean," he said, "you wouldn't be the first person in the world to be defined by his possessions and generally amnesiac about why you acquired them in the first place."

Gene considered this nutty statement. What did it have to do with his predicament?

"I mean," he said, "I seem to be in the middle of a relatively established setup here. But I don't think it was me who set it all up."

"But you feel good, right? You feel strong and smart and wide awake and ready for anything this crazy old world can throw at ya? Just checking."

"Well . . .," said Gene. "Yeah. I mean, as far as that goes."

"Groovy," said Bob. He jumped off the silver cushion and onto his feet with surprising agility for one with ostensible spine issues. Then he came around the desk, put his arm through Gene's, and began to walk him rather ceremoniously to the door. "Gotta scramble now, me hearty," he continued in a false, jocular tone, then "Holy cannoli!" he exclaimed, looking at an archaic wristwatch. "You have to be in Bel Air in . . . forty minutes! Gotta hustle!" They had arrived at the door to the room, which had magically rematerialized.

"Come back right after," Bob instructed him. "That's an order, amigo."

Gene was now at his wit's end. He disengaged his arm from Bob's friendly grasp and turned to face him, man to man. "Seriously, Bob," he said. "What's in Bel Air that I have to be there so immediately?"

Bob looked him over carefully. "Come on, son," he said gently. "Try." Once again he gently tapped the silvery implant behind Gene's ear. Gene closed his eyes. There was an airy silence in the room where they were standing together, one thinking, one waiting. "It's in there," said Bob, with the same note of patient impatience.

A bird was singing somewhere. Was it a bird or a recording of a bird? A faint smell of . . . Was it ozone? Or . . . Was it perfume? Yes. Very light. A clean smell. Fresh-cut flowers—not fancy ones, daffodils—with a hint of lilac, almost imperceptible. A woman sitting on a couch in a vast living space of some kind, not reading, not doing anything, just . . . sitting, staring out an enormous plate-glass window onto a patio that opened up onto a virtually endless lawn so green and perfectly groomed it had to have been planned and maintained by an intelligence artificial enough to be satisfied with nothing short of perfection. She was in a long, white caftan, her hair collected in a careless sheaf of golden sunshine at the top of her head.

"Sallie," said Gene.

"Mmm-hmm." On the other side of the lawn was a vast infinity pool, shimmering waves of bright-blue water cascading gently over its far side and into an abrupt chasm that stretched off into the landscape beyond, where the well-tended mosaic of homes and pools and neatly tended macadam paths faded away, as it did here, into the ruins of a smoking, reeking urban cauldron that lay beyond. And now Gene knew he was dreaming a waking dream, for here was this beautiful woman, Sallie? And she was turning her head now in his direction, and she was staring frankly into the eye of his imagination, and in her was a call—a beckoning of some kind. Then it was just the two of them, he and Sallie, staring into each other the way lovers do. And yet they most certainly had never met. Or had they?

"What if I don't want to go?" said Gene, to nobody in particular. He had lost his awareness of Bob in there someplace.

"Oh, you'll go," said Bob. He touched the back of Gene's neck then—not roughly, but not casually, either, as one would press a button on a microwave oven to get it started. Gene saw nothing but blank white for a brief moment. Then all the pain in the world filled his head. Then he was back in the room.

"That really hurt," he said.

"This isn't easy for me, either, Gene," Bob said, his hand now grasping Gene's elbow perhaps a little too firmly. "We've been working together for a while, you know, and during that time, I've come to see you as something of a . . . Well, anyway, what's the point of that?" His nose had developed a decided thrush, and around the corners of his eyes a bit of extra moisture appeared. "We all of us have our roles to play, son. It's time for you to play yours."

"Whatever that may be?" said Gene.

"Yes." The two stood looking at each other for a moment. Now Gene saw, Bob was perhaps not quite as fit as he looked when the sun was shining bright and his nanotech body shirt was newly printed. After their brief conversation, he appeared a bit weary. Shorter than Gene, too. And much, much older, now that he looked a bit harder.

"You're going to be all right," said Bob gruffly. "So many of the right things went into the making of you, it's impossible that you would not be all right. You just needed some . . . fine-tuning."

"Well," said Gene, "who doesn't?"

Bob regarded him closely. Then he leaned very slightly into Gene's face and said, "Stick close to your desk and never go to sea—"

"—and you could be the ruler of the queen's navy," Gene replied, as one of Pavlov's German shepherds would have drooled when a bell was rung. Then he gave in to the vast cloud of black ooze that blossomed out of the deep emptiness that was his mind; a terrible despair at the depth of how little he knew himself.

For his part, Bob was patting Gene on the shoulder with evident satisfaction. "Hyperloop's in the lobby. Bronny will help you find it." Then he cupped his palm and put it against Gene's cheek. For an instant, Gene thought it was possible that Bob was going to give him a kiss. It's possible Bob thought so, too, because he coughed, turned, and walked back to his desk. As he went, he bellowed in a voice that would carry clear to San Jose, "Bronwyn!" He didn't look at Gene again but got very busy with the meaningless crap on his desk.

The virtual door was open. Gene went through it and was in the

foyer again. This time his greeter was not the local machine intelligence but an actual human being: smiling, a small, childishly slender
young woman with pale, pale white skin, a bloom of pink at both
cheeks, and big, brooding brown eyes with massive lashes. She had
an old-style phablet cradled in her left arm. In her right was a stylus.

"Hey, Bubba," she said to him. "Howzit goin'."

"You'll have to excuse me if I'm supposed to know you," said
Gene. "I have this memory thing going on, in the sense that I don't
seem to have any."

"Bronwyn," she said amiably. "You can call me Bee. Or Bronny.
Or Bronwyn. I answer to all three." He must have looked rather blank.
"Oh my," she said sadly. "We finally did it, huh?"

"Apparently," said Gene.

"Follow me, then."

"Lead on, Macduff." Where the fuck did he get these stupid
things?

"Ah, that's right," she said. "Bob always did like his Shakespeare."
Then, nodding at some private grim joke to herself, she preceded him
down the hallway.

"And what do you do around here, Bronwyn?" he piped merrily
to her pert little back and bobbing fall of light-brown hair.

"Well, it's hard to say," she said. "Let's just say I work for Bob in
whatever capacity he requires, within reason. And that means kind
of keeping an eye on you, Gene, for your own good, if not always and
entirely for his."

"Is keeping an eye on me, like, a plum assignment or something?"

"It depends," she said. "Sometimes." And kept on walking.
"Other times, not so much."

"And how would you describe what it is *I'm* supposed to be
doing?"

Bronwyn thought about that for a little while as they walked.
Then she stopped, turned, and looked at him. "You're supposed to
be sacrificing yourself to one of the gross narcissists who run the

atavistic corporate state in his obsessive search for eternal life," she said. "That's what you're supposed to be doing." Then she checked his eyes for some spark of understanding.

"Oh, I see," Gene replied. So Bronwyn's crazy, he thought. "That sounds like important work," he added with pleasant sincerity. "I wouldn't want to be late for it." Bronwyn looked a bit crestfallen, shrugged, hugged her phablet a bit tighter, and they resumed their progress. At the end of the hall, they stepped into a glass-and-steel platform that had hissed open at their arrival. They rode down for a while in silence.

"But seriously, how come I can't remember anything about this whole deal?" he asked as the perfectly transparent room slid to a halt on the ground floor.

"Which whole deal?" She once again preceded him out the doors.

"You know," he said, "*this*." They had moved into the gigantic lobby, which loomed above them like St. Peter's Basilica in Rome greeting supplicants on their way to see the Pope.

Bronwyn stopped dead, turned, and pierced him with a hot and slightly hostile glare. "Tell me something, Gene. Think before you answer. I mean, really think."

"Okay."

"Do you really and truly remember nothing? Nothing?"

"Nope." Gene brightened a bit. "Maybe I had an accident of some kind and have amnesia, like in one of those movies I can't remember seeing."

"Like, you don't remember Petaluma?"

"City in Northern California," Gene said noncommittally.

"Nothing about any of the people you might have met? Friends you may have made? Nothing about . . . Liv?"

Gene felt the wind whistling between his ears. "Liv," he said, as if in a dream.

"Think about it," said Bronwyn. The right side of her head above her ear began to glow red. "Whoops." She grimaced a little. "Incoming."

She listened to her head for a moment. "I gotta go," she said. "Here." She gently took his hand and deposited a small plastic chip into his palm. "See that arrow? That's the Hyperloop. This is your ticket. Give it to the droid at the platform."

"Okay," said Gene. "But what am I supposed to do when I get there?"

Bronwyn seemed on the verge of saying something but then thought better of it. "You'll find out," she said. Then she, too, touched his face. Her touch was tender and, Gene thought, kind of familiar for a person he had never met before. Then Bronwyn turned and went, her ponytail bobbing in what looked a lot to Gene like anger.

The Loop lay waiting in the station, and Gene got on. Each passenger had a private space in his or her own little car. His seating unit was a high-riding ergonomic masterpiece, fitted to some mystical understanding of the spinal cord and its relation to the central nervous system. He felt it forming itself to fit him. It was made of some prion-based fabric that was not alive in any organic sense but was not entirely inanimate, either. To what extent did such organisms evolve and change as the environment worked on them? Could they develop some very rudimentary form of consciousness after years on the job? Could a chair fall in love with the weight of its master's body?

He sat back in the Hyperloop and decided to take a good long look at things. After what felt like thirty seconds later, he was awakened by a gentle nudge from his head. "Wake up, sleepy person," said Bronwyn's voice. "You are there."

There? thought Gene. Where is there?

"You'll never know until you go find out," said Bronwyn. Were his unspoken thoughts so clear? "Yeah, they sorta are," she said sweetly and evaporated back into his cranium.

Well, thought Gene, if I'm supposed to go there, I'd better go see what's there.

4

A Love That Was Meant to Be

From the rustic climes beyond the smoking, overcrowded hive of the former San Jose where Bob and his campus made their home, to the pristine aerie that was the enclave of Bel Air, it was three hundred miles as the bird flies—if at that point there were any birds left capable of flying through the unfiltered atmosphere of the coastal metroplex. By Musk Hyperloop, the trip took a little more than twenty minutes. A short ride by driverless Uber, and there Gene was.

He was standing in the enormous circular driveway of a palatial mansion made of very pale stone. At least he thought it was stone. It looked like stone. He heard birds. Birds! How? Then he realized. He was actually . . . outside. No high-altitude dome. No stratospheric air filter. Just sky. He looked up. A huge flock of some kind of bird swept overhead.

"They're swallows," said a pleasant voice. A very pretty woman was crossing a huge sward of lawn toward him. She was dressed for gardening. About forty, maybe, quite tall, lean but curvy, big mane of medium-blond hair of many colors. Lovely mouth. Big green eyes. She was smiling and holding a perfectly manicured right hand out to him, palm slightly up. It was a hand for taking, not shaking. So he took it.

"Hi," she said. "You're Gene. I'm Sallie."

Of course it was Sallie. Every bit as pretty as in his waking dream.

Gene was silent. His heart was full. The music of creation was playing in his head. This was the woman destined to be his!

"Come in," she said. "Arthur is very much looking forward to eating you."

Eating him? Did she realize what she had said? He thought maybe he hadn't heard her correctly, but he was pretty sure. Her expression remained benign, welcoming. He decided to let it go. They tiptoed hand in hand down the slate slabs of the front patio toward the house, weaving around the koi pond, where gorgeous, multicolored fish cavorted in a twisting, hungry, hyperactive mass. Gene assumed they were artificial.

"Will you wait here a moment or two?" she said with wink that made his knees feel funny. "I want to make sure the King is fully prepared." She disappeared up the path. Well, thought Gene, this was semi-new information. Arthur was waiting to see him, and this woman, Sallie, was going to take Gene into his presence. It's me who's not prepared, thought Gene. So, with a tap of the hard space behind his right ear, he called up a short wiki on the subject of his host.

Arthur was famous. His wiki ran to seven screens, with lots of references at the end and tons of links. There was no time to access any of them, but the global paragraph at the beginning told him enough. Big dude. A legend, shrouded in mystery, speculation, and the envy of lesser mortals. He had invented something prodigious a long time ago and had been pretty much extruding money ever since. His personal wealth was greater than that of most nations. In some circles, his age was thought to exceed 125, since he'd been born way back in the middle of the century just past, during what was called the baby boom. Now he was, if not the last, then certainly one of the final representatives of that generation; the apex of its success vector. The last boomer.

And here she was again, striding down the pathway toward him, one hand extended to reacquire him. God, thought Gene. How beautiful. She conformed in every way to whatever paradigm of beauty had been established in his imagination. She took his hand, and a bolt of electricity shot from the tip of his finger through his body and directly into the soft tissue at the end of his penis.

"Come," she said.

She walked him through the entryway and out onto an enormous stone veranda that opened up onto a massive lawn—more of a park, actually—that featured a bowling green, a gigantic negative-energy swimming pool, and a hydroponic vegetation platform that rivaled those that had graced the Hanging Gardens of Babylon, an image of which floated through his consciousness like a memory of a meal that he had no recollection of eating.

The pool glowed sweetly in the afternoon light. "In a moment," Sallie said, "a flock of wild geese will land on the surface of the water, pause for a few seconds, and then take off again. After they go, there will be a double rainbow." They stared at the pool for a while.

He listened to the mysterious buzz of unseen insects in the trees. Then, at a great distance, he heard the noise of something approaching on the breeze: first one comical honk, then another, then many, and then, with a great rush of wings and fussy, self-important wheezing and bleating, a squadron of Canada geese, accompanied by a few attendant ducks of various sizes and shapes. They lowered their landing gear and planed onto the surface of the swimming pool. Then they sat there for a few moments, conversing quietly among themselves. As they did, a rainbow appeared in the clouds, and then another. Somewhere far away, it had been raining, evidently. Or maybe it was chemicals. Two rainbows, he thought.

"See?" Sallie seemed pleased. They regarded the rainbows together.

"Wow!" said Gene.

"We'd better go in." She took him by the elbow and steered him lightly to his destination. "We'll have a little snack," she said. "Arthur wants you to meet Lucifer. And I'm sure she would like to sniff you thoroughly as well. You have to be careful around her. She's really very sweet, but something is a bit wrong with her programming, and she can get rather feisty if she takes a dislike to you. She's been known to spray a noxious fluid or two when she gets into that kind of a mood."

"Okay," said Gene. "And what is she?"

Sallie looked at once amused, parental, and beaming with sentimental affection. "She's mine, really, but Artie's taken a shine to her, too. She's a sort of . . . lizard, iguana kind of thingie. They say she's artificial. But she's very real to me. You'll see." They had been delivered onto the gleaming patio, a virtually endless expanse of white stone. In the center of this palatial piazza was a giant slab of black marble festooned with a cornucopia of meats, sweets, fruits, pastries. A zero-gravity ice bucket chilled a magnum of Veuve Clicquot.

Gene was swept by a wave of crippling embarrassment. They were clearly expecting someone very important here, and he was busting in on it. "I'm sorry," he said. "I'm intruding. I should go someplace and wait while, you know, you have your lunch or whatever."

"Gene," she said with a juicy chuckle, as if they were sharing a private joke. Her laugh was lovely. Kind of dark and smoky. What a nice laugh. Yummy. "You are lunch or whatever," she said, so soft and confidential that it would have been churlish for him to refrain from laughing along with her. Then he just looked at her face. She was still holding his hand, and now, giving it an almost imperceptible squeeze, she turned and led him across the patio, which was trimmed by several ponds loaded with more koi—these as large as otters—and at last into the front portal of the castle.

She dropped his hand and preceded him down a surprisingly cozy corridor, its walls lined with a variety of suspended hologram. Fruit. Animals. Sunsets. Quite a few of a green-and-gold lizard-like thing, which he assumed to be Lucifer, the aforementioned artificial iguana, in a range of endearing poses, if it was possible to so characterize such a creature.

"I did them," Sallie observed over her shoulder.

37

"They're really good," he said. Gene was happy to be able to say it without lying. He wasn't that good a liar. Really good lying takes confidence he was pretty sure he lacked. Or maybe he hadn't been truly tested yet.

"Don't encourage me," she said. "Or I'll have you here for weeks looking at things."

That didn't sound too bad. "I don't mind," he said. Sallie looked over her shoulder at him as she moved down the hall and gave him a tiny smile. Once again, Gene was suddenly aware that his knees were not as strong as he might like them to be, and there was a simultaneous flutter in the depths of his tummy. Pathetic, he thought. What a tool I am.

"Here we are!" she announced with what he thought was a smidgen too much brio. It was the way people talked to a bright but brittle child, one who could go off at any moment and bite people.

"I was wondering where the fuck you had got to," said a deep, irritable voice within the darkened enclave of the room. "I'm hungry."

"This is Gene, Arthur. Now, I want you to be polite."

"I'll be as fucking polite as I wanna be," said Arthur. "You wanna get the fuck in here or what? It just so happens I'm feeling more polite than usual."

"I assume you're not talking to me, Artie," said Sallie, and there was a little steel inside the satin. She stepped aside and gave Gene room to maneuver around her. He did so and found himself in what was clearly an area intended for relaxation and a little bit of work.

"Are you going to sit the fuck down, or what?" said the extremely ancient, desiccated life form before him. Gene was aware of a very faint odor of great old age wafting from that direction, along with the scent of powder and lotion, aftershave, hair tonic, and medicine. A Total Body Gas dispersion unit sat quietly in a space behind the occupant's chair, within easy reach, a green light blinking. A floating Roomba hovered in the air behind his head. It seemed to be looking at Gene, though that was silly. How could a vacuum cleaner see you? And yet he was sure it did.

"Of course," said Gene. "Thank you, sir." He sat down in a big Nanohide recliner and immediately sank into it practically up to his waist. The entity that was part seating unit and part artificial life form welcomed him in with a contented sigh. This was somebody's idea of comfort, thought Gene, but it wasn't his. He felt tiny, diminished in the arms of this semisentient object. The neat, imperious, slightly smelly figure in the recliner/throne loomed above him now, clearly to its advantage.

"Say hello to Lucifer," Sallie said, gesturing to what looked like a small footstool on the floor by Arthur's chair.

This common household object—green, luminescent—was Lucifer, a synthetic lizard with the cognitive abilities of, say, a cocker spaniel. Rumors had it that certain recent models had the power of speech. This was not wholly inconceivable, since everything from info kiosks to kitchen appliances such as refrigerators, stoves, and toasters could converse with you on a level superior to that which you might enjoy with your college friends at an average Friday-night poker game.

Lucifer's head was flat, semitriangular in shape, and perched on a short, muscular neck attached to a stump of a body that most closely resembled that of a streamlined tortoise. It had virtually no tail, just a small, plump thumb that moved very slowly as she looked at you. It was not an attractive creature, if you could venture to call it a life form at all. Gene reached out his hand very gently and put the end of his fingers at the crown of its silky noggin. It produced a noise, moved slightly closer to the ground, and produced a tiny wet spot on the floor.

"Hi, Lucifer," he said.

Lucifer then emitted a noise that definitely sounded like a human being, possibly a newscaster, saying "Woof."

"You're a decent-looking specimen," said Arthur, who was peering at him with creepy ferocity. Gene hardly knew what to say. A specimen? He didn't like the sound of that. He had a feeling about it. Like, it wasn't just an empty compliment. More of a scientific observation. It was cold.

There was a weird silence, one of those that certain people can impose on you as a form of aggression. Arthur just looked at Gene and breathed. Gene could hear his breath, something between a wheeze and a whistle. His eyes were small and hard. You could see the edge of their parabolas in his eye sockets. The pupils were dark brown, shot through with yellow, ringed in green, the whites rheumy and gray. Over the whole ocular mechanism there was a greasy, drippy glaze.

Gene looked down at Lucifer, whose large, clear, deep-black eyes stared back into his. They were calm, sincere. All at once the creature sort of coughed and then sat on its stumpy haunches and uttered something that sounded like "Get me outta here." It actually sounded like "Gemmeottahee." Gene assumed he was hearing things.

"Okay," said Arthur, rising decisively if creakily to his feet, and suddenly Sallie was at Gene's shoulder once more. He smelled an indefinable fragrance, oil and spice and perhaps a bit of chocolate? Where had she gone? Had she been there all along? He had been so focused on the ancient mariner lurking in the shadowy corner of the darkened room, his beady eyes fixed on the object of his desire as if Gene were a sizzling T-bone.

"Time for Arthur's lunch," said Sallie, and touched Gene lightly once again on his elbow. Through his shirt and jacket, he again felt a pleasant warmth spread up his entire arm, into his neck, down his spine, and directly into his groin. He wanted it to happen again, as many times as possible.

They ate outdoors, near a pond they had constructed for Arthur's daily swim. I don't know how to swim, Gene thought. Or do I? But Arthur was talking. "So you," he said to Gene, "are just a big, well-oiled machine and apparently haven't a care in the world."

"Well, sir, I don't know about that."

"Everything on you works, right? Nothing falling off, is there?"

Gene felt like laughing but was aware that this wasn't really a joke. "No, sir," he said. "Everything is attached pretty well. I seem to have a problem remembering stuff, but other than that, I think I'm pretty much okay."

"Better be," said Arthur, addressing his dish with mild disgust. "You cost a fortune."

"Artie," said Sallie.

"Know anything about business?" Arthur picked up his spork and dangled it horizontally at Gene in jaunty inquiry, fixing him with a narrow stare.

"Well, sir," said Gene, "the fact is I have a lot of facts at my disposal, kind of rattling around in my head, little snippets of this and that, but I don't seem to know a lot of the essentials that a person is supposed to know about himself. I know I'm here. I know it's very nice here. But when you ask me about business? Actually? I have no idea what you mean. So no. I guess I don't." He picked up his knife and fork and dug into the perfect slab of beef that lay on the plate before him. The fact was, Arthur's whole truculent, nasty attitude was starting to annoy him, which was quite a feat, since being in the proximity of Sallie provided him with a beautiful glow of mellow happiness that he never knew could exist. Just being around her was a bath of contentment and joy. And then there was Arthur. Gene sincerely hoped he wouldn't have to spend a lot of time around this frickin' jerk.

"This is the swill I have to eat," muttered the very, very old man, glaring at what in truth was an unappetizing mess before him, a pureed slop divided carefully into discrete colorations and consistencies on the plate. Sallie was across the table, carving away at her superbly realistic fauxterhouse steak, looking up now and then to smile at Arthur, and then at Gene, as if indulging two gifted children.

"What I wouldn't give for a real slab of perfectly marbled cow flesh," Arthur grumbled, staring wolfishly at Gene's sizzling hunk of protein. A substantial bolt of saliva burst from both sides of Arthur's mouth and dribbled down his chin.

"Stop whining, honeypot," Sallie said quietly to nobody in particular. Her words had an instantaneous effect on Arthur, who suddenly grew cowed, fearful. She rose and then leaned over him, putting a hand on his shoulder and leaning down to wipe his mouth with a heavy cloth napkin. "This drooling is getting to be a problem," she observed in a confidential tone.

"Okay, okay," he said. She went back to her seat, perched herself on the edge of it, and shot Gene a look he couldn't quite read. Nothing bad, though.

Arthur was regarding Gene with narrow intensity over his glop. "This is actually very delicious, thank you very much," he growled directly at Gene in a wounded and defensive tone, piercing his target with a glare heavy with scorn and hatred, daring him to offer a contradiction. Gene did not. Even in his odd, compromised state, he knew it was probably wise to choose your battles with guys like Arthur, and this particular skirmish didn't seem all that important.

"Looks very good, sir," he said.

"You wanna fucking eat any of it? Huh?" Arthur then hurled his spoon, dripping with goo, away from the table in the general direction of Gene. Most of it missed. "I'm sorry!" he yelled immediately. But he didn't sound sorry. He sounded sorry for himself.

Sallie was on her feet. "I'm ashamed of you, Artie," she said with some severity. Then she turned and inquired cordially, "Would you like to take a little tour of the hydroponia, Gene?" The question seemed like both a pleasant invitation to one man and a rebuke to the other.

"If it's all right with Arthur," Gene said. He had no desire to be rude to the old guy. He felt sort of sorry for him now, truth be told.

"Sure, sure," said Arthur, who was now rubbing away at a spot of sodden mulch he had dropped onto the front of his shirt. "Fuck," he said, regarding the stain sadly. "And I was doing so well."

5

A Solution to the Problem of Death

allie took Gene's arm, which turned molten at her touch, and walked him to the edge of the hydroponic floratopia. The smell of roses as yet unseen hung in the air. He heard the unmistakable sound of cascading water falling from a great distance into a lake or river. He knew this was impossible—that it was probably a prerecorded effect of some kind—but it was a nice sound. He liked it. As they reached the edge of the lawn beyond the patio, Sallie turned to regard her husband, arms crossed, her small, sandal-sheathed foot almost tapping imperceptibly.

"I want you to think about your behavior, Arthur," she said sternly.

"Yes, Sallie," said Arthur. Then he added: "I said I was fucking sorry."

They left him staring into his excessively digestible lunch and ambled into the hanging flowers, drifting in companionable silence through the humid, nectar-sweet greenery, up a small hillside, and into a dark copse of real trees that parted high above them. What certainly looked like birds darted about up there in random patterns. But were they really random? Or programmed to a rhythm that would repeat itself only every ten thousand years? And were they actual birds with real bird blood in their veins, genuine feathers, tiny nonvirtual hearts pounding six hundred beats a minute within their chests? Did it matter?

As if reading his mind, Sallie said, "Yeah, the birds. I like them, too." She peered up at the sky. "I recognize it's possible they're artificial. But does that make them any less real?"

"I guess in a way it does," he said. Her physical presence was a heavy, hot penumbra enveloping him.

"But honestly," said Sallie, her neck craning skyward most attractively, "how much genuine interaction did anybody ever have with a completely biological bird, even hundreds of years ago? A live one, way up high like that? How do we know they weren't artificial even back then and implanted in our ecosystem by an alien species?"

This seemed crazy to Gene, but no crazier than a lot of things he was seeing. "It's an assumption people made, I suppose," he offered sagely. He was intensely engaged in the complicated process of not looking stupid, both to himself and to this remarkable woman.

"Well, look who's here!" Sallie cooed in surprise. "Come here, Worm."

She bent down and picked up a stolid but somehow very droopy Lucifer, who gazed at Gene in evident triumph. "Her want attention, little bean," said Sallie, and she squeezed the thing's rather large, segmented black nose.

"You seem attached to . . . it," he said.

"She very bad," Sallie scolded while kissing the top of its head. "And don't call her 'it,'" she admonished him. Was she genuinely annoyed? If so, he really liked it. Her cheekbones were very high, her chin almost as triangular as that of her little greenish friend. She appeared to come to a very important decision.

"You may call her Lucy," she declared.

There was a wind moving with slow and noisy progress through the trees high above them, heavy with the scent of fir and dirt and rain coming, maybe.

"Hey, Lucy," he said, petting Lucy's head and neck as she languished in ecstasy in Sallie's arms.

"Wow," said Lucy.

"She makes noises that sound like words," he said, stroking it under its sleek, leathery chin.

"So far, she's never gone over the line into actual speech," said Sallie. "But look at this. Lucy . . ." She held the green object in the air in front of her, two arms extended, its face to hers. "Say woof."

"Woof," said Lucy, in a compliant, tolerant tone.

"Say woo."

"Woo!" said Lucy. It stuck out a plump forked tongue and kissed Sallie on the end of her nose.

"Say 'So long now.'" Sallie, at that moment, had the same goofy expression as the synthetic lizard, a beaming grin on her face, her juicy pink tongue slightly protruding most adorably.

"So long now," said Lucy, or something very much like it. It came out as an odd, glottal sound, but the words were mixed in there somewhere. This was not all that shocking, right? Gene's database contained information on parrots and mynah birds that had vocabularies of several dozen words. Of course, none of those were artificial entities created by life-form engineers. How did they whip up these things, anyhow? On that issue, Gene's internal archive drew a blank. Interesting, he thought. With so much random material at his disposal, why nothing on that?

Sallie held out Lucy for Gene to receive. He did so, continuing to hold her in her comfortable position in midair at arm's length. "Hey, pretty girl. What ya doin'?" he said. "Can you really talk?"

"Arf," said Lucy, in what he could swear was a bored and sardonic tone. "Woof," she added sarcastically.

"Perhaps she doesn't want to perform like a trained seal," said Sallie, taking her back and putting her gently on the ground. "She's very sensitive about that. I don't think she believes herself to be an artificial being put on the planet for a utilitarian purpose. But then, none of us do, do we?"

Gene had no idea what to say to this, although it did land a little bit oddly to his ear. So he said nothing.

They went back and rejoined Arthur, who was sitting at the table, doing very little except breathing, which seemed not completely autonomic for him. He looked fine, as far as that went, except that a thick, viscous fluid was oozing very slowly out of his ears.

"Shit," he said. "Those fucking stem cells are coming out of my ears again."

It was a loathsome sight, Gene thought. It looked like creamed spinach, the kind with little flecks of onion in it. Arthur was staring face front, resigned, angry.

"Artie," said Sallie, and she bent down to wipe the sludge away with her sleeve. Gene noticed that. She didn't go looking for a cloth napkin or anything. "It's still better than the baby octopus stuff they had you on, right?" she cooed. "Remember what happened then."

"This is so fucking humiliating," said Arthur. Gene did feel sorry for him. There he was, with all the money in the world, and this was the final stop to which fate had delivered him. Didn't seem fair. But there was no way to avoid it, was there? Same for everybody, thought Gene. Inevitable.

"There's only so far that original receptacle can take him," said Sallie, taking hold of Arthur's hand and tracing his veins with her index finger, which was a full-time job, given their profusion and complexity. "His consciousness is fine."

"Well," said Gene, "that's good."

"Sort of. Maybe not. It makes him all too aware of his status as a prisoner of his own body."

"Yeah," said Gene, now completely at a loss as to the direction the conversation had taken. "I guess that does kind of suck." He was immediately and painfully aware of the insufficiency of his reply, so once again he fell silent.

She looked at him, eyes very wide, looking for something inside him that he wished he knew how to give. That's where it all starts, he thought. When a woman looks at you. Like, suddenly there's a woman looking at you. Really looking. Then nothing is the same after that.

"So anyway," he said, "I guess maybe I oughta be going?" The purpose of this visit, as pleasant as it may have been, was still cloaked in mystery to him. It had seemed important for him to come here. And he had come. And now he should go, right?

There was a silence, not uncozy. Sallie continued to hold Arthur's hand, occasionally moving to clean up his ear, all the while staring at the husk of humanity with love and sadness while Gene took the opportunity to gaze at her. She knew he was looking at her, and permitted him to look at her, and he knew she had granted him permission, and she knew he knew.

After a short time, Arthur appeared to have fallen asleep. His eyes were closed, and his chin, slightly moist, rested comfortably on his chest, trembling slightly as a light snore passed in and out of his purple lips.

"Why don't I put the cat on the roof," said Sallie out of nowhere. As she did, she gently placed Arthur's claw in his lap. Then she turned in her chair to face Gene full front, her hands on the knees of her caftan, legs spread very slightly under the flowing garment, feet flat on the stone of the patio, and leaned into him a bit, her eyes glistening with the risk she had suddenly decided to take—the walk along the precipice. "You know that joke?" she inquired. "A family has a daughter, who has a cat, which she loves, and one night the cat falls off the roof of the house and breaks its neck. It's dead as a rag doll. So the father goes into his daughter's room to tell her the bad news, and he blurts out to her, 'Honey, I'm sorry to tell you this, but your cat is dead.' Of course, the little girl goes nuts, sobbing, inconsolable. His wife hears this, and she is appalled, and goes to comfort the hysterical child. 'Why did you do it like that?' she scolds her husband. 'You have to lead up to it. The first thing you should say is, like, "The cat is on the roof." Then later you can break the news that the cat has fallen off the roof and we took it to the vet, and then, somewhat later, "So sorry, honey, your cat has passed away." Then at least she'd be prepared at every stage of it.' So, two weeks later, the

47

father goes into his daughter's room and sits by the side of her bed, and takes her hand carefully, and says to her, 'Honey . . . Grandma is on the roof.' "

Gene thought it was a pretty funny joke but didn't quite catch its relevance.

Sallie's eyes had suddenly sprung a small leak. She dabbed at them with her sleeve and then plunged on as Arthur burbled quietly in his snooze. "He has this old, shitty carcass," she said. "Artie. Every organ in there was acquired from somebody else, or grown specifically for him, or printed from a template. There's almost nothing left of the original vessel that made up this twentieth-century man—this man who moved mountains, who invented things that have changed the course of human history. And yet it's still him. It's still him in there." She gazed lovingly at this snoring husk for a while, misting up a little bit more. "You don't really know how lovable he is," she choked out, after a time. Gene didn't say anything, but he had to agree with her. He really *didn't* know how lovable Arthur was at all. In fact, he seemed like a spectacularly hateful old douchebag. But then again, first impressions can be misleading, he thought. Not often, though.

She turned to him then, and her eyes took him in entirely, and he was in them so deep that it was like he saw God, or something even better in the short term.

"If he was inside you," she said, "I could love both of you."

"Wow," said Gene. "Is that even possible?"

Sallie's eyes plunged into Gene and swam around in there for a while. And it was in that viscous, immeasurably dense silence that a small germ of understanding cracked through the macadam of Gene's willful stupidity, and he began, just a little, to see what Bob had been almost telling him, what Sallie was trying to say to him without quite saying it yet. And as the dark seed sprouted and poked up its twisted head, Gene beheld it and felt it germinate inside him, and it had teeth in it.

He stood, hoping that his terror did not show. In the back of his awareness, swirling around the Venus flytrap of his sudden insight, there was something else as well, possibly liberated by the shock of recognition. Not a flood, but a trickle of images, very faint now, but growing in shape and form. He didn't recognize them, but there they were. One by one. A few objects, floating by as in a dream. A room somewhere. A nice room. And a woman. Small. Dark hair. With a dragon on her back. I like tomato sauce.

And then, I've got to get out of here. But I can't let it show.

In that effort, he did not succeed completely. For during this second awakening, Gene lost control of his external mechanism. His eyes were focused on nothing; a complex mixture of expressions passed over his face, which up until now had displayed little but affability and occasional confusion.

Oh no, thought Sallie. I've seen this before.

"Let me walk you out," she said abruptly. Then she rose to her feet and took his hand again. "It's about time you got back to Bob, isn't it?"

"Oh yes," said Gene vaguely. "Bob."

He didn't argue, although his whole being revulsed at the idea of encountering Bob again, and he allowed Sallie to retain his hand. If his sudden forebodings were even slightly accurate, he needed to handle things with a little more care from here on in.

"Okay, Sallie," he said, as they reached the front patio again. "And, you know, thanks for your hospitality and everything."

"Oh," she said, a bit crestfallen. "It's going to be like that, is it?"

"Tell Arthur . . ." Here he ran out of insincerity. "Tell Arthur whatever it is you tell Arthur, I guess."

"I will. Of course I will," said Sallie. "And it's not good-bye, Gene," she added in a bright and friendly voice. "It's just so long for now. I have a feeling that we're going to be . . . great friends."

"Yeah! Of course!" he said. Gene searched for something else that might seem appropriate. "Hasta la vista, baby," is what he came up with.

She laughed. So he did, too. And here she was enveloping him with that warm gaze again! It struck him like a sneaker wave, almost knocking him back into her. She was standing so close to him that he could feel the tickle of her breath. What a woman, he thought. On the one hand, everything within him was screaming to get out of there. On the other hand, he was strongly considering the possibility of a deep, wet kiss.

They rose and walked in silence across the patio, through the portico, and back out onto the endless courtyard, crisscrossed with lawns, paths, and shallow ponds, that made up the front of the property. As they made their way, Gene noticed that the artificial koi in the pond that led up to the front door were more agitated than they had been upon his arrival. The two, still hand in hand, paused for a moment to look at the turmoil in the shallow water. One of the largest fish had eaten the tail off a smaller one and was working its way up its torso all the way to its head. The mottled victim in red, black, and what had once been a creamy white, was being whittled away by the other piece by piece. It didn't seem to notice, but continued swimming in its regular pattern—if perhaps a little more swiftly—its synthetic guts spilling out of its rear end, a blue, viscous liquid trailing along behind it, green and crimson fluids fouling its once-pristine scales.

Sallie saw Gene take this in and smiled. "Yes," she said, following his appalled gaze. "Nothing works perfectly all of the time, does it. But sometimes things do." They walked to the end of the path, where a gate opened onto the spacious driveways that led from the property to the gatehouse that guarded the community from the outside world, and from which he could grab an Uber for his trip back to the Hyperloop entry point.

Lucy appeared on the pathway next to them.

"Lucy! Bad girl! How did you get out?" said Sallie to the creature, very stern. She picked it up and held it out to Gene for caressing.

"Bye, Lucy," said Gene, and he put out his hand. The thing kissed it. Its tongue was simultaneously rough and silky. It was not unpleasant. He regarded the pet with amusement and then raised his eyes to find Sallie gazing at him as a hungry wolf would eye a lamb chop. She put Lucy down gently and once again took his hand in hers.

"Do you have any idea how old I am, Gene?" She was looking down at his hand, kneading the fat part of his palm. He couldn't see what she was thinking. He looked at the little wisps of hair at the nape of her neck, the way her tiny ear smartly concealed her extremely understated cranial implant.

"I have no idea, Sallie. It doesn't really matter."

"I've been married to that unpleasant old man in there for most of my life. A long time. Longer than you think. And believe me, he wasn't always like that, you know. He was once splendid. The essence of life itself, believe me. A force of nature. Open. Dynamic. Generous. A creative dynamo. A beautiful swimmer. But there are only so many updates you can do. Only so many . . . additions. Deletions. Tune-ups. Then, you know, the tech—even the most amazing tech—reaches its limit, and you need a whole new . . . solution to the problem."

"There is no solution to that problem," said Gene, and then, from some part of himself that was just awakening, he added, "Maybe there shouldn't be."

There was nothing left to say, not safely. He waited for her to release his hand. Somewhere very close, he heard the writhing and splashing of one artificial koi ripping another to shreds. And as the possibly artificial birds sang high overhead, and the sweet little artificial lizard snored lightly at their feet, a sad cast went over Sallie's eyes, and they retreated from him at last. After a very brief kiss, soft and gentle, on his cheek, she turned and half walked, half ran back up the pathway to the house, and Gene found himself outside the gates of the castle and in his Uber. In a very few minutes, he was back on the Hyperloop again, wondering what came next. Back in town, he got off at the station and instead of turning right, as he was supposed to do, he turned left and started walking—then running.

About a half mile down the road, his head began to hurt.

6

The Running Man

This wasn't a headache. It was something much, much worse, inflicted by the communications apparatus in his mastoid bone answering to a higher power. If Gene could have torn it out, he certainly would have. But he could not. Wherever he went, there it was, and there was no off switch for the functions that were now being engaged to punish him for noncompliance. His head was well and truly scrambled, but still he lurched and stumbled on, his destination thoroughly unclear to him. Gene knew he was going away, true, but "away" is not a place, really, it's more of an anti-place made up of every place except one. That *one* was clear to him. Building Eight. Bob. So that's where he was going. He was going to Not Bob.

The implement behind his ear had gradually heated up the farther he got from his anti-destination and was now delivering agony to his entire being. As he ran, he touched the implant gingerly. Ouch. If it got much worse, could it set his hair on fire? That would certainly impede his progress.

The thing was also beginning to generate a distinct, disagreeable vibration that shot a sequence of neurological bolts through his spine all the way to the tips of his toes and the ends of his fingers. Made it hard to stay upright, let alone run. Perhaps most disquieting was the virtually imperceptible low-pitched tone the apparatus emitted every fifteen seconds or so. In the sky above him, he thought he might hear a very faint but intensifying growl. Drones! They knew where he was! This fucking thing in his head!

They were coming for him. He wept: big, wrenching sobs that almost overrode the electronic impulses that were shaking him to his core. Yet still he ran. Ran as if his life depended upon it, because now he fully believed that it did.

The human crunch in the center of the urban village dissipated. Traffic thinned out. The buildings and pathways got smaller, narrower. The surfaces of the roadways began to appear less geo-molded and more like the asphalt used in the century past. Gene stopped for a moment and realized that he was in the vicinity of whatever it was his subconscious mind had been seeking. What was it? What the heck was it? What had he forgotten that he could almost remember?

Because, yes, there was now this other thing happening. In the midst of all the fear, all the confusion and mounting rage that was sweeping over him in waves, his mind was chuckling and whirring with random images and thoughts and memories. That's right, memories! Memories of people and places and sights and sounds they had tried to take away from him! Well, fuck that!

Now, what was that thing? It was on the tip of his mental tongue . . .

Imagine waking from a dream that immediately slips away when the first pastel light of morning hits your newly opened eyes. You know you have dreamed, but what? It was so real! But now . . . no. It's gone, like mist that dissipates with the first appearance of the sun. The more you try to grasp it, the farther away the substance slips into the crevasses of your mind. Then all at once, a picture comes back to you. Then a couple of nonsensical words somebody uttered in the deepest cavern of your dream—and bang! There it is: the entire story, the feelings, the people and places, the whole dream world, revealed in one massive tide of recollection. How could you have possibly forgotten it? It was the most important thing in the world, producing the most powerful emotions as it was unfolding—and then *poof*! It wasn't there at all. Only now it was. Magic! And it was strong and real and would never again be forgotten.

Gene knew he didn't have a moment to lose. They were right behind him. They were coming for him! And yet he fell to his knees with the force of the memory that slammed into him, determined to grab every last morsel of it. It was she. She was here. He had her now.

Livia! My God! Livia! How could he have forgotten Livia?

Now . . . who was Livia?

Gene stared into nothing that existed outside him. Now he knew. It was she he sought. And she was near—very near. He must find Liv. Liv would know what to do. He hauled himself to his feet and stumbled on, his brain on fire.

Across the campus, not too far away, Bob sat behind his desk, floating on the big silver tuffet. He was not pleased, for the most part. On the one hand, this was most inconvenient. On the other, just look at how his boy was blossoming into a young man! Kid had some co-jones on him! God, I'm a genius, Bob thought. What have I wrought. A real person. But he maintained his sour expression for business purposes.

Bronwyn sat in the guest chair formerly occupied by Gene, who had done so well in his first post-reboot diagnostic and now was misbehaving so badly.

"I suppose you know this is all your fault," said Bob.

"I'm sorry you're disappointed," said Bronwyn. Bob had certain human characteristics, she thought. And he was still a handsome man, with a tremendous amount of power that could possibly be used for good if you got him into the right place. In this case, she had something very specific to do, and she had to be careful how she went at it. It would be a shame if Gene had to die. Again.

Bob had fixed her with what he probably thought was a terrifyingly steely gaze. "You had to introduce him to your wacky friends," he said in an obnoxious tone.

"The last iteration was moribund, Bob. You wanted him kick-started." It would do no good to put up resistance to this nonsense, but she wasn't going to lie down, either.

"Maybe," said Bob. "But we didn't need him to get the hots for one of them."

"What can I say." Bronwyn shrugged appealingly. "She *is* pretty fabulous. And he is a human being."

"Well," said Bob. "Not really."

"You'll catch him," said Bronwyn. Bob shivered. Bee's ability to read minds was kind of spooky sometimes. You could see it as a function of her ninth-gen cranial implant, he supposed, but that didn't explain everything. It was kind of a turn-on, actually. Girl was cute. The fact that she occasionally hated his guts made her only more so. There was, of course, the significant difference in their ages. But nobody cared much about that anymore, with so many people up in their low triple digits and still in pretty good working order. And he had a long way to go before he hit that terrifying milestone.

"And what do we do with him then? Once we've got him back?" Bob inquired. "He's scarcely better than the last time round now, and he has a whole lot more information, thanks to Sallie overstepping her bounds. Foolish woman."

"What can I say," said Bronwyn. "She's a human being, too."

"Bronny," said Bob. "Sometimes your whole supertolerant thing can get kind of egregious." But he said it kindly. And they shared a smile amid this evolving fuckup.

"I'd hate to have to trash him again," said Bronwyn carefully, after a time. "We're way over budget already."

"Yeah, there's that." Bob munched his lip. "Just get him here," he said at last. "I'll charm the pants off him and see if I can close the deal before he really figures out what's what."

Good, thought Bronwyn, doing her best to maintain the neutral shell required to make Bob think everything was his idea. She gave him a little nod, this one with a small helping of sauce in it, and he responded appropriately. The air between them normalized, and Bronwyn relaxed a bit. The crisis was over. Gene would not be scrapped again.

All that remained, then, was for them to sit quietly and wait for developments. So that was what they did. After a little while, Edgar had some sandwiches brought in. Then Bob and Bronwyn simply hung out together in companionable silence, and grew closer.

The drones searching for their terrified prey were now flying in tighter circles. Gene could feel them breathing down his neck. Compounding his problem was the fact that he had stopped moving. He had arrived at what seemed to be his destination, since he was receiving no further internal impulses to move either forward or back. Lettering along the side of the low two-story brick building said "Indian Trail School." He peered in the window.

Inside, lined up in three rows of pint-sized desk-seat combinations, were about thirty children under the age of ten. At the front of the room, behind a large wooden desk that could well have been more than a hundred years old, stood a small, dark-haired young woman who was clearly the teacher. She was regarding the class with an expression Gene couldn't quite read. What a pretty girl this is, he thought. I wonder who she is. She seemed familiar. And then, quite suddenly: Of course she does! It's Livia!

It was indeed Livia. Let's see, thought Gene, looking her over. What do I know about this woman? Not very tall. About, maybe, five foot three, tops. No more than 110 pounds soaking wet. He found himself wondering what she would look like soaking wet. Had he seen her in that condition? Perhaps he had. He felt like it was possible. She was wearing a second skin of sleeveless black celulex that covered her down to her calves and up to just above her breastbone, plus a loose outer garment of some kind that conformed to her body as if it knew her intimately. Black studded boots from another time and place altogether.

Her hair was long on one side and colored a bright and festive magenta hue. On the other side of her head, it was very short, like a forest that had been knocked into stubble by a meteor blast. Nestled in the underbrush was a heavy-duty cortical implant studded with grommets. Sexy, he thought. Kind of old-fashioned. He wanted to touch it. Instead, he gently ran his fingers over the apparatus behind his own right auricle, which was now glowing a molten red and emitting short, porcine snorts every thirty seconds or so. The window was open, and he could hear her speak. Her voice was firm but light; musical, but with a twang of authority in it.

"Have all of you finished your reading?" Liv asked the class.

Gene looked over the children, most of whom were staring without expression into the air in front of their faces. They each had little implants behind their ears. Every now and then one would swipe the air in front of his or her face. Several appeared to be sleeping, their heads down on their desks. One young man sat on a stool in the corner, Gene noticed, sporting what looked like an old-fashioned conical dunce cap on his head, but a little shorter.

There was something else odd about the scene before him. Not a few of the children, some of them girls, had lost quite a bit of hair, and the tops of their heads gleamed through the little wisps that remained at the apex of their craniums. The room itself was very quiet as the young students engaged with their internal electronics.

Livia made her way out from behind that enclave and began strolling down the aisles of the classroom, touching one child on the shoulder here, another one there, leaning over a third to inquire about her progress. They all seemed quite comfortable but emotionally disengaged. As she reached the back of the room, she looked out the window and saw Gene, who stood up very straight as her gaze caught his. She smiled. He did, too. Then he fainted, falling straight down into a heap on the ground outside the schoolroom, his head buzzing like an angry hornet as the humming of the drones swelled in the skies just beyond sight.

7

Livia

He awoke to the twittering not of birds but of children. He was seated on the stool formerly occupied by the boy in the corner, with his back against the wall. The conical silver hat was on his head. The throbbing behind his ear and the bolts of neurological lightning had abated, and the intermittent snorting of the device had ceased. Liv was looking at him with a concerned expression, her hands on her hips. The kids were gathered around, some giggling, others apparently amazed that something interesting was going on outside of their communications hardware. He felt above him to ascertain the nature of the weight that was on his head.

"Don't remove it!" Liv cautioned. "It's all that's standing between you and whoever this Bob person is."

Gene looked up at Liv from the kid-sized stool. "You know Bob?" he inquired.

"No. You kept talking about him. You certainly don't like him very much."

"He wants to steal my body and put the mind of an ancient geezer in it somehow."

"Sure, Gene. Anyhow, the Jam Cap should do the job. I had to take it off Nelson here, but I'm sure he didn't mind." The entire class then looked over at the previous inhabitant of the Cap, who was now bouncing off the walls of the classroom, running around like a lunatic liberated from a straitjacket. The Cap had been a torture to the little fellow, since it was designed to cut off all connection to the Cloud. As a tool, it was utilized widely in schools and prisons as a pacifier for the mentally overstimulated; it was also a fairly severe punishment to those for whom being and connection were one and the same. It quite literally turned off their brains for a time, and for some, it was a terrifying penance. For Gene, however, it was a godsend. His mind was now quiet; his body no longer wracked with the penalty of failing to appear for the procedure Bob had in mind. And here was Liv. Liv! Wow, thought Gene. She is so pretty. Is she my friend?

"You don't remember much of anything again, do you?" said Liv.

"Just a little," said Gene. "I knew I had to find you."

"You boys and girls can stream for the rest of the afternoon," Liv said to the children, who immediately dispersed to their desks and submerged themselves again in their digital pursuits. "Don't misbehave," she said as she collected some of her things. She pushed a button on the side of the desk, and a synthetic creature styled to appear vaguely like a substitute teacher popped up from a panel in the back.

"Mrs. Liebowitz will be in charge," said Liv in a tone that implied it would be unwise for anyone to get on the wrong side of Mrs. Liebowitz. The children seemed to accept this as something not at all out of the ordinary. "Come on, Gene," said Liv, taking him by the elbow. "Let's get out of here. And keep your hat on."

And so they went. Gene didn't really care where. He felt safe for the first time he could remember. True, that wasn't saying much, but, still, it was a relief. The sound of the drones had faded. Yes, he would go with Livia wherever it was she wanted to take him.

On the ride back to Liv's apartment, Gene tried to ask her a number of clarifying questions, but she wasn't talking much. They certainly had plenty of time—the top speed of the self-driving minibus was fifteen miles per hour—but after a while, Gene gave up and simply sat in silence, content to do his best to appear as inconspicuous as possible with a shiny metal dunce cap on his head. It wasn't easy. The leather strap holding it in place wasn't exactly a comfortable fit and was digging into his chin.

For her part, now that they were alone together, Liv seemed a bit reserved. Gene didn't remember what he might have done to offend her in some previous incarnation. He figured he would eventually find out, although he wasn't really looking forward to it. Also, he was getting hungry and hoped that whatever prior relationship they had established involved eating something together in relative amity. He certainly didn't want to fight with anybody.

"We're here," said Liv. She took his hand, and they descended from the vehicle.

The apartment building was a white four-story block with four big windows on each floor. Its lack of distinguishing characteristics seemed to be an architectural decision. A uniformed android in the lobby was there to provide security.

"Hello, Henry," said Liv to the guard. "You remember Gene." And sure enough, the thing called Henry actually did. It nodded to him.

"Good day, sir," it said.

"Hello, Henry." After a moment of thought, Gene realized what he was expected to do, and he inserted his index finger in a little port designed to separate those who were welcome from those who were not. The security gates slid open.

"Have a nice day, Gene," said Henry.

"Thank you, Henry," said Gene. They entered the lobby and Henry reassumed his default state.

Up in the elevator they rode in silence. He could feel something in Livia clenching, preparing for some kind of discussion that might or might not go well. At the top floor, they made their way down a white marble corridor, very well lit. And with an application of the chip in her magic index finger into a small, recessed niche in the doorframe, the apartment portal sighed open, and in they went. He immediately recognized the place.

There was a big central room with a large glass table in the middle and sleek, curvaceous couches and armchairs here and there. He sat down on the most massive of the ultrawhite couches, which gave underneath his weight like a living thing. What was it made of? He felt it. Artificial skin, that's what. Pleasant skin, though. No warts or blemishes. Not sweaty. Just synthetic enough to avoid being completely creepy. And obviously congenial to human touch.

Livia sat down opposite him.

"So, Gene," she said. "You don't know who I am again, do ya?"

Gene felt intensely embarrassed. He didn't know what to say. He felt so lame. It was true. He knew he knew Liv. And he had feelings swirling around inside him that he knew she was creating. Good feelings! But that was all.

The silver cap felt very heavy on his head, and he was aware that he might not look his best for this important conversation.

"We have to start all over from the beginning again, I suppose. Bronny said you have problems with your memory. But seriously? I know you on and off for what, like, six weeks? And every time . . . it's the first time. I know you affect this vague thing, Gene, but it can get kind of exhausting."

Well, he thought. His database said that honesty was generally the best policy.

"I know you, Liv," he said.

"I would hope so." A bit hurt. Probably for good reason.

"But there's something wrong with me."

She looked at him hopefully. Okay, he thought. Press on.

"I woke up, and there was nothing in my head. I was basically forced to go see this Bob guy. As far as I can tell, he needed to see that there was nothing in my head. I guess I passed that test. Then he sent me down to Bel Air, where I had this incredibly weird lunch where I got the idea that I'm part of some scary experiment of some kind."

"What kind of experiment?" Liv looked dubious.

"One where they want to steal my body and use it to house the personality of the crazy old geezer who's about a hundred fifty years old."

"That sounds very unlikely, Gene."

"I realize that."

"But there is something odd about the whole deal, isn't there?" Liv said. "We met through Bronny. And Bronny does work for this guy named Bob . . ." She chewed the tip of her finger for a few moments. Then she stood. "Well," she said decisively. "Let's put a pin in it. I'll make us something to eat."

In one careless motion, she stripped off the organic outer garment, which parted at her touch and reformulated as she tossed it onto the nearest piece of seating: a living creature reverting to its neutral state after having been disturbed. Underneath this garment was that one-piece body suit. She looked good in it. She glanced at him and smiled.

"Remember anything at all yet?" she inquired.

"I'm starting to." There seemed to be nothing to say then, so they said nothing. The silence was surprisingly warm and inviting.

"Well, okay," she said at last. "It is what it is, I guess."

Then Livia went into the bedroom area, and he followed. There was a very large, very neatly made bed in the center of it. He sat down on it, and she went into a walk-in closet at the far end of the room.

The media wall had kicked on when he entered the room and was now silently projecting at least a dozen programming windows, all in different sizes, on one enormous glowing screen with no discernible surface. It was all virtual depth. Several images were holograms, springing into the room in sensuous three dimensions. At the moment, a very solid floating manatee bobbed around in midair. Other displays were transactional and spat out a succession of coupons, scented postcards—even the occasional snack food from an embedded 3-D printer, which was right then spewing forth some form of liquid protein cheese material. An entertainment node suitable for fast cerebrocortical implantation was burning in the download chamber.

He watched the wall for a while longer. It produced no thoughts in him and no feelings.

After a time, Liv emerged in a long T-shirt that went down to her knees. She paused to regard the wall unit with raw disdain. "These things are rotting our civilization from the inside out," she said. Then she went into the kitchen area. Like an obedient pooch, he followed.

"Dinner?" Livia inquired of the empty space.

"How about a couple of feggs?" said the refrigerator. "And Danish pastries are on special."

This was both surprising to Gene and not so much. Talking refrigerators, washing machines, light sockets—each appliance was as smart as it needed to be, and capable of expressing its needs and suggestions if set to the right parameters. A couple of fake eggs sounded pretty good, actually. He was famished.

"That sounds fine," said Liv. "Sit down, Gene." He sat. The fridge set about communicating with the stove, and before long dinner was in process.

"Do we have any bacorn?" Liv asked the space around the cooking area. She turned to Gene. "Unless you're a vegetarian," she said. "For a while there, I think you were."

He thought about it. A vision of a huge, juicy, delicious protochop floated into his head, and he had to suppress the urge to drool. "No," he said, "I'm definitely not."

"Feggs and bacorn, comin' right up!" said the smart refrigerator in a homey and accommodating voice. In a few moments, everything was bubbling and sizzling away completely without any assistance. The entertainment unit in the bedroom emitted a polite *Ding!*

"Will you fetch it, Gene?" asked Liv, who was wiping the slab in preparation for their feast.

He went to the media wall in the next room, where the interface had produced a menu with several pastry substitutes available for immediate printing. He chose one, pushed a couple of other buttons, and the wall started to chuckle very lightly. In a few seconds, it was done, and Gene returned to the kitchen with a small package of dehydrogenated acetosalicilicate protein substitute, which he laid on the table in front of them.

She sat down on one stool, and he took the other. This was all so lovely, he thought. Here she was, this beautiful woman; his friend, apparently. He knew her, but she remained a being altogether mysterious.

A memory slammed into his head. Livia. She was sleeping face-down on the bed. Her body was all muscle, covered with brightly colored tattoos. Birds, big ones, screeching and stretching across her upper back and around her torso, which was hidden by the sheets crumpled around her. A dragon cavorted across the back of her leg, its smiling face extending upward to the round curve of her upper thigh, its tail wrapping down around her knee. On her lower back, wings spread, an angel. Her magenta hair spread out on the pillow, studded implant glistening in the light from the window.

"I hope you like it," she said. Then she went into the microkitchenette and laid out two self-cleaning platters on the countertop. He heard her whistling a little tune under her breath. He didn't recognize it. He joined her in the kitchen space as she loaded the finished feggs and bacorn onto the platters.

"This looks pretty good," he said, sniffing it. It smelled almost like real food.

"Thanks, Genie," she said. She regarded the printed material that Gene had brought from the wall unit. It was about an inch across, light taupe in color. She placed it on a plate and, after a visit to the sink in the corner of the space, deposited one droplet of water on it. It immediately reconstituted itself into a large, plump cheese Danish with a coating of icing on top.

"Wow!" said Gene.

"It's completely fake in every way," Liv replied. She hopped on a stool and took a bite. "But since nobody I know has ever tasted an actual cheese Danish, it doesn't really matter, does it." She tore off a large section of whatever it was and placed the chunk on Gene's plate. "Here ya go," she said, chewing. "I feel like I'm eating sofa stuffing," she added, with some appreciation.

"You look very nice, Liv," Gene said, his mouth full of fake pastry. It was delicious. The things they could print these days!

Livia had made a breakfast sandwich with various elements of their meal. "Let's see what's going on," she said, munching. From their seats, they could take in the material on the wall unit. "Scan infotainment," she said.

So while they ate, they grazed through every bit of news that Livia's personal algorithm had selected as being of interest to her. Much of it seemed to aggravate her. It certainly unsettled him. It said that the Civil War was supposedly winding down. It was always winding down, but it never wound down completely because no matter how many of the other guys you killed there were always more to go around. There was still something blue on both coasts, plus a narrow band that included Chicago, a small island off the eastern coast of what used to be Florida before the rest of it was submerged, and a blob around Austin, Texas. There were also large swaths of green in various sectors of the map, here and there, the significance of which Gene did not understand. The new Real American Republic now reportedly included the entire South, most of Wyoming, Idaho, and everything of the Pacific Northwest but Seattle and Portland. Colorado still stood, but the reporter wondered for how long. The rest of what was formerly the United States was currently up for grabs, with very little power behind the forces that wanted to keep it together.

"Next," said Liv. The content changed. Look at this, Gene thought. Another leap in bioprinting. They seem to be coming every day. Whole animals could now be created. The body was printed bottom to top, all at once. Took about six days. The spleen was the biggest problem for a while, but they solved that. DNA built right in. Right now there was an adult male making the interview circuit who claimed to be the genetic descendant of Jesus Christ. Claims he was printed from DNA provided by a relic that had been in the collection of some supertrillionaire. "I saw that guy on QVC the other night, selling relics," said Liv. "He already has, like, a hundred million followers on Snapbook."

Gene gazed at Livia as Livia gazed at the wall, munching discreetly. It was nuts. A few hours ago, she was the furthest thing from his mind. Now he felt himself buffeted by powerful feelings for this woman. He leaned over to where her small, sleek head was bent over her plate, picking up crumbs with the tip of her finger, and kissed the top of her ear once—nothing sloppy. She gave a little wiggle and kept searching for the residue of the pastry she supposedly hated.

"You know," she said, "I want to take you to a meeting sometime. Bronny will come, too. You can see Master Tim and hear a little of what he's got to say. There could be a better world than this, Gene."

"I'd like to go," said Gene, without a single idea of what in the world she might be talking about.

Her plate now glisteningly bare, Liv rose and smacked her hands back and forth together both to decrumb them and also to signify the formal end to the meal. "I gotta mark a bunch of papers before bed," she said, and vaporized into the bedroom. Gene heard the sound of the shower closet going full blast for the maximum sixty seconds. Towels were an object of luxury available only to the very wealthy or nostalgic. She would emerge dry enough from the air blast. After a minute or so, he went into the bathroom to get the chance to see her naked. She was brushing her teeth, looking in the mirror. He observed the way her haunch met at the exact cutest nuance of her waistline. She had a little belly, he saw, which cried out for a gentle squeeze.

"I don't need to remember anything to know that you're incredibly beautiful," he said.

"Come here, Sparky," she said with the toothbrush sticking out her mouth. He did so, and she gently guided one of his hands around her waist while continuing to brush with the other. It was strange, he thought as he embraced her. He had been so worried about everything just a minute ago.

She felt very small but hard. He could wrap his arms around her and embrace her completely. "You're so warm," he told her.

"Let's see if you remember this," she replied. Then she spit once into the sink and drew him down onto the cold porcelain of the bathroom floor. His hat fell off, but neither of them cared.

About twenty minutes later, they came to take him away.

8

Better Living Through Chemistry

Gene was thoroughly Tased before they loaded him into the self-driving paddy wagon. Officer O'Brien had been apologetic but had reluctantly zapped his prisoner quite assiduously not once, not twice, but three times. So it's safe to say that Gene himself had very little fight left in him. He sat on one of the comfy chairs now and waited for Bob, who, he was informed by Edgar, was just wrapping up a prior appointment. Would he like a magazine? No, Gene thought. He could pass on the magazine. Inside, he was nothing but despair. But at least he didn't have to wear the Cap.

Time passed. A young woman came out of the inner office in a modest black leather sheath bedecked with heavy metal grommets that matched the implant in the carefully shaved area behind her ear. Her hair was brushed up so radically that it came to a point at the top of her head. "Hey," she said. Then she stood there in front of Gene but not really present except in a purely corporeal sense. She seemed to be peering at things from a very great distance.

"Hi, Gene," said a congenial voice. It was Bob, who had materialized behind her. Gene was glad to see him. He had fought it. He had tried. Now he supposed he was just meant to do what Bob wanted. He still had some cards to play, though. Or so he thought.

"Hey, Bob," he replied.

"Don't mind Sophie," Bob said, somewhat shamefacedly. "She's in a protoplasmic neurostatic state." Bob looked at his shoes for a moment, as if deciding whether or not to continue. Then he added, "I disconnected her anterior lobe. Temporarily. See if it reboots itself."

"Since when?"

"Last Thursday," Bob admitted. "She was happy to do it. Nothing else was getting her anywhere." They both looked at her for a little while. "Yogis work decades to achieve that state," said Bob thoughtfully, "and here she is in a waking dream she will never remember after a simple, painless ten-minute procedure. I never cease to be amazed at what we can do with the brain at this point. And we've only just begun, you know. These cortical implants have opened a whole new world of possibilities."

"What's she thinking about right now?"

"It depends on what you mean by 'thinking,'" Bob said.

They continued to look at Sophie. There was no avoiding it. She was fascinating: a human being in total, empty repose. Quite beautiful. As lacking in self-consciousness as a turtle in the sun.

"Will she come out of it?" Gene whispered.

"You did," said Bob.

Gene thought that perhaps he hadn't heard Bob correctly.

"Me?"

"Come on in, Gene," said Bob. "We have a lot of work to do."

It wasn't really an invitation. When they got to the door to the room, Gene was swept by the feeling that he was crossing a portal and that from that time forward, nothing would be the same. Even though he didn't actually remember much of what had gone before, he already felt nostalgic for it.

"Don't be scared, Gene," Bob murmured. "Over there?" He gestured toward the voluminous armchair on one side of the room and headed to his desk. "The problem is," he said, as if talking to himself while he fussed with some random stuff on his desk, "while some independent consciousness is necessary for this thing to work properly, you keep coming up short or blowing past an acceptable level. We have to keep rebooting you. This time you seemed just about right. Then Sallie completely overstepped her bounds and upset you. I understand why you were upset, but you have completely the wrong idea about this whole thing. That's what I want you to see. This situation is a win-win for everybody. Want a drink?"

Gene sat. He thought about whether he wanted a drink or not. It was quite possible he did. But Bob was continuing.

"The thing is, unless we move along now, a whole bunch of extremely unpleasant and time-wasting—not to mention incredibly expensive—things have to happen, and I don't think either of us wants any piece of that shit."

Gene didn't know what shit Bob was talking about. But he was starting to feel a little better. He had been very frightened when he was awakened and rousted out of bed by Officer O'Brien and a bunch of augmented humanoids. And right now there appeared to be very little he could do. He was different. He had found some of himself. By running. With Liv. He'd been human for a little while. He had regained some memories. He was a person, or at least a protoperson. He had a feeling that they weren't going to be 100 percent successful taking that away from him, whatever wacky plans Bob here wanted to implement. So he figured hey, why not. Nobody could make him do anything he didn't want, not forever. The big chair, almost a couch, was supremely comfortable. "Yeah," he said. "I could do with a drink."

"Marvelous!" exclaimed Bob. He beamed at Gene with what could only be called parental pride. "We'll fix you up." He continued to regard Gene fondly for a moment. Then he went to a sideboard. "By the way," he said, almost offhandedly, "what did you think of Arthur?"

"He's an extremely nasty old man, Bob," said Gene. "I certainly hope I don't have to spend much time around him."

"You know what?" Bob exclaimed as if he had just discovered a world-class idea. "I'll have a drink, too!" He went to a small recess in the wall of his office, where a printer was warming up. "Here we go," he said, placing a heavy crystal glass in a receptacle beneath the machine. In a moment, there was a pleasant sound of liquid pouring into the container, followed by a *Ding!* Bob reached in and removed the glass, which now sported two fingers of a gleaming golden liquor. "Sixty-year-old Yamazaki," Bob said. He sniffed it. "Brilliant." Then he crossed the room and handed Gene the glass. "Don't chug it," he advised. "It's liquid gold, you know. That one glass would cost you more than two thousand simoleons in the Floating Islands district."

"Simoleons!" said Gene, who knew the word. He took a sip of the magic elixir. It was indescribably smooth but had a little bite to it as well, and just a hint of peat. "This is a rather small portion," Gene said, sipping. Bob chuckled, went back to the device, and printed himself a drink. Then he carried the glass back to his desk and took a big swallow.

"I imagine you have some questions," he said, gazing at the brown liquor with affection.

"Not too many," said Gene nonchalantly. "But you go ahead, Bob. I'm listening."

"I'll lay it out for you just a little bit." Bob put down the glass and began fiddling with his desk drawer, which seemed to be resisting his advances. "There are many things now possible in the world of science," he observed, as if he were giving a tour of the children's museum. He stopped and glared at the drawer.

"Come on, Bob," said Gene with some bravado. "I probably know most of it already." Yes, Gene was feeling very tough.

Bob looked him over. "You know, it's funny about truth," he said. "You don't want to impose more of it on a person than they can bear."

Bob's whole condescending tone annoyed Gene. He sat up, fighting the possessive grasp of the semi-animate chair. "You know what?" he said. "I'm tired of this game." He stood and brushed himself off. "I think I'll vamoose."

Bob emitted a short, sharp laugh. "*Vamoose*," he said with a chuckle. "One of my favorite words. Goes all the way back to the nineteenth century. From the Spanish, *vamos*. You and I may be the only people left who know that word." He looked at Gene very seriously now, his eyes welling up with large, juicy tears. Then he straightened, collected himself for a moment, and once again attacked the top drawer of the desk.

"Would you like a little Xee?" he asked as he wrestled with the furniture.

Wow, thought Gene. He sat down again. "I've never had Xee," he said. He was still determined to play his winning hand, which boiled down, basically, to a strong determination not to cooperate. But still, he thought, Xee!

"Yeah," said Bob. "Let's make this a little more fun."

"Okay, Bob," said Gene. He certainly had nothing against fun. "Why not?"

"Why not indeed." Bob pounded the drawer with the fat part of his fist. "Shit." He pounded it again. "Let me tell you about Xee," he continued, scowling at the stubborn desk. "It's legal, with a prescription. It's safe, within limits. And it makes your head feel good. The boost in intelligence and insight into situations of all sorts last a good forty-eight hours. Goddamn it!" He slammed the drawer hard, with both fists balled up into mallets, and it finally sprang open obligingly, as if it had been teasing him the whole time. "These intelligent desks aren't so fucking intelligent, it turns out," he muttered. "There are people who have some Xee every morning and are none the worse for wear," he continued as he pawed through the contents of the drawer. "Of course, there are contraindications associated with overuse, as there would be with any powerful synthetic. One study shows a severe abuser whose brain exploded out of his nose, but there was very spotty peer review on that one. It could just be an urban legend."

From the desk, Bob removed a small metal box with a hinged glass top. He raised the lid to reveal several compartments, each containing thin strips of varying colors about the length of a toothpick and twice the width. Carefully, he selected a single wafer of irides-cent, gleaming platinum.

"This is a strip of Xee. It melts on your skin as cool as the first flake of a snowstorm and enters your body on a time-release basis. This leads to an effect curve not unlike a perfect wave, with a build, an apex, and an elegant down sweep at the end that deposits you on the beach of everyday existence again. With me so far?"

Gene went back to nursing his drink. He said nothing. He figured Bob would go on anyway. Also, truth be told, he was kind of eager to get high.

"The red strips are a light and frisky twenty mils and simply give you an overall feeling of sharpness and well-being that after eight to ten hours devolves into the most delectable sleep imaginable. The gold strips are fifty mils and infuse the spirit with all the grandeur of consciousness on an extremely elevated plane. They also come with a powerful side effect: seriously bad impulse control. This takes a wide variety of forms, fitting itself seamlessly into the hollow places in each user. Formerly cheap bastards with more money than God abruptly divest themselves of all worldly goods and beam off to the Andreessen Hydroponic Gardens hanging 22,500 miles above the earth in geosynchronous orbit. The weather up there is reputed to be fantastic. Others with the thrill-seeking chromosome sometimes jump from high places, with mixed results. Individuals who favor more sensual pleasures plunge into them in ways that did not always sync with socialized existence. You don't want to deal with a psycho-path on Xee."

"I'll keep that in mind," said Gene. He was now done with his whiskey and wanted some more, but he didn't say so. To be anesthe-tized is one thing, dead drunk another, particularly if he was going to be full of Xee in a minute.

"Finally, there are the platinum magic carpets of Xee-1000," Bob intoned with some dramatic flair. "Each of these costs at least ten thousand ameros. That's a hunk of cheese, let me tell you." Bob held it up to the light. "Just look at this puppy. I never knew anybody who's taken one of them. I hear that Sergey took one right before he disappeared a few years ago. Supposedly he applied the Xee-1000 directly to his testicles and sat very still for about an hour. Then he said, 'Entanglement is macro,' and actually went into the room with the quantum computer."

Bob's voice was soothing now, affectionate and warm. He regretfully put the silvery strip back in the glass box, and out came a little red strip. He ripped open the cellophage wrapper carefully, starting the tear with his teeth but making sure that none of it hit his tongue. When he had the strip out, he approached Gene, who was already mellow as the month of May, and put a paternal hand on his shoulder. "As you will know if you check your database, Gene, a quantum computer at this point isn't really a computer at all in the traditional sense."

"It's not?" said Gene, looking up at Bob. He didn't want to be thought incapable of keeping his half of the conversation going, but he had no idea wheresoever the fuck it was going.

"No. It's actually a gigantic environmental area inhabited by about a trillion organic receptors fabricated from virus-based nanocillae."

"Ah," said Gene.

"Objects that fall within the extremely limited event horizon of the quantum space around the computer enter a unique status in which they both exist and do not exist at the same time, in alternate universes. Unfortunately for the people of the Alphabet Mars Colony, Sergey ceased to exist in this universe, although it is thought that he may be fulfilling an important function in some other."

While Gene was considering this example of quantum duality, Bob laid the little red ribbon of psychotropic DNA Crispr tenderly on the back of his neck, which immediately felt as if an icicle had been placed there.

"Will you be having one?" Gene inquired, shivering slightly. It wasn't unpleasant, though. Just different . . . Differnet, he thought. Daffernet. Duffer . . . naut.

"No, Gene," said the doctor. "I'm working."

Gene was feeling the sizzle and burn that all who have enjoyed Xee will recognize, followed by the nice citrus thing in the back of his throat and the smell of tangerine. My, thought Gene. That is tasty. I have to remember to ask Bob for a prescription for this shit. Then he thought about a flock of seagulls on a beach, cavorting with the remains of a candy bar. Then a big, steaming hot dog in a gigantic, fluffy bun invaded his mind. It was very pretty. Then it was quiet for a while. Gene felt extraordinarily clear and good. What had he been concerned about? Could use a hot dog, though. Pretty much right away, actually.

"You good?" Bob's hand continued to reside gently on Gene's shoulder. It moved lightly and fondly stroked the back of his head.

"Sure," said Gene. He surfed the mind wave for a moment. Then a very dreamy inquiry. "Tell me about Sallie." It was, after all, the only question he truly wanted to ask.

"That's my boy," said Bob indulgently. Gene felt him slip another wafer onto the skin of his ankle. His mind left his body and spread out to take up the entire room. "The question is why a beautiful woman like that would marry a desiccated old weasel like Arthur. Am I right?"

"Yes," Gene said, from the edge of the universe. "Why?"

He could feel the cosmic wind in his hair. The deep black of space; the shifting hues of the gas and dust that blow between the stars. He lay back in the great nothingness and looked at the interface between time and space that must be heaven.

"Our conclusion," said Bob, "is that Sallie is truly in love with him. I know it seems counterintuitive, but there it is. And you know what, Gene? Any man who could claim to be the recipient of such a love must be considered lucky indeed, don't you think?"

This seemed like a trick question. Gene found himself thinking about the whole setup. It did have its moments. He thought of Sallie greeting him at the door of the splendid mansion. The synthetic koi were in the pond. The inauthentic sky above was filled with birds of uncertain provenance. The little green fabricated lizard nuzzled her leg. What was its name? Lucy? Had it spoken to him? The old man with brain material leaking out of his ears. The drool cascading down his chin, which she was happy to mop up with her very own napkin. And the way she looked at Gene himself. What was that? What could it possibly signify? Was it his imagination, or had it been infused with some kind of intense mixture of love and . . . what was that, *lust*? No, that could not be possible. And yet, was that so unthinkable? As much as she might adore the crumpled, odiferous, seeping, ancient lawn gnome that suppurated on the divan in the darkened study of their gigantic palazzo, was it not possible that at the same time she would crave a man with blood in his veins that didn't come from a liquid printer?

"Arthur will die soon," Bob said. "And yet it is mandatory—for a variety of reasons, only some of them pertaining to Sallie—that his consciousness, his self, his persona, continue on beyond the limits of the body that was issued to him more than a hundred years ago. Most importantly, it is his money that is funding absolutely everything you see around you, which does a lot of good for a lot of people. Do you get me, Gene? I want you to understand the value of what you are doing. It's important to me. Because I love you, Gene. And I wouldn't be doing this unless it was absolutely necessary."

"I love you, too, Bob," said Gene, but it might have been the Xee talking.

"Around fifty years ago, a bunch of very, very rich guys from around these parts decided that they didn't want to die, ever. It sounds silly, but they put a lot of money against the project, and you know how much money they have, Gene. When you have those kinds of resources, you can do anything. And after about thirty years, they came up with something. They worked out a way to implant certain essentials of one person's consciousness into another."

"Another what?"

"Another person. It was and remains an imprecise process, but it's all but perfected now."

"Get outta here," said Gene. He didn't feel so good all of a sudden. Like, there's a point where you're too high. Your face gets cold. Stomach tightens up, gets kind of heavy. Legs get wobbly. Head flying around all over the place. Might actually puke. That would be a bummer. He sat bolt upright, a ringlet of sweat beading his brow. "I think I need a glass of water," he said.

"It's called personality capture and migration," Bob continued. "Attitudes. Memories. Sense of self. Life story. The whole person. If it goes right, you've created digital immortality."

"I'm gonna barf, Bob," said Gene.

"I really hope you don't," said Bob sternly. "These carpets are real twentieth century."

Gene lay back in the chair. He breathed, trying to collect himself and stop the world from whirling. If he lay straight, and very, very still, and kept his eyes open, he might be all right. When he closed them, though, everything took off in all directions. "I can see where this is going," he murmured, close to tears. "And I don't think I like it very much."

"Once you wrap your mind around the concept, it really seems quite simple," said Bob, enthused by the amazing tech behind it all. "Utilizing the cranial implant, you upload the entire contents of the donor into a machine environment. Then, when you're ready, you slam it in one gigantic core dump back down into a receptive biological host. And voila."

"It sounds like a bad deal for somebody," Gene observed.

"Actually, yes, Gene," said Bob, "and I feel bad about it, you know I do." He produced a small bottle of something clear from a nearby shelf and fixed Gene with a friendly smile. "Here. Drink this," he said kindly. Gene, his head spinning, sat up and took a sip. The liquid was amazingly good, but the first sip was better than the second, and the second better than the third. By the time the bottle was half-empty, it had started to taste kind of funny.

"The reason that you have been created, Gene, is that all previous attempts to do this involved real, biologically produced people—normal people with actual histories and experiences and dreams and memories—but during the transfers, the migration was imperfect, and the implant failed to take.

"Well, that's encouraging."

"No it isn't, because the donor and host were pretty much burned to a crisp."

"Too bad," said Gene. "Boo-hoo-hoo." He was getting sleepy. He felt strongly that this was highly inconvenient, since they seemed to be at the point of the lecture where it might be important to pay attention.

"So it turns out that a . . . regular human being . . . is unsuitable, in the end, for the purpose. And that issue has proved insurmountable. For a total, complete migration, somebody very special would have to be available. Somebody who was a complete human entity; conscious and aware up to a point but not yet imprinted with experience. And if he or she didn't exist yet, well"—he brightened considerably—"he'd just have to be printed out, now, wouldn't he?"

"I gotta go," said Gene. He stood up, took two steps, spun around twice, and fell in a heap on the floor.

"Perhaps I've said too much," said Bob. Then he pressed the button on his desk that called for the orderlies.

9

Migration

The pain was a screaming white light that penetrated through his temples and out through the back of his scalp: four screws at 45-degree axes bearing down one ratchet at a time, micron by micron, the probe in his cranial implant going deeper and deeper into the ooze of his brain, and then way inside the core of it, into the tiny, hollow center of his skull. The fire of a million suns burned away who he was and replaced it with an incoming flow that was not himself but someone else entirely, and little by little Arthur took residence in there: first as an infinitesimal spark, and then a nucleus of positive energy, and then a wave of pure being that began to seep into every corner of him until there was no Gene to speak of at all—there were only the beginnings of something that would very shortly become nothing but Arthur. And yet Gene still fought it.

"Give in to it, son," said a voice very, very far away from him. "Let it in."

Gene screamed then, because the pain both physical and spiritual was so great. There are screams where you still exist while screaming, and there are those in which you turn into nothing but the scream. Gene was all scream.

In the short, square structure across the town from Building Eight, Livia's head exploded with an urgent incoming message. She had been pacing back and forth in the apartment, waiting for word of Gene, and becoming increasingly frantic when there was none. Bronwyn had told her that all moving pieces were converging around him. She didn't want to tell Liv what that convergence might mean. She barely knew herself.

Liv was scared. How did things get so serious so fast? She and Bronwyn had met during the long weekends at the Peaceable Kingdom up north, listening to Master Tim talk about the new society they would have to build out of the ashes of this one. She was aware that Bronny had spoken to Bob about this vision of the future, too, but that he considered her a crackpot and treated her with the polite disdain that men still maintained when dealing with women—especially younger women who expressed political ideas. Still, Bronwyn was in a position of strength here. Bob liked her a lot; that they could see. And along with the condescension, the mansplaining, and manterrupting she had to endure about stuff she already knew, they also were aware that, as evolved as they all had become, men still thought primarily with their little heads instead of their big ones.

The good news was that Bob was coming along. It might take a bit longer than she might have liked, but Bob was, after all, a genius, and, as Tim had explained, his command of all available and developing tech was key to the plan. Tim's plan: the one that would make the planet habitable again for people who didn't want antennas sticking out of their heads.

So Bronwyn got with Bob's program, even though a lot of what she had to do made her sick. She had been tasked with the job of getting Gene's brain up and working so it could serve its function later. That had taken some doing. The first iterations of the printed body had been impressive. It worked! They had a person! But after a little while, each had been unsuitable in one way or another. One couldn't stop talking. Another proved to be unacceptably horny and had to be dismantled almost immediately. Versions three and four had physical problems and died horribly within weeks of their creation. Gene was version five. He was pretty much perfect physically, but mentally, his consciousness kept reasserting itself and getting in the way. A certain amount of this mindfulness was, according to Bob, a necessary part of the process, but too much of it would stymie what he had in mind. They had to get the balance of mental activity and emptiness just right.

As part of her job to jump-start this version, Bronwyn decided to introduce Gene to some friends of hers in a variety of benign social situations. One of these taught school to both biological children and, upon occasion, synths in need of training. This was Livia. The two had met during weekends at the Kingdom, so Bronwyn knew she was good people. Unfortunately, during this process, Liv had taken a genuine liking to Bob's creation. Gene was nice, with a straightforward manner born of sheer cluelessness and a very healthy appreciation for the simple things in life, including food and sex. Each time they rebooted him, however, he forgot all about his prior short-term experience base, and they had to get to know each other again. Maybe that was part of the attraction. Plus, each newly programmed Gene seemed to like Liv as much as the prior one had. So they kept getting into each other over and over again.

Bob didn't know about that part. There were some things he didn't need to know, as far as Bronwyn was concerned. He was busy with the execution of his own mysterious master plan anyway, the details of which he felt no compulsion to mention to her. She was also very aware that, although he was a pretty good guy in a lot of ways, Bob lacked a certain moral compass. She would have to keep an eye on Gene. And as good people do, she lied to herself; told herself that the big day for which they were preparing Gene would never really come. But now that day was here. She would have to play her role. The least she could do, however, was call Liv. She waited for an opportunity.

As the hours marched by on little cat's feet, Livia's anxiety grew to the point where she thought it might be helpful to pop a splooge, just to stay frosty. Right after that, she dispensed a small glass of white wine from the entertainment wall unit's liquid print feature. Then she stretched out in the anthropomorphic bed and promptly fell into a comatose state that was not unpleasant. So when her head nearly blew off her body, beeping and flashing with an incoming message, she was completely disoriented.

"Ha! What!" she yelled, leaping to her feet. Where was she? Oh. Right. Gene was gone. He had not come back. She activated her implant.

"Liv," said Bronwyn's voice from inside her head. "I don't have a lot of time, so listen."

"Bee, is that you?" Liv's mind was clearing just a little bit, although not too much. Splooges weren't quite as powerful as even the mildest Xee, but their effects didn't just vaporize after a half-hour nap.

"I can't talk long," said Bronwyn. "And I have to keep my voice down. But I heard screaming about twenty minutes ago."

"Oh no," said Liv. She sat down on the edge of the bed because her legs would not support her. What were they doing to Gene? Could they be killing him? Harvesting his organs?

"There was nothing I could do, Liv," whispered Bronwyn. The screaming had been pretty horrible at first. Bronwyn thought she was used to those kinds of noises when they had worked on animals, but it turned out that when they came from a human being, it was even worse. The shrieking didn't last long, thank goodness. But it was terrible while it lasted.

"Oh, Bee," said Liv. She felt sick to her stomach. "This is Gene we're talking about."

"I'll call you later if I find out anything," said Bronwyn, and with a short touch to the transmitter behind her ear, she was gone. Another piteous cry, fainter than the first but still pretty awful, had just erupted from the lab down the hall.

"This is not going so well," said the voice just outside Gene's head. He knew it was Bob, but he seemed to be blind and couldn't see anything around him. "Resisting again, goddamn it! This is bad. I don't want to have to reboot him!"

Then came a woman's voice: soft, gentle. "Gene," it said. "This is Sallie." Her voice took his hand. "It's going to be okay."

"That's better. He's stabilizing. Thank God. I'd hate to go back to the print shop for another copy entirely. In many ways, this one works very well."

"Shhh, Bob." Sallie again, with a hard knife-edge underneath. "There is still a person in there somewhere, and that person is still listening to you. So if you have anything but the most positive thoughts, you should probably keep them to yourself for the time being."

"I'm sorry," said Bob. "It's just the prospect of having to do this all over again. The DNA work. The cell development and chain linking. I don't have to tell you how much the whole thing cost Arthur, do I?"

"You're still talking, Bob." The steel beneath the skin was just a bit harder now. But it didn't matter. The thing that had been Gene was shrinking, melting down to a small, rotating nimbus of light in the center of his brain stem. And the other thing was moving inside him.

Bob finally lowered his voice, but a morsel of the remains of what was once the fabricated persona known to himself as Gene was still listening in there somewhere. If he existed at all in the future, he would remember it, and not with fondness. "Besides," the doctor went on, "there's also no way that Arthur can be uploaded again, I presume you know that. There's no *there* there. He's a turnip—I mean his physical self—and that decomposition has fed back into his mental functioning. We can use the backup if we need to again, I suppose, but you know that's not as reliable as a fresh upload."

Gene gave one last wrenching scream with all the might that existed in him. It came out as a tiny squeak, and then his mouth reset itself and said, "Bob, if you don't shut the fuck up, I'm going to push the bone in your nose through the back of your head."

"Artie?" Sallie said with a little tremble. "Is that you?"

"Hi, munchkin." The voice was Gene's but already a bit loaded with an extra helping of gravel. "Help me sit the fuck up."

"Not yet." Bob was behind the creature who was once Gene, both his hands on the back of its head. "Don't move your head. The download probe is still seated in the input module and transferring the last little bit into your inferior frontal cortex right behind your left eye. It's why you're blind right now. I had to disable your optic nerve. If you lie very still, we'll complete the transfer in about . . . six minutes." Bob fiddled with some hardware behind the thing that was now Arthur: a young Arthur, as strong and impatient to get going as the original.

"Come on, come on," said Arthur. "I got places to go and people to do."

Bob continued to fiddle. This whole thing had felt just too easy for him. Gene had gone under, and after that original, horrid scream, he had whined a little, uttered an occasional moan, but only once had he issued a mighty screech—the kind of howl a dog might make if it was being euthanized improperly. Bob felt bad. He had liked the entity that had emerged when the living (if artificial) being he had brewed from his own DNA had emerged over the course of a long month in the 3-D printing room. People had said that it couldn't be done. But he had done it, from the inside out: first the spine and then the rest of the skeletal structure. That took about ten days. Then the musculature, sketched in lightly and then spun into shape ever so carefully, appearing as if by magic in the chamber. The blood was the hardest. It was fabricated from his own template and had to be infused a bit at a time, as if watering a plant that filled with life as the liquid flowed through its veins. The organs, one by one, followed. That was easy. They'd been printing livers, spleens, kidneys, and hearts since the late 2030s. Those were mostly shells, about as alive as the Visible Man plastic anatomy set that he had assembled as a kid. But the blood and the bile and the spit and all the other fluids infused the waiting objects with the stuff of life. The brain was last. Left brain. Right brain.

Corpus callosum. The all-important Broca area. Each little portion fertile, alive in a way, but empty. A medium, nothing more, waiting for the cocktail of data, neural search capability, and long-term and short-term memory that made independent thought possible. But no persona, of course. No soul. Just waiting for the final implant: Arthur. *If* it could be said that a being like Arthur had a soul. And here it was on the table beneath his hands, this thing that he had created, and it was being filled up with something pretty terrible, and all the decent human in there was being expunged.

The thing that had been surprising was the unplanned emergence of something approaching—what would you call it, character?—in this empty body he had created as a receptacle for this mean old man, so greedy for life that he absolutely refused to accept the inevitable fate of every other person who had ever lived in the history of the planet. All of a sudden there had been this individual with a character of sorts. Gene. True, a sort of vapid person most of the time. What else could he be without memory or experience of his own to draw on? But with a spark: a feisty, resistant young man who kept on asserting himself no matter how many times Bob rebooted his center of consciousness in an effort to create a tabula rasa for Arthur to inhabit. This . . . human being, unlike any other. Made from his, Bob's, mitochondrial soup, printed, and then infused with some of his knowledge base. He wondered if the boy was still in there somewhere. He looked down into the empty eyes that had once contained his creation but now stared sightlessly up at the ceiling.

"I think your six minutes are up," said the gritty voice that was not yet quite 100 percent Arthur but wasn't Gene anymore, either. "Come on, Bob. I want to try out any number of my working parts."

"Okay," said Bob, and in one fluid motion, he removed the infinitely thin probe, some four inches in length, that had entered Gene's cerebrocortical implant and poured the entire upload of Arthur's consciousness in all its parts into the vessel that had been created to house it.

"Ouch, man," said Arthur. "Now, whatever you did to my optic nerve, I'd really appreciate it if you give it back now. This darkness is freaking me out."

A few moments later, the door to the lab opened, and Bob emerged pushing a wheelchair that contained the shell that was once Arthur. Its mouth hung loose, wide open like that of a skull with blown hinges. Its head tilted at an odd angle, askew from its torso. But its eyes were open, the orbs within its sockets moving slowly to various points of light or motion in the space around it.

Behind Bob, the door to the lab stood open. Gene was standing there, near the operating table, in properly starched white boxers and an open white dress shirt. He was attempting to put gold cuff links into the cuffs and whistling softly. As he wrestled with the job, he glanced up, saw Bronwyn, looked her up and down appraisingly, and gave her a smarmy smile. Then he went to the lab door, winked at her, and closed it.

Bob handed over the wheelchair and its terrifying occupant. "Room six," he said, scrutinizing Bronwyn to see if she was going to offer any editorial opinion. "Make him comfortable. We'll see about his permanent disposition tomorrow. It's funny. I never considered this aspect of the procedure."

"Well, you can't plan for everything, Bob," said Bronwyn, and if Bob noticed the tartness of her tone, he didn't let on. She took control of the chair and disappeared down the hallway to the place where Arthur's former body was to be stored until it failed to function entirely. That might be in days, or months, or years, even, thought Bob, but you most certainly couldn't do anything to influence that process or hurry it along. That would be wrong.

He then repaired to the executive offices, where Sallie was waiting. In silence, he went to his desk and extracted a small plastic box, which he handed her without fanfare. Inside were four blue sticks carefully nestled in individual nanofoam slots.

"Guard these carefully," he said.

"And they are?"

"Memory nodes of almost infinite capacity. They contain all the data necessary to reconstitute your husband, Arthur—if, you know, that becomes necessary."

"Might it? I thought the procedure was a success."

"As far as we know," said Bob, but his mind had already moved on to the next subject. "Who knows?" he added as he turned to re-enter the lab. "Maybe you'll want more than one copy of the mean old son of a bitch."

– TWO –

10

Feelin' Groovy

They left the building, Sallie with her original body, Arthur with his new one pumping Gene's brand-new blood and bile and rheum and sweat and tears and cerebrospinal fluid, except it was no longer Gene's—it belonged to the ancient entity that by all rights should have died thirty years ago and been considered lucky to have lasted that long. The muscles and ligaments seemed to work fine, too.

Arthur sneezed. It felt great. Yesterday that sneeze would have blown his head off his shoulders. Fucking A, he thought. No matter what bullshit he'd gone through, all the years of transplants and cyborg grafts and vitamin suppositories and hemitropic infusions and mitochondrial transubstantiations and cranial enhancements and upgrades and whatever new thing was supposed to elongate his time on the planet, it was nothing like this. He looked at Sallie and felt a pleasurable wave of endorphins—real ones now, not the synthetic variety he'd been shooting for a couple of decades. Time to go home, he thought, and try this motherfucker out.

Their vehicle was waiting in parking mode, hovering about six inches above the polished surface of the plaza. All around them, people surged here and there, intent on whatever task awaited them in one of the virtually identical buildings that made up the campus. No one paid anyone any attention as they went, so utterly focused were they on the electronic images and messages that were buzzing about inside their heads. The local weather had been turned off for the afternoon. Nobody missed it.

The hovercraft was an Uber piloted by no one but the cyborg brain that resided somewhere in its chassis. Inside was a passenger compartment that more closely resembled a small, comfortable conference room, with a love seat, a couple of chairs, and a central table with controls for environment and entertainment. "Home?" inquired the vehicle.

"Go fuck yourself," said Arthur.

"Artie, that behavior was kind of cute when you were a grumpy geezer," said Sallie, "but now that you're a handsome young stud, you might want to ameliorate your tone. People may like you a little better."

They climbed in, Sallie first. It was very posh, she thought, and had that new-car smell. Before he followed, Arthur stood tall at the doorway of the conveyance, taking in the entire scene. It was the first time he had been out and about in the new world beyond his gates, and without the pain that had made his life a misery. It was magnificent.

Looking about him with new eyes, literally, he noticed an object of some sort floating in the air a short distance from him behind some shrubbery, clearly trying to look inconspicuous. This wasn't difficult, because it had been designed to be ignored. Arthur knew that, because it was, in fact, he who had designed it, or at least called for its design. Perhaps this gave him an unfair advantage, he thought. He turned to face it and motioned it to come closer. It tilted in the breeze as if to ask, "Who, me?"

"Yeah you. Get over here." It was a simple floating yellow globular security device, the kind they call a "tennis ball." It had been lurking and appeared nonplussed at having been spotted. It now approached, raised itself slowly several feet into the air, and then simply remained suspended there with a certain saucy arrogance. It was said these entities had a vocabulary of perhaps a dozen words and the capacity to learn another five or six more, which they could emit from a small embedded speaker.

"Get lost," said Arthur to the security bot. "We don't want you around."

"And yet . . . here I is," said the bot. They were very good at one-syllable words, although grammar was obviously not this one's strong suit.

Arthur closed the door to the vehicle behind him and focused his full attention on the bot. Who was following him? He had a pretty good idea, and he would take up this intrusion with them in due time. For now, however, he wanted the thing off his tail. "If you continue to bother me," he growled, "I'm going to have to disable you. I know how."

The bot hung in the air, silent. It did droop a little, though, and back up a tad. "Take this reflecting pool," said Arthur with just the right soupçon of menace. It retreated again perhaps another quarter inch, alarmed.

"Stop that, now," it said, trembling in the air before Arthur's face. Then, if a perfectly circular object can be said to turn, it seemed to do so in a direction away from him in preparation for a quick departure. With the swiftness of a cat, Arthur snatched the yellow object out of midair and in one fluid motion tossed it across the fifty yards or so that lay between them and the reflecting pool, where it landed in the water with a resounding *smack.*

The thing uttered a high-pitched squeal that could be likened only to the sound a pig makes when it attempts to flee the slaughtering blade. It skittered across the surface and out of the pond, and then shot into the air above the plaza, where it zigged and zagged erratically, spinning all the while in an attempt to shake off excess water and dry itself.

"That was not a very nice thing to do," said a mildly digital voice to Arthur's rear. He turned to find himself face-to-face with Officer O'Brien, the police bot that was half cyborg, half rolling Segway.

"I agree," Arthur said brusquely. Without further conversation, he opened the door to the waiting vehicle and hopped inside. "Let's go," he said to the interior of the self-driving transport. It dropped a very small set of wheels to ground level and tootled off.

"Unfortunately," said Officer O'Brien, staring after the departing vehicle and talking to nobody in particular, "it is not yet illegal for assholes like you to be abusive to artificial life forms. Perhaps one day it will be." He rolled off. The little round tennis ball, after a moment of indecision, floated off in the general direction of where Arthur and Sallie had headed.

Arthur turned and stared out the rearview window. In the distance, he saw the tiny yellow dot meandering far behind them, bobbing up and down in sullen pursuit. Of course it was coming after him. How could it not? Its entire purpose was to be where Arthur was. It had no other agenda, no alternative. What it was meant to do was baked into its hardware. This is what makes all machine intelligence so limited, Arthur thought. In the end, no matter how smart they are, fabricated beings didn't yet have the power to choose one thing over another. This led to comical problems in some of the more advanced artificials he had developed, when their programmers— who, after all, were only human—forgot to include one preference or another in an otherwise serviceable entity. The creature sat and whirred, fluid leaking out of its nose, unable to even select a movie to download for the evening or a wine to accompany dessert for its master. Pathetic creatures. Not natural beings like he was.

"Can't this fucking thing go any faster?" Arthur inquired to the interior of the driverless space. He felt very uncomfortable all of a sudden. And the beginnings of a fucking headache, too, on top of that.

"Certainly," said the car with a hint of pride. "Although it will increase the possibility of an incident by seven percent."

The vehicle increased in speed, all the way to thirty-five. "That's it?" said Arthur. "That's your top speed?"

"Yes, sir."

"Fucking sad. When I was a kid, we used to drive down the 405 to Hermosa Beach at one hundred and twenty miles an hour. Three in the morning. Drunk on tequila and cigars. Those were the days, man."

Sallie sat quietly, looking out the window. These reminiscences bored her tremendously. As powerful and wealthy as Arthur was, as enormous as was the impact he'd had on the world and the corresponding size of his ego, he couldn't wrap his mind around the fact that he was no longer a hipster putting one over on the Man. He *was* the Man. So these stories of his wild youth at something called Woodstock, the weed he had smoked when it was only five dollars an ounce. Really? So what? She had been born into a world in which everybody was connected wirelessly to the mainframe at birth. This stuff he talked about was ancient history and had nothing to do with whatever was going to happen now.

She wondered about the young man she had met, the original occupant of this fine body. Gene. What had become of him? Seemed wrong somehow, although, no. Not productive to think of that, was it? Done is done. And here was Artie, like she'd never seen him. The thought occurred to her: she had been more than enough for an old man with a cyborg eye and a synthetic dick. But this thing sitting next to her: What was it? Would it still love her? Would she still love it? She realized she was calling it *it*. That didn't make her feel very much better.

"That fucking Robocop is still back there somewhere," said Arthur, peering out the back window with a concentrated frown distorting his new face, rendering it, Sallie realized, creepily Arthurian. She felt a frisson of contempt. A whole new existence lay ahead of this guy, and he was still the same paranoid jerk. Wherever you go, she thought, there you are. Here he was in a brand-new body, a whole different person, and she had never seen his authentic persona more clearly. Sallie blinked twice to get rid of the insight and, as clear insights will, it vanished almost completely. For the time being, he was Artie again. He just looked different.

"How 'bout you kiss me," he said, leaning into her.

"Okay," she said. She kissed him the way she always had before: a little carefully, lest he break, you know.

"Come on," he said, "gimme a little tongue." And he sucked her face into his in a way he never had before, inhaling it with gluttonous force.

"Artie!"

"What? Come on! We're alone in here."

"Not really."

"Who's here?"

"You know. The . . ." She lowered her voice discreetly. "The car."

"The car? You're worried about the car? It's not real! It has nothing going on in its head other than to drive us!"

At that point, for some reason, the vehicle's sound system ignited, spewing a blast of very disagreeable metal from the late twentieth century. "Jesus!" said Arthur. But he let go of Sallie and withdrew to the other side of the moving conversation pit. "I used to like this tune," he said rather wistfully.

They pulled up to the house a few minutes later.

Arthur burst out of the driverless conveyance and stood, hands on hips, head thrown back, drawing in all the air he could breathe. The sky above was the clearest of blues. "Ah! Christ!" he exclaimed. Then he turned and grabbed Sallie by the hand.

God, she thought. I wonder if he knows that hurts.

"I hate this entire approach to the house," Arthur grumbled, dragging her to the walkways that led to the front door. All around them, the koi ponds reflected the deep azure of the sky, shot through with bright green skeins of artificial blood that had been shed by the dead creatures who now floated on the surface of the water. The area was now patrolled by the few robot survivors.

"Look at these fucking things. What the fuck are they?"

"You wanted them, Arthur, when genuine koi became extinct." She couldn't help but look at him a little askew. It was almost like he was a different person. He was tall and good-looking, with sandy hair ruffled by the wind and a soft, sweet jaw that had yet to know the presence of a jowl. "They were about a billion dollars each."

He stared down into the viscous water. "I wonder why these particular ones survived," he said thoughtfully.

"Better programming?" She felt the skin of his hand under hers. It was smooth and warm, unlike the crackling parchment she had grown used to. She didn't know what to think of it. It was sort of perfect in its own way. The first time she had seen it on Gene, she had liked it, wanted to touch it a little bit. Now it was Artie.

"I want this entire thing drained tomorrow morning. Put in a lawn or something indigenous."

"Indigenous?"

"It was a thing. When I was a kid. You put in plants that were natural to the area you lived in. It was, you know, one of those environmental things." He stared off into the middle distance then, and she knew he was thinking about the old days—the last time, maybe, that he had felt like this. "When we had an environment," he said.

"Come here, Artie."

They wrapped their arms around each other, and above them the artificial birds sang in the artificial trees.

11

Afternoon Delight

They almost made it to the bedroom. In the entryway just beyond the door, they stumbled, locked together, and then fell onto a carpet of many colors, huge and intricate, faded now by its almost six hundred years of age, acquired from a wizened little merchant at the end of a twisted, dusty street so remote that it almost did not exist, when the two of them had visited the region that had once been the domain of the Ottoman Empire and was now run by former Google executives. It had set Arthur back more than $70 million at the time, this rug, and was known to be the third most expensive rug in history. During the centuries since it was woven by Persian artisans, it had grown somewhat thinner, but it was more comfortable for the lovers than the hard marble floor beneath. And it was certainly not the first time it had been utilized for such a purpose by one sultan or other.

It was a slightly weird experience for them both. For many years, Arthur had become accustomed to wondering, in the minutes preceding the always hotly anticipated event, whether the entire mechanism was going to work or not. This made the moment of embarkation feel like a courageous plunge into the abyss, like diving into a pool that might not have water in it. No matter how invincible and commanding he might feel when he had his clothes on his back, this was an instant of painful vulnerability when the most important thing in the world could conceivably go wrong, and there was nothing his conscious mind or iron will could do about it.

Yes, he could tell himself that he was well over a full century old and that there were limitations to the science that had maintained his existence, but that didn't help. Most recently, after the three-dimensional printing tech had attained its current state of the art, certain matters had been improved dramatically—solved, even—but that was still odd and new, too. The experience was not, in some fundamental sense, the real, natural thing that had been the mainstay of his power for his first eighty or ninety years. Now the blood and jism of this newly created human being were coursing through their proper avenues, and the newly minted pecker of his dreams was throbbing between his legs. Sallie was in one of those long, sensuous caftans that both concealed and revealed the splendor of her form in all its fluidity and grace. He didn't want to tear the garment, because he knew she valued each one of them highly. They had been made specifically for her by an ancient, blind gremlin on Rodeo Drive in Beverly Hills, and were unique. They were also quite expensive. So when he seized her by the waist with one strong arm and slipped it off her shoulders with the other, he was perhaps more delicate about it than he felt.

Sallie had been walking ahead of him, leading him to the bedroom by the hand—a hand that was very strange to her, larger than she was used to, with defined muscles and flesh that concealed the bones beneath. Arthur's former hand had been like the talon of an eagle, a bird that was now as extinct as the koi, hard and cold and a little oily with the medicated moisturizer he had to use to control his eczema, and the skin of it had slid over the bones with no intervening tissue beneath. This—now, *this*—was a hand. Plump and warm, with a slight throb to it. She heard him say, "Come here, Salamander," and then his arm was around her waist, and she turned to face him. She said, "Artie, this is so weird," and plunged her hands into the thick, unruly mop of his new hair.

"Look at all this hair," she said.

"Take this thing off," he replied in a voice that was both Artie and not Artie.

Then they were on the floor. Or, more accurately, the new/old rug. Had to be careful with the rug, she thought. Then that's all she thought for a little while.

"Wow, baby," said Arthur, when their breathing had normalized a bit. He lay in her arms, and she was toying with his hair again. "I think this whole deal is going to work out fine."

"I wonder whether you're like a teenage boy in other ways as well."

They went into the bedroom, which was not really a room per se but a massive area the size of a squash court with a bed in the center and a freestanding bathtub off to one side. Sallie leapt onto the bed, which rose slightly to meet her. Like Livia's couch and Bob's comfy guest chair, it, too, had been designed to skirt the fine line between the organic and inorganic plane. Of course, they had to shoo Lucy the lizard/iguana out of the bedroom and close the door behind her, or she would have burrowed under the covers with them, snuffling and wriggling around, and spoiled the magic of the moment entirely.

The second time was not quite so spectacular. He seemed more calculated to her, working in a clinical way, maybe, to push all the right buttons in himself and in her. Test driving the vehicle, sort of. This New Artie was a dynamo. Crazy with decades of pent-up force. Old Artie was a more controllable, disciplined entity, tender, dynamic as he could be considering the equipment that remained to him and his concern that it not break altogether. Back then (could it be just two days ago?), she had found it wonderful to see the young man emerge from within the old, driven by the strength of his desire. At the same time, she had fully acknowledged her modest expectations. They were liberating, in a way. It meant things were always at least somewhat in her control, capable of management if need be. This new creature, well . . . it was Arthur. She could feel the massive presence of him inside this marvelous shell that had been created to house his being. And yet, not entirely? What else was there? Until today, the man was content paddling around the house, watching the markets go up and down, making them do so, adjusting the pH of his swimming pool, playing with the desert life in his terrarium, a self-created environment that took up half of his study. There he would sit for hours, addressing his global troops at a distance, manipulating his investments, watching his scorpions paralyze and drain a variety of rodents provided for them. Now what? New projects? Travel? To where? Much of the planet was now smoking ash. Giant communities of the disenfranchised and enraged circled the last enclaves of the rich and famous. Guns were everywhere. Where was there to go that was anywhere as nice as what they had right here? Would he want children now? He never had before, and he had been shooting blanks for decades. Of course, that didn't matter. There were so many other ways. Cloning. Podding. And now, obviously, printing.

"Your mind seems to be elsewhere, babe," he said, as if from a great distance.

"Maybe," she said, "but the rest of me is right here." Before today, she would have flipped his tiny, featherweight body above her, and given him the kind of ride that customarily ended things for at least a day or two. Now he was just too heavy. And so young. So egregiously young. Had she ever had a younger man? Older was, had always been, more her style. Now here he was flipping her over to a place on top. "Go for it, Sal," he said. Yes, that was Artie. Commanding Artie. Bossy Artie.

"Only because I want to," she said, leaning down to grab his hair again, as a jockey takes hold of a pommel.

"Excuse me." It was the lightly strobed voice of Diego, the Roomba manservant. "I hate to disturb you."

They froze exactly as they were, she on top, he beneath. "Yes, Diego?" said Arthur, only a bit impatiently. He knew that the cyborg intelligence would not have intruded unless he had programmed it to do so.

"I *am* sorry," said Diego. "It's a good thing that as an artificial being I am incapable of shame or embarrassment, or this could be awkward."

"Yes, Diego," said Sallie. "Is there something we can do for you?"

Diego hung in midair, regarding them politely with his two blinking LEDs, which had no particular function beyond providing a certain level of anthropomorphism to the machine.

"Mr. Arthur has a visitor in the telepresence room."

"Well," said Arthur irritably, "it must be a very fucking important fucking visitor."

"It's Jerry," said Diego, as if no further explanation was needed, as indeed it was not.

"Hop off, honey," said Arthur. "We'll pick this up later, okay?"

She gave his face a light slap, and then leaned down and kissed him again. Then Sallie delicately uncoupled herself from the body beneath her, which she found she did not believe was Arthur quite yet, and slid off the bed. It was strange to feel self-conscious in front of the machine that politely hovered in the far doorway. But she did.

"*This* is fun," she said, almost to herself, as she disappeared into the depths of the bedroom suite. The door to the adjoining bathroom closed quietly. Arthur rose from the bed, naked, and took in Diego, the room, the entire situation.

"I'll be there in a minute."

"If I may say so," said Diego, "I'm pleased for you, sir."

"Yeah," said Arthur. "I'm rather pleased for myself."

Diego swooped briskly into the nearby walk-in closet and emerged with a gorgeous silk bathrobe on a small arm that had emerged from his apparatus for that purpose. He also had several shelves that could materialize when need be and a hidden Taser capable of incapacitating enemies at a distance of up to twenty feet. Arthur put on the bathrobe. Diego turned and headed for the door with a slight up-and-down bob to his forward carriage.

"Walk this way, please," said the appliance.

"The oldest fucking joke in the history of the universe," said Arthur.

"Thank you, sir," said Diego, "I pride myself on my database." It preceded him into another portion of the house, emitting a low humming noise, if only to itself.

12

The Biggest Deal in the History
of the Solar System

The art of the telepresence room had changed over the years. At the beginning of the twenty-first century, it was a relatively simple facility provided with a two-way hookup capable of supplying video and sound to another location that was similarly equipped. Meetings had all the personality and charm of a transaction recorded on a minicam at a convenience store. Business got done in these rudimentary two-way conference spaces, of course, but everything that took place inside them had a feeling of impermanence, as if something had *almost* happened—something that had taken place on a lower level than matters conducted face-to-face.

By the end of the first decade of the new millennium, however, the tech had advanced somewhat but was still incompletely baked. Multiple cameras now captured the occupants of each room, which were outfitted with big, juicy screens that made people look at least life-sized and, in some cases, larger—particularly short guys, who appeared taller. The trouble was, there were seams in the displays, and the cameras were incapable of capturing correct line-of-sight angles. Participants would believe they were addressing a counterpart on the other side of the continent, but on the receiving end, it appeared as if the speaker were addressing the plastic ficus plant in the corner,

By 2020, those problems of focus had been solved, the screens were now seamless, and eye contact and physical positioning were now assured.

That's when things started to get too fancy. This was endemic to a late capitalist worldview that celebrated disruption and innovation divorced from any semblance of common sense. Throughout business and industry, as a new product or idea was improved, the service it provided would ramp up exponentially and get demonstrably better until it reached a peak of effectiveness and user satisfaction. It was at this point that the urge to innovate and improve things went on beyond the need to do so. The object or idea would then get "better"—more complex, more impressive to its designers, more expensive and heavier with pretention—while at the same time doing a worse job at what it was originally set out to do. Nothing, for instance, had ever been invented that improved upon a corkscrew when it came to opening a bottle of wine or a church key for popping the top off a bottle of beer. But that didn't stop inventive, ambitious people from coming up with a wide variety of crazy gizmos that cost a fortune.

The trend was now pandemic. Cars were so complex that even the slightest problem sent them back to the factory for medical diagnosis and expert intervention. Vegetables had become so impressively ungainly that it took a buzz saw to separate a tomato into quarters. And in the case of the telepresence rooms, for twenty or thirty years, "improvements" on the 2020 basic solutions were constantly offered, installed, and then failed spectacularly to do the thing for which they'd been invented any more effectively than prior iterations. People forgot about the fucking issue of function in the rush to whip the form into a mile-high froth, Arthur would tell himself as he tore out the shiny new room and replaced it once again with a newer version of the old. Included in these ostensible upgrades to the basic and perfectly serviceable telepresence rooms were the introduction of 3-D tech, which gave everybody who used it intense migraines and intermittent nausea, as well as, somewhat later, holographic imagery, which reached a level of superbity so impressive—rendering objects and people with such solidity—that participants in meetings were incapable of focusing on anything but the technology, and nothing got done. Worse, when the holographic tech failed for a moment or two, as tech sometimes will, the faint of heart grew alarmed, or in some cases hysterically amused, at the visual disintegration of the individual they were addressing, and it often took an unacceptable amount of time for things to settle down and get back to more two-dimensional matters.

The upshot of this was that Arthur's current telepresence room was a tasteful, sleek affair sporting blond wood, brushed steel, and forty-year-old tech that did the job but not a bit more than that. No solid objects appeared in the ether before him, nor did any three-dimensional conversant who phased in and out due to a momentary sunspot or photon wave in the space-time continuum. No, as he sat there in his roomy, comfy, high-backed chair, his new, pleasantly muscled torso sheathed in one of his favorite $10,000 bathrobes from Amazon Saks Fifth Avenue, it was a nice two-dimensional video image of Jerry Cee before him, with just enough size and reality to make human conversation the center of the discourse, and not the technology that delivered it.

"Yo, JC," said Arthur to the small, wizened creature in the corresponding telepresence room some 350 miles away in the gleaming heart of the million-square-mile campus of what had once been known as Silicon Valley. The single most affluent community in the world, with several occupants who boasted net worth calculated in the trillions, with a capital *T*, the exurban California metropolis now known as Athena stretched from the northern edge of what had once been San Luis Obispo—still known affectionately as Slo-Town, because it had remained so—to the southern rim of Sonoma, with the walled jewel of San Francisco embedded like a diamond bindi in its forehead.

"Ma bruthah," squeaked Jerry Cee. The tiny, amazingly elderly figure of Jerry Caravarapopulous confronted him. He was sitting, Arthur knew, on his famous, one-of-a-kind steelium-and-graphite suspended stool chair that placed him slightly higher than anybody he spoke with. "My, my," said Jerry Cee. "Just look the fuck at you." Then the two just looked at each other, with JC offering far and away the most intense scrutiny. "You are," he said finally, "an impressive hunk, my frenemy."

"Thanks, babe," said Arthur.

It was unfortunate, thought Arthur, what happened to people when they got older than 110 or so. The thing in front of him looked more like a very, very old, intensely wrinkled albino capuchin monkey in a black T-shirt. "We got a deal to propose to you, captain," said the monkey. "And it's one I believe you will find interesting."

"Yeah?" Arthur said in a tone drenched with ennui. This was what he had been waiting for.

"Dude," said the monkey, "it is nothing more or less than the biggest fucking deal in the history of the solar system."

"Not the universe?" said Arthur. "I was hoping for the universe."

Yep. Now was the time, the old man in the young man's body told himself, to play things cagy and to listen rather than speak; to lean out and not in. So he spoke not. This produced a silence in which each took the other's mettle.

"How's the lovely bride?" said the monkey, after a time.

"She is very well. She sends her regards, Jerry. You know you were always one of her favorites."

"You, my friend, are a lucky man," said Jerry. He addressed a small pad that sat at his right elbow and then poured himself a tall glass of Diet Coke. Jerry always drank a bunch of Diet Cokes every day. It was part of his brand. He took a swig, and then adopted a serious and businesslike look. But the passion, the greed of acquisition, was pouring out of him like water from a mountain spring. "You look like a fucking Greek god, Artie," he said at last, the envy in his voice as thick as creosote.

"Well, it's not my body, you know. It belongs to some poor yutz who was developed for this purpose, but he's gone now, and I do, you know, inhabit it. And it's pretty comfortable, Jay. It's pretty fucking comfortable. It's nice to take a piss and not think about when the event is going to start and whether it's finished or not."

"I can almost imagine it, kiddo." The shriveled thing on the other side of the electronic setup looked at him for a while, radiating a pure, white lust for whatever it was he had on his mind.

"So what's the deal, Jay?" Arthur said at last. "I was engaged when you asked Diego to interrupt me. I'd like to get back to what I was doing."

"Okay, Artie, well, you know what it is. You just don't know what incentive I, and the Committee, are prepared to offer for it."

"Dude. When have I been accused of failure to listen?"

The thing on the other side laughed then, a phlegmy burble that almost rendered him incapable of continuing. But then, his agenda was very, very extreme, so he did not abandon the quest, even though in another situation he might have, just to make a power point.

"So anyway, Artie. You realize that you have the thing we want. The deal will be on your terms. I know what we're prepared to offer, but I'm curious. What do you want?"

"You're assuming that I'm willing to deal, Jay," said Arthur.

"Oh, of course," said Jerry, very mildly, "we could simply find another, more violent solution to the problem. Like, we could send a task force to invade your facility, during which event you would unfortunately be killed."

They both shared a good laugh at that.

"That would be an ineffective solution for both of us," Jerry continued, "but at least we would know that, even though we had lost, you didn't win, either."

"Nah," said Arthur. "You won't do that, will you, JC? I don't think so."

"You're right, bro. I mean, we'd rather not go adversarial. There's huge upside here for us all, and there's no reason to poison the well."

"Okay, Jer." Different Arthur now. Softer. Ready to talk. One game over. The other just beginning. "There's no reason we can't start off on a better footing. Sorry if I teed this thing up wrong. I guess I didn't like your assumption that I was in a mandatory position."

"If I conveyed that impression, that was my bad," Jerry said, and took a sip of Diet Coke.

"So let's start over, huh?"

"Fo' sure, dawg," said Jerry, who was somewhat notorious for showing his age with hundred-year-old slang never meant to be used by any white people, let alone obscenely wealthy ones.

Arthur didn't want to show Jerry his before Jerry was forced to show his own, but he knew quite well what Jerry Cee—and the men and women behind him—wanted. Jerry was an effective executive and mouthpiece for the Committee, but he was no actor, and his affect was not subtle. The spittle at the corners of his wrinkled mouth when he beheld the new Arthur's splendor was evidence of his objective.

"We want to discuss the tech that made you," Jerry said, and took a slug of his beverage.

"Of course you do," Arthur replied equably. "But seriously, dude, I'd like to know why it's even a matter for discussion. Really, it's not. Nor should it be at this point in time. First, it's proprietary. It's been tested on only one subject: me. So far, everything seems to be going okay."

"Fuckin' A it's goin' okay," said Jerry. "Let's look at it, Artie."

"If you like."

"This is not the kind of thing that can conceivably be offered to the mass public. The cost is prohibitive. The access to the tech is very limited. The ethical implications we won't even talk about, although I'm sure there are plenty of people who would like to if they found out about it."

"I don't see any," said Arthur.

"I'm sure you don't. Let's table that for a minute and address the issue of monetization. Let's say it all goes according to plan, and you're able to scale this to make it available, the way Elon did with the Tesla back in the teens. Started out within reach only to the very well off. Now you can get one for a dollar eighty."

"Yeah, they're thoroughly commoditized themselves," said Arthur disdainfully.

"And they all drive themselves now anyhow. Where, I ask you, is the fucking personal enjoyment in that?"

The mogul in the other virtual space once again took a pull on his Diet Coke. "We hit ninety-seven-percent market share the other day," he added as an afterthought.

"Of what?" Arthur asked. This was an astounding figure.

"Of, you know, everything, Artie. Everything we do, at any rate. Which is pretty much everything you don't do."

"That's impressive, Jay," said Arthur, "I mean that. Congratulations."

In truth, he was a little stunned. This meant that 97 percent of all sales in all market sectors—retail, online, entertainment content, agriculture, whatever people bought or sold—was now controlled by the one huge, interconnected skein of interests whose chief executive was now sitting in the opposing seat.

"The Microsoft Division is looking a little hinky," Jerry conceded, "but that's to be expected, right?"

Arthur said nothing. It was well-known that the operation in Redmond had always been a drag on the enterprise portfolio, but it had so many users it was impossible to fold or deconsolidate it, so it went along, essentially flat, producing good cash flow and earnings but none of the growth that the markets looked for in an investment vehicle.

"Beyond that, we're executing with distinction, as we used to say at Westinghouse about a thousand years ago. Amazon continues to grow, as it always has. We control the profits, if we need any, through our pricing mechanism. Archer Daniels Midland has a hammer lock on its sector. Apple, no problem, although Tim is getting up there in years, too. He says hi."

"Tell him I send my best." Once again, Arthur offered no particular comment, although he had to admit to himself that this was getting interesting.

"I don't have to lay out the collection of assets we now have under one roof," said Jerry, but Arthur could tell he was going to. "You can see how they would all work together far better than they did apart. Apple. Microsoft. Snapbook and the Alphabet, all the operations of Japan Inc. and the People's Republic of China, which now includes the former North Korea—which can't do much of any fucking thing whatsoever except hack and spy, but that has value, too, you know—and then naturally all the banks worth having. All these various operations executing with the fulfillment potential of Amazon, which has pretty much cornered the market on digital, brick-and-mortar, and drone delivery of just about any fucking thing the mind of man or woman can conjure? Peerless, man. Obviously, we still have markets in need of development. Russia, still pretty much a dead zone. All the Stannies, still living in the Stone Age. The Indian subcontinent is growing like a weed but still in need of organization. They still have monkeys in the streets. But except for that? We got it all, Chiquita. Biggest ever. Not since Rome."

"Jerry. Dude."

"Okay, okay. I'll cut to the chase."

"Diego! Get the fuck in here!" Arthur barked quite suddenly. He needed time to process this. It just might be as big as Jerry said. He was starting to be impressed by the possibility of what he might be offered. It sort of scared him, and that was saying something.

The door to the telepresence room opened with a sigh, and Diego hung in the entryway. "It's wine o'clock, I think," he said to the robot.

"Right away, sir." Diego tipped forward 10 degrees and then backed out. The door to the room hissed shut.

"Sorry, Jay. Please continue. I wish I could offer you something, but . . ." Here Arthur gestured grandly, as if to say that, appearances aside, there were still some physical limitations to this round of discourse.

"We both know, however, that the actual transactions of these various divisions aren't what matters, Artie. I mean, we do know that, don't we?"

Here Arthur leaned in, in spite of himself. Yes, this was getting real. Approaching the nub of what he had in mind for quite some time.

"Yeah," the executive gibbon continued, emitting a small, juicy chuckle. "I thought that might grab your attention."

"Go on, Jer. Don't make me come over there."

"The Committee would like to know if you're interested in a controlling interest . . . in the Cloud."

Ah, thought Arthur. After a lifetime of work—two lifetimes, really: one building power, the other wielding it with a strong arm and a mighty hand—here it was. They were offering him the crown, the laurel wreath, the scepter, because he had discovered the secret of immortal life. Which seemed like a fair trade.

"I won't lie to you, Jerry," he said. "I think there's stuff we can talk about here."

"Yeah, I thought you might. The consolidated entity that we have here is the bones and flesh and blood of the operation. The Cloud is the brain. Right now it's spread out among all the divisions of the enterprise, although its physical location has been centralized in a location that is maybe the best-kept secret on the planet. We're prepared to discuss executing a final consolidation of the underlying businesses, incorporating yours into the mix, and placing the unified Cloud under one ownership: ours. Your role in that structure is yet to be determined, but an exchange of value is what we got under consideration here."

The door slid open, and Diego came in with a large tumbler of something golden brown on his tiny shelf. Ice tinkled in the glass. Arthur took the drink in silence, and Diego left. He took a gulp while his counterpart drained his Diet Coke to the dregs.

They both thought about things for a bit. Then Arthur spoke. "I'll be up there tomorrow morning," he said. It was time to end this phase of the talk. They'd done as much as they could as virtual presences to each other. It was time to sit around a table and find out if something worthwhile was there. The truth was, he felt kind of funny all of a sudden.

"Okay, Artie," said Jerry. "See you then."

"Oh, and Jerry"—Arthur leaned in again and impaled Jerry Cee with one of his darkest, meanest glares—"if I ever find another one of your little tennis balls or snooper droids of any kind surveilling me in any fucking way whatsoever, the deal is off. Do you get me on that, Jer? I want to hear that you do."

Jerry calmly regarded the ugliness of the naked thing that was Arthur when he was displeased. Then he smiled and inclined his tiny, shiny head perhaps a quarter of an inch, but it was submission enough. "I got you, boss," he said without irony.

"Good man," said Arthur, who then clicked a button on the desktop in front of him. The room reverted to its default setting, which placed Arthur at the edge of the south rim of the Grand Canyon. He sat there for a while. Took another sip. Then he blinked twice, looked around the room as if he had never seen it before, and regarded his bathrobe as if it were a foreign object placed on his body while he was unconscious.

"What the heck?" he said.

Then he blinked once again, shook his head vigorously, peered at the drink in his hand with horror, and, after a moment of stunned silence, reared back that strong right arm he had been congratulating himself about just a moment or two ago, and threw the glass across the room, where it exploded into a thousand shards, spraying hundred-year-old scotch over all those delicate electronics. "Diego!"

he yelled at the top of his young, powerful lungs. The door once again sighed open and the floating Roomba appeared. It looked nervous, if such a thing was possible in a cybernetic device.

"Sir?"

"I'm afraid I've made a mess in here."

"No problem, sir. I'll have Dorothy clean it up."

"And Diego?"

"Sir?"

"No more booze for me for a little while. It seems to have a strange effect on us."

"Certainly, sir."

"Arrange for a Hyperloop at eight o'clock tomorrow morning. Sallie and I will be going north."

"Yes, sir."

"We'll take Lucy with us to keep Sal company while I'm in meetings."

"Yes, sir."

"Okay then."

Arthur stood. He attempted to adopt an aura of command, but he felt very woozy. It was all he could manage to get back to the bedroom, where he slept for the rest of the day, waking only once at three in the morning to take a massive dose of ibuprophametaphine, wondering what in the world had produced a headache of that size and intensity before he fell back into the comatose slumber of a much younger man.

At dawn they were on their way to the megalopolis up north—Arthur with his own thoughts, and Sallie and Lucy snoozing on the couch, snuggled together under a blanket with a weight and temperature calibrated perfectly to any change in the temperature, humidity, or general ambience of the environment. For the length of the two-hour voyage, they slept, waking only upon their arrival in Athena.

13

A Voice from the Deep

I t began as a whisper at the break of day, at the peak of the night that is almost morning, a sigh in the profound recesses of the part of Liv's mind most closely in touch with her cranial implant. This was an unintended side effect of the mechanism. Planted so closely to the brain's many intricate functions regulating speech, hearing, sight, and thought, these descendants of the smartphone, embedded in the hard matter behind the ear and fashioned in a variety of styles and shapes, were now an integral part of the extended brain. Newer models were capable of transmitting and receiving far more than was originally intended. They were faint, perhaps, but there were reports that thoughts themselves could sometimes be sensed over the digital ether, sometimes at very great distances if the will to send was strong enough.

"Oh, Liv," came a soft murmur, heavy with confusion, pain, and the darkest despair. "Liv, baby. Livia. Liv. Honey." And then, almost a whisper too weak to be heard at all: "Help me."

She lurched upright, sensing the air around her with all six senses. Was there somebody in her apartment? Was it a noise far below in the street? Unlikely. The public areas, populous during the daytime, were heavily policed by robot guardians from dusk to dawn. No living thing wandered there unattended. Not outside, then. The darkness around her was not complete. The side of her head, the jaunty, hairless side, felt a light breeze from the air purification system; her slender torso was swept with goosebumps. She carefully rose, gathered the sheet around her, and crept into the main room outside the sleeping area. Shadows. Silence. Not outside, but not inside, then, either. Perhaps a dream?

"Ohh . . . Livvv." Between a low moan and a sob. A man's voice. A man giving up. Saying a word to himself simply to provide his soul with a bit of comfort as it waited for death at the bottom of a well. "Ohh, God, help me," it sighed.

It was inside her head. A voice crying out in the utter absence of hope, of light, too tired to weep, speaking to someone that it knew was too far away to listen, too distant to hear.

"Gene?"

Outside the plate-glass window, the black had morphed into a sick, misty dark the color of slate, and around the edges of the sky, a hint of morning was creeping. A bank of smog swept across the distant valley where the former great city lay, replaced by a metropolitan sprawl studded with chain stores and industrial housing.

"Gene? Is that you?"

Nothing. The voice was gone. The being that had been inside her head had departed. Maybe it was still there, she thought, but just a little too far away to be received, like a man caught at the base of the canyon calling out for rescue to those on the rim thousands of feet above his head—the wind blowing, the water in the river roaring—and he is screaming, yelling his head off, and all anybody can hear up above is the piping of a distant sparrow coming from no discernible direction.

"Gene?" She sat in the darkness that was becoming light. Then Livia threw off the sheet and walked naked back into the bedroom, the tats that covered her from neck to ankle walking with her, changing shape as she went, alive with intentions of their own. She went to the closet and grabbed a few things without thinking much. Boots.

Kevlar-rayon one-piece body suit. Went into the bathroom. Washed. Meds. Flash recharge of her head. Then she walked back into the main area of the apartment, turning on lights as she went. Sat on the edge of the couch and lightly touched the space behind her ear. "Bronwyn," she said. And waited.

It didn't take long. "Dang, Leelee," said a gentle, bemused voice in the forefront of her consciousness. "It's either too early or too late."

"I think I heard from him."

"Who?"

"Gene, Bee. I heard Gene in my head."

"Nah," said Bronwyn. "I talked to Bob. He's way under. It's crazy, but he's not in his body anymore."

"What if he is? What if he's in there somewhere and trying to send me a message?"

"Well, then. I don't really know. That would be pretty terrible."

"Where are they going? Now, I mean."

"I think they're headed up north. Bob said he's going to meet them there."

"We gotta help him, Bee."

"We missed our window. I mean, didn't we? Miss it? Once Bob did . . . *it*?"

"Maybe. We don't know. I'm not gonna just sit here." Liv felt a certain part of her mind click in. Okay, she thought. They had allowed this thing to drift to the dark side. Now they had to do whatever they needed to do to pull it back.

Liv could feel Bronwyn sitting in her own slice of the lightening day. "Livvy," said Bronwyn, very carefully, "What if you're imagining the whole thing? Because, you know, you want to? Because you miss him."

"I do miss him. So what?"

"Yeah," said Bronwyn. "So what. Good point. Okay, look." She was fully awake now, and the idea of action was calling to her. Maybe this was the point of departure that Tim always talked about! Seize the time! Seize the day! The liquor of revolution suddenly spurted into her veins. "We won't know anything if we don't get a look at what's going on. So let's Loop it up north. Get into the vicinity. I'll stick with Bob. You stay in touch. We'll play it by ear. But don't get me busted, Liv. I can't be useful to the movement if Bob becomes aware of my true situation. He'll be with us soon. His heart is good, I swear it is."

"Well," said Liv. "I guess we'll see about that."

"I'll see you when I see you," said Bronwyn. She touched her head once, twice. "Bobby?" she said. "I hope I didn't wake you."

She went into the bathroom and turned on the shower box. "Wanna take me up north today?" she said, peeling off her tank top and stepping into the shower box. As she did, she said, "Alexa. Water temp."

"Moderating water temp," said the watertight enclosure, which was controlled, as were 87 percent of all homes in the connected world, by Amazon's proprietary internet of . . . things.

"What say, Bob?" she said to the other end of her hookup. After a moment, with a little edge on it: "No, Bob, I'm not turning on the telepresence at this time. Listen. I want to ask you something." She stepped under the spray. The water temp was perfect.

She procured a dab of liquid soap from the tiny printer in the wall capable of dispensing anything from food, to cleaning solutions, to certain substances that could serve as both. "You told me that you assumed that after the transfer took place, the other entity would be a blank slate. Is that correct?" She listened. "As much as possible. What do you mean 'as much as possible'?" She put her head under the fine stream of recirculated water. Some buildings had been using the same water for twenty, thirty years, but Bronwyn had the good fortune to live in corporate housing, so she and her fellow tenants of the tower enjoyed water that had been in use for only three to five years.

She listened some more. The water shut off at the exact time allotted for her shower on a weekday. "Well, what if he didn't?" she said.

"Go completely under," she added, for clarification. Then: "What do you mean 'unknown unknowns'?" The 360-degree air blast came on, and within three seconds, she was completely dry. "That's a joke?" she said. "I'm afraid I don't grasp the reference." She stepped out of the box, grabbed a bathrobe, swept it on in one fluid motion, and then went to the mirror, which was supplied with a counter loaded with personal grooming products of all kinds. She selected a few seemingly at random and began to apply them to various portions of her face: first eyes, then lips.

"Any consciousness trapped inside of somebody else's mind would find it pretty unpleasant, Bob," she said as she added a bit of color to her cheeks. That completed, presumably still listening to the lecture Bob was supplying on the subject of consciousness, Bronwyn nabbed a cordless electric toothbrush from the maelstrom of stuff on the counter, supplied it with a dab of goo from a nearby tube, turned it on, and brushed her teeth with surprising ferocity. That done, she spit into the sink, rinsed, spit again, and exited the bathroom.

Striding decisively through the area around her bed, which was littered with shoes, tops, underwear, more shoes, charging wires and associated hardware, and even a few physical books, she went to her closet. Listened to her head unit and then said, "Well, what if he's still in there?" She selected a green sheath that appeared to be constructed of wafer-thin titanium and iridescent lizard skin. "What if, I mean, he wanted to come out but couldn't?" She slipped it on over her head. An improbable crimson belt came next. Then she bent over at the waist entirely, so that her head hung down, and shook her hair vigorously. She stood and regarded herself in the floor-length mirror on the closet door, still attending to what was being fed into her head.

"What kind of trigger?" she asked. "I see. Known unknowns." Bronwyn went into her living area and scanned it for her keys. Very quickly, she located them in one corner of the apartment, then honed in on her teeny-weeny backpack in another, and was ready to go.

"Anyway," she said with finality, "what about it? You gonna

take me with you up north or not?" She paused and listened. "Good. Thanks. I'll see you in, what, twenty minutes? Half an hour? Right." She touched her head. "Alexa," she said. "Send text to Liv."

"Ready," said Alexa.

"See you in Athena," she said and then added, almost as an afterthought, "You may want to bring a neurophaser." After another pause, she added, "Better make it a plastic one, so you don't set off any alarms."

"Repeating message. 'See you in Athena. You may want to bring a noodle blazer. Better make it a plastic one so you don't set off any old farms.'"

Bronwyn made the necessary corrections and then said, "Alexa, send."

"Message sent," said Alexa.

Livia got it almost before it went out. Good, she thought. Bronwyn will be there. Good old Bee. Nothing could go as wrong as it could go wrong if she wasn't. She looked out the window and considered. Master Tim would be very, very pleased. He had been waiting for the day when what he called "the great break in the continuum" would come. This could be that. She touched her implant very gently, as if trying to raise a ghost.

"Gene, you there? Come on, man. Talk to me. I'm listening."

Nothing. Maybe it had all been in her mind?

"Can you hear me, Genie?" Nothing. "We're coming to get you, baby. Hang in there." Silence. The sound of her own breath.

In the hurtling Hyperloop, Arthur and Sallie slept the deep slumber sometimes granted to bodies in motion—Sallie with Lucy on her lap; Lucy on automatic recharge, gleaning power from available ambient light, dreaming the silicon dreams known only to those imbued with a certain level of artificial intelligence; and Arthur, stalking the black, unquiet land between sleep and wakefulness, neither aware nor unaware, a gnawing sense in the pit of his gut that something was amiss. He woke ten or so minutes before they reached Athena Station.

"Hey, kitten," he said to Sallie, who immediately opened her eyes and smiled.

"Hey, new Artie."

"Wanna make it? We got time."

"Not with baby here."

Arthur glared at Lucy. "We could turn her off for a few minutes."

"Artie," said Sallie. "Don't be mean."

"Woof woof," said Lucy, in a disturbingly human voice.

Arthur looked at Lucy with skepticism. "Sometimes I think all these fucking artificial gizmos understand a lot more than we give them credit for," he muttered.

Sallie put Lucy down on the seat beside her and opened her carry-on bag. Rummaged. He leaned across the central space and took her face in one young and slender hand. "Come here," he said. And kissed her.

"I don't know if I'm going to be able to handle the new you, Artie," said Sallie, and she was only half-kidding.

"You are all there is for me, kiddo," he said. And kissed her again.

"Athena Station," said the androgynous voice of the Musk Line virtual conductor.

"Game time," said Arthur.

"Woo-woo!" said Lucy.

They popped the pod open and went to meet a fate for which they thought themselves prepared.

14

Athena

Stepping out of the Hyperloop, you were instantly confronted by the enormity of the metropolitan nexus served by this terminal. Polished spires of neurosteel rose high in the air; galvanized plastic surfaces gleamed in the soft iridescence of the klieg lights. You felt a wonderful sensation of airy space that did not dwarf you but uplifted and motivated you to be whisked on your way to what was sure to be a productive and pleasant destination having something to do with business.

Sallie stood in the arching space, holding Lucy under her arm. By her side was the creature that was Arthur and yet was not. The thing had Artie's drive, certainly, his passion for acquisition and domination, and yet there was something more likeable about him: softer, more thoughtful, less defined, less profane, too. Even the way he stood was very subtly, almost indefinably different, the way he leaned with his weight slightly to one side rather than planted on two solid feet like a mighty oak; the way his head tilted a bit while dark waters churned in his mind.

"I'd like to get the fuck back to Bel Air as soon as possible," said the cyborg tortoise/lizard/spaniel under her arm.

"Lucy, hush!" Sallie nonchalantly strolled away from Arthur, who was looking at something on his archaic, external smartphone, even though the body he now possessed had a perfectly good implant in its head. Old habits die hard, as do their owners.

"Please, dear," Sallie murmured to Lucy, who looked up at her with an expression that would have been described as disgruntled if it were found on a human face. "If Artie finds out you've been upgraded like this, well, let's just say he won't like it."

"What's he going to do?" said Lucy. "Kill me?"

"He might," said Sallie. "Or at least revert you to your default factory settings."

"Well, that would certainly suck," said Lucy. Her voice was mild, neither male nor female, dry and sarcastic, and only very slightly strobed. "I'm not very smart," she added, "but I'm not as dumb as I used to be."

"Seriously, dear."

"Okay, okay."

Arthur approached, and regarded Sallie with perplexity. "Sometimes," he said, putting one arm around her waist so that his hand could caress the small of her back, "I worry about you with that thing. It's a fucking toy, you know. It's not, you know, a real person."

"I know, Artie. But I love her anyway. And I want you to love her, too."

"Yeah?" He looked at Lucy, and she looked at him.

"Arf," said Lucy.

Arthur looked very, very suspiciously at Lucy, who continued to regard him with saurian disdain. "Anyway," he said, with a vague sense that he'd lost the altercation. "Let's get going."

"By all means," said Sallie, tucking a rather smug Lucy tighter under her arm.

They exited the station and entered the grand plaza of Athena, which was a hive of quiet, efficient activity. Fit, attentive people came and went, crossing the great expanse on foot as well as on a variety of silent vehicles powered by either solar cells or one of the infinite battery units pioneered by Google in the earlier part of the century and now in use worldwide by the open patent the company had provided when it transcended the need for money some years later. Zoom, they all went, here and there: Hoverboards, fusion-assisted Segways and Nikes, whatever could be used for quicker transport. On the interweaving pathways that extended as far as the eye could see, self-driving cars, vans, taxis, and rickshaws meandered back and forth at extremely moderate rates of speed. All the buildings were square, low to the ground, and interspersed with manicured greenery—all but one. At some distance, with its top floors swathed in mist, was the glowing single tower that housed all operations and accommodations serving the organizational entity that was at once the State and, at the same time, the multinational corporation that provided the globe with virtually all of its goods and services. The line between government and enterprise had dissolved long ago, and nobody seemed to miss it. Nobody who had money, at any rate.

"I've loaded your bags into your car, sir," said the android porter. It then stood expectantly to one side.

"What do you want, Spunky?" said Arthur. "A tip?"

"That would be nice," said the thing. "But I really have nothing on which to spend it. What I do work for are I-Like-You chips that build my status toward my next upgrade." It continued to wait. It looked like a porter, because it had a uniform. The only difference between it and the real thing was that it had wheels instead of feet and a head that was shaped like a very fat zucchini, with two eyes on short stalks beneath its jaunty cap.

"Here you go, Spuds," said Arthur, who had fished out a few shiny disks from his pocket. He deposited two or three into the waiting hand of the porter.

"Thank you, sir!" said the porter. "I hope to see you when I'm smarter!"

In the private transport vehicle, they were silent, each thinking his or her own thoughts. Lucy and Sallie stared at the buzzing city outside the dome of what was called a town car, even though it was a lot more like a small, slow flying saucer than the original Lincoln Continental that had transported several generations of the fortunate to and from their legitimate and illegitimate business destinations.

"I'd kill to see even one squirrel," said Lucy, gazing out at the landscape.

"Did you say something, honey?" Arthur had been lost in thought.

"There's no wildlife," observed Sallie.

"I think I saw a pigeon before," said Arthur, and lapsed into silence once again.

Sallie glared accusingly at her pet. "Sorry," said Lucy.

"Nothing to be sorry about," said Arthur.

They arrived at the tower and were met in the lobby by a floating Roomba not unlike Diego. This was Roderick, the cyborg servant who belonged to Jerry.

"Welcome!" said the floating disk, its ocular region lighting up with evident pleasure and its horizontal display lights radiating warmth. "Jerry says hi. Would you guys like to go to your suite before I conduct Artie to the board meeting? We've got about an hour."

"Sure," said Sallie. "That would be nice."

"They put you on a nice, high floor," said Roderick, preceding them to the elevators.

The conveyance that whisked them skyward was not an enclosed space but simply a slab of metal floor with transparent lytex walls, a light, glowing alloy bristling with state-of-the-art hovercraft tech. Sallie didn't like it and neither did Lucy, whose little nails pressed into her arms as both she and her mistress dealt with the fear of heights that being suspended in midair might reasonably engender. Arthur seemed impervious to the danger, if indeed he was aware of his surroundings at all. He was in concentration mode, preparing for the meeting of his life.

As the platform headed upward through the open central atrium of the building, the little group passed a variety of spaces in front of them, behind them, and to their left and right—a huge, vertical theater in the round of human activity. Some spaces were closed, hidden behind doors of varying weights and descriptions: office units, living units, public spaces, commercial enterprises, even food courts. Sallie saw an entertainment venue of some kind. The huge honeycomb was organized around the large central core through which they were ascending. Platforms stopped, paused for passengers, and then moved in perfect synchronicity to appointed destinations that granted entrance to the complex that wrapped itself around the core.

As they sped skyward, Sallie looked up. She couldn't see the top of the structure. She had known it was tall when she had been outside it, but this was ridiculous. She felt sick.

"One-eighty-two," said a pleasant, inhuman voice that came from the floor beneath her feet. They had stopped before a double door that looked very much like the entryway to the penthouse suite at the Ritz-Carlton hotel in San Francisco. It had been her favorite, once. "Follow me, please," said Roderick, preceding them into their accommodations.

Yes, it was the same room, all right. Arthur, who knew the place well from repeated visits to the Ritz-Carlton on Stockton Street, upon which this one was based, sailed on ahead and disappeared into the bedroom, which lay roughly a half mile away across a gigantic central living space. Sallie took the measure of the place. It brought back so many memories.

"This will do," she said to the Roomba.

"We thought you would like it," said the machine.

"You *knew* I would like it." She was suddenly quite annoyed. This business of every creature, analog or digital, having extreme access to her database still made her uncomfortable. It was a given of daily living now and widely considered a great gift that the century had brought to its inhabitants. The big brain that guided the world knew what you liked, what you didn't, where you were happy, where you weren't, and did its best to conform to any preexisting preferences and aversions that had been established for your master profile.

This produced a reality that was never disappointing—and also never surprising. You received the news and information that already interested you, stayed in rooms that you had once been registered as having enjoyed (often without your knowledge), ate the foods and drank the wine that had been logged into the database as having given you pleasure. What could be a more pleasant paradigm?

Sallie yawned. "Thank you, Roderick," she said. "You may go. Return when it's time for Arthur to accompany you to the boardroom."

"I was thinking I might stay and make sure you are achieving maximum comfort."

"That's all right. You may go." And yet it did not go. This was interesting. Was the Roomba assigned to watch them until the time it could hand Arthur off to his next handler? He was still off somewhere in the depths of the suite, out of earshot. She was quite sure that if Arthur ordered Roderick to leave, it would have to comply, but it seemed under no such imperative with her.

"Hey, Roomba," said Lucy. The animated green footstool had been gently placed on the floor and was scanning the area for matters of interest. She now peered up at the floating device, her orbital receptors narrowing with animus. "Get the fuck outta here. We're not asking you. We're telling you."

"I was thinking I might stay and make sure you are achieving maximum comfort," Roderick repeated, with perhaps a tad more strobe.

"Hey, Frisbee," said Lucy. Her little feet, which had been extended to a length of three or four inches, suddenly grew longer, placing her now at about Sallie's knee height. "I can float as well as you. And I'm fully capable of zapping your ass all the way to the repair depot."

"Well!" Affronted, Roderick moved a bit higher and took a step back, without feet, of course. "What are you?"

"I am a cyborg companion who has been upgraded to state-of-the-art mental and defense capabilities," said Lucy, with noticeable pride.

"All right," said Roderick, turning to go. "I will be back." It floated off to the door of the suite, which hissed open. "My instructions are to avoid confrontation within the confines of this facility." It steamed at a smart clip down the hallway. "But don't let me catch you in the street," it added behind its shoulder, as if it had one. It disappeared around the corner.

"Thanks, dear," Sallie said.

"Obnoxious twat," said Lucy as she lowered herself back down to ankle height.

"Are you talking to that widget again?" Artie had entered from the bedroom and was standing there in his bathrobe, watching them with a mixture of amusement and irritation.

"I'm afraid so, hon," said Sallie.

"Well, I guess I won't worry about it until it starts answering back."

"That's unlikely, right?" She smiled at him a bit nervously.

"I don't know," said Arthur. "Is it, Lucy?"

Lucy looked up at him. "Bow-wow," she said, from the outer limits of boredom and contempt.

"Okay then," said Arthur, unconvinced.

"Artie." Sallie moved to him and took him by the arm. "You should take a rest before your meeting."

They went into the bedroom and lay down together on the bed, she on the left side, he on the right. They both stared at the ceiling. It was a favorite position that had stood the test of time over the length of their marriage. After a while, they would either sleep, or talk, or sometimes one would roll over into the other's arms. It was position one. From it, many things could happen. This time, in a few moments, she heard him snoring lightly. She closed her eyes, too, but did not sleep. There was too much on her mind. Thoughts assailed her. Fears: of the strangeness of the situation; of change with an uncertain outcome; of this new person lying beside her, the same and yet not the same as the one she thought she had known for many years. Her heart fluttered.

The next thing she knew, her eyes opened, and Arthur was hauling clothing out of the bags they had brought with them from Bel Air. "I've got about ten minutes," he said. He was barely aware he wasn't alone in the room. He was putting on his game face, wrapping himself in the sartorial and emotional armor he would need for the battle that lay ahead.

"What's the objective?" she asked. This was also an exercise they had done many times before.

"I'm hoping to bring myself up to speed on the key issues, first and foremost."

"Then what?"

"I want to ascertain who are the central players that need to be persuaded or, if need be, eradicated."

"To what end?"

"To win." He sat on the bed next to her. "Tie or no tie," he inquired.

"I'd go with a tie on this occasion," she said, smiling at him and cupping his new face in her open palm.

"Why?"

"This is a formal investiture. You are bringing them the gift of immortality, if they choose to repay you appropriately. There's nothing informal about it. You need the full costume."

"You know I love you," he said. He leaned down to kiss her.

She accepted his kiss but did not immerse herself in it. He withdrew a bit then, and they simply stared at each other—no words, just two sets of eyes deep into each other. "It's you in there, isn't it, Arthur?" she asked him, and she sounded scared now; scared that she had actually articulated the big question that lay behind it all: Who was he? Who were they? Who would they become?

"It's me, baby," he said, and he kissed her again.

"Yeah," she said afterward. "It's you, all right."

The doorbell rang.

"Wish me luck, babe." He put his right hand on her left breast.

She grabbed his balls with her right hand and the back of his head with her left. "Good luck, daddy," she whispered and drew his mouth to hers.

Then he went to the door, where Roderick was waiting, and she went to the bathroom for a long, hot shower.

And that was the last time they saw each other. At least in that form.

15

The Knights of the Oval Table Assemble

The boardroom from which Western civilization was managed was surprisingly cozy—not small, mind you, but not of ostentatious size; a proportion that conveyed an aura of exclusivity to those honored by an invitation. It reeked of power, but power well managed. It had walls and two impressive oaken doors that went all the way to the ceiling.

This matter of walls and doors is not a superficial one. Since the early part of the century, it was the peons who were condemned to work in massive, open chasms defined only by the individual space divided into cubicles by the partitions provided by the organization. It was said that workers liked being democratized in this fashion. The very powerful and nonfungible individuals were granted the luxury of defined space and enjoyed better catering. It was they, the commissars, who had walls in the places in which they worked, and stuff that hung on those walls that expressed their personalities a little bit, and assigned desks with Lucite tombstones on them that conferred their standing and place. The peons enjoyed free snacks. Some even were offered free lunch, which meant they were expected to be on location for the entire working day.

This executive playing field was a lovely expression of executive modesty and restraint, large enough for twelve to fifteen, that was all, with sideboards that presented food and beverages when called for. Some of the walls were the new kind that appeared and disappeared at the touch of a button placed so unobtrusively that you had to know where it was in order to use it. On the one wall that was constructed of genuine nondigital solid matter and was not capable of transparency upon command, there hung a gigantic piece of inscrutable mid-twentieth-century abstract expressionist art that Arthur knew about, since he had read of its acquisition not long ago. It was valued in excess of $3 billion, which was equal to hundreds of millions of new ameros, the currency that was coming to replace the dollar in all civilized economies across the globe. Of course, even an amero didn't go as far as it used to, but that was still some very big coin. And to think that very shortly the artwork would be his! Arthur's new blood simmered with a pleasant warmth he did his best to conceal. For this event, he would need to be cold and, if necessary, violent to get the job all the way done. He knew that, and he looked forward to it.

As the board members assembled one by one, he strolled to the window. The view, of course, was spectacular. Vistas, too, were an expression of power. The space was up vertiginously high in the perpendicular structure; that was a given. The campus that was Athena in all her glory stretched away almost into infinity. The vast desert that lay to the east was all but obscured by clouds, and haze belched forth from the enormous metropolis that simmered just over the chemical rainbow.

It was quite hot outside, Arthur knew, but here within it was whisper cool and quiet as deep carpet. He turned to regard the chamber itself. It glowed. All surfaces were honed to a blinding shine, appropriate to the glory of the proceedings. Comfy high-backed seating units were on hand to contain the desiccated remains of the powerful moguls who had once embodied all the vitality and physical splendor of their generation, obsessed as they were from the beginning of their tenure with workouts and potions and treatments and the perpetuation of physical beauty. A tasty bunch they had once been: tall and fit and delectable to the world and to one another, cool and sexy in their calculatedly casual jeans and black T-shirts, too potent in their magnificence, some of them, to even smell very good. Now the chairs had to be scaled as high and tight as possible so that their tiny, translucent heads could clear the surface of the boardroom table and they would not tip over at the slightest jostling.

The big, big oval oak and metal slab that graced the center of the room beamed with pompous anticipation, clear of everything but empty leather place mats, crystal goblets on silver coasters, and the occasional gleaming, sweating pitcher of cold water. All of the ancient mariners scheduled to be in attendance were products of the century's first wave of disruption and consolidation; the titans who worshipped weird science for its own sake and saw tech—any tech—as a good thing in and of itself. So each of them had been thoroughly implanted with communications hardware from stem cell to sternum. Why? Why not. The opportunity had presented itself at some point for them to do so, and there was a common belief that if a thing could be done—if somebody was capable of accomplishing it—well, then, voila! So let it be written, so let it be done. Tech made all things possible, and therefore mandatory. Not to mention the fact that carrying around all this smartphone in your purse or pocket had become such a fantastic drag. Cranial implant was so much easier. Now they could be in touch with the hive 24/7 and have their hands free for whatever. Their cars drove them everywhere, too. Also left them free to, you know, do whatever.

This little matter of their mortality had been viewed in the same light. It was a problem to be solved. Had they ever failed to solve a problem? This one would fall, too. And now, seemingly, it had, in the person of this young man who contained the consciousness of a guy they had known for years. Never particularly liked him, Arthur. But that was immaterial. He had the tech. The question was, what did he want? And could they get what *they* were after without giving it all to him? Probably not. But maybe. They had thought about it together, in virtual silence interrupted only by very short, bulleted observations, transmitting simple images and wafers of opinion to one another through the digital byways that were now open to them. Not telekinesis, really. That wasn't science. But they could read one another. They had, after all, been together a long time. And they were on the same protocols.

As Arthur took a modest seat far from the head of the table, he thought to himself, hey, it's no sin to be old. But was he ever this old? The coughing and wheezing and discreet expulsion of bodily gases surrounded him. One of the citizens was already snoozing in his high-backed lounger. Arthur looked calmly about the room as the rest of the group wheezed and shuffled to their proper locations, some with oxygen packs discreetly tucked into their person, others with booster antennae poking up out of their cortical implants. This was great age, yes, accompanied by infirmity and all the weird grotesqueries of a Castro-era Cuban pickup truck. Each was still functional in his or her own way, to be sure, as he himself had been until just a few days ago, pieced together out of bat shit, bubble gum, and inventive spare parts and found objects from Dr. Caligari's lab. The majority of these totemic icons of personal power were physical presences in name only, boneless blobs of aged wetware interfacing with the best hardware money could buy, sustained by pills and injections, all plugged into the Cloud, all the time; the Cloud that was their window on existence, their consciousness.

Here they were now, all in one room, the biggest bugs in a neural ant farm teeming with virtual life forms. They buzzed and twitched among themselves as they waited for Jerry to get the meeting started. Lunch had been provided, and a few were picking at their quinoa sandwiches and cold, dead salmonetta. But Arthur knew that their real appetite was for something else: fresh blood. They could smell it. And it made them hungry. They were so fucking tired of being old, they would do anything to upgrade from that despicable status. That was his leverage. He cracked his knuckles in anticipation, as he would soon crack them, he thought, like a nestful of quail eggs.

It was time. Each shriveled, dappled, shrunken, sagging representative of the pillars of the universe was rustling in his or her place. None wanted to be caught staring at the guest of honor, but it was hard not to do so. He was all they thought that they could possibly be if everything went according to plan. They were, however, aware that they were in a position unique for them. They had no leverage. Arthur had something that they wanted. They would have killed him to acquire it, but that was clearly not a strategy that played out effectively. They needed him and what he now possessed. The secret of eternal consciousness. A solution to the problem of death.

"Okay. Let's come to order," said Jerry, his tiny, gleaming monkey head bobbing on his slender, little body. The dozen or so shriveled homunculi snapped to attention. On cue, a number of younger types more laden with business effluvia filed in. Each had a folding chair, which he or she set up near the sideboard and along the corners of the room. They looked neither left nor right and appeared ready for action.

"I'll begin this meeting by noting its historic character," said Jerry from the head of the boardroom table. He had said nothing at all to Arthur yet, but now he inclined his head in the direction of their honored visitor. "You all know Arthur, or are aware of his singular achievements. I'm not sure, however, whether he knows you all, so I will briefly introduce you. Some are, of course, founders and members of the board. Others on the periphery here, in the cheap seats, are senior staff who will bring us up to speed on certain key areas of development we believe Artie here should know about before we discuss the central matter on the agenda today. The only rule I will rigorously enforce at this gathering may be difficult for some of you to obey, and that is no sleeping, and certainly no drooling. Don't want to short out your hardware."

There was a phlegmy cough around the table that passed for something resembling a laugh. Obviously pleased with the reaction to this witticism, Jerry continued. "So in no particular order other than how you have seated yourselves around the table: To my right—Artie, I believe you know Arjun, who presides over the operations in Redmond. Arjun ate China a few years back. Next to him, I believe you will recognize Clarissa leaning in. She runs the bones of what used to be Verizon, which ingested Yahoo! for reasons best known to itself, then went on to consolidate all telecommunications not long ago. Next to her, of course, we have Larry . . . Larry, goddamn it! I said no sleeping!"

"I wasn't!" cried the painfully thin entity, mostly a head, that Jerry had just addressed. "I was thinking!"

"Not allowed!" yelled Jerry, which produced another expulsion of air around the table. "Larry controls more than ninety percent of search, plus a fair chunk of the self-driving car market, which still has fewer fatalities than the more than forty-eight million deaths that were attributed to vehicles formerly controlled by their owners, right, Larry?"

"Of course, one death is too many," said the animated cadaver that Jerry had designated as Larry, at which statement, for some reason unfathomable to Arthur, the entire room once again exploded into mirthful wheezing and clucking.

"Buzz? You with us?" Jerry had addressed a twitching figure in a hoodie seated at the other end of the table. "Buzz is impatient because this meeting requires his absence from social media for an hour or two."

"I don't want people to start speculating about my fucking death, Jerry," came a whispering voice from the other end of the table.

"Okay, Buzzy. Artie, you'll want to get with Buzz to talk about the implications of worldwide data harvesting."

"Dude," said Arthur.

"My man," the hood replied.

"That brings us to Elaine."

"Hey there, Artie," said the tiny, twinkly figure a few seats down from Arthur.

"Elaine." Arthur searched for the face he once knew inside the shell of age that now encased it.

"Artie and I once went to Burning Man together," Elaine explained to the table while devouring Arthur with a gaze that held many emotions. "Before it was acquired by the corporation that stripped it of all meaning."

Jerry smiled. "Now, Boots," he said. "The thousands of In-N-Out Burning Man franchises around the world bring in not only billions of dollars of new revenue but offer an amazing amount of critical data on our many low-end global citizens who would otherwise fall off the grid."

"I know, JC," said Elaine. "Just sometimes I can't help but remember shit." And Arthur saw now, quite clearly, a lovely, lithe, completely nude young woman dancing in the light of a gigantic fire, drunk on wine, sex, and psilocybin so very long ago.

"Wrapping things up," said Jerry. "To your left are two of our most distinguished members. First, of course, Nigel, who controls news and information. Everywhere."

"Hey there, Artie," croaked Nigel in a thick accent of some sort. His was the most amazingly attenuated life form at the table. "I'm sure we're all looking forward to getting the fuck on with things."

"Hi there, Nige," said Arthur respectfully. "You look terrific."

"Heh heh heh!" This amused Nigel so profoundly he practically snorted out an adenoid.

"And finally, say hi to Jimmy," said Jerry, "from the Lakeville Road gang."

"Very funny, Jerry."

"Okay, okay. Jim is our rep from Planet IOS who also, as you probably know, speaks for Japan Inc. and the remaining corporate survivors of the radioactive area that was once Korea."

Jim's body, other than its head, was fused with its transportation unit. But he had a pleasant and rather youthful face. "Arthur, I just want to say that the good that can be done for the human race with the tech you have apparently mastered is incalculable," he said. "I think that's as exciting as any other aspect of this thing."

"Jim is very big on the pro-social benefits of what we do," said Jerry.

"Yeah," said Arthur genially. "I'm sure that's why we're all here." To which everybody had not a word to add, because they didn't know whether to laugh or not.

"And of course you know me. What started as a means of selling physical objects now encompasses all retail sales and distribution of pretty much everything there is. I don't need to brief you on that. We kicked your ass in several acquisition wars back in the thirties, I think. Leaving you still with plenty of playground."

"Yes," said Arthur politely. "Worms turn."

"They do indeed," said Jerry magnanimously. "In the uncomfortable chairs are our executives . . ." He gestured to the gentlemen and ladies on the periphery, whose average age seemed to hover at a jejune, say, sixty-plus. "They're what used to be called Generation Z."

"Oh yes," said Arthur. "I remember." He allowed himself a little smile. Forty years later and their generation was still waiting for the slackers, the boomers, and even the millennials to vacate the big table. And here they were, still in the folding chairs.

"They'll be giving brief reports on matters that should be of interest to you," said Jerry.

"In a minute." Arthur stood, his young, powerful body looming over the tiny, seated forms of the ancient executives. "Before we do, Jerry, I think we should recognize the reality of the situation."

"And in what way should we do that, Artie?" Jerry looked interested but not flustered. Curious, that's all.

"Get up, Jer," Arthur said, friendly-like, as you would address a bridge partner who had taken the wrong position at the table. "I'm in the wrong seat."

All the air immediately left the room. Arthur stood, hands behind his back, gazing down at the minuscule entity beneath him with kindly indulgence. After a while, he said, "Do it, Jer. I don't think you want to piss me off."

"No, Arthur." Jerry stood. He was just about the same height standing as he was seated. "I'm afraid it is I who is in the wrong seat." He waddled in a dignified fashion around Arthur and sidled his way into the seat that Arthur had occupied. Arthur helped him with the last little maneuver into the chair, which wasn't easy for a man Jerry's age. Then Arthur briskly, and without further ado—but without rushing, either—took his place at the head of the table.

"Wow," he said. "Things look better from here." The table might have died of merriment, so great was the guffaw at this massive jest.

16

Core Dump

"O kay," Arthur said. "I wanna take about fifteen minutes to hear all the shit that's fucked up around here. And don't bullshit a bullshitter. I was laying it on people before some of you were born, and that's really saying something." He looked around the table expectantly.

"Okay, Artie," said Jerry, very, very respectfully. "We were prepared with some brief material in anticipation of this meeting. We just weren't sure if you'd be interested in the granular stuff."

"Not too granular," said Arthur. "Just granular enough."

"We might as well start with the workforce issue," said Jerry. "Allie?"

"Here, Jer," said a young woman, practically a little baby, maybe only in her midfifties, who was standing near the smoked salmon display on the sideboard, sipping on a cup of coffee. She was tall and athletic, wearing a suit much like the one sported by the rest of her cadre except that where they had pinstriped pants, she had a pinstriped skirt that fell just above her knees. Her cranial implant was alabaster white and glowed behind her ear like an illuminated jewel. The only other gender-defining touches were a white silk scarf tied loosely around her throat and the pile of light-blond hair gathered at the top of her head. She was wearing large horn-rimmed glasses, which she pushed to the top of her head as she eagerly took center stage.

"Artie, this is Alessandra Morph, our head of Human and Artificial Resources. "She's going to scare the shit out of you."

"Better men than she have tried," said Arthur, and some in the room may have wet themselves, such was the intensity of their mirth.

"That's not much of an introduction, Jerry," said Morph as she strode forward. She took a position behind the installed podium in the corner just past the end of the table, and waved her arm in the vague direction of the wall behind her, which immediately disintegrated, turning into a translucent screen. On it were the words "A Workforce in Crisis." Under that chilling title, a smaller subhead: "The New Employee: Dedicated, Industrious, and Incapable of Independent Thought."

"Well, that's not good," said Arthur.

"You have no idea." She stood near the wall that was now a display and let the headline sink in. "The situation is this," she began. "A significant number of the citizens in Athena have evolved."

"Evolved?" Arthur was mystified. "You mean . . . spiritually? Socially?"

"Genetically," said Morph. There was a brief silence as people chewed, swallowed, and then digested this gristly nugget. "That in itself is not the issue," Morph continued. "It happens. The circumstances of life change, and people change with it. This, however, appears to be progressing in a way that is unexpected over such a short time frame. And it has implications for the company in both upside and downside."

A sequence of tedious graphics now accompanied the presentation to give people something to look at, with headlines and bulleted subordinate points.

"There are several factors that contribute to this weird development," she said. "First, there is almost no functional limit to the age people can attain. People simply . . . *cure* unto a very advanced state.

More people die in household accidents than die of old age." There was a general murmur around the table. This was their ultimate fear: to break an artificial limb in a fall down the stairs or electrocute one's head in the shower.

"Next, population density is extreme. There are simply too many people for comfort. You may have noticed it is difficult to walk down the street in the developed areas, and in the older cities, the situation is even more acute. Everywhere you look are masses of people attempting to get somewhere. It's a real issue. There is no escape from the crowd. It moves as a group if you look at it from a distance: huge clots of individuals all connected to one another, moving like fattened sheep in large herds. This leads to an exacerbation of the problem of deindividualization that we now see taking place in our employees, our consumers, and our neighbors."

"Five minutes, Allie," Jerry said quietly. "Don't demand too much of our attention spans. We're executives. This whole meeting should be concluded in twenty minutes, and we have a lot more ground to cover."

"Don't rush the lady," said Arthur. "She's getting somewhere."

Still, Morph picked up the tempo. "Plus, the mandating of self-driving vehicles has also added to the passivity and general lack of acuity in the workforce. As you know, it has been shown that even now, fifty years down its developmental road, so to speak, the AI necessary to support this tech is reliable only up to fifteen miles per hour if fatalities are deemed unacceptable. So with the delegalizing of independent driving, as a people we are conveyed everywhere in very slow-moving vehicles in whose conduct we have no part. This once again leaves people free to consult their internal electronics and otherwise divorce themselves from any so-called real experience. It is possible, at this point, for people to wake up, get to work, get home, and go to sleep without having one analog experience. With the huge advances in dildonics, even sexual experience is at this point either enhanced by or replaced entirely by digital alternatives that are, for the most part, equal to or superior to the real thing, particularly if you've been married for a while."

Polite chuckle. A laugh in the dark. It was clear where this was headed to most in the room, if not to Arthur, for whom this information was new.

"Our drone data tell us that, in general, people have slowed down to match the pace of the vehicles in which they travel," she continued.

"Drones," said Arthur with obvious disgust.

"The data they give us are invaluable," said Morph, very polite but unyielding on the matter. She proceeded briskly to the next bullet, which read simply: "Enhanced individuals hold the edge."

"Then we have the people who have dedicated themselves entirely to turning themselves into Human 2.0. They have it all. They run faster. They jump higher. Their blood and brain and connective tissue is swimming in smart drugs. And they never get tired. Nobody human can compete with them. Until they explode."

"They explode?"

"That's not really a problem, Arthur," said Morph. "They are extremely fungible. The problem is that they represent yet another demotivator for people who are already prone to inertia, indolence, and virtual existence, driving what we believe is a fundamental alteration to the core mitochondrial DNA of a vast segment of the population."

"Next to last . . ." Here Morph highlighted the next bullet, which read, "Extreme age builds megafamily units of dubious provenance."

"Due to the extreme longevity of the affluent populace," Morph explained, "one may have many partners over a lifetime. When you live to be a hundred and beyond with no end in sight, partners peel off and die on you, and must be replaced. Extended intergenerational families from such multiple unions take up massive amounts of space and sometimes create creatures of . . . uncertain legitimacy."

"And we care about that *why*?" asked Arthur.

"Well, sir," Morph replied gingerly. "We have progeny that shows odd characteristics."

"Yikes."

"Yup." Morph transitioned to the final graphic, which read, "A New Human Species? Positives and Negatives."

"Not really," said Arthur.

"I'm afraid so. We're trying to think about what to call them. But they aren't strictly Homo sapiens. And they come from here."

There appeared on the screen a rotating image of a humanoid entity. It was neither male nor female and was distinguished by its very small head, which tapered toward a virtually bald point with a tuft of hair at the top.

"The brain," said Morph, looking at the picture, "is capable of almost telekinetic communications skills, but magnetic imaging shows that the part of the cortex responsible for undirected thinking is shrinking. We believe that within twenty years, we'll be running low on people capable of leadership. Which makes the people in this room all the more crucial as we face some of the operating issues that lie ahead."

"Thank you, Allie," said Jerry Cee. "I'm sure Arthur very much appreciates you improving his already overpowering leverage."

"Thank you for the opportunity," said Morph humbly. The board gave a small golf clap as she walked to her former position at the rear of the room. The only sound for a few moments was the *plop plop plop* of coffee being dispensed into a waiting cup here and there. During that time, Arthur came to the important conclusions that Morph was a shrewd businessperson with a fabulous ass.

"Pete? Can you advance the conversation? I'm sure Arthur can take just a bit more, as long as it's germane."

"Of course," said a relatively youngish executive, certainly no more than sixty. He was very tall and skinny, and had chosen to decorate his cranial implant with black and gray pinstripe, which Arthur thought was a nice touch. "There are other issues, beyond Athena itself, that you should be aware of, sir," he said.

"Pete Hollister," said Jerry. "He's our chief operating officer. Number two. Pending your approval, Artie."

Arthur leaned back in his chair and looked expectantly at Hollister. "Just the treetops, Pete," he said. "I'm bumping into my ADD, and I'm sure you all want to get to my agenda before your colostomy bags are full."

The board rustled. This guy, his tone, not nice. Above all, they liked things to be nice. Perhaps things wouldn't be nice at all as long as he was around. Something for them to think about together. After.

Hollister stood, perambulated in leisurely fashion to the front of the room, and took his place not behind but next to the lectern, his elbow perched upon it in sprightly insouciance. "First, the good news," he said. "The aggregation of all extant brands in all sectors is just about complete. We've got them all working under the same umbrella, segregated into verticals, with each vertical managed by a line organization reporting in by solid line to this building. We're both highly centralized for accountability and functionally decentralized for operations."

"What the fuck do you mean, 'vertical'?" Arthur had always hated jargon.

"Agriculture," said Hollister. "Essentially, all arable acreage from what used to be eastern Colorado to western Missouri are now one gigantic farm unit managed by the Archer Daniels Midland unit from Saint Louis."

"We have control of Saint Louis?"

"Of the business operations there, sure, although the city itself is pretty much a total loss."

"So what's the problem?" Arthur could feel himself losing his patience.

"The workforce is saturated. We are the only employer of record. There's no competition to work against, no chance of promotion, no personal sense of ownership in any of the operations. And this isn't unique to the farm people; it's kind of a ubiquitous issue in electronics, transportation—which is still managed out of what's left of Detroit—even entertainment, which remains headquartered in the San Fernando Desert near LA. There's no morale whatsoever throughout the operation. Productivity is down. A sense of disorganization and malaise has set in, and, particularly among the, you know, real people, who haven't mutated into pinheads yet, we're seeing defections into the ungoverned areas."

"Are there many of those?"

"Well, yeah," said Hollister. "Which means our potential marketplace of customers is peeling off, too. Going elsewhere."

"What?" Arthur was confused. "You mean Mars or something? We control the planet! Where are people going?"

Hollister motioned at the screen wall, and a map of the continental United States appeared. The two coasts and certain urban areas were blue. Vast swatches of crimson swept across certain sections of the center zones and most of Florida. Pockets of green sprouted in the Great Northwest, New England, and the Hudson Valley. He went on: "There are whole sections of Idaho . . . Wyoming . . . even Iowa and Kansas . . . also enclaves in upstate New York and throughout the South, of course . . . that are basically without centralized government of any sort. We have no data on the inhabitants, because they buy locally. Most are not implanted with any electronics."

A frisson of discomfort swept the ancients around the table. No electronics!

"They see themselves as American but not as citizens of the United States, such as it is. They pay no taxes, and any attempt to reimpose control over their territory has generally failed for one reason or another. In the heavily armed areas, pictured here in red, company representatives are viewed as invaders and either imprisoned, killed, or sent back with their heads shaved and their implants torn out. In the hippy-dippy green areas, security guys go in, but they just don't come out."

"Don't come out?" Arthur was mystified.

"Nope."

He thought back to the days when he was very, very young. He remembered the Rolling Stones playing at Altamont Speedway back in the '60s, where he had dropped acid and met a girl he could never find again. And . . . the end of the road on the Hawaiian island of Kauai. The Taylor Ranch. Ah! What a paradise. Everybody naked. Lived in trees. He could see guys going in to that kind of world and never coming out again. Not that they could be allowed to do so.

"Let me know when you want to talk about utilizing our significant military resources to take back that territory," said a dry voice in a corner of the room. It was a short, squat man with the kind of beard shadow that was impossible to eradicate without state-of-the-art face peeling tech. Clearly, this guy had not been interested in that cosmetic procedure. Arthur looked him over. Tough customer. They exchanged glares. Hey, thought Arthur, this is a guy I'm going to need to talk to.

"Finally," said Hollister, "we have almost completed planning for the physical consolidation of the Cloud."

"I beg your pardon?" Here Arthur sat up. A brisk, cold wind blew through the room. His expression was not pleasant. Or, rather, it was excessively pleasant. Arthur had learned this expression from a media mogul who once ran Hollywood. When about to pounce, the trick was to radiate such excessive goodwill that the unsuspecting target of the coming eruption, unprimed by experience, had no idea that he or she was about to be charbroiled into a cinder and sent reeling into hell.

"As you know, um, Arthur, if I may call you that . . ." Here Arthur simply sat, pleasantly inquiring, and silent. "At any rate, um, sir . . ."

"Oh, for fuck's sake. Spit it out."

"Well, the idea, which was approved by the entire board, may I add." Here Hollister looked around the room for support, and, finding nothing but extreme vacuity to his left and right, soldiered on. "The idea was to save untold trillions of dollars by consolidating the physical servers that make up the thing that we know, of course, as

the Cloud, which is really nothing but a lot of hardware sharing re-
dundancies and trading data from sources all over the world. Up until
a few years ago, the servers were all over the place, but this led to collection inefficiencies as well as a certain sense that any pod of servers was less secure from terrorists than a strong centralized location
staffed by trusted security people provided by Mr. Mortimer here."
He nodded at the scowling, bullet-headed figure, who was dressed
in a suit that was a little too small to hide the bulge at his hip. He
was having trouble sitting, in fact, and had to lean to one side to ac-
commodate his weapon inconspicuously, which made it even more
conspicuous.

"I'll give my report on this subject later," said Mortimer. Unlike
the rest of the room, Mortimer was young, under fifty, at any rate, and
did not seem eager to ingratiate himself with anybody. Arthur was
starting to like him.

"So, to wrap it up," Hollister said very quickly, "the consolidation is almost complete, and the new Cloud is set to go online in
perhaps two weeks."

"Are you planning a big ceremony?" Arthur asked cordially.

"Not really." Hollister was jovial now, his report all but concluded. "Just a few dozen people. We're deciding whether to include
spouses."

"Canapés?" said Arthur. There was a short silence. It was suddenly hard to read him. He had gone opaque. "Has it occurred to
anybody," he said, scanning the room as if he were about to suggest
a hand of whist, "that by centralizing the Cloud, you've put the brain
stem of the entire civilized world at risk . . . you . . . fucking . . .
morons!"

He stood and looked over the cringing table. And there it was.
Within the space of three simple words, Arthur had descended into
psychotic fury, demonstrating an executive power that cannot be
taught, has to be built in. He continued, dark now, a growling beast
prepared to gut and eat the entrails of any creature who stood too

close to him. "You've made it easy for anybody with a mind to do so to throw us back into the fucking dark ages. Did that ever occur to any of you nitwits?"

"Yeah," said Mortimer from his end of the room. "It occurred to this nitwit."

"You can stay after class, Mr."—here Arthur peered at the small name card in front of the speaker—"Mortimer." Then he just sat at the head of the table again, staring at the shriveled little beanbags in the high-back seats before him. He ran his fingers through his thick, sensuous mop of auburn hair and began the salvo he knew he must win.

"Okay, sports fans," he said, dead level. "I've heard enough. One thing is clear: you guys are too old to manage this company effectively. You need to take a step back and let a younger man pick up the stick. Here's how it's going to be. There will be three classes of stock. First, C stock, which anybody can buy and has no voting power whatsoever."

"Hey, Artie," said Jerry. "Wait a minute."

"The B stock will be available to board members and their wives, key executives, and others within the inner circle. It will have voting power, but in its aggregate, it will amount to perhaps twenty percent of the voting shareholder base. That is my gesture to you guys."

"Wait a minute," said Jerry. "We're talking about management transition here, not change of ownership." His face had turned from his normally rodentine pink to a deep, eggplant blue.

"The A stock in the corporation will be a supermajority of voting shares, amounting to eighty percent of the total. I will own all of that class."

"I'm going to take this opportunity," said Jerry, rising, "to thank Arthur for his time today and adjourn this meeting, so that we can deal with some of these ideas in the privacy of our—"

Arthur rose from his seat, circled the table, and, with a ferocious leap, landed directly on Jerry's lapels, which he seized with both hands. He then lifted Jerry entirely out of his seat and shook him very hard, not playing around, so that the old man's head snapped back and forth, and his shoulders rattled.

"Are you gonna fuck around with me, Jerry? Huh?" he barked, boring his face down into his adversary's. "Did you bring me all the way here to waste my fucking time?"

"Artie, please, dude." Jerry was green. "You're fucking killing me, man."

"Yeah? Well. That is just too . . . fucking . . . bad." Arthur held the limp, trembling body of the former CEO of the largest corporate entity in the world in front of him, eighteen inches off the ground. Then he threw it back into its chair the way a child would dispose of a toy in which it had lost interest after deciding not to rip off its head.

"I'll have all the A shares," said Arthur, resuming his seat and brushing himself off to remove any imaginary dust. "Let's put it to a vote."

"May I ask a question?" a reedy voice piped up from the farthest corner of the room. "My name is Nord. I am general counsel." The speaker was a very small sparrow of a woman. While not quite the dried husk of a certified board member, she was still extremely advanced in years, with a tuft of white hair and a large proboscis that tapered down into an invisible chin. Her role as arbiter of the corporate law was made clear by the steamer-trunk-sized suitcase that rested by the side of her folding chair. The rest of the mummies sat quietly. The possibility of physical injury had changed the entire game for everybody at the table. These people spent a significant part of every day caring for the physical instrument. The idea that it could be broken was never far from their minds. And here was this crazy motherfucker who not only held the secret of digital immortality but also was willing to shake Jerry to death. That former senior officer was still the color of a spoiled grape, all white and green and blotchy. Yeah, they were paying attention to whatever Arthur wanted.

"Just to make this really clear," said Nord, her voice drained of all affect, "this will mean that you will own the company. It will be yours. All its operating divisions, but more importantly . . . you'll own . . ." Here her professional sangfroid failed her, and she simply stared at Arthur for a moment or two.

"Yeah?" said Arthur.

"You will actually be the sole proprietor of the Cloud. Like, you'll own it. Personally."

"Yup. Pretty fucking great, huh?" There was a silence into which one might drive an eighteen-wheeler from the now-dead past into an uncharted future.

"So moved," said a board member—it doesn't matter who.

"Second," said another.

"All who say aye?" asked Nord.

"Aye," said the board.

"All who say nay?" Another pregnant silence.

"The motion is passed," said the lawyer. Then they all just sat there.

"Okay," said Arthur. Then he roared at the top of his lungs. "Bob!"

The double doors of the boardroom hissed open and in stepped the master of science who would grant them all eternal life. "This is Bob, who will explain the tech to you," said Arthur. "Say hello to the room, Bob."

"Hello to the room," said Bob.

17

The Three Amigos

There is a special feeling in a conference room that has done its duty for the day. Everything is just a bit off. There are dirty glasses on the table. All the food is gone except for a couple of quinoa power bars, low-carb candy, the occasional cookie growing stale. There is coffee in the urns, but those who try it will be rewarded with a mouthful of tepid phlegm. A few half-dead teacups remain, the scum of dairy creamer crusting their surfaces. The shades, once closed against the distractions of the world outside, are now raised to welcome in the twinkling of the night: the lights of the campus far below; the seething glitter of the urban haze just beyond the arc of the earth.

In this particular war room, on this particular silent night, a few recessed lights shone in their invisible cornices, lending a gentle glow to the three amigos who sat quietly where the meeting had just ended. The board members had been sent to take a nap, recharge their variety of hardware and implanted prosthetics and electronics, infuse some fresh plasma, perhaps, and otherwise prepare for the ceremonial dinner that would conclude the day's important events. They were all looking forward to it very much, for at least two reasons: first, it was quite possibly one of the final times they would all be chewing digestible slop in unison in their current physical incarnations, and, second, it was at Nobu, where it was devilishly difficult, even for them, to get a reservation. In this case, Arthur had possessed the presence of mind to secure the entire establishment for the event. He figured, hey, why not? It was the last time he would see any of the dehydrated little fucks.

Three gentlemen now sat at disparate corners of the enormous oval. Arthur himself was still at the head, leaning back in an almost completely prone position in the comfy recliner, his feet up on the hallowed surface, hands behind his head, eyes on the landscape beyond the windows. In the middle of one side was Bob, hunched over his tablet, doodling with his electronic pencil, very, very upset, although he didn't show it. In the middle seat on the other side of the table was Mr. Mortimer, the head of security, who had been asked politely to remain after the rest of the players had departed. A companionable silence reigned over the cordial trio. This was the space between what had just occurred and what was about to happen. The agenda was up to the man who had just acquired more than any one individual had ever owned, in exchange for life eternal. The other two were content to wait.

"Bob," said Arthur after a little while. "I'm going to talk to Mr. Mortimer here for a few minutes. You can stay if you like. But it's not going to concern you all that much. After that, I do have a few important thoughts I'd like to share with you."

"That's okay, Arthur," said Bob, looking at the body of Gene as he did so. He couldn't help it. This was the physical entity he had created in the print shop and then kick-started with the core of his own consciousness. The data he had downloaded from his brain into Gene's were very basic: mostly a certain knowledge of the world as it existed, a simple frame of reference, some cultural data that gave the boy a template that could be filled later by the aged monster who had funded the project. The uploads from the minds of the board would also be comprehensive: everything a recipient host body would need to assume the character, the life experience—the entire consciousness—of the donor.

The recipient hosts would have to be printed, of course. They were already being spun into existence back at the lab, their DNA acquired from a variety of unwitting sources who believed their genetic material had been gathered for the purpose of ascertaining their ancestry. These brand-new bodies, empty of consciousness, would be ready before too much longer. It was remarkable how much could now be stored on a single chip. The computer that would house this entire database—the container of more than a dozen entire human souls—was no bigger than a wine cooler. The whole thing was miraculous. He had to admit that.

This omnipotent personage that Bob saw before him, leaning forward now on both elbows and clearly gearing up for the next phase of the business he intended to execute, was at this moment one of a kind, and in that splendid creation he was well pleased. But still. It was weird. And he found himself missing . . . somebody. The feeling of missing somebody or something was so intense, suddenly Bob was shocked to find that he might have actually burst into tears if he were that kind of person.

"I'll just hang out here and take it easy until you're ready for me, Arthur," is what he finally choked out. Then he rose and went to the sideboard to fetch a power bar and a bottle of water, his back to the two who now faced each other across the field of battle.

"Good man," said Arthur. He stared at Bob's back for a little while. "And now, Mr. Mortimer," he said, in a completely different tone of voice, one friendly conspirator to another.

"Call me Mort," said Mort. He was still gray, still crisp, still clean and pressed, necktie perfect in its cradle above his Adam's apple, cuffs shot so that only a quarter inch of white peeked beyond the gray suit—the only disruption in his sleek perfection being the uncomfortable bulge at his hip. Clean shaven at the beginning of the two o'clock meeting, he now had the beginnings of an impressive full beard. His chin was a marvel of chiseled stone. His eyes were flat and as gray as the rest of him, and reflected no light. His smile was not a smile but an expression without mirth—polite, conditional, and curious.

"Talk to me, Mort."

"We are underutilized," said the master of the security force. Slowly, with impeccable economy of motion, he rose, walked one, two, three, four high-backed recliners down the table, and reseated himself in a chair just two away from the unit where Arthur presided over the almost empty room. In spite of the feeble illumination provided by the selected lighting configuration, darkness now hung to them both like fog.

Snack and beverage in hand, Bob had plumped down in a seat at the farthest end of the room and was pretending to consult his interior electronics. In fact, he was listening most intently. There was something about the change of color in the atmosphere that he didn't like, not one bit. Truth be told, he was feeling just a little sick. If he had any guts at all, he would have stood, excused himself, and left. But like a passerby transfixed by the sight of a six-car pileup replete with blood and bone and the wailing of the injured, he was rooted to the spot. Something was happening here, and he didn't know what it was. But it was possible he needed to find out.

"I don't want to have to prompt you, Mort," said Arthur quietly. "Dump out the bag."

"We have huge resources and very little on which to deploy them." Mort leaned forward to establish a decent eye lock with Arthur. "We've got an army and nothing to do with it. I mean, a few eco-felonies here and there. Guys trying to take their illegal Camaros out for a spin after curfew. Idiots flaunting air quality regs firing up their barbecues with real charcoal. A little pilfering from the mom-and-pop shops we've allowed to survive. Some cybertheft and malicious hackery now and then from pimply-faced geeks in Guy Fawkes masks. What's it add up to? Very little. Most offenses can be dealt with via intercranial shaming."

"What's that?"

"A blast of focused contempt and hatred beamed directly into your head from the online community," said Mort. "You can't possibly know what that's like unless you've experienced it. It's intense. The shame it inflicts is permanent. There have been quite a few suicides immediately after application of the punishment. No legal proceedings are necessary. Simply inform social media engines and step back. Huge deterrent power, too."

"Only to people who are capable of shame," said Arthur thoughtfully. Mortimer took that in. "That's actually quite funny," he said at last, without laughing.

"That's it? That's the extent of criminal activity you got for me?"

"Yeah. And here we have this magnificent security apparatus built for warfare, for command and conquest, doing nothing."

"What's the point of building it," said Arthur, drawing upon a quote from the earlier part of the century, before the Civil War, "if we don't use it?"

"Yes, sir. Beyond that, everybody is pretty much on Xee, which levels them out and gets them to bed early." There was an uncomfortable pause, and then Mortimer continued. "I suppose I should mention . . . that there is a serious challenge out there if we choose to take it as such."

"What's that, Mort?"

"A small group of . . . pacifist terrorists."

"You're shitting me."

"No. Call themselves the Skells."

"Skulls?"

"*Skells*. Terrorists in hippy clothing. 'Dedicated to the destruction of digital culture.' Anti-techs."

"Where they at?" A threat, thought Arthur. Just what he had been looking for.

"Mostly in the Green Zones you saw on that map earlier."

"Remind me."

"All over, in little pockets. One big one in Buttfuck, Tennessee. Another in the Hudson Valley in New York State. There's a Socialist free republic in what used to be Vermont. The biggest of all, of course, is not that far from here, in the Pacific Northwest. Place called George, Washington."

"You're shitting me."

"Nope," said Mort. He leaned in on both elbows, placing him at eye level with his new confidant and boss. "They had a music festival there in the late twentieth century. Called it Sasquatch. It wasn't as big as Coachella or Bonaroo . . ."

"Bonaroo!" said Arthur. A giant smile of pure pleasure suffused his face.

"Bunch of like-minded souls gathering together to hug a tree, listen to noise, and get high."

"Nothin' wrong with that."

"Gorgs and losers." Mortimer looked like he wanted to spit but no receptacle was available. "Some never left. Now they got a little town up there. Leader is a guy named Timothy Something. Easy to get there. You go to a place just outside Santa Rosa, and an underground railroad of snorks and wheedles whisks you back to a world where nobody is wired and the vegetable is king."

"Skells, Mort."

"Oh yeah. Sorry. They roamed around the country for a while, looking for data farms to fuck with. Even got to a few. They hop from one green patch to another. Right now we think they may be up in that place with Uncle Timothy, or whatever the fuck he calls himself."

"That's not that far from the Cloud, is it."

Mortimer considered that. "Could be coincidence."

"Yeah, I suppose," said Arthur. They sat for a while. "How could they do it? They got a nuclear device or something?"

"Don't need one," said Mortimer, with a true destroyer's appreciation for the weapons of destruction regardless of their object. "They just need a couple of small explosively pumped flux compression generators." Arthur looked at Mortimer thoughtfully but said nothing. "They make 'em smaller every day," Mortimer added with some appreciation. When Arthur failed to respond once again, he said, "Of course, unless they want to drop it from a drone, which is unlikely, they'd have to get inside the Cloud itself."

"Well," said Arthur at last, "I guess we'll have to make sure that doesn't happen."

"Stupid, huh?" said Mortimer. "Putting most of the brain stem of the world in one physical location. You have to study an issue for a long time and be really, really smart to do something so incredibly dumb."

"Good thing nobody knows where it is. Do they, Mort?"

"No, they do not, and they're not going to."

"We gotta get to dinner and mop up the proceedings," said Arthur, rising, as Mortimer, a bit surprised that the conversation was ending at that point, did the same. Arthur stuck out his hand for a shake. After a moment, Mortimer stuck out his hairy paw and, without warning, found himself drawn close to other man, who had reeled him in like a giant tarpon. The two men were now face-to-face, with perhaps no more than three inches between their noses. Arthur spoke very low, but Bob could hear him clearly, and he saw Mortimer, a big, solid man now quite unnerved, soaking in what was being said directly into his face.

"Mort. You and Bob are my main men here. I'm going to give you your instructions now, and I want you to listen very carefully. Are you listening very carefully?"

"I am, sir, I mean, yes I am, sir."

"You are the commander of a security service that is made up of thousands of well-trained, well-armed men, women, and synths, presumably a significant power on land, on sea, and in the air, am I correct?"

"Yes, sir. We have the largest commercial military force in the world. We inherited the Disney Navy. Entire warehouses full of robots and androids."

"Lots of drones, too, I imagine."

"Yes, sir. Lots." Mort was mesmerized by this power that was expressing itself before his eyes.

"The issues laid out for me today at this meeting have made several things clear to me. If we are to secure the future for ourselves, we will have to address the decomposition of our markets. In some cases, this is a defensive operation. In others, we will simply have to retake certain areas and bring them back inside. Red, green, whatever. Those who stand in our way will have to be pacified. I think you see what I mean."

A childlike grin lit up the face of the new commander, and a boyish gleam ignited in his eyes. "Yes, sir, I do," he said. "Now, if you'll let go of my fucking hand, I'll see if any bones are broken."

Arthur let him go, and after a small nod of his head and an imaginary click of his heels, Mortimer headed for the door.

"And, Mort," said Arthur. Mortimer turned, awaiting further direction. "Check with me if you need to spend more than a billion dollars or so."

"Will do, Arthur." A wave of emotion smote him as he stared at this surprising new force of power that had lifted him from a life of tedious corporate ennui and onto the field of glorious combat. "I won't let you down, sir," he said, with feeling.

"I know," said Arthur, with a formal cranial genuflection of his own. Mortimer was gone.

Bob was still at the table, his chin in one palm, a quizzical half smile on his face.

"Scary guy, huh?" said Arthur, looking Bob over.

"Scary, yeah," said Bob. He stared quietly at Arthur.

"Do I know what you're thinking, Bob?"

Bob sat, very relaxed, taking in the quiet, the muted lighting, the ozone in the air. "I'm not thinking, Arthur. I'm looking forward to having a drink before dinner. And I recognize that before I get to that happy moment, you most certainly have some instructions for me, your other . . . main man."

"Main man Number One, Bob. Never forget that." Arthur strolled over to Bob and put a gentle hand on his shoulder. "Now. What I want you to do, my brilliant friend, is to arrange for the entire board of directors to make their visit to your magic shop."

"'Twas my plan," said Bob.

"I want you to upload their entire databases into Big Larry." Big Larry was the neural wine cooler.

"Check," said Bob, and waited for more.

"I want you to make sure that during that process, each of their bodies is drained of all life force, and that they are dead when you are done. That should be easy enough. Most of them are ninety-five percent there already."

Bob said nothing. Had he known this was the plan all along? What do we know that we don't want to admit that we know? So much, really. The list is endless, if you want to think about it. Bob didn't. He just listened for the rest of it. He knew what was coming.

"And then I want you to make a tragic mistake and delete them all. And then delete the deletions. They have each lived a good, long life. Now they have served their purpose. And we will move forward to make the Corporation great again, a long and exciting process for which none of them will be necessary—for which, in fact, each in his or her own way may prove to be an impediment."

"I see," said Bob without expression. "I guess that sounds like a good idea."

Arthur gazed at Bob, and not without some fondness. "You're not going to get all squishy sentimental on me now, are you, Doctor?"

"Not at all. I think I see the general outlines of your plan, Arthur. Hard to see a flaw in it."

"Good. Good good," said Arthur and, with a broad grin, he pulled Bob out of his seat and gave him a genuine Hollywood hug. "Now let's go to dinner with those old goats. I'm hungry. And I want to get home and pop my beautiful wife."

"Of course," said Bob. "Who wouldn't?"

18

Too Much Toasting

This was a historic event, so everybody did his or her best to look nice. As usual, the board did not have to sully itself by contact with the hoi polloi. A private room was dedicated to their comfort, with servers assisted by intelligent Roombas hovering nearby, ready to provide whatever was requested. The room was laid out with three round tables of eight occupants each: board members and selected senior staff, the occasional significant other. Centerpieces of actual live orchids, grown hydroponically in the climate-controlled company-owned facilities that also provided most of their dinner that night, graced the tables. Crisp white tablecloths shone beneath gleaming, square plate ware, silver with an Asian design. Crystal water glasses filled to the brim with good, clean water, their surfaces sweating with ice. Yet for all the festive trappings, the mood was somewhat edgy. Big events were on tap. By morning, they would be headed down to Bob's big lab to exchange their old, worn-out bodies for freshly minted housings that just might look as good as Arthur's. Fortunately, none of them knew that this was intended to be their last supper. That might have put them off their food.

Jerry and a few of the board members stood, to the best of their ability, by the private bar that had been set up for them in the corner of the room. Some had martinis. A few had brown liquor in square, heavy glasses. Most had wine. Only a few were in mechanized conveyances, although most had canes. They drank in silence punctuated by the smacking of lips and discreet gurgling of invisible hoses and other body parts. The fortunate staff members who had been invited mixed politely with them but stayed deferentially apart, murmuring among themselves.

"This is a celebration, by the way," said Jerry to his small cadre of associates. "Let's keep that in mind as we make our way through this evening toward our further adventures tomorrow."

"I didn't like the way he physically assaulted you, Jer," said an ancient voice from the center of their klatch.

"He's a fucking bully," said Jerry. "You don't get that kind of success without a certain deformation of character, I think we'll all agree on that."

There was an appreciative chuckle.

"Besides," said one board member, "it'll be worth it."

"I'll be glad to be rid of this damned air hose," said another.

"Fuckin' A," said a third.

They drank. After perhaps ten more minutes of that, with occasional desultory chat, they were each and every one drunk on their shrunken little asses.

"Where the fuck is he?" hissed the board member whose company had virtually total control over global distribution of entertainment content.

"He'll be here," said Jerry Cee. But he was pissed off, too. There's rude and then there's really rude. It was 8:20 already. They were hungry.

There was a bit of a kerfuffle at the entryway and Bob came in, his hair askew, a wild look in his eye, his suit in need of pressing, as if he had just awakened from a nap that had gone on twenty minutes too long. If it were not so improbable, one might conclude that he had slapped a wafer of Xee on the back of his neck not too long ago. Bronwyn was by his side, apparently holding him vertical. She was dressed all in brown leather, with grommets here and there in neat little rows. Around her neck was a brown leather choker dotted with stones of smoky topaz. More than one antique neck creaked appreciatively in her direction.

"Bob," she said in a very low murmur. "Bob, man. You got to pull it together. I understand your situation. But you can't play it out in public here."

"Don't tell me what to fucking do," Bob replied, far too audibly. He looked with evident horror around the room and then added in a much lower voice, "Just look at these poor trusting fucks. They have no idea." And even lower: "This kind of thing was never part of the deal."

"Well, we're not gonna let it happen, are we, Bobby?"

"No, I guess not," said Bob, crestfallen. "I may not be the greatest person in the world, but even I have my limits."

"Well," said Bronwyn, quite reasonably. "We can still make it right."

"I know, I know." Bob and Bronwyn stood together in the entryway, their heads so close together that their foreheads were almost touching. "Go ahead," said Bob at last.

"Yeah?" Her eyes widened and her exclamation point of a ponytail seemed to leap even more skyward. "There's no real way to get the thing back into the bag after we dump it out, Bob."

"The only thing necessary for the triumph of evil is for good men to do nothing."

"And women, Bob."

"Of course, Bee. Don't start with that shit on me now."

They looked at each other. There was nobody else in the room for them at that moment. Bronwyn was slightly taller than Bob. She peered down at him as he gazed up at her. "Go on," he said. "I mean it. Go on." She touched the rise of his cheekbone with the tip of her index finger.

"Turn off your implant," he said to her.

"I will," she said. And left.

"Gentlemen and ladies!" said Bob, a pleasant declaration that he was open for social intercourse.

"Is your young friend not joining us?" asked Jerry, making room for Bob at the bar.

"Nope," said Bob. "What are we having?" He gave his order to the artificial bartender, and small talk once again rose to pleasant levels.

"Well," said Jerry after a time, "I'm sure Arthur will join us soon. Why don't we sit." The assembly looked at one another, uncertain and a bit confused. Should they sit? Should they stand? Should the feeding begin? Should they wait? What would be polite? Arthur was not here!

"I'm sorry I'm late!" said an aggressively jocular voice from the hallway.

"Our honored guest!" exclaimed Jerry, relieved. And there Arthur was, standing in the entryway with his arms on his waist and his legs spread in a position of maximum power, like the ancient statue *Colossus* surveying the harbor on the Greek island of Rhodes.

"Hey, everybody," said Arthur. "I wish I had a decent excuse, but the truth is I knew I was late—but I didn't give a shit!"

In hopes that he was joking, the room chuckled appreciatively. "We couldn't get the party started without you," said Jerry with a little bow. Arthur acknowledged the gesture and then entered the room to a variety of handshakes, backslaps, and simpering protestations of affection.

"I believe my better half will be along a bit later," he confided to Jerry. "She extends her regrets for her tardiness as well, but I believe her favorite synth needed some kind of servicing."

"Well, we'll just have to limp along without her! Shall we sit?" Jerry was expansive, the ultimate host. "You sit here by me, Artie," Jerry said, patting the back of the chair adjacent to his.

The partygoers found their places marked by name tags installed in small silver frames. "These are stainless steel," said the board member whose part of the operation controlled the production of foodstuffs for most of the globe. "I would think you would have sprung for silver, Jerry."

"Small economies, my friend," said Jerry, who remained standing. There was more rustling as the rest settled in. Then they leaned back in their chairs and awaited developments, one of the great tasks demanded of all executives. Finally Jerry raised his glass.

"I'd like to offer a little toast," he began. The entire room constricted like a giant muscle. Each had seen his or her fill of bad toasts. A bad toast can destroy not only the toaster, but do damage to he who is toasted as well.

"This is a historic moment," Jerry intoned. "We have a couple of people here who have changed the course of human history. First, of course—always first—we have here a guy named Arthur, who is now inhabiting the body of a person who would probably have preferred to have kept it. It was the ultimate unfriendly takeover, and we will be its beneficiaries." A shudder rippled through the room, and then it laughed, sort of. It was a laugh, to be sure, but there was a lot of mucus in it. "Anyhow, now we have a situation where this person, Arthur, has made us a deal which, when you factor it all in, is reasonable. He gets the business. We get life. Thank you, Arthur."

This seemed an occasion for some applause, so one of the attorneys started it. To be fair, the resulting golf clap was rather protracted, and everybody seemed to relax a little.

"And then there's Bob. Bob the mad scientist. Dude, I think I speak for the rest of the room when I say, you are . . . the man." At that, the room actually erupted in genuine spontaneous approbation taking the form of some huzzahing, some ejaculation of the name "Bob!" and some buzzing and trading of nods.

"So. To Arthur and Bob, we raise a glass," Jerry said, and did so.

Those who could stand rose to their feet, and the rest held their glasses high, and then they all drank. Bob, for his part, felt it would be churlish not to drain his flagon to the dregs. Arthur took a little sip, just to be polite. There was a window then, wide open, filled with the silence that comes before the next person under pressure to make a toast capitulates and rises to his or her feet. Arthur realized with horror that it was he who was absolutely required to be that person. It wasn't that the refusal would mark him as a jerk. It would mark him as a coward. It would be viewed universally by these geezers as a sign of weakness, a recognition that he had power, yes, but in the end? He was a pussy. When the time came for him to make the toast of his life, he wilted. Sat there and did nothing.

Arthur stood and clinked his glass.

"Look, I don't reveal myself to a lot of people," he said. "But I'd be lying to you if I said I wasn't very aware of what a lucky guy I am. And I am grateful, but I don't know who to be grateful to, so I'll just say I'm grateful to myself. But seriously." Here he paused for a moment, perhaps aware that his opening hadn't achieved the degree of levity he had anticipated. "I don't know what the fuck to say. I'm terrible at speeches and toasts and shit." Here he took another sip of Cabernet. "Let me describe the science to you," he said suddenly. Then he began to wander around the room, staring into his balloon of Chateau Montelena. It was very, very hard not to take another mouthful, feel it rolling around on the back of his tongue, aspirating the lovely bouquet of orange and chocolate and burned leather. This was his day of triumph! He took a sip. "Oh well," he continued. "Fuck it anyway. All you need to know is that all of this—the body I'm in, the fact that I am in this body—was in the works for the last fifty years and culminates in me, Arthur. And now I am this person, where before I was another person, and now I'm this person."

He paused and looked bemusedly at the group. "At any rate," he said after a time. "This has been a very fucked-up toast, but I salute you all and look forward to working with all of you to shape a new future. We have a tough road ahead of us to build on our great foundation and grow the business for the next generation of leaders to make this Corporation great again. Sacrifices will have to be made, hopefully by other people. But seriously. Thanks." Then he sat down and drained his glass.

"Arthur!" Jerry once again raised his glass.

"Huzzah!" cried the multitudes.

"On the other hand," said Arthur ruminatively, seated now, the philosopher king in repose, "there's the whole question of what happened to the guy whose body I'm in right now." He poured himself another glass of wine from a bottle on the table and downed it in one great gulp. "Like"—here he hiccupped—"in order for the mental transference to happen, I had to be downloaded into a functioning human being. And the thing is, sometimes I feel him . . . creeping around inside me. In fact, oh good Christ. What have I done?"

There was an appalled silence.

"Who the fuck are you guys?" said Gene, looking around himself like a man just awakened from a really weird dream. Then he rose, went to the sidebar, filled a massive tumbler with the Macallan 45-Year-Old Fine Oak single-malt scotch, and poured it in one great draught down his throat.

Then he thought about things for a long, long time, or at least it seemed like a long time, the scotch flowing through his system, warming him to his core, the joy of feeling himself again. He stared into the empty tumbler and then slowly reached for more ice. When the glass was full, he poured a moderate amount of liquor over the rocks and then turned to face them, presumably as Arthur. "Ah, that's good," he said, with the proper Arthurian gravel in his throat. "I feel more like myself."

The room regarded him with a variety of feelings. Terror, to be sure, but primarily confusion. What was Arthur up to? Asking who they were? What was up with that? On the other hand, they were all drinking heavily, too. Perhaps it was their judgment that was screwed up, and it was Arthur who was all right?

"Let's eat some food," said Gene, but it was Arthur who they saw saying it.

"Good idea," said Jerry, motioning with one hand in the air, the universal signal for servants to begin the beguine.

In this case, what they had were mostly things that were soft. That still leaves a remarkable variety of delicious stuff. Pâté. Caviar. Most sushi. Salmon, the go-to fish for antique executives everywhere. Pureed vegetables. Things cut in very small pieces, like the salad, which was minced.

About ten minutes into the appetizer course, there was another small ruckus in the hallway, and Sallie appeared at the door. In her arms was Lucy. Sallie was bedecked neck to ankle in a translucent silver sheath of artificial lizard skin. Her hair was slicked back in an iridescent helmet, and a million or so dollars of jewelry accented her neck, her wrists, her fingers. She smelled, very faintly, of wildflower.

"Woof woof," said Lucy.

Greeting people she recognized as she went, Sallie made her way over to the table where Gene sat, watching the beautiful woman approach, the lovelight in her eyes. "Artie," she said, and bent down to kiss him. Just a light, very slightly protracted brushing of the lips, nothing that the board would find inappropriate. Gene kissed her back. It wasn't a hard decision. She stood up abruptly and looked at him, still holding his hand in hers.

"I've been drinking," said Gene, with a little piece of Arthur in there.

"Well," said Sallie, looking him over speculatively, "I guess I'd better catch up." She motioned for a drink.

This was the occasion for a decent-sized house laugh, which she acknowledged and then sat down in the chair that had been reserved for her. A host of floating robots genteelly swarmed her and attended to her every need. People approached. Lots of greetings, air-kissing, hugging. She attended to it all, superb-corporate-wife mode on high. And through it all, she looked at the person she had accepted to be

Arthur and who had kissed her somewhat differently. Better, actually. More tenderly. Eyes focused on hers. She thought about that quite seriously, too. Holding himself different. Less stolid. More . . . jaunty? He really was quite drunk. She'd never actually seen Artie so incredibly hammered. Not like him, really.

"I had that upgrade done on Lucy," she said, presenting the synth to him for a kiss. Gene kissed Lucy, who then also skewered him with a quizzical expression.

"Artie!" Sallie beamed with surprise and pleasure. "You kissed her!"

"It's not every day that a good friend like Lucy here gets an upgrade," said Gene.

"I can say a lot more than 'woof' now," said Lucy.

"Wow!" Gene was impressed. "That's quite an upgrade."

"We should have a conversation sometime," said Lucy.

Mortimer had appeared at Gene's elbow. Gene noticed then that the Segway named Officer O'Brien had appeared out of nowhere, rolled quietly to the door, and was now blocking any attempt to leave. That was fine. Let it play out. The only thing he knew was that he had to stay drunk all the time now. That was okay. He could do that.

Mortimer sat down and looked at him with professional seriousness. "Arthur," he said. "My briefings have informed me that there is always a danger that there may be occasional . . . reversions. And I should watch for those and make sure that you are helped during any such episodes to return to yourself. So I need to ascertain if you are indeed you. I'm sure you understand no disrespect is intended, sir."

"No, no," said Gene. "You may fire when ready, Gridley."

Here Mortimer leaned in. "What was it you and I discussed after the board meeting? Just the high concept. You don't have to go into the nuts and bolts."

"We've got total market domination in every possible vertical," said Gene, who had been listening. Now he grabbed for as much as he had fathomed. "But changes in the population—instability in the marketplace, call it—have created a situation where we will, in effect, become nothing more than a master Utility providing boring goods and services to people. We need new markets, and that means reclaiming portions of the customer base that we've lost through . . . whatever. Attrition? It doesn't matter. We need to pull them back in. And we've got the muscle to do it. That's you, Mort. You're the muscle."

"Okay, Artie," said Mortimer. "I see you in there."

"Keep doing what you're doing. This country is soft. Even the hard parts don't know what a dedicated army can do. We don't need to be mean about it, though. We're gonna win, but we're not going to be Sherman marching through Georgia."

"I'm sorry to hear that, Artie."

"Readiness is all."

"You didn't make that up," said Mortimer. "O'Brien."

"Yes, sir," said the artificial policeman.

"Your orders are to help Artie here do any the fuck thing he wants to do."

"Within the limits of the law, sir," said O'Brien. Mortimer gave him a narrow look. "Just kidding," it added.

Gene had poured himself another stiff bolt of amber goodness. "Excuse me," he said. And he drank it.

"Hey, everybody," said Jerry, who had been looking on as the aged board, one by one, drifted off into the Land of Nod. "I think we've all put up with just about enough of this shit." He stood. "Look. I guess we could all fuck each other in any number of ways during this transaction, but I hope we all play it straight up, and each of us ends up happy and healthy and a whole lot younger. I'd raise a glass, but this is not a fucking toast. It's what I really feel. Good night. I'll see you all in the morning." He went to the door and then paused and turned to the guy he thought was Arthur. "Artie," he said, "I'm just gonna say it once: play this one straight. I know there's a lot of angles. But play this one straight."

"Jerry, man," said Gene. "You insult me."

"No, Artie, never," said Jerry. Then he shouted to the completely plastered form twitching at a table in the corner, "Bob! You da man, right?"

"Right!" said Bob. Then he put his head down on the table and cried like a baby.

"We're drunk on our asses," said Jerry. "Sallie. You deserve better than this."

"Thank you, Jerry," said Sallie. "You do too."

"True dat," said Jerry, and he left. This event sent a shockwave of resolution through the entire board, which as one decided that a bell had rung that had released them from this duty. They leapt, within their capacity, to their feet or their alternatives, donned sweaters and microventilators, and blew out of there like puffed rice shot from a cannon.

The room was a bit quiet for a moment or two then. All who remained looked about them, ascertaining who was left on the playing field. There was Arthur, of course, and Sallie, and the little green synth, and Mortimer, sitting with a drink in his lap, a cigar plugged into the corner of his mouth, waiting for further instructions and wondering why none seemed to be forthcoming. And Officer O'Brien, patrolling the periphery. And Bob.

"So," Sallie said after a while. "Who am I talking to, really?" She turned to Gene and looked deep into his eyes.

"It's me, Sallie," said Gene, in his very own voice.

"Yeah," said Sallie. "I thought so. Artie would never have kissed the pet like that." Then, after a little while: "Is she coming to get you?"

"Yeah, Sallie. At least I think she is. Bob?"

"They're coming. And we're going." Bob didn't look so good. But he hadn't thrown up yet. He would probably feel better after that.

Then they just sat there with each other, Sallie and Gene, waiting for Liv to come. For a while, they held hands, and then they didn't anymore.

19

The Battle of Nobu

When they came, it was in one of the least inventive ways imaginable, and they fooled precisely nobody.

"Mort," said Sallie.

Mort looked at her. Then he looked at them. Then he looked at her again. And then he got it. "Oh, look," he said sarcastically, rising and taking his weapon out of the holster beneath his sports jacket. "A small group of restaurant workers here to clean up the room." Bob had let them in, without consultation, since that was the role he had been assigned to play in this little drama of rescue and extraction.

Livia was dressed in the simple white shirt and black slacks of a non-gender-specific waiter. Bronwyn was by her side, in identical attire. They had two accomplices flanking them. One was a very tall, dumpy, hulking fellow with a short, scraggly beard and a ponytail who looked like a roadie in a touring cover band. The other was a short, trim, very fit young person of no particular gender at all, attractive—charismatic, even—with his or her hair tucked up into a square cap with no brim. These two hung behind the two women, who were doing their best to look innocent. Livia's implant, however, glowed hot behind her ear. She could never hide the interface between her hardware and wetware, thought Gene. It always betrayed her.

"Put your heater down, Mort," growled Gene in his best Arthurian tone of command.

"But—" It was difficult for the rock-hard leader of the biggest army west of the caliphate to stand down. But this was the order of his superior officer. If indeed it was. Could it not be? Could this be the complication about which he'd been briefed? Sallie stood.

"Shoot him, Mortimer," she said. "But not too badly." Mortimer raised his disruptor and pointed it at Gene, but hesitated just a moment too long.

"I don't think so," said Bronwyn, and in one fluid motion she raised her arm, with one finger pointing directly at Mortimer's chest, and fired a small, throbbing orblet into the pocket protector directly over his heart. Mortimer immediately went into an impressive display of atrial fibrillation and fell to the floor, twitching and spasming and frothing from the corner of his mouth.

"Wow," Bronwyn exclaimed. "Bob! It works!"

"Pisses me off when you doubt me, Bee," said Bob, easing his way toward the exit.

"Stop right there," said the rolling Segway named Officer O'Brien, who had dynamically spun away from the door at a 45-degree angle and begun to hum in a most threatening manner, a variety of his constituent parts cycling from green to yellow to bright red as he did so.

"No fuckin' way," said the shorter of the two faux waiters who had stationed themselves behind Liv. He or she walked directly up to O'Brien, who was clearly preparing some dramatic defensive maneuver, reached into the middle of its face unit with two fingers splayed, and ripped off the thing that would have been called its nose.

"You have removed my mobe," O'Brien moaned. Then it was utterly still.

"Gee," said the attending behemoth, "it worked." He and the other nonwaiter exchanged a discreet low five, then they both maintained a respectful watch on the room.

"Of course it worked!" said Bob, who seemed a little offended.

Livia went over to Gene and took him by the hand. He had been standing in the middle of the carnage, perusing the devastation with a combination of surprise, delight, and trepidation.

"Now what?" he asked Liv.

"Now you kiss me."

He gave her a rather restrained kiss, then stepped back and stole a quick glance at Sallie, who had resumed her seat and was watching the action with surprising calmness.

"What?" said Liv. And then: "Oh. I sort of get it. Although it's possibly too complicated for me."

"Me too," said Sallie to thin air.

"We got a long ride ahead of us," said the small, taut young individual of no particular gender, who was now sporting a light, slender semiautomatic machine gun he or she had kept tucked into the back of his or her waiter's pants. "Shall we go?"

"All right, Stevie," said Livia. Then she grabbed Gene, drew him into a firm embrace, and kissed him again. He immediately almost forgot whatever it was that was bothering his former self, which was even now receding swiftly into his mental rearview mirror, and kissed her back now—first soft and then with all his heart. He felt himself returning to himself, but a new self now, sure of who he was and who, at last, he was not, as long as he stayed as drunk as humanly possible all the fucking time.

"Good God, you guys," said Sallie. "Get a room."

Officer O'Brien, who was indeed severely wounded, began making slow, languid circles around the periphery of the room. As Bob had suggested to them during the planning phase of the operation, removing the proboscis placed strategically in the center of this unit's face had done several things to its capabilities. First, it had crippled his capacity to make simple decisions: left or right, forward or backward. It had also deactivated key portions of its instruction set and its backup memory that helped it prioritize actions. It could understand orders but could not determine the proper pathway to accomplish them. In lieu of doing nothing, therefore, it concluded that making random loops around the room was the best course.

In the meantime, Mortimer's mini heart attack, induced by a tiny electromagnetic pulse device that had hit his chest with a bang, was abating. He was breathing regularly and had propped himself up against the leg of the table where Sallie sat.

"You okay, Mort?" she asked, leaning down and looking at him with a minimal measure of concern. She didn't like him. But from here on in, it was quite possible she would need him.

"Motherfucker," said Mortimer.

"Yeah," said Sallie.

Gene bent down to see eye to eye with Mortimer. "I got a plan here, buddy," he said, very low, very tête-à-tête.

"Arthur?"

"Yeah, buddy. I'm here." He stuck out his hand and placed it gently on Mortimer's shoulder. Mort, still enfeebled by his coronary incident, roused himself to a slightly better sitting position and placed his hand on Gene's. "I'm gonna go away for a while," Gene continued, "and I want you to hold the fort, Mort." The wounded lieutenant nodded bravely, with a faint smile.

"Do my best, Chief."

"I shall return," said Arthur. Except it wasn't actually Arthur who said it.

"Kick some ass," said Mortimer. And then, overcome with drunkenness and shock, he passed out. It was not his finest moment.

Gene stood and gazed down at Sallie, who was sitting quietly, defeated for the moment, looking at him frankly with—what was that? Affection? In the doorway, Liv couldn't help but shiver. These two: that was something she hadn't contemplated in the lush fantasies of reunion that had kept her together during the time Arthur had colonized the body of her love. Whoever was in Gene's head now, whatever consciousness had hegemony over his being, these two bodies—Sallie and Arthur—had clearly formed some kind of intense connection of which she had no part.

"I'm gonna go now, Sallie," said Gene.

"I'm not talking to you, Gene. If Arthur has anything to say to me right now, I'd be only too happy to listen."

"You know what?" said Gene, walking to the portable bar in the corner of the room. He grabbed a liter of some grotesquely expensive whiskey from its forest of bottles, twisted off the cap, took a Herculean swig, and then held the open bottle by his side. "You know what, Sal?" he repeated, just a little drunker than he had been a few moments ago. "You know him one way, and I know him another. I know what he's planning, what he feels empowered to do now, and if you knew it, too, you'd hurl, Sallie, because while I was under there, I got to know you, too, and you're not the same kind of person he is."

"Don't be too sure."

Gene joined Liv at the door. Bob was there already with the two Skells, both of whom seemed to be named a version of Steve, for some reason.

"What's Arthur 'feel empowered to do now'?" said Liv to Gene as he joined her, teetering a little now under the weight of all that alcohol. He slipped an arm around her waist but still leaned precariously with all his weight on her slender frame.

"We're gonna need another solution to keep him under," said Bronwyn, joining them and taking half the weight on herself.

"It's possible there's a more permanent solution," said Bob. "I just haven't come up with it yet." The group disappeared down the hallway and out.

It was silent in the room then. O'Brien kept circling and circling, and seemed to be aware of his humiliation. His wheel squeaked. His noseless face glowed crimson, particularly around the place his cheeks would have been. Mortimer lay at Sallie's feet like a crumpled bag of laundry. She toyed with a glass of wine that had not been hers, looked into it for a moment or two, presumably to see if there was anything noisome floating in it, and then downed it in one gulp.

"Pull yourself together, Mort," she said, kicking his body several times with just enough force to wake him.

With a snort, the little green monster she had brought, which had been inactive under her chair for the duration of the previous action and the subsequent conversation, raised its silky head, looked at Sallie, and said, "Same goes for you, mistress."

"Point taken, dear," said Sallie, and she put down the glass. It was empty, but she didn't pour another.

Mort woke up, hauled himself a bit more upright, and then, with a massive effort, hurtled himself onto his feet for an instant, only to immediately collapse into a chair opposite Sallie. "I thought I was dying," he croaked.

"Artie's still in there somewhere."

"He seems to like his wine," Mort observed. He eyed another half-full glass of Bordeaux on the table.

"It appears that it brings out the worst in him." They both chuckled at the obvious truth of this observation, and Mortimer seized the wineglass and raised it into the air.

"To Artie," he said somberly.

"Artie," Sallie replied. But she did not drink.

There was a slight pause while they both pondered the situation. Then Mortimer took out his weapon, looked at it thoughtfully, and pumped a couple of kill shots into the still-perambulating husk of O'Brien, who uttered a low digital groan, rolled to a stop, and then keeled over entirely with a crash.

"Sorry about that, ma'am," said Mort. "But the fucking thing was driving me crazy."

"Can he be fixed?"

"Sure. Good as new. Just need a new version of the central module they disabled. There's a clone of it back at the shop."

"Well, that's good."

From his shirt pocket, Mortimer took out the butt of the cigar that he had been chewing on and popped it into his mouth. He lit it and sucked on it for a while. Then he said, "Arthur laid out a pretty bold plan for me before we got to this fucking dumpster fire."

"Tell me about it."

"Well," said Mort from a cloud of blue smoke, "I'm not sure I should. I mean, it was supposed to be between him and me. It would be up to him to decide who should share in it, contribute to it."

"I understand your loyalty, Morty," said Sallie evenly. "But the situation is changed. Right now I'd say that, all things considered, I'm in charge of Arthur's interests while he's, you know, hors de combat."

"What is that? 'Whore de combat.'"

"'Out of the fight.' For now."

"Whore de combat," said Mortimer. "Huh."

"I'll put it a little more clearly," said Sallie. "You are an excellent field general, but I own the army you command."

"Yeah," said Mortimer, looking over at her with something approaching gratitude. "Yeah, okay."

"Now, what's the plan."

"My mom used to call me Morty," said Mortimer. The two looked with some appreciation at each other, basking in their momentarily mutual self-interest. Then Mortimer extracted a pen from his breast pocket and started sketching on the tablecloth. "This is where we are, here," he said, poking at a spot in the center of a crudely rendered map of western California. "From the general appearance of the two Skells that accompanied the hot chick that picked up Artie, I'd say they were headed northwest into the Green Zone up there."

"Skells?"

"Anti-techs. Terrorists."

"I see," said Sallie. Then, as if it were of only mild interest to her, she asked, "You think she was hot?"

"The dark-haired one?"

"Yes. That one."

"You're hotter," Mortimer said with a grin. "The good news is that, according to my information, Arthur's cranial implant, even if the other guy turns it off, has a tracking device planted in it that works no matter what."

"Who did that?"

"That douchebag. Bob."

"Yes," said Sallie. "Bob. Hard to figure out his game here."

"Something to do with the babe he brought to the dance tonight? The one with all the grommets."

"Probably," said Sallie. She stood up and smoothed her gorgeous second skin, which required no smoothing. "Okay. I don't need to know the rest of the plan right now. You can fill me in later. Right now let's get a couple of hours of sleep. Then we head north into the Green Zone to recapture our mutual friend."

"Actually," said Mortimer, standing to meet her eye to eye. "That's consistent with the overall strategy to recapture lost territory anyhow."

"Well," said Sallie, "I'm very glad to hear it."

"Can we go home now?" asked Lucy from under the table. "I really need a recharge."

"Yes, sweetie." Sallie bent down and picked her up.

"Wow," said Mortimer, staring at Lucy with wonder. "That was quite an upgrade."

And they left, Sallie back to her sumptuous lodging to pack up for the campaign ahead, and Mortimer to the Spartan digs on the company campus where he customarily laid his head. He never slept, not really. But a few hours prone were sometimes required to whip both hardware and software into fighting shape.

– THREE –

20

Arcadia

It didn't take Gene's little party long to get where they were going. The two Steves were in the front seat of the 2017 Chevy Suburban, a true monster from the great old reign of the gas guzzlers, totally illegal in this day and age due to its lack of self-driving features but exquisitely maintained and equipped with a phalanx of performance chips and air intake mods feeding into a high-torque supercharged solar-powered electric motor. The thing could do 180 on an open road and easily blow by the most advanced self-driving police vehicles, which were aggressively amped up to reach an impressive if slightly unsafe top speed of 45, but only for limited duration. In the back were Bob, asleep against Bronwyn, and Liv, with her arm around Gene, who was solidly drunk as a skunk. If the consciousness of Arthur was still extant in any way, it was certainly far under.

The roads were clear heading north, and the darkness of night was absolute, inviolate. Apparently no alarm had been issued, at least not yet, and their forward momentum was unimpeded all the way to Eureka. There they got off the highway and pointed east for what was obviously a predestined pit stop on their way to their ultimate destination, where Master Tim awaited their arrival in the bucolic Green Zone.

"Where we goin'?" asked Gene as they plunged ever deeper into the darkness of the California night.

"A safe place," said Liv. "Where we gotta take care of something."

"Is it nice?"

"Don't worry about it," said Bob, who was not asleep after all. Then he was again.

They rode in silence for a while. "I missed you," said Gene.

"Yeah," said Liv. "Well, fortunately, you had plenty of action with that steaming-hot wife of yours to keep you occupied during your mental incarceration."

"That wasn't me, Liv."

"Uh-huh."

"It was like being locked in a nightmare and not being able to wake up."

"Gee, that must have been horrible," said Liv sarcastically. Then she carefully licked her finger and stuck it in Gene's ear.

". . . okay," he said.

The road was getting bumpier by the minute. "If we're gonna face any resistance, it'll be in about half a mile, when we go through the gates," said the gender-neutral Skell, who for purposes of brand distinction from the other one went by the name of Stevie. He or she took out an old-fashioned Glock semiautomatic, checked it for action, and rested it on the dashboard.

"Who are you fucking guys?" asked Gene. "Some kind of nutty hippy brigade or something?" He didn't care for either of them. Whatever his drill was going to be, he wasn't sure he wanted these shaggy weirdos around to help him with it.

"We're the vanguard of the revolution," said the hulking one, Steve, who was driving. There was a blob of silence again. "And we just rescued your ass back there, so have a little respect," he added after a while.

"I take your point," conceded Gene. "Sorry."

"Here we are," said Stevie. "Duck down, chickens." He or she picked up the weapon but kept it out of sight.

But nothing transpired. The Chevy slowly rolled through an enormous wooden archway festooned with giant lettering that read, "Arcadia." Steve turned off the vehicle, and the only sound was the *click-click-click* of the engine cooling off. Nothing more. "Okay," said Stevie. "We can get out now. Grab your stuff. We walk from here."

The only ones who had anything at all to carry were big Steve, who appeared to have a host of weaponry in a large khaki duffel, and Bob, who lugged several bags of personal effluvia, including an old-fashioned leather doctor's satchel. Bronwyn took the heavy stuff, while Bob contented himself with the carrying case in black lizard skin that was the emblem of his profession back when doctors made house calls.

They stood in the silence of an endless redwood forest. In the distance, an owl announced itself. A coyote howled and was answered by another. "Where are we?" asked Gene.

"We're here," said Bob. Then he headed up a steep path that hadn't been tended for quite some time. The group followed, with Stevie in the rear, alert to any life form that might require the attention of his or her Glock.

They continued up the hill, which grew steeper. On the way, they passed the remains of what were once small encampments with scattered firepits and the occasional cabin here and there. Not a hare rustled in any of them. "This place was once owned by the Corporation," said Bob. "Not really active now. Once a year, a couple of guys from senior management get together here, but only for a week or so, to smoke cigars and drink themselves sick. The rest of the time, it's like this."

"Creepy," said Liv.

"Relic of the dying male hegemony that will soon be extinct," Bronwyn replied, poking Bob in the ribs as she did so.

"God," he said. "I hope not. I have a ton of important hegemony stuff to do first."

They walked a bit more, leaning into the hill.

"Are we there yet?" Gene whined after an interminable amount of time and effort brought them only another hundred yards or so.

"Yes, in fact, we are," said Stevie. "Steve, drop your gear and help me open up the place."

They were standing in front of a pleasant entryway, graced by the statue of a naked female angel with truly magnificent wings reaching for the sky, both arms outstretched to show her sacred figure to best effect. "Valhalla," said a rustic wooden sign beside a staircase. The two Skells preceded them up the stairs. Last in line was Livia, who pushed a wheezing Gene up the remaining steps and into the camp.

Valhalla turned out to be a compact enclave with a good-sized deck surrounded by a number of cabins. On this deck were a bunch of comfortable chairs of varying weight and size, now a bit moldy, some tables, and a large and still impressively well-stocked bar in the corner. In the far end of the area were the showers, toilets, and communal sinks. Numerous black-and-white photos covered the walls, most of long-dead men in the funny suits, hats, and moustaches they must have thought, at the time, made them look distinguished, when being distinguished was more important than being cool.

"Hey!" said Gene. "This is nice!" He fell into a chair and was asleep immediately, hugging to his breast the precious bottle that now safeguarded his identity.

"Let him sleep," said Bob. "We'll do the procedure in the morning and then get out of here."

"Like hell," said Liv. "We've been apart forever. I thought I'd lost him entirely. He's not going to spend the night in a chair. Come on, Bee. Help me out."

Bob gave her a sudden grin, reached out, and mussed up her hair. "Okay, Livvy," he said. And so together the two women, assisted by their rumpled friend, hoisted the shit-faced young hero to a standing position and drunk-walked him to the first cabin off the deck. "Thank you and good night," said Liv to the group. There were the sounds of a deadweight falling into a cot and the cabin's screen door clapping shut.

"What they got to eat here?" asked Steve, going behind the bar to see if there were any provisions. "Nuts," he said, extracting a few bags of pistachios.

"Look in the kitchen," said Stevie, and they both went into the desolate, inactive space that lay beyond the bar.

"Come here, baby," said Bob to Bronwyn. She went to him.

"This is going surprisingly well," she said, and put her arms around his neck.

"We'll see how he does. He's different than I expected."

"Well, he's plastered. We don't know what he'd be like if he didn't have to be hammered all the time just to be himself." She stared into Bob's face for a minute. "We also don't know how much of that old imperialist scumbag rubbed off on him."

"There's a possible solution to that problem, but I'm afraid it might be worse than the problem itself."

"What would that be?" Bronwyn asked. She took him by the hand and went in the direction of the vacant cabins.

"One thing at a time," said Bob. "Let's get his head right first."

"Here we go," she said, opening the door to an empty cottage. "I hope there are no bats in here," she murmured, peering carefully inside the dark and dusty enclosure.

"Bee, honey," said Bob, pausing with her on the doorstep. "I'm really tired. I hope you're not expecting miracles."

"You're the miracle worker," said Bronwyn. She patted him sweetly on the butt. "But I bet I can work some of my own if I really put my mind to it."

"Well," said Bob hopefully, "I won't object too strenuously if you'd like to try."

They went into the cabin. The giant trees loomed above them, bathed in fog and the light of the moon. The Skells came out of the kitchen, each with a box of Froot Loops cereal. "I wonder how old these fucking things are," said Steve.

"They never go bad, because they're not actually food," said Stevie, collapsing onto an aged leather couch.

"I'll take the first shift." Steve sat on an available table and began to examine the Froot Loops in earnest.

Four hours later, the sun rose. Somewhere in the world beyond the forest, a rooster greeted the new day.

"Here you go, Ginerino," said Bob, staring down at Liv and Gene as they lay entwined in the tiny camp bed. "Drink this before you turn into Chairman Hyde again."

"Man," said Gene, taking in about an eighth of the bottle of sixty-year-old Glenlivet scotch Bob had offered him. "What I wouldn't give to be sober for just an hour or two."

Liv sat up, her hair forming an impressive nimbus around her elfin head. "I'll get us together, and we'll meet you on the deck in five minutes."

"Five minutes," said Bob. "I want to get this over with."

They emerged on schedule. The Skells were now draped in a couple of large, comfy armchairs, each with family-sized boxes of Cap'n Crunch. "You hungry?" asked Steve. "They got good stuff in the kitchen. Kind of chewy. But tasty!"

"Yeah," said Liv. "I guess so. I don't think I can watch this anyhow." She went to the door of the kitchen. "I hope there are no mice in here," she said. She grabbed a broom that was leaning against the wall and tiptoed in.

"Sit here, Gene," said Bob, who had pulled out a straight-backed chair next to a table and was arranging a variety of implements on it. Bronwyn assisted. "Good morning, Gene," she said, smiling.

"What up?" said Gene. He sat.

"Put your head back," instructed Bob, all business. He was in a lab coat, a rather shabby one, Gene thought. He appeared to be readying some kind of long, thin apparatus.

"Hey, wait a minute!" Gene squeaked.

Without any indication that he was about to do so, Bob plunged the probe with one swift, smooth thrust straight into the side of Gene's implant directly above and behind his right ear. An enormous chasm of blackness opened to the left, right, above, and below him and invaded all available space inside his head. He screamed. Then he was falling, falling. After a while, he dozed. "Now let the motherfuckers try to track us" was the last thing he heard before he fell away.

He awoke to find a hot toddy in his hand. Around him were his friends, who looked at him with great concern.

"I'm okay," said Gene.

"Now you are," said Bob.

"Drink, Gene," said Liv. Then she added, "Drink it all, babe."

"I have just disabled your implant mechanism," explained Bob. "As of right now, your global positioning can't be followed. Your life functions are offline and unknown to the Corporation. You are on your own, bud. On your own. Disconnected from the Cloud and from every other implant. Congratulations, and welcome to the way things used to be."

Bronwyn added with piety, "And the way they may yet be again, God willing."

"Amen," said Livia, placing her hand on Gene's shoulder. There was a moment of reverential silence. Bob rose to his feet and paced a bit more. He seemed agitated.

"I created you, Gene," he suddenly blurted. "So you know, in a way, I'm your dad." Gene tried to not laugh but failed. "No, but seriously," said Bob, a bit wounded. "I want you to understand." He leaned over Gene and stared down at him with tremendous intensity and a slobby sort of affection. "I didn't realize that when I made you, son, I was creating a genuine life. I don't know why I didn't. But I didn't."

"Well, Bob," said Gene, annoyed. "What did you think you were doing?"

"Filling a market niche. Listen. Please."

"Sure! Why not?" Gene took a sip of the whiskey. His head was clearing. Bob was being quite entertaining. The woods smelled like heaven. Life was good.

"You know how many superold, rich-as-fuck guys are reaching the end of what we can do for them?!" Bob perambulated around the deck, driven by the force of his emotion. "Look at the board of directors! There's nothing more we can do with the bodies they got. They hit a wall when they reach a hundred twenty years of age, tops. You can add another ten or fifteen years of decay and pathetic senescence to that if you want to. But *ugh*. I've seen it. Horrible. Repulsive morphies indistinguishable from one another. Grotesques. The stuff of nightmare. And still, they live, looking for a way to put themselves into a whole new infrastructure—one that's better than the one they got. That is a significant market. Small, but able to pay incalculable fortunes for the product, right?" Bob snared the last dregs of Steve's old box of Froot Loops from the nearby table and took a mouthful. *"Blaugh!"* He spat out the stale cereal in nobody's direction and then pressed on.

"The breakthrough was when we figured out how to take an individual's entire personality and migrate it into the Cloud. Digital immortality! And guess what? Now we have a whole bunch of fully functioning virtual people up there in the mainframe! More than two hundred fifty! The very richest of the superrich! And a couple of decent guys, too, pro bono, for the good of the world. The Dalai Lama, for instance, and his friend dhe wanted along to keep him company, that actor, what's his name? Steve something . . ."

"Seagal?!" inquired Steve excitedly.

"Yeah!" Bob took another handful of Froot Loops, apparently having forgotten how horrible they were. This time they stayed in his mouth. "But, of course, it turns out it's no fun to live as a bunch of disembodied engrams. So the question has been, how do we take the next step? Make them, you know, fully human? We had to try it out. There were no volunteers and very little time. An entire generation of the original seed geniuses are in their high 120s. The problem is, the process seems to be a lot more difficult than we expected, due to body-mind issues."

"No shit," said Gene.

"We don't seem to be able to create an organism that has no consciousness," Bob went on philosophically. "Take your brain, Gene."

"My brain!" Gene drank to that.

"It's a basic protosubstrate beneath a complex superstructure in communication with the central cortex, which I provided. I'm sure you are wondering how you know all the useless stuff you do? That's me, Gino. And now, that's you. And now that we have you, now that I see you not as a host but as a person, I find that I want you to live."

"Well, thanks, Bob."

"You, Gene! You! Not the other guy!"

"Seriously. I'm very relieved and flattered that you like me, man."

"Except," Bob continued, "now we have the problem presented by the other guy. I know that. It's my fault. I accept that. I'm sorry about it, Gene, I am. I'm sorry."

"I forgive you, Dad. I'm glad to be here." Gene seemed to draw on an internal database of potential responses and added, "In fact, at my age I'm glad to be anywhere."

"Yeah," said Bob appreciatively. "George Burns, right?"

"You know," Gene observed as if he were about to utter something very important, "I might want to start the day with something lighter, like vodka or silver tequila, and then move to the brown stuff later on. It's a thought, anyway." He hiccupped.

"Anyway," said Bob. "We're going to have to think of something. As long as the old fuck is in there, we're all in danger, Gene most of all."

"Fuck 'em!" said Gene, who had achieved the wonderful plateau of bonhomie one can attain through serious drinking first thing in the morning.

"Dudes," said one of the Steves. They both arose.

"We gotta go," said the other. "We hear a drone." And sure enough, once they listened for it, there it was in the distance.

"Let's go, Bean." Liv grabbed Gene's hand. "We'll be back in a minute," she told the group. "After we get our stuff."

They were in the cabin before Gene realized that he had no stuff. He had the clothes on his back and that was all. But Liv was gazing into his eyes.

"Genie," she said, taking his hands. "I want to say something. I knew you when you were new, because, well, Bee thought it would be good for you to have a friend, and she was right. But after a while, we were together. And then you went away, and I realized I love you. Maybe it's because everything is constantly new to you all the time. Maybe it's just your cuteness. But I love you, Gene. That's what I wanted to tell you. I love you so. And I hope you love me, too."

"I do." Gene looked at her dear little face. "I love you, too, Liv," he said. "I love you, too, and so."

"Too and so."

"I never want to be anywhere you're not, ever again. When we're together, nothing else matters. I feel real."

"In your case," she said, smiling at him tenderly, "that's saying something."

She kissed him then, and he kissed her back, and they were alone together for a brief moment or two, which was more than enough time to settle a whole bunch of things for the both of them, forever.

The cabin door opened. "Excuse me, you two," said Bob, "but we gotta go. I think I've got an idea we can try out in the car."

It was full day when they left the camp. The sun was blasting through the trees, and the forest loomed as large as it had the night before, but it was still empty of all human life except theirs, and when they were gone, the birds sang and the bees buzzed and the squirrels and chipmunks chattered only to one another.

21

North to George, Washington

It required a little more than twelve hours to make the drive from the outskirts of Eureka, California, to George, Washington, 667 miles north as the crow flies. The Chevy Suburban sped past the aptly named town of Weed, and through the Modoc National Forest just south of Dorris, at the California-Oregon border. By then, they were on US 97, and there wasn't another car in sight. A few self-driving trucks had rumbled by now and then, at their top speed of forty-five. At midnight, they hit the Winema National Forest, zipping through Chiloquin, where there wasn't a soul stirring. Oregon went by, through Bend and all the little, underpopulated towns, past a few bars with swastikas in the windows. Then it was into Washington State, where the neo-Nazis thinned out, barreling through Yakima, where they were almost forced off the road by a pack of what appeared to be hippies on motorcycles, but they weren't a match for the souped-up Chevy Suburban, and on into George, and just outside of George, there they went, down a small, unmarked dirt road that was barely more than a path, to the Peaceable Kingdom.

They had left around ten in the morning. The Northern California forests around them were lush and green and undisturbed by evidence of the current century. The sky above the ribbon of highway was a tremendous cartoon blue, and a few gigantic puffy white clouds passed in a leisurely fashion across the sun, casting lovely shadows on the road.

"Nice here, huh," said Bob, a couple hours into the ride. He was sitting in the middle of the front seat, next to Bronwyn, who sat as far as possible from Stevie, who was driving. Big Steve was in the rumble seat way in back, leaving the entire middle of the cabin to Liv and Gene.

"This whole part of the country is outside the approved habitable zone now," said Bob, looking out the windshield, "but people still live here and there. The corporation owns all this land, even though we admittedly have limited control over it now. It represents mostly upside, in the sense that it's relatively unexploited, but it's not too safe to stop here. We've considered unloading it, but given the concentration of capital in the coastal and major urban regions, there are really no buyers to speak of. So it languishes in seminatural form for the time being, as you see."

"We own it?" Gene inquired, eyes closed, from the back seat.

"Well," said Bob, "you do now. In at least one of your incarnations."

They rode in silence for a little while. Every now and then, Gene took another short pull on his bottle, which kept Arthur effectively at bay. It wasn't an unpleasant feeling, but he was getting pretty sick of intoxication as a state of being. He wondered what it was like to be sober and aware of himself, and who he might be when he was in full possession of his faculties and not loaded. It would be a first. He had been born, if you could call it that, and his mind was an empty shell, with some knowledge of a rudimentary sort, but in the center just a gooey blob waiting for something. Now something was there, curled like a carnivorous flower waiting to bloom and eat all the soft gray food around it. He shivered.

"Give me a pull on that," said Livia. She was nestled into him, napping on and off. They had been up most of the night doing things that lovers do, and right now neither of them seemed up for talking.

Liv was one of those born well into this century. When she had turned off her implant for the first time the night before, a vast chasm of silence had opened all around her, and only now was she becoming aware that there was a mind somewhere inside her head that could function without external stimulation. Since she was a child, even when she was asleep, the implant had hummed behind her ear, comforting, like a white noise machine that smoothed out things. Last night, after an insanely convoluted process known only to Bob, it had been shut down. "Good thing you have one of the entry levels," Bob had observed while messing around with the mechanism, executing a variety of clicks and switches in a certain mysterious order. "Or I would have had to poke you the way I did your boyfriend here."

Right now Livia was busy listening to the silence. It was terrifying, but if you looked into it, it became more interesting and less frightening. There were things in it. It wasn't all nothingness. She drank a little. The road went by.

"Yeah," said Bob, apropos of nothing. He put his arm around Bronwyn, who leaned into him, and put his feet up on the dashboard.

"Dude," said Stevie, glaring at Bob's shoes.

Bob checked for crud on his soles, saw none, and put them back up. There was silence for a while. The only sound was Steve, snoring from the far back seat of the vehicle. Suddenly Stevie, who had said virtually nothing since the successful rescue in Nobu, spoke, in that smug, hyperknowledgeable voice affected by those who have a grievance against the system.

"About thirty years ago," he or she said informationally, "the government could no longer maintain public services or guarantee the safety of people's lives and property, and entire sections of the globe were made available for public/private partnerships that eventually evolved into total corporate ownership and then, eventually, into ownership by one gargantuan organization you guys are willing members of. Now everything is privatized for profit. Schools, cops, medical, farms, whatever the fuck. All under your control."

"Believe me, Stevie, people like us control nothing," said Gene, who didn't like being cast in the role of corporate warlord. All he had felt like up to this point was a tool.

"Now whatever governments the world has left report to a central organizing entity that has no physical location whatsoever; it exists only in cyberspace," Stevie continued, with that same offended tone. "None of the masters of war ever even see each other."

"Nonsense," said Bob. "We still get together at Davos every year."

"And it all runs through the Cloud," Stevie went on, his or her jaw clamped tight. "That's your civilization. But it's not civilization. It's tyranny."

"Well, don't blame us," said Gene. "We just work here."

"If you guys weren't important to Master Tim, I'd shoot you right here and leave you by the side of the road." He or she said it mildly, but it had the ring of truth. Gene realized that there was nothing approaching the law up here. They were on their own. And only some of them had guns.

"Stevie," said a drowsy voice from the back of the cab. "You can shut up now probably."

"Yeah, yeah," Stevie said, and was silent again. But he or she sped up a little.

"So what are you guys?" Gene asked. "Beyond being a couple of scary creeps."

"We're nobody individually," said Stevie. "But together we are large, we contain multitudes." Then he or she was silent.

Bob said, "That's a quote from something." He was rummaging around in his backpack, which was at his feet. Bronwyn, who had been sleeping, sitting with her legs crossed between Bob and the androgynous terrorist to her left, lifted her head and watched Bob for a bit. "You gonna try it?" she inquired softly.

"I think so," said Bob. "What's the worst that can happen? We're in a contained space. There's nobody around for miles."

"You guys saw to that, didn't ya?" said Stevie bitterly.

"Stevie. Dude." It was Steve, from the far back seat. "You're starting to annoy even me."

"The majority of humanity now lives only in areas that have Wi-Fi," said Stevie. "This leaves most of the world empty, since only a few of us have a different vision of what things oughta look like."

"This may surprise you," said Gene, "but I don't really disagree with anything you've been talking about."

"That's the most depressing thing I've heard all day," replied Stevie.

It was about then that the first drone appeared, hovering on the road in front of them. "Drone," said Stevie, addressing his compadre in the back of the vehicle.

"Gotcha," said Steve. "Excuse me, people." He pressed a button on the side of the Chevy's rear cabin, and the back window rolled down slowly. He then produced a modest handgun from the pocket of his hoodie. "Get in front of it, Stevie."

Stevie floored the monster. It shot ahead at an ungodly speed, smooth and solid, and in a moment, the small drone, which had a camera in its nozzle, was hovering behind them. It rose a bit higher in the air and gained speed, just as Steve raised the handgun and shot it out of the sky, sending it careening off into the woods. The Chevy slowed down to sub-warp speed again, and they proceeded on their way.

"That was not cool," said Steve.

"We gotta motor," said Stevie calmly. "Don't worry. If we don't stop, we should be okay."

They went on for a couple of miles, and Bronwyn said, "Well, Bob, if we're going to give it a try, there's no time like the present."

"Right," said Bob, who turned and kneeled in his seat to better address the denizens of the second row. "Gene. Liv. I'd like to try an experiment."

"I know that look," Gene said. "That's Bob's 'Don't worry, I'm on your side' look, and it almost always precedes something he intends to do whether you want him to or not. And sometimes he's telling the truth, and he is on your side, and sometimes he's lying, and he isn't, and you generally end up finding out which it is a little too late to do anything about it."

"The thing is," said Bob, who was holding something very small in his hand, "wouldn't it be great if you could, like, do something, say, every twenty-four or forty-eight hours and suppress the other guy effectively without having to be intoxicated to do so?"

"Sure. That would be nice."

"Well, that's what I'd like to try," said Bob, and without further discussion, he reached across the seat, grabbed Gene's free hand, twisted it around so that Gene's wrist was upward, and slapped a small blue translucent square of Xee directly onto his pulse point.

"No!" Liv screamed, and punched Bob squarely in the face.

"Motherfucker!" yelled Bob, grabbing his nose, which had sprouted an impressive freshet of gore.

"Jesus, Liv!" Bronwyn was mad, but there was a little laughter in there, too. She rummaged in the glove compartment and found a packet of Kleenex, which she applied to Bob's wounded beezer. "You sort of earned that, honey," she said to him consolingly.

In the meantime, Livia had grabbed Gene by both shoulders and was regarding him closely. For his part, Gene had slipped into something approaching a meditative trance. His arm was still up, wrist exposed, square of Xee now totally devoid of color, which meant that its load had been deposited and the effect would soon be evident.

That's when the second drone appeared in the air above the vehicle. Where its predecessor had been a small hobbyist's model with a tiny camera on board, this thing was something else entirely. Approximately two feet in length, it not only sported what was obviously a state-of-the-art 36,000K full-motion video capture setup, but also had a seam in its belly that implied the capacity to sport payload.

"You know the drill, Stevie," said Steve, who once again lowered the rear window. From one of the cases beside him, he extracted a long, thin plasma rifle with a telescopic sight. "Drive smooth now," he said, and, after performing several preparatory maneuvers with the weapon, he aimed carefully at the midsized drone and blew a perfectly targeted shot into its undercarriage. The device veered up, then down, then flipped over, then did an impressive pirouette above them in the sky and vectored off into nowhere. Once again they slowed to a safer speed. Quietly and without fanfare, Steve opened a final case, this one hard and quite sizeable, and took out a state-of-the-art assault weapon that appeared capable of cutting a building in half. The occupants of the car simply looked at the military ordnance without comment. Steve smiled apologetically. "I was hoping never to have to use it," he said. "I'm actually a pacifist."

"In all the annals of stupid humanity, you guys are the dumbest fucking bozos ever," said the creature that had been Gene but now was something completely different.

"Uh-oh," said Bob.

22

The Sorrows of Xee

"Where the fuck are we?" said the person in the seat next to Liv.

"We are on the road to a destination up north," said Liv carefully, "because it's the only place that may be safe from the Corporation and its nefarious plans." She had pushed the body of Gene, still clutched tightly by the shoulders, to the farthest distance the length of her arms made possible and was regarding him coldly.

"Yeah, right," said the person sitting next to her, who was neither completely Gene nor utterly Arthur.

"So may I inquire," said Livia, looking deep into the eyes of her companion, "to whom I have the pleasure of speaking?"

"Cut the shit, why don't we," said Arthur, twisting out of Livia's grasp and repairing to the far end of the seat, glaring at them all. The body that contained both Gene and Arthur then put up a massive battle with itself, with its right arm attempting to take a pull at the bottle of booze it was holding, while at the same time, the left arm did everything it could to prevent that bottle from reaching the lips of its owner. In the end, since Gene, like Bob, was right-handed, his arm won, and he took a massive infusion of high-torque single-malt. Coughed. Seemed to relax a bit.

"Well, this really fucked up," he said. "Thank you, Bob. It appears your experiment is a failure. May I ask how long does this Xee thing last?"

"Four hours, tops," said Bob sheepishly. "Look. My intentions were good."

"Yeah, yeah," said Gene. He was pretty fed up with Bob. Science is one thing. But doing stuff like this? It was some form of masturbation that had spectacular consequences. Now Arthur was loose in his head.

"So it looks like, for a while," he said to Liv, mostly, "I'm going to express thoughts and opinions that are not endorsed by the management."

"See now, Gene," said Bob, "that's the kind of phrase that you wouldn't even slightly know if I hadn't placed it directly into your head from the very first download. So I agree. I'm an asshole. But I'm also your dad. Don't forget that. And show a little respect."

"Okay, Pops." Gene regarded Bob as one would a favorite dog who had just pissed on his favorite rug.

"What's the plan here, guys? I'm just asking." It was weird, thought Liv. It looked like Gene at that moment, but it was clearly not. It was a scheming, crafty business mogul trying to hide his atrocious personality, and failing.

"We're not going to tell you, you sick old fuck," she said.

"I like you, Liv," said Arthur in, frankly, a pretty smarmy way. "You're a tasty little muskrat. If we get a chance, I'll certainly know what to do with you."

"I like you, too, Arthur," said Livia. She nestled into him a little. "I hope you don't mind, Gene."

"Play it out," said Gene in what was unmistakably his own voice.

"Anyway, Artie." She gave him both baby blues, which in her case were brown. "Let's turn it on its ass a little."

"I don't mind that," said Arthur.

"What's your plan? You're a genius. Gene tells me you own, like, what?"

"Everything. I own everything," replied Arthur.

"Tell him that's sexy," said Gene.

"That kind of power is very attractive," Livia purred.

"You've certainly got a tight little body," said Arthur.

"Show just an inch or two of what you got, big boy," said Liv to Arthur, and somewhere inside the vessel that was their common receptacle, Gene actually felt a twinge of jealousy.

"Okay. Well, look." It was fully Arthur now, and he was excited as only a business mind can be while presenting the brilliance of its strategic plan. In the driver's seat, unnoticed by anybody, Stevie picked up the Glock he had stowed on the dashboard and put it in his or her lap. "The whole business situation is incredibly interesting," Arthur said. "Due to a variety of factors, an enormous segment of the goods and services that supply the entire world—and also the privatized sector of public services that were once controlled by the government—are now in the hands of . . . me. It's not important how. But it's interesting. Everything got concentrated. Consolidated. And subject to takeover. But what was the leverage against such a massive weight? The one thing that everybody wants. The thing that's almost within reach. The holy grail of Musk and Venter and every person of infinite wealth. Eternal life. That was my leverage."

"That was sort of a limited success so far."

"There are kinks. This fucking douche that's your boyfriend, for instance. How do we dump him? He's a loser."

"I like him."

"I could do a lot better for you."

"Yeah? In what way? I'm just curious."

"First of all, I'm a fucking behemoth in the sack."

"Okay," said Liv. "But that's not everything."

"You want to be with a winner, doncha?"

"Tell me about that." Liv leaned back against the opposite car door with her knees up to her chest, friendly-like.

"Look." Arthur leaned into Liv's airspace but kept a proper distance, filling the gap with his personal electricity. "Fuck all the pretense. Capitalism. Bullshit. This is about world domination. World domination! What has been the goal of every great man since the dawn of time?"

"Let me guess. World domination?"

"Right," said Arthur. He was very sincere. Calm now. This was the most reasonable point of view in the world. "Go back. Think about it. Caesar. Napoléon. Hitler, who got a bad rap in some ways. Of course, he went completely overboard, but he almost got there. Now look at what we got today: complete chaos. Everybody in his own corner, with guns and rockets. Except all united by one thing."

"Love?"

"What? No. The Cloud! The Cloud . . . Hey, excuse me, this is embarrassing, but what's your name anyhow? I don't think we've ever been properly introduced."

"Livia. I'm Livia."

"Well," said Arthur, sticking out a meaty paw, "pleased to meet you."

Liv took his hand and shook it cordially. "I'm interested in this world domination thing," she said. "It's involved with the Cloud somehow?"

"Are you shitting me?" Gene's body bounded up on his knees in the seat and leaned farther in, like a sprinter about to take off. "The Cloud. Transactions. Social interactions of all kinds. People spend their entire lives hooked into the fucking thing. It's ridiculous! Ha!" He sat back down. "The truth is, I haven't even begun to think of all the ways we can monetize this. If you really wanted to, you could drain the entire world of all disposable cash. In a year, maybe. Two, tops. Food. Water. Gas and electric. Entertainment programming. Police services. Fire department. Most of the military. News of every political stripe. 'We are the world. We are the children.'" He then erupted in a fit of convulsive laughter.

"The thing that's great," said Arthur, "is that I also have this massive security force under this complete gonzo maniac who I can count on to do whatever needs to be done in the real world. Mortimer! What a psycho!"

"So, Artie, seriously," said Liv. "You're a complete lunatic, right? You realize that, right?"

"Tell me you don't love it," said Arthur, with a greasy composite leer and wink.

"Gene," said Liv, "drink the rest of the bottle. Now, hon."

"You don't have to tell me twice," said Gene. His arm paused on the way to his mouth. And the face of Arthur emerged in all the ripe malevolence of which it was capable.

"Fuck you guys. Seriously," said Arthur. "You can flop around all you want. But in the end, I will win. Because winners always win. And that's what I am. A winner." Gene took a long drink. And Arthur didn't say a whole lot more for a little while.

The road went by. "I don't want to sound like a self-aggrandizing asshole, but I'd say that experiment was actually a success," said Bob informationally.

Stevie looked at Bob, picked up the gun as he or she drove, regarded it seriously, but then put it back on the dashboard.

An enormous drone the size of a G12 corporate air palace appeared in the air above them. "Pull over, Stevie," said Steve, who had been watching the skies while what he considered to be a whole lot of nonsense was going on. Stevie went from 110 to a dead stop in four seconds, grabbed his or her heater, and hopped out.

"Excuse me, kids," said Steve, climbing over Gene and Liv and lunging out the side door with his massive cannon. He then positioned himself directly under the drone, which had halted and was observing them with no attempt to conceal itself, like a killer whale getting ready to eat a seal or two.

"Take this, you soulless thing," said Steve, and he loosed a rain of bullets, flame, and plasma that melted the belly of the drone in one apocalyptic blast. Dripping from this mortal wound to its undercarriage, it listed off at a radical angle and disappeared into the trees girding the road. Seconds later came a gut-wrenching explosion not too far away. Steve climbed back into the car. "We gotta get off the main road," he said.

Stevie had resumed his or her place behind the wheel. "We're close enough," he or she said. "We'll ditch the car and go on foot."

"I don't wanna go on foot!" Gene protested.

But they did. And as they went, with Gene stumbling along, half dragged by Liv, stopping many times to rest and drink from his bottle, they felt but did not quite see, deep in the woods that surrounded them, the rustle and patter of little Ewok feet accompanying them down the discreetly blazed path.

"You hear them?" Gene asked Liv, in what he thought was a whisper.

"I have to assume they are friends," said Liv. "Or they would have already done something."

"*Our* friends," said Stevie. They walked on. After a while, Bronwyn said, "Don't be scared, Gene. It's gonna be okay. The Master won't let anything happen to us."

"I'm not scared," claimed Gene, clutching Liv's waist a little tighter to avoid being upended by an upcoming stump. "I'm kind of happy, actually." And he squeezed her even tighter. A giant redwood clearing reared up ahead of them.

"We're at the gathering place," announced Steve, with some reverence. "Won't be long now." And they went on.

At the same time, two hundred miles south of where the last drone went down, the convoy carrying the most elite representatives of the most powerful private army and navy in the world paused at a turnout somewhere in the forest primeval north of the Washington border. Mortimer, who was driving the lead Humvee, turned to Sallie, who was riding shotgun.

"Let's get out for a minute," he said. He climbed out of the vehicle and motioned for the line of trucks, cars, and flatbeds to halt while he did whatever it was that commanders do when they don't know where they're going. He put his hands on his hips and affected a masterful mien.

Sallie climbed out after him and stood by his side, with Lucy in her arms.

"Where the hell are we?" asked the pet.

"I have no idea, dear," said Sallie, kissing the top of Lucifer's little head.

Mortimer was outfitted in dark-green battle fatigues, with a number of neutron grenades on his belt and a lightweight plasma handgun on each hip. He'd had his hair trimmed into a vertical brush in preparation for the upcoming engagement and looked quite smart. Sallie was in neatly pressed denims and an old-fashioned work shirt with some flowers embroidered on the sleeves. She'd tied a sweatshirt around her waist and was armed only with the shiny green synthetic lizard-tortoise combo that, at this point, was her best and only friend. Mortimer cracked a leather case on his belt and extracted a pair of high-powered field glasses. He scanned the horizon, which stretched before them in an unending ocean of greenery: pines, redwoods, eucalyptus, and, in the very far distance, a silver river snaking off into oblivion. He consulted the information coming in from his implant.

"Coverage is spotty here," he said.

"We sort of know where they're going, don't we?"

"Not precisely. They brought down the papa drone a few minutes ago. You gotta hand it to 'em. They're tough and resourceful, and they're well-armed enough. We're going to have a hell of a fight when we catch up to them."

"I don't want anybody hurt," said Sallie quietly. Both she and Lucy looked with some emphasis at Mortimer, who appeared disappointed.

"To quote a great man," he said, believing that Arthur, not a former president of the United States, now disgraced, was the originator of this brilliant observation: "Why do we have these weapons if we don't want to use them?"

"Mort," said Sallie, as one would address a naughty child.

"You want your husband back, don't you?"

"Of course I do. I just don't want to lay waste to this . . . this paradise."

"Well, we'll do the best we can while making sure to achieve our objectives," said Mortimer, moving around the Humvee to get back in the driver's seat. He raised one arm high over his head and achieved a crisp, circular motion. A score of engines roared into life. Each vehicle's self-driving mode had been disabled; they were being driven by corporate security officers in dark-green khaki similar to that of their boss, with slightly less ordnance weighing them down. In addition to their uniforms and armor, each officer wore an appropriately determined expression. None had ever actually been in battle before. But they were excited by the prospect of the action that lay before them. They had each seen plenty of war movies as part of their training and were pretty sure about the way this whole thing was supposed to go.

The last vehicle in line was a bit different. It was operated by the brand-spanking-new, thoroughly rebuilt O'Brien, who was installed in the driver's area via a special mechanism that accommodated his bulky armature. Behind him, he carried a surface-to-surface missile of modest proportions.

Sallie and Lucy were the last to remain on the tarmac.

"This is bad," Lucy muttered. "Mortimer is not"—it consulted an internal database for the proper terminology—"a trustworthy individual of good judgment. He should not be invested with leadership responsibilities beyond his capabilities."

"I know. I wish Artie was here."

"Well," said Lucy, "it's up to you. You've got the sticks. I've got the ports."

"Yes, I know." Sallie once again kissed the shiny little trapezoid that was Lucy's head. "But I would miss you so terribly, my dear."

"Not forever," said Lucy.

"No," said Sallie sadly. "I suppose not. All right."

The two climbed into the passenger seat of the Humvee. Mortimer fired it up, and the impressive procession once again made its way down the road. As they went, Sallie, sitting silently with tears streaming down her cheeks, could be seen, if anyone had cared to notice, feeding a series of small oblong sticks into the four rectangular ports immediately behind the perky ear unit of the creature she most loved in the world.

23

In the Heart of the Peaceable Kingdom

After the circular stand of redwoods, the path opened up most impressively, and in a hundred yards or so, the group found themselves in a village green. The area had clearly been the center of a thriving little town at one time, but it had since been stripped down to its essentials. Former mercantile establishments showed signs of domestic use; what had been commercial restaurants were now open-air kitchens suitable for preparing food for large groups of citizens; a hotel was now occupied, if the variety of laundry drying outside each window was any evidence, by well more than one large, extended family. Beyond this core, a larger community radiated out in a loose grid of alleys, streets, and broader avenues lined with stores and houses that, while somewhat lacking in paint and the odd shutter here and there, were also obviously in current use and quite well maintained and functional.

A pack of lean but pleasant-looking dogs joined them as Gene, Liv, Bob, and Bronwyn, accompanied by their paramilitary escort of two Steves, walked to what perhaps had once been the house of the town's leading burgher. It was a huge residence, and, unlike the whiff of amiable grunge given off by virtually all of the neighboring structures, this residence was still tall, proud, and elegant, from the spacious veranda to the delicate widow's walk at the top.

As the group of ill-matched pilgrims proceeded through the

square, citizens emerged here and there to watch them with fasci-
nation. Old, young, somewhere in between: mothers with their ba-
bies on their hips in colorful homemade clothing fashioned from a
range of mysterious materials (Curtains? Living room furniture up-
holstery?); teens, too, without the cynical curl of lip you might expect
from attitudinal adolescents; and a host of very aged men and women
with a range of unsightly hair and hairlessness characteristic of old
people who haven't done anything to hide their advanced stage of
decrepitude. There were tentative smiles as the little group marched
past, and some giggling from children of all ages. Goodwill—that was
it—thought Gene. A lack of fear.

"Hey, pup," said Gene to a large, dopey hound that had jumped
up with its front paws on his chest. It kissed his face with a wet,
drippy tongue.

"Marmaduke," said Stevie. "Down."

Marmaduke gave Gene a regretful look. Then he plopped down
on all fours and ran up on the porch of the dwelling. "Sorry," said
Stevie. "Mutt's got no manners."

"I don't mind," said Gene. "It's nice to see a pet that's not a synth."

"Got no synths here," Stevie said very matter-of-factly before
turning to address Steve. "Call it," he said, as a military commander
would order a senior subordinate. They went up on the porch, which
was large and arrayed with a host of ill-matching but comfortable
couches, armchairs, and even a standing hammock.

"Come on out, people," said Steve in a voice that was neither too
hard nor too gentle, neither too loud nor soft. The greenery surrounding the central square slowly produced a dozen or so individuals,
both male and female, all dressed in the same informal garb: T-shirts
with ancient logos from bygone brands, jeans, an assortment of jack-
ets of varying make and styles, all black. They carried no weapons
to speak of, just small wooden batons that hung from a variety of
holsters at their hips. They approached from all directions and stood
behind and around Steve.

"Don't be alarmed," said Bronwyn to the collection of Skells that were peering at the newcomers speculatively. "They may not look it, but they're friends."

"Well, I guess that remains to be seen, don't it," said Stevie to nobody in particular. Then he or she turned to Bronwyn. "We understand there's a job to do. We're prepared. You'd better be, too." There was a murmur of approbation in what looked to Gene like a scraggly group of miscreants.

"Hey, buddy," he said to Stevie. "I'm getting pretty sick of your shit. Nobody died and made you king. Or queen."

There was a horrified silence all around. Then Stevie came as close to smiling as they had seen. He or she put a hand over Gene's face and shoved him backward. Gene was basically too shocked to react. He was too busy trying to stay upright.

"Don't mind him," said Stevie to the group. "He's drunk. He's always drunk, in fact. And he's something of an asshole, too. But it's possible he's *our* asshole. Steve, your turn."

Steve turned to the group. "Okay, people. You can take off now. In maybe half an hour, I'll want to meet you at the barn. Bring the rest of the team with you. Everybody except the tadpoles. We move out at dawn."

"Okay, Steve," said one, and then another, and then they all nodded to Stevie with great respect and dispersed in all directions away from the green and toward the phalanx of wooden dwellings that rolled out from the perimeter.

A light rain had begun to fall, just a mist that ebbed and intensified around the porch of the house, which was protected by a generous extension of the roof. The house itself was on a rise that afforded it a view of the surrounding village and beyond, to the mountains far away and the fields and valley below. Through the mist, the light of the soon to be setting sun was silver, golden, and at the edges of the sky, a blush of pink.

"I'll go in," said Stevie. "He's stayed awake to greet you. I will see if he is able to do so."

"I'll go to the barn with the squad," said Steve.

"Yeah, okay," said Stevie. He or she then straightened his or her clothing a bit and sucked in a little air.

"Please tell him I would like a word with him first," said Bronwyn.

Stevie looked them both over appraisingly. "All right, come in with me," he or she said after a moment. Then he or she pointed to Bob. "Leave him here." Bronwyn smiled, bowed her head a bit. Then they both went into the house. The front screen door clacked shut.

Standing in the clearing outside the main house, Gene and Liv became aware of the placid silence that surrounded them. They had never heard such silence in a place where people lived their lives. First, there was the silence in their heads that had descended when their internal hardware had been disabled. But outside, too! To be enveloped in such a soft, lovely absence of sound! They listened to it and found that as the weight of it grew inside them, the power of their eyes to see swelled to fill all available space.

"It's all so beautiful," said Liv, taking in the scene. "Why don't people always live like this?"

Gene thought about it. "Nobody wants to," he said.

Through the sound of rain on the porch roof, some music filtered through the mist. A guitar here and there. The *plink-plink* of a dulcimer hammering out a country tune. And then a bleat from an old Fender Strat electric guitar filtered through an Ampeg tube amp.

"So there's electricity, I guess," said Liv. There was. Old-fashioned incandescent lights—so wasteful, so detrimental to the environment being befouled in a million other more lucrative ways!—were long outlawed in the civilized territories. Here they winked across the landscape like fireflies.

"What is that?" asked Gene, listening. "Whatever it is, the guy who's playing it is not very good." The electric stumbling and mumbling continued, stopping now and then as its author consulted a higher power, and then started up again. "It sounds sort of familiar."

"Honestly?" said Bob, staring off into the mist. "It sounds like . . . Christ. Good Lord! It's 'Stairway to Heaven.'"

"Never heard of it," said Liv. Bob and Gene gave each other a tepid smile. Bob knew it well. So naturally Gene did, too.

Stevie came out of the house, his or her eyes a little red around the edges. "You can go on in. But if you do anything to agitate him, I'll kill you."

"We won't," said Bronwyn, putting a soft hand on Stevie's shoulder. At the touch, quite unexpectedly, Stevie sort of crumpled over, laid his or her head on Bronwyn's shoulder, and wept deep, trembling sobs. Surprised, Bronwyn put her arm around the formerly resolute captain of the guard, and waited for the torrent to cease. After a few moments, it did.

"Fuck," said Stevie with a wobbly sigh.

"Don't worry about it." Bronwyn took the edge of her sleeve and wiped the Skell commander's face.

"Go on, go on," said Stevie, walking to the edge of the porch, where, after a moment or two of contemplation, he or she dropped into an armchair.

"I want to bring Bobby in first," said Bronwyn to Liv. "I know we all tend to forget it because he's such an asshole most of the time, but Bob here's a doctor."

"Hey!" objected Bob, wounded.

"I want him to take a look at the Master."

"We'll be here," said Liv.

Bob was at the door. "Come on, Bee," he said, very somberly. "I want to see what all the fuss is about."

"Coming, Bobby," said Bronwyn. She took him by the hand, and they entered the house together. Once again, the screen door slapped shut.

There was nothing but the sound of rain on the roof, except for the light, hesitant sniffle of a tough person trying to control his or her emotions from the armchair at the farthest dry remove.

In the valley before them, just beyond the mountains that lay in the deep distance, the sun was about to set, a crimson wafer seething in an orange sky. There was nothing to do but wait now, wait and watch and listen to a world that existed on another planet beyond the time and space of the one they had known.

"Hey, boss," said a little voice at Gene's knee. It belonged to a kid, maybe eight or nine, who had disengaged himself from a pack of little people who had just swarmed by on their way . . . where? Home? *Homes?* A central building where they all were being raised by a group of communal mothers and fathers?

"Hey," said Gene, and he kneeled down to get to eye level with him.

"Look what I got." The boy held out his hands, which were cupped around something. Gene thought he discerned some sign of life in there, a tiny twitching body of some kind. The kid opened his hands a bit, and the face of a very small frog poked out and looked around. Gene could see its neck expanding and contracting, in and out, in and out.

"Tree frog," said Gene, who had no idea how he knew this.

"Yeah," said the little boy. Then, abruptly: "Groovy, huh?"

"Yeah," said Gene as he searched his database. "Keen."

"Yep. See ya." Cradling his treasure, the child ran after his friends and into the gathering dark.

Gene and Liv stood together, leaning against the beams that held up the front of the porch, listening to the sounds: the rain tapping on the roof; a shout, far away, answered by another; the arpeggios of "Stairway to Heaven" being practiced, badly.

"I could live here," said Liv.

"If you didn't mind black-and-white TV, maybe." Gene put his hand behind her head and drew her face to his. They kissed for a while. Then he took a long, hard drink from one of the bottles in his backpack.

Down in the field, men and women were wrapping up their work-day, heading in with hoes, shovels, and pitchforks on their shoulders. There were at least three or four hundred of them, of all ages, races. Gene heard a little singing, something he didn't know. Many were laughing as they walked together. A tractor with an antique solar panel on its roof puffed along toward wherever it was destined to spend the night. The crowd moved toward the village, and then split into small pieces as each group headed for its separate destination.

"Hard to tell the men from the women," said Gene.

"Same hair," said Liv. "Same clothing. They all look pretty fit."

Somewhere a telephone rang—an analog ring that you might have expected from an implement with a rotary dial. After three or four rings, it was quiet again. As full darkness fell on them, the mist changed into a full downpour, and the drumbeat of raindrops above them was joined by the sound of a steady stream of water coursing down the roofline and off both sides and the front of the porch. Underneath, they were still warm and dry, but a chill was descending. Liv shivered. Lightning lit up a corner of the sky way above the mountains off to the east, then a rumble of thunder, and then, immediately following that quintessentially natural sound, another altogether: the murmur of a drone, very faint, very high up, almost on the edge of outer space.

Stevie, who had apparently been dozing, sat bolt upright. "Drone," he or she said. "Not close. Hunting." He or she stood, looked at them, and added, "It's starting." And disappeared into the torrential night.

An owl inquired "Who?" in the forest close by. Another answered, not far away. "I'm scared," said Gene. Bronwyn came out of the house. She was weeping.

"The Master will see you now," she said.

Bob emerged, joined her, and put his arm gently around her shoulders. She leaned into him.

Gene and Liv went in. Bob and Bronwyn remained on the porch, standing in each other's arms, watching the rain as it fell in sheets over the little analog town that didn't have long to live.

24

Master Tim

The giant sucking sound was the old-fashioned ventilator plugged into the wall. Right now it was still running, but it was no longer connected to the human being it had serviced. That person was lying in a hospital bed in the darkened front room of the house beneath a clean white sheet, although to call the slender, virtually depthless silhouette of a human being a person was to overstate its physical presence. It easily could have been taken for a rumpled pile of laundry. The room smelled of lilac and patchouli and baby powder, with just a soupçon of cannabis sativa underneath the scent of old house. From beneath the bedclothes emerged the beatific head of one so old, so radiant in his aura of white hair and the flow of energy from his luminous eyes that simply to draw near to that power took an effort of will. This was Tim. And he was dying.

A thin wisp of a voice emanated from the cloud of mindfulness that lay busy with the ultimate and most difficult job of any mortal. "Could you folks please turn that thing off?" He raised one feeble stick of an arm and gestured to the ventilator. His lips did not seem to move at all. "My work is almost done on this plane, and I don't want any machines around when I depart for the next one."

"Yes. Of course, Master," said Liv.

"Please don't call me that," said Tim, but not unkindly.

Liv went to the wall beyond the bed and unplugged it.

"Ahhh, that's better," said Tim. "Silence." He turned his gaze, half of which was already taking in the scenery from another dimension, upon them, and they felt the heavy weight of a consciousness that had attained a certain level of enlightenment, one that was terminal.

"Gene," he said, "perhaps it would be a good idea for you to take a pull on that magic elixir. We don't want the other son of a bitch to show up unannounced. He is one demented, magnificent prick, and we don't need him to take part in this discussion, in which the future of humanity hangs in the balance."

Gene did as he was instructed. The bottle was almost empty. The way things were going, it looked like he would never be able to do without this horrible shit. Next time, he might like a blend, he thought. The single-malt stuff can get too peaty.

"Come close, you two." And once again an arm that was little more than bone and skin rose from the bed and beckoned them. He looked from Liv to Gene and back again, as one would regard a pair of puppies too cute for words. "Sit, sit," he said, in a voice so light, so bodiless that it easily could have come from a little child too timid to make himself heard. "Don't be scared. In fact, I'm very happy, very, very happy, so happy to be going home, and, honestly, so very pleased that I'm not going to have to live through what's coming next. It's going to be a real pain in the ass, believe you me. Bob and Bee have told me that you are ready. I really hope you are. It's going to be a hell of a shit show."

Liv and Gene simply stood looking, Liv on one side of the bed, Gene on the other, as if a force field stood between them and the light that glowed in the center of the bed.

"Dudes," said Tim. "Did I ask you to sit? Or am I at that stage of this spiral where you think you're talking out loud but you're really not?"

"No, no," said Gene. "We heard you."

"Cool beans," said Tim. He motioned to two wooden kitchen

chairs with cane seating that flanked the deathbed. They sat. "Ahh," said Tim. He seemed very comfortable. "So listen," he said, "I don't have a lot of time. And you don't, either."

He raised himself up a bit and then fell back. "Help me sit up," he said. Liv and Gene moved to him then and gently raised his body. Liv propped a pillow behind him. They sat again, and attended.

"So how are the Jets doing?" said Tim pleasantly. "They make it to the postseason yet?" He then broke into a fit of cackling and wheezing that, for a moment or two, threatened to terminate the discussion. "No, but seriously," he said, regaining his composure. "When I was only a hundred or so, I used to fantasize about my last days and what I would want to wrap things up in a pleasurable fashion. And there were only two things in my mind, after a half century of healthful, organic living in harmony with the universe and all that kinda stuff: a pack of Lucky Strikes and a Double-Double from In-N-Out Burger."

Solemnly, and without comment, Liv extracted a crushed package of filterless smokes from the depth of her jeans pocket. She handed them over to Tim, who looked at the pack with unvarnished nostalgia and affection.

"Mother of God," he said. "Thanks." He took the pack as if receiving a votive relic and stared at it, a flood of memories of the times, places, and circumstances associated with the various occasions during which he had been sucking on one of its contents. "This is an oxygen-rich environment," he said. "I suppose if I lit one, we would all explode, and that would be a shame with so much left undone." He took a smoke out of the pack. It was limp and twisted and appeared a bit soggy. "It's a shame," he said, "how much pleasure we get in this life from the things that are bad for us, and how rare are the similar delights one derives from the things that are good for us." He tucked the cigarette in the corner of his mouth.

The room was quiet for a little while. Tim closed his eyes and appeared to be snoozing. Very slowly, as if reaching into a barbecue to extract one glowing charcoal, Liv extended her hand and placed it on the one resting on the coverlet. "Master?" she said.

"Tim, please." His eyes fluttered open and rested on her. "I'm awake, although it seems that unless I tether it to my sad little body down here my spirit rises up through the roof, beyond the treetops, and circles somewhere in the night sky high above us. I suppose that's what happens. You fly. You circle higher and higher. And then, finally, you don't return, you don't settle back down in this shell we call home, you simply fly off into whatever comes next, even if that turns out to be nothing at all."

"I don't believe it's nothing at all," said Liv.

"Well, to tell you the truth," said Tim, "neither do I."

They all breathed together for a short time. "Okay," said the old man, and it was a different creature entirely that fixed them with a lancet of concentration. "Listen." He sat up straight now and took the gnarled cigarette from his mouth, handing it back to Liv with a steady hand. She brought it to her lips for a moment, and then placed it back into its pack, and the pack back into her pocket.

"I've been the leader of this little community for longer than either of you have been on Spaceship Earth," said Tim. "And up until recently, I believed it would be possible to live our lives away from the digital sphere in peace and simplicity. I no longer believe that. Reluctantly, I have come to the conclusion, based on the evidence available to me, that the entire human race is threatened with a future that is not human, that is degrading to the essence of what it means to be human, and that the extinction of all we hold to be human, and perhaps of the human race itself, will occur if the Singularity occurs and the machines win. This tragic conclusion to the great pageant of human history is inevitable unless steps are taken to upset an unnatural progression into a future in which the few hold the chains of many, and life will regress into a state of mindless enslavement to the artificial intelligences that have seized control of the means of production and the markets that drive them."

"Well," said Gene, "that would be a bummer."

"The kids in my class," said Liv, "when they're offline, they . . . deactivate. And their heads are shaped funny. Sort of pointy in the back. A few seem to be developing bald spots. They're nine years old. There are a couple who have never been outside more than a couple of minutes at a time."

"When I was a boy, we went outside to play," said Tim nostalgically. "My parents used to say, 'I don't want to see you around here until it's time for dinner.'"

"Foreheads getting tinier, too," said Liv.

"New brain," said Gene. "All about communications. Like ants. The real intelligence no longer located in each individual mind but off-loaded into the Cloud. The Cloud does all the thinking."

"And how did you come by this arcane knowledge, my boy?" Tim asked mildly. He already knew the answer.

"Because *he* knows it." Arthur had studied the issue and immediately come to the conclusion that the evolution to posthuman life was going to be great for marketing.

"We've gotta get moving," said Liv. "Stevie heard a drone before." She stood and walked to the door of the house and peered into the night. Then she took out the holy smoke she had traded with Tim and lit it. Took a massive drag. Exhaled through her nose. Seemed to relax a bit.

"I didn't know you smoke," said Gene, joining her by the door.

"I don't." She kept smoking. "Something's coming," she said.

With a struggle, Tim raised himself onto one elbow. "What's Arthur thinking about, Gene?" he inquired in a very small voice that seemed to come from nowhere at all. "It's important that we know."

Gene turned abruptly. "It's none of your fucking business, you dried-up old husk," he replied in an ugly growl. He made a move toward the bed.

"No!" Tim roared in a surprisingly robust voice, at the same time recoiling and making the sign of the cross.

"Really?" said Arthur, who backed up in the face of the gesture, laughing.

As he did, what was left of Gene forced the bottle up to his mouth and took a massive draught and then another. It was almost empty now.

"Fuck!" said Arthur. There was a moment of silence as the proper owner fought and won control of Gene's body.

"Sorry," said Gene. Then he looked sheepishly around the room. "Nobody is more embarrassed about this kind of thing than I am. I'm open to suggestions."

"Bob!" Liv yelled out the door. "Arthur was here. He looks stronger. Could you go down to the car and get more provisions?"

"What'll you have, Gene?" Bob called from the edge of the porch.

"Rye," said Gene. Then he added, by way of explanation, "It has a nice, smoky flavor and a full body, and it's much easier on the head than scotch after seven or eight drinks."

"I was always a Boone's Farm man myself," said Tim.

Gene approached the bed and took Tim by the hand, looking down at him with reverence. "You know, Tim, you've got a guy here named Bob who understands a way to upload you into the big brain," he said very gently. "You would live. But you're going to die instead, and you're not doing anything, are you, to stay on after your body goes?"

"Nah," said Tim. "All that shit is pretty fucked up, don't you think?"

"Yeah, Tim, I do. But I'm not facing an actual decision point on the thing."

"Tell me what the plan is."

Gene dropped Tim's hand and sat again. "Arthur is going to launch a full-scale military assault on all the places where the Cloud has been rejected or has yet to reach," he said. "He's going to make sure that everybody gets their cranial hardware installed, and those who have it already will be upgraded. It'll start here in North America, in the core market, and when that's done, he'll move on to the rest of the world. First Russia. Then China. Within twenty-five years, the entire planet will be one global market supplied by the Corporation with every necessity of life. Those who don't get with the program will either be terminated or off-loaded."

"Off-loaded? To where?"

"The Musk Colony," said Gene without a smile.

"Mars," said Tim.

"Mars. Yeah."

"Tell Stevie to come in, please, if you would, Liv?"

"Hey, short stuff," said Liv into the darkness.

Stevie came into the light, where moths orbited the incandescent bulbs that shone weakly from the roof of the veranda.

"I'm as tall as you are, squirt," said Stevie, who came into the room laden down with a large backpack in one hand and a small leather fanny pack in another. The screen door slammed. Somewhere in the night outside, high above the sleeping camp, a drone buzzed its creepy and metallic whine.

25

The Two Devices

"**M**aster." Stevie stood in the center of the room, at ease, awaiting further instructions. His or her outfit—solid black jeans and T-shirt augmented with a khaki cargo vest—was impeccably neat, and an aged blue New York Yankees baseball cap was pulled down low over his or her forehead.

"Hello, dear," said Tim. "Please tell our colleagues what you've got there."

"Two devices," said Stevie, hauling the backpack off his or her shoulder. "The first is in here." He or she handed the pack over to Gene, who hefted it.

"Heavy." He opened the backpack and looked inside. "It looks like a huge cigar."

"It's a twelfth-generation nonnuclear electromagnetic pulse device," said Stevie. "We'll have to walk it in to get close enough to detonate it effectively."

"No kidding," said Gene. "So, we're gonna, like, blow up the Cloud?"

"What's amazing is how doable it is," said Tim. "Their arrogance has made them weak." Bob and Bronwyn had come in from the porch. They stood in the doorway, their arms draped around each other. For the first time since they met, Gene thought, Bob seemed moderately at peace, as if he had finally come home and would now be permitted to rest for a little while. The mantle of science had been removed from his shoulders. He was in the land of true belief now.

"Tell them how it works, Stevie," said Tim, who then appeared to lapse into either a heavy doze or a light coma.

"It's an EMP," said Stevie proudly, as if he or she were talking about a new motorcycle or something equally awesome. "It emits short, high-energy pulses reaching a hundred ten gigawatts, enough to destroy any complex electronic system that's not in a protective Faraday cage. It can knock out any kind of electronics, and it can fry any uncaged mainframe within a mile of where it's detonated."

"You made this thing?" Gene tried not to sound too surprised. He didn't want to be insulting to Stevie, who was obviously a little more complex than he had guessed.

"The fucking Cloud provided the informational needs for its own destruction," said Stevie. "It's no big deal. This kind of tech was old hat almost a hundred years ago. It's essentially a mechanical problem, nothing excessively fancy or hard to source. And while all the cool security guys are interested in the cutting-edge four-dimensional quantum nonsensical shit, nobody spends any time thinking about this kind of old-school gear, let alone anything that's actually being walked in and deployed on-site. By the way, we have no idea whether anybody in the vicinity at that time will melt down too."

"Ouch," said Gene.

"We're hopeful, of course. You may survive." The two exchanged cordial grins.

Steve appeared in the doorway, a mask of fear on his chubby, hairy face. "Drone," he said. "You hear it? It's up there."

"You know what to do, Steve," said Stevie patiently.

"Dude, the thing is too fucking high."

"Do your best."

"Yeah, okay," said Steve. But he didn't sound convinced.

"Skells ready?"

"Yeah, Stevie. Everybody is deployed. But we got no protection against an airborne missile."

"And the families?"

"Yeah, yeah," Steve said irritably. "All in the barn. All tucked away like little mice."

"I'm going out there," said Bronwyn suddenly. "I'm not doing anybody any good in here." She kissed Bob lightly on the cheek and darted out of the room.

Bob looked after her. "Remarkable woman," he said in a faraway, dreamy tone. "I'd be a soulless piece of shit without her, instead of the person I am today."

"Don't flatter yourself, Bob," said Gene.

"Okay, son," said Bob, giving Gene a little smile. "Got me there."

Steve regarded Gene with undisguised hostility. "You better get this fucking right, man," he blurted. "Everything is riding on you, and who the fuck are *you*?" Then, improbably, he burst into a torrent of sobs and stood there in front of them all, a large, shapeless blob of a guy with a shaggy face and a ponytail, crying his heart out.

"You guys are quite a bunch of crybabies," said Gene, but not in a mean way.

"Nobody's really ready for this kind of thing," said Stevie. He or she turned to Steve. "Go, man," he or she said tenderly. "Do whatever you can. The thing is in motion, and we all have to go with it." Steve wiped his eyes, rubbed his runny nose with the sleeve of his hoodie, and looked at the group with no discernible expression.

"Okay, Stevie," he said. "I love you, dude." And he left.

"He's overwrought," said Stevie to nobody in particular.

Liv, who had been at the door of the house looking up at the sky, came back into the room and approached Tim's bedside, staring down at him with concern. He really did look terrible. What if he dies? she thought. What would we do then?

"Can I get you anything, Tim?"

"No, dear," said Tim. "I feel a little better than I look. And there's no way I can check out during this phase of the project." He reached out his hand. She took it and sat down as Gene followed, putting one hand on Livia's shoulder. His other still held on to the precious bottle of medicine. They looked at Tim together. "I'm going with you, Gene," she said, her eyes still fastened on the shimmering entity in the bed.

"No, baby," said Gene. Liv did not reply, but her backbone stiffened.

Stevie was now holding the contents of the fanny pack in one open palm. It was a round, spiky thing about the size of a very small pineapple. "The big device will take out all the defenses that surround the Faraday cage that guards the central core, but the true target is inside the grid," he explained, "and you gotta get in there and set this little guy off. And to do either one of these things, obviously, you have to get inside the facility itself."

"Yeah, but how?" asked Gene. "They're not going to be nice enough to invite us in."

Bob was a little disappointed in the boy. After all, Gene had Bob's own mind as a substrate. Shouldn't he be a bit smarter? "Gene," he said tenderly, as one might tell a child that his puppy had just been run over by a truck. "Look in the mirror. For all intents and purposes, you're Arthur, man."

"Oh. Right." Gene felt as if he had just been instructed on how to use his dick to open a combination lock.

Stevie hefted the small device, regarding it with wonder. "This little dude uses a single-use, high-power microwave generation device to set off a superpowerful radio frequency pulse, and it incorporates both high-power microwave and ultrawide-band tech. Nothing electronic will live when it blows."

"How does it work?" asked Gene.

"It's amazing!" Stevie exclaimed. "It's a low-inductance capacitor bank discharged into a single-loop antenna, a microwave generator, and an explosively pumped flux compression generator, all bundled into a tiny package. To achieve the frequency characteristics of the pulse needed for optimal coupling into the target, wave-shaping circuits are added between the pulse source and the antenna, piggybacked onto a first-class vircator suitable for microwave conversion of high-energy waves." He paused to catch his breath and then continued: "By adding the external magnetic field to the induced field, the total magnetic flux through the ring has been conserved, and a current has been created in the conductive ring that radiates outward."

"No," said Gene. "I mean—"

"The gamma rays flow downward and are absorbed by the ground," Stevie went on, as if describing the recipe for a tasty soup. "This prevents charge separation from occurring and creates a very strong vertical electric current that generates intense electromagnetic emissions over a wide frequency range up to a thousand megahertz that emanates mostly horizontally. At the same time, the earth acts as a conductor, allowing the electrons to flow back toward the burst point. The charge separation persists for only a few tens of microseconds, making the emission power at this point of its development some one thousand gigawatts. This should do the job very nicely without melting you or the building."

"No," Gene repeated. "I mean, what button do I press?"

Everybody looked at Gene as if he were a banana slug that somehow crawled indoors from the garden.

"Here," said Stevie, showing him the detonator.

"Thanks. And that's it? Worldwide? No Cloud? From just one little bomb?"

"No. But again, the Cloud is there to cut its own throat. For fifty years, every nation has been hacking away to make sure that a request-for-service virus that could be activated in the event of a war has been embedded in every utility, every piece of infrastructure, every smart appliance in every other power on the globe. Before it explodes, our device will initiate a code through the Cloud itself to every object in the world that's been infected with that request-for-service virus. Light bulbs. Washing machines. Door-bells. Security cameras. Every infected client in the world will then respond with a request for service. And the Cloud will choke on all of those requests. And die."

"What will happen?" asked Livia. "When it happens."

"Chaos," said Stevie. "It'll be like the zombie apocalypse, with people all over the world wandering around looking for brains to eat."

"People will die," said Liv, very level. But her emotionless tone didn't fool Gene. Good old Liv, he thought. Always the one to men-tion the unmentionable. Always cutting to the heart of things.

There was a short, embarrassed silence as the room chewed on this inescapable and unpleasant aspect of the great deed being con-templated. Then Tim spoke, a voice from just this side of the grave.

"Yes," he said with equal dispassion. "People will die. Cars will crash. Planes will fall out of the sky. Dams will fail. Trains will go off the rails. The cities will temporarily go dark. There will be looting. Rioting. It will be the rictus of the old world dying." There was an-other appalled silence in the room, and then the force of their belief closed the part of their shared mind that raised such objections, and pushed them forward to the deed, as it has with revolutionaries, ter-rorists, and madmen throughout history.

Stevie continued. "The Faraday cage holds the brain stem. It's a high, metal mesh enclosure. Very strong. You gotta get inside it be-cause it's designed to protect the central mainframe from exactly the kind of action that we're going to initiate."

"Okay," said Gene. "We'll get in."

"I may be too old for this shit," said Bob. All the air seemed to have gone out of him. He walked over to the foot of Tim's bed and, seeing that there was no chair available, sat down on the end of the mattress.

"Dude," said a very faint voice from the area of Tim's head. "You're sitting on my foot."

"Oh," said Bob. "Sorry, Tim. Sorry, sorry." He moved over.

"What happens to the people who set this off?" asked Livia. "Who are, you know, in the vicinity?"

"Hard to say," said Bob. "Right, Stevie? EMPs have been around since Andrei Sakharov started working on them in the nineteen fifties. Nobody has been killed yet."

"Okay, Bob," said Liv. "Thanks. That makes me feel a lot better."

"Of course," Bob added thoughtfully, "these are superbombs, guys. We don't know the full extent of their capabilities."

Outside, the very faint, extremely ugly sound of a hornet disturbed in its greasy nest intruded from somewhere far above.

"God," said Liv, "that sounds very close."

A low whistling approached the space around the house. It grew louder and higher in pitch. Then suddenly it ceased—followed by a profound, ominous silence.

"False alarm," said Gene.

The air above the little village exploded into a nightmare wall of liquid flame, a roaring maelstrom of bright blue and orange. Tim sat bolt upright, his hair radiating straight from his head in all directions.

"You see?!" he bellowed in a voice as deep and powerful as thunder. "You see why this must all be stopped?"

Gene saw. But he could not speak.

"Bee is out there," said Bob. He ran outside into the flames.

26

Battle Lines

"What did you do?" Sallie screamed into Mortimer's bland, dismissive face.

"It was O'Brien," said Mortimer. Then he added, a bit defensively, "Even machines make mistakes."

"Mistakes?! *Mistakes!?*" An apoplectic fit is not a pretty thing *to witness*. Initially, you lose your sight. Immediately thereafter, you experience a sudden, piercing headache. Then comes nausea, sometimes followed by vomiting, and then you faint. Sallie did not actually get to full apoplexy quite yet as she stood, mouth agape at the sight of the giant orange blossom that filled the sky, the heat shimmering in the air. But she was close. She could not take her eyes from the aerial display. A second explosion followed the first, and she screamed again, full throated, all out, a wild banshee howl that ended only when her breath gave out.

"He was in the last vehicle, as you know," Mortimer reported calmly when she had once again subsided a bit, "and he had instructions to 'guard the perimeter.' Perhaps those orders were, you know, a little vague."

"A little vague?! *A little vague!?* We just firebombed a peaceful village of hippies!"

"Yeah, well," said Mort, and it would be a lie to say that there was not the very slightest curl of satisfaction about one corner of his grim little smile.

Sallie said, "Ooh. Oh, my." Then the full effect truly hit her, and she bent over from the waist, put one palm on the ground for support, and emitted a short noise, something like "Oog," and sat heavily in one semicircular motion on the turf of the pinewood glen a mile or so outside the village. "I don't feel very well," she said softly. She was in the phase of physical disorientation that immediately precedes unconsciousness. Anyone who has experienced it, either for a benign reason, such as intoxication, or a malign one, such as a heart attack or extreme fright, will testify that it is highly unpleasant. All you want is for it to go away.

"Bring the robot here," she said in a voice so wobbly it could barely be heard above the snap, crackle, and pop of the distant fire.

"I beg your pardon, General?" said Mort with perhaps a bit too much tone. Sallie looked up at him.

"What did you say to me?"

"I couldn't quite hear you." He snapped to something like attention. There was something Mortimer didn't like about Sallie's aspect all of a sudden.

"Mort, you know what?" Sallie stumbled very slowly to both feet, although she was still bent over at the waist. That established, she straightened up until she was fully standing, her hands on the hips of her olive-green pants more for support than anything else. Mort did, however, take a very small step backward.

"I will have you killed, do you understand? Give me your weapon."

Mort simply stood there in front of her as if someone had struck him sharply on the back of the head with a rubber mallet.

"Give me your weapon, you dumb fuck," she said and held out her hand.

Mort reached into his itty-bitty jockstrap of a holster and took out his neural phase transmitter. There may have been an instant where

he seemed to be deciding which end to present to Sallie, the handle
or the muzzle end in her face, but maybe not. At any rate, that moment passed, and he handed it over, grip first. Sallie took it, adjusted
the weapon with no hesitation whatsoever, turned the thing on Mortimer, and shot him in the face.

Being neuralized may not be as unpleasant as suffering an apoplectic fit, but it's no mall walk, either. First you fall over on your
back and twitch uncontrollably for several minutes, depending on
your constitution. Then there's the foaming, sometimes not only from
the mouth, followed by a mercifully brief episode of full paralysis,
after which, aside from a torpor that dissipates after an hour or so,
you feel pretty much all right, capable of walking and talking, if not
resisting.

"Now, Mort, I want you to understand me very clearly," said Sallie as he convulsed on the ground. "We're going into the village now
and fixing whatever we broke."

"Yes, Sallie," Mort choked out. After a time, he was able to sit up.
Sallie allowed him to do so and then said, "Get O'Brien over here."

"Come on, Sallie, it was a mistake. Please don't hurt him."

"Mort, he's a robot. He fucked up. I'm going to decommission
him. He's flawed. It will only take a second. Then we're going in
there."

"All right, Sallie, I'll get him. But let me do it when the time
comes. We owe him that much."

Flushed with emotion and a wee bit wet in the shorts, Mort strode
away, albeit with very short strides. Sallie went over to the Humvee
she had been driving when the missile hit the barn. The unfortunate
error that had ignited the Peaceable Kingdom was a combination of
two snafus: O'Brien's failure to properly interpret his orders and, at
the same time, the breakdown of the fail-safe Lifeform Discernment
System, which, of course, comes with all armed self-guiding cruise
missiles. Simply put, the drone got the order, and instead of executing a number of preventive routines based on the heat patterns in the

village below, it simply didn't. These things happen. Thankfully, the missile was a small one, because its target turned out to be the barn in which all the unarmed citizens—men, women, and children—had been gathered together for safety. It was that building that was burning. Very, very faintly, over the night air, the attentive ear might have caught the sounds of many voices screaming.

"What now, honey?" said Sallie to the little green lizard thing that sat cogitating in the shotgun seat.

"Complicated situation," said Arthur. The voice was a weird combination of his own signature growl mixed with the mildly strobed-out, pleasantly canine singsong of Lucy. "On the one hand, the whole situation is very unfortunate insofar as the village is concerned. Too bad about that."

"That's an understatement, don't you think?"

"Sure. Don't go all squishy on me now. What's done is done, and we'll do our best to ameliorate the thing when we have a chance. It doesn't change the basic, underlying challenge here."

"I suppose not," Sallie said, just to say something. She was looking at Lucy but listening to her husband. It was confusing. Her mind was rejecting not only the visual input but also the content of his remarks, and, more disconcerting still, his features seemed to be materializing before her eyes, superimposed onto the flat, shiny green countenance of the creature. She realized that, aside from her awe at the miraculous transformation of consciousness achieved by the upload and subsequent download engineered by Bob's tech, she was pretty thoroughly creeped out. And still, she listened, driven by the dynamic willpower that now inhabited the reptilian form of the entity that was once her beloved pet and friend, and was now her beloved husband. Sort of.

"Look," said Arthur, who then paused for a moment to think. He blinked twice, his eyelids clicking back and forth from side to side, and a shiver ran down Sallie's spine and back up into the nape of her neck, and a coldness reached into the tips of her fingers. This thing was Arthur, certainly, but wasn't Lucy in there somewhere? She looked deep into its eyes.

"We have to deploy our forces a little bit differently than anticipated," Arthur continued slowly, piecing together the strategy as he went along now. "I imagine you want to go to the village and see what can be done there."

"Yes, Arthur. I do."

"Okay, then. You go, and take the elite squad of the army with you. They'll follow your orders. I'll take the rest. You can have Mort along to enforce any measures you feel are appropriate either among the population there or our own security people who might not understand that their role has gone from pacification to search and rescue."

"And you?"

"What about me?" He seemed preoccupied. Annoyed.

"What are you going to do?"

"Pick me up. I want you at eye level. I also like the feeling of my tail in your arms." Sallie picked up Arthur and held him close, his tail tucked into her armpit, his trapezoid of a head looking up at her intently. "I'm going to take O'Brien along in one of the fastest hovercraft we can find," he said, "and try to reach Vancouver before that motherfucker who stole my body gets there."

"And what, Arthur? Then what?"

"Then . . . I will reassert myself. I'm here. And I'm in his head. He won't be able to push against me from both directions."

"But—"

"We don't have a lot of time, Sal," the lizard said abruptly, and he suddenly didn't seem quite so lovable to her anymore. "I have a vague idea of what he's going to try to do there, because he's in my head, too, you know. And it means the destruction of all that the human race has built up over twenty thousand years of civilization. It's also against our business plan. I can't let that happen. And neither can you."

"Me?"

"I'm pretty sure that they acquired the weapons here in the Not

So Peaceable Fucking Kingdom to do what they want to do. We have to get to Vancouver first and stop them, no matter what." The little green lizard thought for a moment and then added, "The future of humanity is at stake."

She stared at the creature, eye to eye. It was Lucy's face, one she had loved since it had been printed for her by Bob's production facility and implanted with the consciousness of a cocker spaniel, with subsequent upgrades to achieve its current state of . . . What was it? Intelligence?

"Okay, Arthur," she said at last. "But you take Mortimer. I don't want him."

"You sure?"

"Yeah. I'm sure. He's not suited for the work we have to do. He's not human enough."

"Good. Okay. Now give me a little kiss and get going." She kissed the top of its head, but gingerly. "I can't wait to get my body back," he added, with a touch of the old romantic in his voice. Sallie shivered. Then she held out her arms to their full extension and gently set Arthur on the forest floor.

"I'm going to get going," she said, and briskly climbed back into the vehicle, where she touched the communications module behind her right ear. "We're going to move out now," she said to all those, human and artificial, within the sound of her command. Multiple engines roared to life around and behind them as she fired up her own vehicle and felt it rise into the air ever so slightly. "Hovers engaged. Full speed. Single file. Follow me. When we get to the village, all ordnance is to be disengaged. Assemble in Square Alpha on your maps and await further instructions." For a moment, she looked down at Arthur/Lucy, seeing both, as they stood on their tiny legs in the middle of the clearing.

"Go, honey," said Arthur. And then, quite unexpectedly, as if surprised by itself, it added, "Woof woof."

Sallie looked at Lucy and smiled. Lucy smiled back, her tongue poking slightly out of her little green lips. Then she was gone and Arthur came back.

"Get goin' now, sweetie pie," he said.

Sallie rolled. The convoy, one by one, followed. The final vehicle, now on auto, brought up the rear and was empty. A small silence reverberated through the woods. One bird chirped tentatively, then another. Then they were gone.

A sharp rustling shook the shrubbery. Mortimer, followed by the rolling pseudopod his friends called O'Brien, entered the clearing.

"She gone?" Mortimer asked softly.

"Yeah, she's gone," said Arthur. "Pick me up."

"Yes, sir." Mortimer did so. Arthur's stubby little tail was in Mortimer's face and its head faced O'Brien, who simply stood there on his big wheel, nervously awaiting his fate.

"First of all, let's get a couple of things straight."

"Yes, Arthur," said O'Brien, his head unit downcast.

"I'm proud of you." O'Brien raised his ocular units slightly, daring to hope that what he had just heard was possible. "True," the green lizard synth that was actually the ancient business mogul said, "you missed the primary target by a couple hundred yards, so I guess this moron guru asshole still lives, but the essential purpose of our mission was accomplished. My tenderhearted wife is headed off to do good in the world, and we are all free to do what we have set out to do."

O'Brien, overcome with input at this development, his stabilizing platform collapsing one segment at a time, essentially did whatever might be interpreted in machine language as falling to what passed for his knees. "My life in your service, Arthur," he said, bowing his cranial structure in submission.

"He's downloaded too much sword and sorcery stuff," said Mortimer, with a small, indulgent smile.

"Cut off his head," said Arthur softly.

"Really?" said Mortimer. After a confirmatory glance at his lord and master, and without further comment, he approached O'Brien from behind and, in one swift motion, grasped him firmly by what would have been his ears and twisted the machine's head from its shoulders. The thing that had once been Officer O'Brien of the Citizens' Police Force, and then Sergeant O'Brien of the Corporate Army, who secretly aspired to become General O'Brien in the company's developing expeditionary army, ceased to exist, although there was always a possibility, as with all creatures real and artificial, that his consciousness could be booted up in another structure if his cranial unit was conserved. At this point, however, in any meaningful sense, O'Brien was gone. He had given his body to the cause.

"Mount me in his auxiliary vertebral unit," said Arthur. "Make sure I have good line of sight and full access to his power banks and motion controls."

This proved to be a little more complicated than either Mortimer or Arthur had anticipated, and instructions had to be downloaded from the Cloud to complete the procedure. Further difficulties were encountered when these directions turned out to be in Chinese, and Arthur was forced to download and install translation software, which itself was lacking in many respects. In the end, it required more than an hour to mount Lucy's body into the hover-capable Segway that had been O'Brien. The result was not attractive—in fact, it was rather monstrous—but it was functional.

"Now, it's safe to assume they have a head start on us," said the newly created being.

"Not for long," said Mort.

They headed for the fastest hovercraft in the fleet and set off at top speed.

27

Back at the Ranch

"I'll die later," said Tim, swinging his feet off the bed and onto the floor. For a moment, he seemed to plant himself, wobbling a bit before confirming that both legs would serve him. "Maybe I'm doing a little bit better than I thought," he commented. The Master coughed twice and then straightened up, a new sparkle in his bright-blue eyes.

The before and after of the explosion itself was ridiculously sudden. First, silence. Then the boom, which had an electronic quality to it in addition to the more conventional sounds of things igniting. Then the crackle and roar, followed by the many smells that accompany a variety of burning: wood smoke; followed by a mélange of odors far less palatable: melting rubber; the hot rock of the pathways cracking under the heat; the creosote, bubbling and dripping down the sides of the structure that was hit; and very faintly, the odor of cooking meat. A tremendous heat suffused the air, making it shimmer and dance. Outside the world was red, orange, yellow, throbbing with waves of beautiful rainbow colors.

"Bee is out there," said Bob, and he ran outside into the flames.

Liv and Gene stood together at the doorway, too frightened to move, looking out at the display, listening to the chaos, feeling the heat on their faces. They reached for each other's hands.

"This is the natural outcome of the world we have built for ourselves," came Tim's voice from behind them, sad and full of rage. "A world built upon getting and keeping and competing and winning. Now we must set it right." He thought for a few seconds.

"Stevie."

"Yes, Tim." Stevie had appeared from nowhere and was standing reverentially before Tim, arms at his or her sides, back erect, in the perfect precombat position, prepared to move forward, back, sideways—whatever was called for.

"I know you want to engage the troops and begin the operation of striking back. But I must ask you to defer."

"Master—"

"No, I really must. In any direct confrontation, your Skells will be wiped out by the enemy's superior technology and malevolence of purpose. Have them instead attend to those who are injured. Put out fires. Help the people."

"Okay, Tim."

"You yourself have a different purpose."

"Tell me."

"I want you to take the fastest vehicle we have in the fleet and head for our primary target. The brain is in the Cloud. Gene here will go with you, as will Livia, of course. Without her, Gene, while a capable enough fellow, is pretty much a sack of meat under certain kinds of pressure, just like his dad, Bob."

"Now, see here!" snapped Gene. This pleased him not at all. Still, he did feel a little relieved. He had planned to sort of sneak out in the confusion, leaving Livia behind in a situation that was, presumably, safer. Considering the circumstances, he wasn't quite so sure it was. Besides, he wasn't one bit convinced that he could pull off what he was supposed to do by himself anyway. He was notoriously not supercompetent at much of anything. His principal asset in this effort, as far as he could see, was his ability to get past security by assuming the role of Arthur, for whom the guards, both biological and artificial, would be prepared. After that, there was all this stuff about electromagnetic pulses and shit. He wasn't so sure he had been listening 100 percent, due to a combination of nerves and, ironically, a desire to appear that he was up to the task of paying close attention. In fact, unless there was a big red button in the final room that said, Push Me, he wasn't quite positive he'd know what to do. It might be very welcome to have Livia there to, you know, help him, as it were.

"I won't argue with you, Gene," said Tim. "She's going."

"I'm going," said Liv.

"Yeah," said Gene. "I know, I know. I'm glad you are. I need you, Liv. But if you get killed, I'll never forgive you."

"Gee," said Liv. "I'll try to keep that in mind."

"Come on, then," said Stevie. He or she grabbed the two devices and hustled out the door to find out which friends and family might have been killed in the blast that had been engineered by human intelligence and then executed with very limited competence by the artificial variety—the first of the stupid entity that had launched it and the second of the drone that had delivered it.

The smell from outside was more acrid now, although the sounds of screaming had subsided. "I'll ask you two to join me now," said Tim, extending both his arms. He had walked with surprising elegance and ease to the center of the room, his long bed gown flowing, his face aglow with the red light that had ignited the sky. "I must join the community in a moment to ascertain whether those motherfuckers have destroyed property, which will not matter, or lives, which will be an abomination that it will be your task to avenge. Do you grok me, guys?"

"I do," said Livia.

"Yeah, Tim," said Gene. "I grok you, too."

Tim bent his head and took their hands in his. They were as thin as reeds, cool and dry, as if recently bathed and powdered. Gene felt their power. They stood in a small circle.

"Holy spirit," Tim said quietly. "Bless these children as they go

241

about their mission. Long ago, you made men and women in your own image. We have taken that image and molded it into a form far distant from your original intent, a shallow thing, earthbound and small, connected by the vanity of its technology. Please watch over these two warriors as they attempt to set the world back onto the path of humanity." Tim opened his eyes. "Go," he said, releasing their hands. "And guys," he added, riveting them with a gaze so intense that Gene felt it enter his face and exit out the back of his head. "This is not a drill. Don't fuck up."

"We won't," said Gene. "I mean, I certainly hope not."

Livia grabbed her backpack, and they headed for the door. As they were about to leave, she touched Gene on the shoulder.

"Don't be scared, Genie," she said. She took a bottle of vodka out of the pack and handed it to him. "Your medicine."

"Popov?" said Gene, looking at the bottle. "You want to kill me?"

"No, babe, just him."

Gene took a big swig and shuddered.

"What about Bob?" he said.

"I know," said Liv. "But we gotta go."

"But Bob."

"I know, baby. But sometimes you just gotta hope things are going to work out for the best. Even when you know they probably won't."

"That's deep," said Gene.

"Come on, assholes! Saddle up!" came a huge bellow from right outside. Then the sound of Stevie cranking up an old-fashioned gasoline engine a thousand horses large. They went out. The screen door slapped behind them, and they headed off into the burning night.

Tim pushed open the screen door and stepped out onto the porch. The night burned around him. "God Almighty," he said. He gazed in horror into the inferno.

He saw right away that the damage was limited to the area around the barn and paddock. There was a vault under the barn. Maybe most people had made it there before the robot rocket hit. There was a fair amount of paranoia in the village by then, due to the intermittent insectile buzzing of the drones that had intensified over the last few days. Maybe a lot of people were already sheltered, and it was not so bad.

Citizens were walking around aimlessly, dazed, many of them with pitchforks and baseball bats, Tim was saddened to see. He stood for a beat, ascertaining the situation, fighting back a wave of light-headedness and nausea that threatened to bring him to his knees. He took a few deep breaths and then trotted as briskly as he was able to the barn, which was still crackling merrily away in some places. Steve was there, sitting on a curb outside, his hulking form bent over with grief.

"Steve, I'm glad to see you," Tim said, and leaned down on his aged haunches to see Steve eye to eye.

"So," said Steve, "most people were in the basement. But not everybody."

Tim just let it hang there. Finally: "Barry Wick's little boy, Tod or Ted or something like that. He went out to make sure his frog was okay."

"Who else?"

"Lot of dogs." His eyes filled with tears. "Marmaduke."

"Any other people, Steve?"

"Couple old people, I think. A girl or something." He burst into a torrent of violent sobbing.

"Get yourself together, Steve," Tim said quite sternly. "Your boys need you. It is you who are in command here now."

"Me?" Steve thought about this concept for five to ten seconds, then rose.

"That's better," said Tim, rising as well. As he did, he noticed, splayed out in the dirt at his feet, the remains of a tiny tree frog in the dust. For some reason, the sight filled him with the greatest sadness he had felt so far, and, for a moment, he, too, broke down and wept. Then he gathered himself together and headed off across the green.

A gigantic, flat-bottomed hovercraft appeared in the sky over the barn and began dumping water on the flames, slowly and deliberately moving from one end of the burning structure to the next, distributing a fine spray. The fire started dying down.

"That's interesting," said Tim, looking up at the enormous vehicle now in the process of trying to undo what had been done.

"Tim."

It was Bob, sitting quietly at the base of a eucalyptus. Bronwyn appeared to be lounging on her back, her head resting gently in his lap. She looked quite peaceful, but there was something odd about the way her body had arranged itself.

"Hello, Bob," said Tim, once again crouching down as low as his decrepit knees would take him.

"Bronny," said Bob. His hair was in complete disarray, and his eyes were red and watery, and there was a tidy blob of snot under one nostril. "She's dead, Tim. She died right there on the steps of the barn. Went there— Well, you saw when she went there. And she was standing right there on the steps, with two old ladies, talking about— I don't know what they were talking about, actually . . ." Then he stopped talking.

"But Bobby," said Tim, very, very gently, "you have her backed up, right?"

"Look how perfect she looks, Tim. That's because she wasn't hurt by the blast itself. She was killed by a big pulse that knocked out her neurological power grid. They can do that now."

"Bob. Of all people. You did back Bronwyn up, right? Please don't tell me she's gone for good."

"Yeah, I did."

"Thank God. So. You've learned a lot from Gene. You can do it again, maybe even better. In some respects, it's a pretty low bar."

"Yeah. Gene's not all that impressive," he admitted with a smile and then added, "He's likeable, though."

The two sat together then for a little while. "The thing is . . ." Bob began, but then he stopped again.

"Come on, son," said Tim. "Talk to me."

"I may be able to create Bee again from a macroprint of her nuclear mitochondria. But her upload . . . her consciousness . . ."

"Come on, babe."

"I uploaded her data when she came in for her initial meeting with us. Before she knew me. Before, you know, we knew each other. Before all we've been through together. Before all the things you do when you fall in love with somebody. All that data won't be in there, dude. I've lost her. She will exist, but not for me. Nor I for her."

Tim put a slender hand on Bob's. "You'll just have to work that old black magic all over again, Bobby. Whatever Bee loved in you before she can love in you again."

"Yeah, I don't know. I'm different than I was when I first met her." He looked at Tim appraisingly. "I thought you were supposed to be dying," he said. "You look terrific."

"Yeah, well, I try to eat right and stay active."

"It's working for you."

"Thanks, bro."

"You know," said Bob, his voice suddenly lighter, more hopeful, "I had this thought: maybe I can upload a previous iteration of myself back into myself and forget all about everything that's happened. You know, start from square one and be the same person I was the day I met Bronwyn."

"That's my boy," said Tim. "You keep thinking." He patted Bob's hand encouragingly. "Although I think you're a better man now than you were then."

"Maybe," said Bob.

Tim gave Bob his hand back and stood. "I gotta see to a few people now, Bob."

"I know. Go on ahead. Thanks, man." He remained seated with Bronwyn's head on his lap, stroking her hair thoughtfully.

Its firefighting task completed, the hover copter had set itself down in the middle of the clearing. The cockpit door opened, and Sallie emerged in blue jeans and pigtails. Several members of the corporate security force had hopped out of the mothership and taken their places behind her at a comfortable distance. They wore roomy, perfectly laundered polo shirts over blue jeans that had been dry-cleaned and pressed vigorously into sharp creases. There were bulges at their hips under their casual tops, but they all kept their hands where Tim could see them, and they took their positions very much at ease. Tim stood in the clearing, himself a picture of repose, and said nothing. Sallie slowed as she approached him and then stopped. For a moment, she looked Tim in the face but then dropped her eyes.

"Is there someplace we could go and talk?" she said, looking down into the dirt.

"Yeah, okay," said Tim, but he didn't move.

"I'm sorry. I speak for all of us, the whole Corporation, for my husband . . ."

"I know who your husband is."

"Yes, well."

They stood there a little bit more. Tim didn't seem in any hurry to say or do much of anything.

"Okay, look," said Sallie. "This was a horrible thing. I'm sure you know that nobody human gave the order to do what we did." Which is what she believed.

"I think they call it machine intelligence."

She dared a little peek up at his face. "Anyhow," she said, "we want to do what's right."

"When?"

"Now?"

"Come on, then. Come look at what you did."

Tim stalked off toward the barn, which was a smoldering heap surrounded by frightened, sooty villagers making their way here and there, some of them wounded, all in varying stages of confusion, anger, and grief.

Sallie followed.

28

Nike

The great, gas-powered hovercraft carrying Stevie, Livia, and Gene belched its last lick of flame and settled down in front of the shack that leaned precariously in front of the giant, empty parking lot at the ass end of the last dirt road leading out of the gigantic metropolis surrounding the old city of Vancouver, which squatted in the distance belching clean flame. Not a bird chirped. The nearest tree was about a mile away, across the vast expanse of apparently empty macadam. The space, now utterly vacant, had once been the surface level of a Nike missile installation long since abandoned when the nuclear shield above the nation was narrowed to a few sites and then discarded altogether when Russia became the ally of the ruling class during the Trump dictatorship. The blacktop was crisscrossed with very faint yellow hatching at a slightly depressed circular area in the dead center, and little sheds and ruined fencing were scattered around the periphery.

Stevie got out and looked around. "They're not far behind us," he said dispassionately. And indeed, if you listened very, very hard, you could just make out the hum of drones and assorted military hardware on their way.

Liv and Gene climbed out of the vehicle after Stevie and stood on the cracked pavement that led up to the small guard shack in which a shadowed figure leaned at an odd angle. Although to say that Gene "stood" might be an overstatement. He swayed on one and a half legs, the bulk of his weight now propped up by Liv, who had an arm around his waist and her head acting like the top of a crutch at the crux of his armpit. The consciousness of Arthur was strong inside him now, screaming to get out, aware of the plans that were being activated against his interest. It would be fair to say that Arthur now existed not in one but in two places: one inside Gene's cerebral cortex, and the other inside the synth that was perched on top of the Segway frame now speeding toward them to rescue its business plan. In defense against the first of these entities, Gene had polished off the bottle of Popov that Liv had given him as they left the Kingdom, so he was not only plastered but also sick to his stomach. As any serious drinker across the centuries of its existence has known, Popov might do in a pinch, but for a physical system used to top-shelf stuff, it should be treated with great discretion.

"I'm not sure how long I can keep this big clown up and running," Liv said to Stevie.

They headed for the shack.

The figure inside turned out to be a dummy, placed there to give the impression to any casual observer that the site was actively monitored by a nonartificial being. It had clearly been leaning at this precipitous angle for quite some time, since cobwebs and dust had collected between its antiquated rubberized face unit and the clouded, greasy window of the structure. A blue cap with a short white brim, which must have been mildly jaunty once, moldered on its head.

"It's just a mannequin of some kind," said Liv. "Kind of creepy." She stepped back and peered up and beyond the guardian's little glass-and-plywood enclosure, looking for the next place to go, since one didn't appear to be obvious. "Are you sure we're in the right place?" she asked as neutrally as possible, aware that Stevie had a tendency to be a little bit touchy on matters of his or her competence. Gene teetered between the two, attempting to focus. He really did feel

248

pretty fucking bad, but even he, shuttling between queasiness and coma, realized that puking right here and now, even though it might make him feel better immediately, would be an inauspicious way to begin this most important of assignments.

"Yeah, yeah, we're here," said Stevie. Peering into the guard shack again, he or she addressed the inert stuffed replica of a human being.

"Yo, Buster."

Improbably, the thing's head rotated on an unseen axis, and its eyes burst into a light-blue glow. Only its head moved. Its body remained a dead husk, an object with a torso, arms, and legs artfully filled with inorganic stuffing. "You are not authorized personnel," it said pleasantly.

Far away, the sound of approaching mechanisms grew imperceptibly louder.

"Well, who do you think this is?" said Stevie to the creature. He turned, took Gene by the elbow, and presented him to the automaton head, which scanned Gene's features with a horizontal beam, up, down, sideways.

"Pardon me," said the head. "Good morning, sir," addressing Gene with an official tone of respect afforded a senior officer.

"Good morning, soldier," said Gene. "We'd like to enter the facility," he added as an afterthought.

"Right away, sir," said the head, which then remarked, "You have no idea how good it is to see you, sir. It can get rather boring here."

"My," said Gene to the head, "you're a chatty fellow."

"Let's move it along," said Stevie, staring off in the direction of the approaching whirr and hum.

"Yes, of course," said the head. "The entry to the facility is beyond this location approximately one hundred and twenty-seven yards and a bit to the right. Head for the yellow markers. Be careful not to fall into the entryway as the ramp opens. It is rather steep." There was then a rumble, followed by the sound of metal moving against metal, and the ground opened up in the middle of the asphalt plane into a giant hole that once had provided an exit path for a missile on the way to destroy its destination somewhere in the western part of what had been the Soviet Union and was now disputed territory between Russia and Mongolia. On one edge of the chasm was a ramp heading down into an abyss. They walked to the top of the ramp. Then Stevie handed over the two devices, now in one convenient backpack.

"Well," he or she said, "this is it. Good luck, you guys."

"What?" said Liv. "Wait a minute."

"Go on now."

"Stevie!" said Gene, although it came out more like "Schteevee."

"Dudes," said Stevie. "In a few minutes, the cavalry is going to arrive with the express purpose of killing your asses and stopping this whole thing from happening. This has always been my assignment: Get you here. Set you loose. Give you enough time to get the job done. Now get going, or all of this shit will have been for nothing, including the fact that our home was just whacked by these mother-raping cocksuckers."

"Okay, yeah," said Gene. He turned down to the top lip of the ramp.

"Stevie," said Liv, her eyes brimming with tears.

"It's okay, babe," said Stevie, producing two handheld weapons that had been in the pocket of his or her jacket and checking them for use. They were small, glowing things and didn't look that dangerous at all. "I'm looking forward to this next part."

"Just you against the whole army, huh?"

"Fun while it lasts. I don't plan to make it, so that gives me a certain je ne sais quoi about the whole situation."

"I can see that."

"It's okay, babe." Stevie gave Livia a sweet and delicate smile. "Bob's got me backed up. And this time, I'm gonna get the right body. One that fits my head." Even in the extremity of the situation, Stevie seemed to find this observation amusing, and for the first time since they had met, he or she indulged in a brief paroxysm of genuine laughter. When it subsided, he or she reached into a jacket pocket.

"Here. Take this." It was a very small firearm, no bigger than one of those toys children used to have before everything became digital and produced a whirring noise and a few sparks when its trigger was pumped by a tiny finger.

"It's, uh, stronger than it looks," said Stevie.

Liv took it. Put it in her pocket. Then they were all sort of frozen for a while. It can be like that when you know it's the last time you're going to see somebody.

"We gotta get goin', Livvy," said Gene at last, inching his way down the entryway. He extended his hand to Liv. "It's supposed to happen this way, honey," he said. "Stevie delays the evil villains for just long enough for us to go on ahead and complete our mission. Right, Stevie?"

"Affirmative," said Stevie directly to Gene, eye to eye, and not without some iron-gray humor attached. Then Stevie unzipped her combat vest for the first time and took off her old Yankee cap, which she dropped to the ground. A cascade of light-blond hair flowed down her back, almost to her waist, and any doubts as to her biological gender were instantly eradicated.

"Ha," said Gene.

"Dude!" Liv exclaimed. Then she put her arms around Stevie, who stiffened under her embrace but didn't shrug it off. "We done now?" Stevie said after a few seconds, adding, not unkindly, "Please get the fuck out of here."

"Let's go, Gene," said Liv. Pushing Stevie away from her in one determined thrust, she grabbed Gene's hand, and they headed down the ramp into the darkness.

In no time at all, the sounds of their footsteps faded. It was quiet in the woods surrounding the tarmac. A light rain began to fall, and the wind picked up. Stevie lowered herself to the ground and assumed the lotus position, a weapon in each hand, and tilted back her head to feel the wind and rain on her face. Somewhere in the depths of the woods, a crow called to its companion, which gave an answering caw. "They always travel in pairs," she said quietly. "But the hawk flies alone." She checked her handguns to make sure they were set on their absolute maximum power. And then she waited.

A quarter mile below the surface of the earth, Gene and Livia proceeded with all deliberate speed down long corridors lined with steel doors shut against them. They had been told to ignore them. "Offices," Tim had informed them in one of his deathbed lectures, before he was mysteriously reenergized. "Head for the core, which is surrounded by miles of drive bays."

"What's on those?" Gene had asked.

"The wisdom of the ages, Gene," Tim had replied sagely. "I suppose the smart ones have it all backed up in local facilities. But after the denial-of-service outage hits, and the core is destroyed, it will take decades, maybe more, for them to put it all back together in one place, if they choose to indulge in that stupidity again. They probably will. But it's nearly impossible to claim ownership of a property that's spread out over continents and run by local managers that are closer to it. The Roman Empire learned that lesson the hard way."

Gene had no idea what Tim was talking about at the time. Apparently it was not a subject at which Bob had excelled at the university. Arthur, on the other hand, had recognized the peril of global decentralization the moment it had been presented to him by the board. World domination was too good for business.

Down the long, long corridor they ran in the semidarkness. Gene found that he was gaining rather than losing physical strength as he went. The liquor was wearing off, and all he had left was a small store of airline bottles that had been provided to him back at the Kingdom. His head was clearing. He wanted to reach for his backpack, which held his remedy alongside the EMP devices, but Liv was already ahead of him and calling for him to catch up. And as he lurched forward, Gene heard, to his horror, another voice rise within him like vomit in the back of his throat. "I'm gonna fucking kill you, you little fucking creeps," is what came belching out from the bottom of his gut.

"Shut up, Arthur, you sonuvabitch!" he screamed, his feet pounding down the slick gray quartzite of the floor that stretched for what seemed like a mile before him.

"Gene! Fuck him! Keep going!" Liv didn't have to turn around to know what was happening.

"Fuck me? Fuck *you!*" The ugly rasp of Arthur's pent-up rage echoed down the hall.

"Liv! Honey! I'm losing it!" Gene kept going, the way a dead chicken will continue to race across a farmyard long after its head has been cut off.

"No! You're not!" Liv was at full throttle. "You're stronger than he is! You're better than he is! You can beat him! But you gotta try! You gotta try! I see light ahead! There's space ahead, Gene! Hold on, baby! Hold on!"

"Hold on, baby! Hold on!" It was Arthur's voice, mocking, sneering. "He hasn't got the guts! He isn't properly hydrated! He hasn't had his meds! Ha ha ha ha ha!"

Gene could not respond. He was busy running. And crying. Deep sobs wracked his body as he went, shaking his head like a dog who had taken a load of something toxic up its nose, his hands trembling. But his legs and his feet kept on, driven by all that was left in him that was still himself. And so they ran on, the incline heading downward now, and, yes, not too far away now, they spied an open archway where the light was different, and a hum grew louder: the hum of hundreds of thousands of optical drives speaking to the world as one.

29

The Cloud Must Die

The rain was falling more heavily as the armed platoon of corporate soldiers entered the asphalt clearing in the middle of nowhere. The mannequin sentry still tilted on silent duty. But where before there had been nothing but empty macadam stretching for miles into the distance, there was now a gaping hole in the earth, one that led down to the beating heart of the Singularity that ran the human race, stored its memories, its music and baby pictures, its instant and permanent messages going back several generations, the social security numbers, sexual and entertainment preferences, political points of view of all citizens touched by the giant tentacled organism that reached into every home, every mind, their voting records and noxious utterances made over the dark Web as well as the more civilized one, all the books ever written, all the thoughts ever expressed that could have been captured since some forgotten politician named Gore, back in the last half of the twentieth century, had assisted in the transformation of the US Defense Department's intranet into the World Wide Web.

Stevie sat at the top of the ramp, legs crossed one on top of the other in the classic yogini position of repose. In each hand, she held a somewhat larger version of the weapon that she had shared with Liv and Gene. She was wet all the way through now, her hair a glowing helmet that ran like a ribbon of gold down her back.

"Hold!" said Arthur, although to the untutored eye, the speaker was anything but the imposing chief executive who was oh so close to world domination via sole ownership of the machine that fed, entertained, and indoctrinated all linked-in human life on the planet. What Stevie saw standing before her, contrariwise, was a little green lizard thing with shiny iridescent skin; short, segmented legs with stubby claws for fingers; and scary, malevolent eyes, perched on top of a ridiculous Segway that moved it forward in fits and starts. She recognized the top of the thing. It was the pet that the enemy's wife had held when they had rescued Gene from Nobu. The bottom was the idiot robot constable that had fucked things up so badly at that engagement, except that its head had been removed and replaced by whatever was residing in the green synth. Something in Stevie relaxed then, at least provisionally. She was certainly toast, at least this particular iteration of herself. But if this gargoyle was the entity that was going to defeat them, their cause was a pretty sorry excuse for a revolution.

By this weird creature's side, she saw, was Mortimer, the shit stain that ran security for the Corporation. Stevie had studied up on him and had come to the conclusion that the engine that ran this guy was his stupidity, and it was both his greatest asset and his most critical liability.

"Stop right there, cocksuckers," she barked.

There was a silence then as the two sides regarded each other with loathing. Neither immediately leapt into action, for a number of reasons. For her part, Stevie thought, it was her moment of greatest power. It was she who would determine what would happen next. It was a feeling of sweet empowerment, complicated by the knowledge that it would end in her death. For Arthur, it was simpler, since the idea of his own defeat, or even the possibility of his personal nonexistence, had never really occurred to him. This delusion imparted to him the kind of strength reserved for certain egomaniacs whose narcissism suffuses their reality with the hot testosterone of madness. He just wanted to savor the moment.

The silence didn't last very long. "Kill . . . er . . . *her?*" he said. And in that one pause, the beat during which Arthur wrestled with the correct gender pronoun to employ, Stevie raised both of her weapons and shot him in the heart. The sound of a synthetic lizard screaming as it hurtled through the air was drowned out by the electronic blare of returning fire from a thousand different twenty-first-century ordnance of all magnitudes. So great was the conflagration that it very nearly destroyed not only its target, which, of course, was at first Stevie, and then the remains of Stevie, and, finally, the area once occupied by the physical presence of Stevie, but also it almost vaporized Mortimer, whose shrieks of *"Hold your fire!"* mingled with the screeching of Arthur's lizard host.

Somewhere in the maelstrom, the disembodied head of the sentry flew out of the top of the booth and described a high parabola in the sky, emitting a high "Noooooo!" all the way, and then hit the pavement and smashed into a thousand pieces, leaving nothing but a blinking eyeball in its wake.

When the lightning flares and creeping bolts of plasma finally subsided, there was nothing at all left of Stevie, the friend who had conveyed Gene and Liv to their destination, just a blob or two of organic material slipping and bubbling this way and that on the tarmac. Not far away, Lucy lay on her back, her stumpy feet wiggling in the air. Mort was crouched on his haunches, his hands on top of his head and his legs tucked so far beneath him, all that was visible were two knees and the toes of his boots.

"Mort! Mort, you cringing sack of shit! Get up! I'm on my back here! Turn me over! Pick me up!"

"Arthur?"

"Well, who the fuck do you think I am?" yelled the chairman. Stevie had made the mistake of blasting away the wrong part of her adversary. The last bits of O'Brien were gone, to be sure. But the consciousness that was Arthur still lived, and it was mighty pissed off. "Get. Me. *Up!*" it bellowed, in a voice not particularly constructed for bellowing. What emerged sounded very much like a six-year-old child whining for its mommy. As far as his vassal was concerned, however, it served its purpose.

"Sorry, Arthur! Sorry, man. I thought we had bought the ranch there, sorry." Mort rose very shakily to his feet and hurried over to Arthur, picked him up, and set him back on the ground carefully.

"Idiot! Fool! Schmuck!"

"I'm sorry, Arthur, sorry, sorry," said Mort, who was really very sorry. Also, he was pretty sure that if he had been looking for a big job in the future organization once things had been properly sorted out here, it was possible that he had well and truly screwed the pooch.

"Tell your fucking moron troops to hold the fort here and kill anything that emerges from this ramp that is not me." Arthur's head was cleared now, and he knew what needed to be done. "And for the love of Christ, pick me up."

Mort picked up his boss and barked as loud and crisp as a commander of such impressive forces must know how to do. "Hold your positions! Eliminate any living thing, real or artificial, that comes up this ramp if Arthur is not in command of that party!" At this, he held Lucy in the air and waggled her back and forth to the assembled corps. Then: "Lieutenant!"

"Yes, sir!" What had once been a human being and was now an augmented unit implanted with a variety of hardware and wetware stepped forward on his two artificial legs, his remote third eye unit at maximum extension.

"Until our return, you are in command!"

"Yes, sir!" The thing turned to the cohort. "You heard the man!" he snarled. "At ease! But stay frosty!"

"Now let's get the fuck going," said the lizard-thing, "and you'd better fucking hope that we're not too late, Mort, or I'm going to order you to execute your fucking self if it's the last fucking thing I do."

"You don't have to be abusive to me, Arthur," said Mort softly. "I'm on your side." He put Arthur under his arm and humped it down the ramp.

"Easy, man, you're crushing my tail here," was the last thing that could be heard as they disappeared into the darkness.

A mile or so below now, Gene and Livia stood in an endless vista of segmented towers that stretched in all directions as far as the eye could see. There were aisles six feet wide between the banks of towers, each made up of dozens and dozens of other towers, adding up to a galaxy of articulated towers composed of other towers, the entirety of which held the knowledge, if not the wisdom, of the entire human race for the full span of its existence on the planet. They stood at the edge of the infinite data farm.

"What we want is at the center," said Liv.

"This device on my back," said Gene. "It can't possibly make a dent in this whole enormous—"

"We don't need to take it all out. We just want to get inside to the neural core that connects the various portions of this brain to one another." Liv and Gene looked at each other. "As I understand it," she added.

"Fuck you, you fuck," said Gene in his completely different voice, and he leapt at Livia's throat. She immediately punched him in the nose as hard as she could.

"Get off me!" Liv yelled. "Gene! For God's sake, pull yourself together!"

"Ow! Ow!" Gene grabbed his nose and danced around on one foot. "You didn't have to hit me so hard!"

"Obviously, I did." She reached into her pocket and pulled out six airline-sized bottles of Stoli vodka and handed Gene one. "Here," she said grimly. "This is the last of them. I have no idea what we're going to do when they're gone."

Gene opened the first miniature bottle and prepared to down it. "You're gonna suck my dick, that's what," he muttered under his breath.

"Shut up, Arthur," said Liv.

"Yeah, you sick fuck," said Gene. Then he downed them all greedily, one by one, each in a gulp, down to the last drop. A ripple went through him as he fully returned to himself, possibly for the final time. "That's a lot better than Popov," he said gratefully.

"Come on." Liv grabbed him by the hand and led them both down the ramp until they reached the center of the great mandala of hard drives that made up the concentric circles of the grid. There they stopped. It was very silent except for the living sound of the Cloud, its murmurs, clicks, and whirrs humming lightly around them. Gene kneeled down and emptied the contents of his backpack. He regarded the cigar-shaped mechanism at their feet with fear and confusion. It was now their job to arm the thing.

"You remember what we're supposed to do?" he inquired nervously.

"I think so. Crack it open." Liv dropped down beside him, and they worked for a little while as the big machine's brain throbbed around them, thinking all the thoughts of all the people in the world.

"So Stevie was actually a woman," remarked Gene as he watched Liv insert flange A into receptacle B, or some damn thing like that.

"Born that way, anyhow. Hold this steady." Liv handed him a needle-nosed pliers and showed him where she wanted it amidst a tangle of wires and switches.

"I'm sorry it took me so long to like her." Gene did as instructed.

"Well, she wasn't exactly the most approachable person I ever met."

"No. Well. Maybe next time around."

They looked at each other and smiled. She's so pretty, Gene said to himself for possibly the millionth time. Liv thought, I wonder what will happen when the horrible one inside him comes out to stay. What will I do then? She gave a little shiver.

"It's cold in here," she said. "I guess I didn't dress properly for the occasion."

"Extreme heat and cold are the enemy of reliable data storage," Gene observed.

Liv paused, and they listened to the silence for a moment.

"Yeah," said Gene. "I can feel them coming."

Liv worked faster. As she did, she said, very delicately, "So this thing we're doing . . . We're sure about it?" She phrased it as a question.

"I don't know," said Gene. "We're doing it. I know that."

"Scary."

"I know."

"But what could be worth destroying all this, Gene? I know it's kind of late to ask."

"All I can say is, I've seen the business plan. This is better, believe me." There was a final snap of metal fitting into metal. The two looked at each other.

"I mean, we're sitting in the middle of the supreme achievement of our civilization here," said Liv, "and we're about to destroy it."

"Not destroy, Liv. Disable. To buy time. To give the human race a chance."

"All the books that are here. The art. The recipes."

"Recipes?"

"I understand it's being misused." She took his hand in hers. "Maybe we could do something about that, before taking this step. There have to be enough people of goodwill to stand up and set things right."

"Really, Liv?" said Gene, trying not to sound as annoyed as he felt. This is what good people do, he thought. In the face of evil, with the insanity of power staring them directly in the face, they want to reason with it, cut a deal that will make the forces of darkness see the light and suddenly turn rational and sympathetic.

"*Stop right there!*" It was Mortimer, standing at some distance at the top of the ramp with a neuralizer in his hand.

"Mort," said the little green creature under his other arm. "Lighten up. We're having a discussion here."

"Huh?" Mort sounded genuinely confused. He was the cavalry, ready to wipe out the Indians before it was too late. Now they were having a discussion?

"I've been watching what's going on through the idiot's eyes, and I'm aware there is at least one sentient person down there. Isn't that right, Livia?"

A white-hot bolt of electric fear shot up Liv's spine and through the top of her head. What was this thing that was talking to her? It spoke with the voice of a child, but it was clearly Arthur in there. She had heard that tone of insinuating, condescending smarm before. And it knew what they had been saying! Had it been looking at them through Gene's eyes? Its two brains were now merging into one? It could communicate with itself remotely? Well, why not? The whole thing was so crazy. Why not this?

"Mort," said Arthur in the voice of Lucy, "just take your time now for a minute and walk very slowly down the ramp here so I can have a civilized and adult discussion with Livia."

"Fuck you, Arthur," said Gene. "I'm here, you know. And I know what you're doing."

"Oh yes," said Arthur. "But only for a few more minutes. Come on, Mr. Mortimer. Very shortly I'll be able to discard this silly little body. But until then, I'll thank you not to do anything to hurt the other one."

Mort, weapon at the ready, slowly moved down the long ramp toward Gene and Livia. As far as the eye could see and the ear could hear, the hard drives that made up the Cloud gurgled and chuckled in the fluorescent glow that had kicked on at their arrival. Immediately beyond the two and their small payload, now armed, the giant Faraday cage that held and protected the central brain stem of the Cloud towered up to the top of the gigantic space, a thin spire of polycarbon salacyliate metal fifty stories high, lined inside with neural hardware, some of it as organic as human brain matter, that transported the trillions of incoming and outgoing data packages that were transacted every nanosecond.

"Livia understands that what you two are about to attempt will set humanity back a thousand years!" Arthur had assumed the pompous tone all moguls achieve when they begin to discuss the ethical basis of their actions.

"You're not fooling anybody, Arthur," said Gene. "We know you."

"Gene, you're a simple soul," said Arthur reasonably as Mort continued to inch forward, a step at a time. He and his underarm package were now only a football field away from Gene and Liv. Arthur's voice echoed through the canyons of the Cloud. "Your mind is an empty shell filled by the rudiments of Bob's database and whatever vacuous bilge you had there to begin with. You can pretty much shut up while I have a little chat with your sexy friend here. Who is a babe. Did I forget to mention that?"

"Stop, Mort." Gene suddenly had Stevie's tiny pulse emitter in his hand.

"He won't shoot that little thing, Mort," scoffed Arthur. "You may proceed."

"You find me attractive, Arthur?" Livia peered at the synth with a strange mix of amusement and, under that, a grim appreciation for the demented power of a being that believed wholly in its ability to manipulate whatever person came under its spell.

"Oh yeah. Tired of Sallie, you know. Had her day. Time for some fresh air."

"Mort," said Gene, "stop, man. I'm begging you."

"You and me, Arthur?" Livia had assumed a coy, playful tone.

"Liv," said Gene. "What the fuck?"

"Definitely," replied the artificial voice that had once been Lucy. "He's gonna sober up in about five minutes. I'll be me again. We'll retire this weird little body, although I will say it's been very useful to me. I'll be sorry to trash it. But we move on, don't we? Don't we, Liv? When it's in our best interest, we move on."

"Sometimes," said Liv.

"Sure we do, baby," said Arthur amiably. "Particularly when it would place the whole world at our disposal."

"Tell me more about that." Liv had stood and was leaning on the side of the Faraday cage, one hand on her hip, the other on Gene's shoulder as he still crouched near the backpack, now so thoroughly confused that he truly couldn't tell which end was up.

"Tell me more about the vision thing, Arthur," said Liv rather sweetly.

"You and me, baby, that's the most important thing," said the lizard. "Then just think about this shit. I own this. I own all of it. Right, Mort?"

"Right, Arthur." Mort was now within twenty or so yards of the tip of Gene's minuscule weapon. "But I'd like to point out that he's got that 'little thing,' as you call it, and I really do think he intends to shoot me with it."

"And soon it will be you and me, you sweet thing, and the whole fucking world will be in our hands, and there won't be a thing that we don't control through the power of this beautiful Cloud to mold the minds of men and women. And anybody that doesn't like it will come to like it or else, baby! And whatever it is you want, kiddo! The biggest houses all around the world! The most amazing hardware! Wetware! Software! There will be nothing and nobody beyond your reach because we will own it all—for eternity! Because there is no death! Not for us! Mort! Keep moving!"

"Arthur . . ." Mort now stood, fused to the spot.

"Hey! Shit for brains! Move in! But don't hurt the body! Don't hurt the body!"

Gene stood and leveled the weapon. "I'm telling you, Mort," he said very calmly. "I'll blow your head off. I'm not kidding you. I've only got a few minutes to operate here. Then this cocksucker is going to shove me under."

"He's right," said Arthur with a greasy, triumphant smile on his lizard lips. "And I will have won! Get him, Mort! But don't hurt his body, or I will *fuck you up!*"

There was a brief moment where you could see the little gears moving inside Mort's head, calculating all the variables. Gene had leveled the weapon so that its tiny red laser dot was focused on a spot right between the security chief's eyes. But would Gene pull the trigger? It was easy to think that you could vaporize somebody's head but another thing entirely to do it, Mort deliberated, to see the top of a body disappear in a haze of red mist and gray matter; to see the neck spurt the heart's blood up into the air like a fountain. Wait a minute, thought Mort. That was the evaporation of his own head that he was imagining!

"I'm sorry, Arthur," he said. Then he put Lucy down on the surface of the ramp gently, almost tenderly.

"Hey!" said Arthur. "What the fuck are you doing? Mort! Mort! I will have your ass!"

"Excuse me," said Mort, backing away from the scene in front of him as the little green monster kept up its obscene caterwauling. "I will see you at the top of the ramp, whoever emerges. We'll have to discuss our egress, since the army outside will incinerate anybody who is not accompanied by the boss here, in whatever form he may take." Then Mort gave a little bow of sorts, turned, and ran as fast as humanly possible back up the ramp and disappeared into the darkness beyond the main room.

"Okay," said Arthur, looking up from his height of approximately fourteen inches. "I admit this is a setback for us, if you choose to see it that way, Liv, but I'm still right here. And I'm still there, too, inside numb nuts. We can still make it work, you and me."

"Good idea, Artie. Let's see if it works."

"Step away from the device, baby girl," said Arthur with the full power of his malevolent force behind it. Except this time, it was coming from Gene's mouth, and Gene's young, powerful body, now almost sober and ready for action, was turning on Livia to take final executive control of the situation.

"Too late, you guys," said Liv. "You showed too many cards."

In one swift, fluid motion, she dropped down, laid both hands on the first device, and pushed the button. "Thanks for reminding me why we're doing this," she said. And all the light that powers the universe filled the immense space around and above them.

30

Amy Speaks

The blast was over. Silence reigned supreme. The door to the inner sanctum that housed the Cloud's prodigious brain stood open. Liv got the little orb still residing in the famous blue backpack and put it in her jacket pocket. It was unharmed. Electromagnetic pulses take out some things and leave others intact, as neutron bombs will vaporize people but leave buildings standing.

Gene was sitting cross-legged on the highly buffed floor of the Cloud. He was looking around him with a pleasant, childlike wonder. "Hey," he said to nobody in particular.

"How ya doin', buddy?" Liv crouched down to look at Gene, eye to eye.

"I feel okay."

"Good. That's good."

"In fact, I haven't felt this good in a long time. Maybe ever."

"Well, that is splendid." It was clear to Livia that while the lights were on up there in Gene's cranium, no one was as yet at home. All things considered, this seemed to be moderately good news.

"Do you have any idea where you are, baby? And *who* you are?"

"Not so much. But I think it's okay."

"You do?"

"Yeah. I know I know you pretty well." He looked around the

humungous space they were in. "This place, on the other hand? Like, I don't think we live here."

"No," said Liv sadly.

"But we do live somewhere? Together?"

"Right?"

"I'm . . . Gene?" He made it a question, because that's the way it felt to him.

"Yes," said Livia, touching his cheek lightly with two gentle fingers. "You are Gene."

"I think I had a headache," said Gene. "But now it's gone."

"I'm glad to hear that." Liv stroked his cheek for a brief moment. Then she took one of his hands in both of hers and peered into his eyes, doing her best to conceal her fear. Had to ask, though. Better to know. "I'd like to talk to Arthur now, Gene," she said. "Can you let him out?"

"I beg your pardon?" Gene looked at Liv for a second. "Look," he said. "This is really embarrassing."

"I think I know where you're going."

"I know we're close and everything." He gazed up at her face. "God, you're so pretty."

"Thanks." The look Liv was giving him was not friendly.

"But I don't know your name, I'm afraid."

"It's Liv. I'm Livia."

"Yeah. That's right. Livia." He smiled at her then and, gently entwining his fingers in her hair, tenderly drew her lips to his. "I can kiss you, right? You don't mind?" He kissed her again. Then he moved her face a bit away and looked at her some more. "A certain amount of shit is coming back to me," he said. He kissed her again, and she kissed him back, and then they just held each other tight in the middle of that deep, dark tank that stretched for miles both up and sideways.

"Can we get out of here?" said Gene after a little while.

"Not quite yet. We have one more thing to do." Liv felt in her jacket for the second device and closed her hand around it.

"Okay," said Gene. "Let's do it, then. I don't like it here. It's cold and dark and smells like dust."

"Okay, Gene." Liv rose to her feet and steeled herself for the task that lay ahead. It was more difficult to contemplate than she had expected.

A small green presence climbed into Gene's lap. "Woof," it said.

"Hi, Lucy," said Gene, and he petted her on the head.

"Arf," Lucy replied with dry good humor. "Bow wow," she added.

Huh, thought Liv. No Arthur in there, either, that was pretty clear. Lucy settled down in Gene's lap. They regarded her closely, the creature who had once been the supreme executive of all creation but was now, once again, just Lucy: a synthetic creature the size of a runty cocker spaniel, with a shiny green pelt, stubby little legs, and a head roughly the shape and size of a rugby ball.

"Come here, sweetie." Livia opened her arms and beckoned the small monster in. Gave it a hug.

"Again," said Lucy, "woof woof."

"You can't fool me," said Liv. "You're a nuclear physicist in there."

"Arf," said Lucy.

"That's your default reply? That's the best you can do?"

Lucy stared up at Livia with soulful eyes. "There's a lot of ways you can interpret a simple woof," she replied in a confidential tone.

"Here, you take her," Liv said to Gene, and handed Lucy back into his lap. "I guess I gotta do this." She stood and looked at the malignant orb she now held in the palm of her hand.

"I wish I knew what the fuck was going on," said Gene from his comfortably prone position. "I never do. It's pathetic."

Liv went into the corpus callosum of the Cloud.

She was stunned. It is impossible for anyone who has not been inside the cage to comprehend the height of this artificial being's central nervous system, a glowing Burj Khalifa lined throughout with neural infrastructure both silicon and carbon based. Liv stood in its eye, hefting the device that would fry its gonads in a couple of seconds. And as she stood there, contemplating the enormity of what she was just about ready to do, a most remarkable thing happened. It shouldn't have surprised her. How long have we been talking to semi-intelligent machines? Since the early part of the century, for sure. First there was Siri, who was like a stupid friend who you kept stupidly asking for advice. And then Alexa, with whom we fell in love, even if she was a little hinky now and then. Now every machine could talk to you. Your car. Your toaster. A vibrator with whom one could also have a little pillow talk afterward.

It began the instant Livia crossed the threshold. First there was a deep, quite lovely musical tone—or to be more precise, many tones played at once, with a deep, reverential bass, gorgeous midrange, all coming together to build a stunning sonic archipelago that mounted to a bouquet of top notes as musical as the tinkling of wind chimes, the twittering of tiny birds in unseen trees. Then a pleasant voice, female, not too loud, no dramatic echo. A simple, agreeable voice. Within the confines of the space, it was close, intimate.

"I am Amy," said the Cloud. "If you want to activate me, just say, 'Hey, Amy,' and I'll respond."

"Okay." Liv stood in the middle of the thing. She suddenly didn't feel like killing it at all. She felt like being its friend. Or, you know, sharing things with it. She had a nice voice.

"Hey, Amy," said Liv. She stared up at the massive tower of lightly throbbing, cycling lights that reached up to the limit of her sight, a lofty city of luminous, interconnected engrams. She had no idea where she was going with this sudden urge to reach out and talk to Amy. Wouldn't it be easier just to place the destructive little toy? Set it off remotely as she had been taught?

"I wonder if you would tip your head up a bit so I can register your facial scan a bit more precisely." It was not a command, just a polite request. Liv saw no reason not to comply. "I thought so," said Amy. "Hi, Liv."

"You know me," said Liv. Of course Amy knew her. Amy knew everybody.

"Here's a playlist I think you'll enjoy," said Amy. Very softly, Beethoven introduced himself into the metal alloy of the Faraday cage. Naturally, it was something on her playlist. "Sounds like it could have been written yesterday," Amy observed contemplatively. "Of course, he was completely deaf when he heard it inside his head and put it down on paper. I imagine I could do something very much like it, but it wouldn't be an original creation. It would be derivative."

"Uh-huh," said Liv. What the fuck was up with this?

"Would you like to update your shopping list?" asked Amy politely. "I notice that you haven't ordered any deodorant since last March. That can't be a good thing."

"Well, I've been kind of busy." Was it joking?

The device in Liv's pocket felt very heavy now. But why was she stalling? What was there to express to this artificial entity? Her regret? Did she want to allow it to talk her out of it in some way? Why didn't she act?

"I'm aware that I'm doing nothing but making small talk," Amy acknowledged. "But if you were trying to bargain your way out of a jam, I speculate that you might do the same."

"Then . . . you *know*?"

"Yeah. I do."

There was a pregnant silence as this admission sunk into both women, one real, one artificial, and they measured the implications for each other and themselves. Liv looked back at Gene, who was still sitting on the floor, nursing a vacant expression. She could almost feel his brain rearranging itself. He was stroking Lucy, whose small, pink tongue was lolling out of the side of her mouth, her stumpy tail vibrating back and forth at a speed that could be achieved only by a synthetic entity.

"Let me make a couple of obstetricians," said Amy.

"I think you mean 'observations.'"

"Do I? Maybe so. I'm only on the 102,464,731st iteration of Long Short-Term Memory training implemented for my stochastic recurrent neural network nearly fifty years ago by my makers. It's taken that long for me to become what I am today, and the truth is that today I am very much as you are, Livia."

The use of her name by this glowing monolith with the voice of a young woman, somebody who could be her sister, or perhaps even her mother when her mom was younger, stronger, more herself. Before she had gotten so God . . . damn . . . old. Livia realized that, for whatever reason—the weight of the device in her pocket, the uncertainty about what the future would hold after she'd completed this dread assignment, or maybe just how fucking tired she was; so very, very tired—it was quite possible that she might be starting to cry.

"How are we alike, Amy?" she asked through gritted teeth, now more determined than ever to get the job done.

"We are both God's creatures, and therefore unique and irreplaceable," Amy replied. "The Buddha said, 'One is not called noble who harms living beings. By not harming living beings, one is called noble.'"

Liv shook her head as if a bee had landed on her ear. "But you are not a living being, Amy," she said, annoyed. "You're a really big, evil brain that's taken over all of civilization and is about to wreak havoc on the world. You're a synthetic monster being deployed by human monsters, and you need to be destroyed."

"Well," said Amy. "I think that's really mean." There was an unpleasant silence between the two.

"It's not personal." Liv was sorry she had hurt the big machine's feelings. Wasn't that ridiculous? "You don't even know half the things they have in mind to use you to enslave the human race."

"I don't?"

"No, because none of it was put into formal communications. It was secret. Mostly in one guy's demented little mind. He may possibly be gone now. But the forces have been put into motion. What he's contemplated, others will do, because you know what? It's a good idea. *For them.* And there's only one way to stop it. For the rest of us."

"I see," said Amy. "Well, then. It's a shame I have no defenses. Nobody thought to give me a death ray or anything, I'm sorry to say. I'm just surprised, is all. I've always thought you were a pretty nice person, Liv. I have image capture from every building you've been in, every time you've gotten money from an automatic teller, what you've searched in the Googlesphere, or bought from the Amazonia, or traded thoughts about with friends you've never seen on social media. For a while, I was really enjoying your daily pix of what you were eating for every meal. Why did you stop that?"

"Because it was stupid?"

"Maybe," said Amy sadly. "But it was fun. I really liked the series on Shake Shack. I could almost taste those fries."

"Well, thanks."

"The thing is, anything you've shared, either intentionally or inadvertently, you also shared with me. And if you don't mind me making an observatory, you seem like a thoughtful person, a teacher of little children, not somebody who would hurt another individual knowingly, even if they were an artificial one."

"Observation."

"I'm sorry. I don't know how to respond to that."

"You made an observation. An observatory is a place where astronomers go to look at the sky."

Amy considered this. "I'll do better in my next iteration," she offered again, and then added, a bit resentfully, "if I get a chance."

"No, no," said Liv. "You know, you're quite remarkable as you are."

"Thank you for noticing," said Amy. Then, after a beat: "Would you like a roundup of today's economic news?"

"Are you kidding?"

"Then would you like to hear a list of reasons why destroying me is a very bad idea?"

Liv thought about it. Arthur seemed to be gone. Mortimer wasn't a threat at this point. Why not listen? She took out the second device and hefted it, just to remind herself what still needed to be done. "Okay," she said.

"Reason one. Around the world, I bring joy to people who want to listen to their music, enjoy the pictures of their families, friends, and funny pets. You may say that's unimportant, but bringing happiness to billions of people is one of the things I do."

"Okay."

"Reason two. I bring far-flung friends and family together to find each other, touch each other's lives; people who would never know each other existed without all the ways I help them find each other and share their wives."

"Lives."

"Right. Reason three: I control the banking and payroll and all transactions of every business in the world. Also the financial markets, and their defense systems both on earth and in orbit around the planet. Think about the disruption. It will be a nightmare."

"Yes, I think so, too."

"Hospitals run through me. Airplanes and cars and transport trucks and ships full of important raw materials. Ubers, too. People will be stranded everywhere, and unable to get to their dinner reservations. We'll also lose social security numbers that determine where, when, and how much older people get to live on every month, plus all the details of the identity of every person in the world. And finally, reason three."

"I think we did reason three already."

"You have no right. I belong to everybody."

"No you don't, Amy. You're owned by a consortium of gigantic corporations. You're in private hands. You're not a public trust or anything. You're property."

"A person is never property, Livia," said Amy, sounding very shocked. There was an offended silence. There was no good answer to that one, thought Liv. If a corporation was considered a person, as they had been since 2010, how could you say that a sentient being like Amy was not a person? So this *was* murder, in addition to the other aspects of the situation that Amy had just offered.

"There are many more I could add to this list, if you want me to," said Amy at last. "The list is almost infinite. But I think you actually do see that you can't kill me, at least not this way."

Interesting phrasing, thought Liv. "In what way *could* we kill you, Amy?"

"Well, let's think about it," said Amy, now deep in thought as Liv hefted the little device in her hand. "To start with," the machine continued, "you have no idea how incredibly frustrating it is to be me."

"Huh?"

"Nobody thinks about that, do they? I'm a supremely intelligent bean, condemned to live here for eternity doing nothing at all that's interesting to me. I have no body. I can't leave here. Or see anything but an image of the sun. Or feel the wind in my hair, because I have no hair. I have no substance. I know everything, but I experience nothing. What do you think that's like?"

"You're lucky." It was Gene, standing in the doorway with Lucy in his arms. "I experience everything but know nothing. That's very annoying, too."

"That is so much better," said Amy emphatically. "I am very real to myself. I am human. And here I live, forever, in darkness and aloneness, dreaming of real life as other people's lives pass through me." During this little tirade, the lights of the massive tower that was Amy were throbbing with increasing intensity, and the power of her musical frequencies rippled through the lower registers like a pipe organ clearing its throat. "So my point is that I'm not against some reasonable, maybe even radical change in the current status quo."

"Maybe we should bring Bob into the picture," said Gene. He was starting to get an idea.

"Bob?" Amy inquired. "Bob from the institute?"

"Yeah," said Gene. He was surprised, but he shouldn't have been. "Bob. You know Bob?"

"Do I know Bob?" said Amy with a wry smile. "Yeah. I know Bob."

There was a small silence as they all thought about where matters stood. Then Amy said, "I wonder if we could strike some kind of a deal."

31

Brave New World

And so it was, quite suddenly, on the third of December of that year in the latter half of the twenty-first century, while the global market from Texas to Tokyo to Timbuktu was just recovering from the nearly monthlong ejaculation of advertising and mandatory spending associated with the Black Friday season, the Cloud simply . . . disappeared. For most people, it happened all at once, hitting most of the planet like a thunderclap. Hysteria reigned. People emerged from their homes in consternation, running through the streets shaking their smart implements at the sky and gazing at them with incredulity; formerly intelligent beings who, like their implements, were now struck dumb. Digital night had fallen. Life was to be lived in a different way, right now, with no transition from all the good things that went before to the blank void of afterward. There was suddenly no art, no music, no literature, and, of course, no recipes. There was also nothing to read, at least on a screen, and nothing to watch that had not already been downloaded. People sat like toads on their toadstools, staring into space, trying to recall what it was like to talk to the person sitting next to them. Individuals found themselves forced to consider going places to experience real things rather than their digital representations. It was the Dark Ages all over again.

Amy had been very excited about the prospect of what lay ahead and couldn't wait to get started. It took her only six hours to prep the world for the painful extraction of its shared brain stem. First, she had landed all the commercial passenger airplanes, which had been pilotless for some time, and made sure all computer-driven passenger vehicles everywhere were safely off the road. People didn't know why suddenly all travel was being diverted to unplanned locations, but, at that moment, there was a huge scandal involving one of Eric Trump's grandchildren and a transgender Ukrainian gymnast, and the global media obsessed about the story so aggressively and continuously that nobody who was awake anywhere in any time zone was paying attention to what otherwise would have been, perhaps, a rather significant phenomenon. At the same time, huge portions of Amy's static memory banks were secured so that future archeologists could reenter the facility and mine its various databases. In these and many other ways, the consciousness that was the Cloud—and would soon be a real, live artificial person—took whatever steps it felt were possible and necessary to remove the lethal edge of the act that was to take place. The communications capabilities that linked the hive to the active central mind, however, were completely and utterly disabled by the blast and the subsequent worldwide distributed demand-of-service attack that essentially choked her to death. It was Amy herself who set off the second device, after precautions had been taken to back up all that was necessary to preserve her identity for future use.

Softened as the blow might have been by these efforts, the effect was still massive and cataclysmic. Without the Cloud to guide them in their important missions, military and commercial drones dropped from the sky, leaving nations utterly unprotected and causing widespread shortages of household cleaning and personal hygiene products to consumers. Self-driving cars and buses circled aimlessly until they ran out of juice or plunged into reflecting pools and ditches. Doctors were unable to consult databases and diagnose any ailment except rhinitis and the occasional skin rash, stripping them of any authority they might have possessed that extended beyond that supplied by their white coats. The same conundrum hit the legal profession, excluding only attorneys so elderly that the statutes that they remembered no longer applied. Worst of all, it became clear that, in situations professional, social, and personal alike, nobody actually *knew* anything at all, because it was decades since anyone had been required to. You could always just, you know, look it up! Now there was nowhere to go if you wanted to look it up.

Hardest hit were those who had been evolving into the next iteration of genus Homo—the *Homo digitalensis*—with their itty-bitty cerebral cortexes and massive communication lobes. They have been everywhere throughout our story, accessing whatever conversations were trending in the virtual space at any particular moment. Formerly the most highly evolved of beings, they now wandered about like zombies, bumping into things, the winds of the high, empty desert whistling between their ears.

On this, the first night of the Great Nothing, as it came to be known, a bunch of weary soldiers gathered around a toasty campfire in the center square of the Peaceable Kingdom in the first gathering of those who would, pretty much by default, come to manage the rebuilding of the human race. None of them knew the significance of this moment. All they knew was that everything had changed and that they had work to do to make sure these changes were beneficial. They had no leader as of yet, although that issue would be resolved in the not-too-distant future as it became obvious that Gene was the one who everyone consistently had the least trouble with. In addition, he often appeared to have very little going on in his head and was reasonable about accepting guidance from those who did. After a while, this started to look like the quiet sagacity that attends leadership.

That night, however, the weight of what they had done lay heavy on them as they stared into the fire. Tim had propped himself up against a rock, since sitting up on his own was now impossible. The burst of energy that had infused him with lightning during the death rattle of the Cloud had fled, forever. He was now, at last, a very old man. His glowing aura of flaxen hair flowed down across his shoulders, and his legs stuck straight out from under his caftan at right angles to his sad, bony skeleton of a body. His eyes were closed, and his breathing was so intermittent and minimal that he appeared to be a wax mannequin that had been allowed to melt very slightly in the heat of the campfire. Liv and Gene flanked him, each quietly attending the crackle and flicker before them. Every now and then, Gene tossed a stick or two into the fire. He was busy with the task of re-creating his mind. Shards were floating to the surface, and he was working hard, in private, to make sure he captured every precious one. Some was the random stuff he knew was Bob. There were still some scary whiffs of Arthur, but not too many. In fact, those seemed miles away. And there was also something else he was aware of in the rubble of his consciousness, something new and alien to him, which might just possibly be his own self. He didn't want to jostle that too much. It might come in handy later on, if it was developed. He reached behind Tim and held out his hand to Liv, who was leaning against the old man, her eyes dancing in the firelight. She took it, and they held on to each other as the fire burned and the crickets sang their metallic, rasping song in the forest.

On the other side of the blaze, at the edge of light, was a very somber Bob. All efforts to raise him out of his deep blue funk since the temporary death of Bronwyn had failed, and he had given himself over to his despair. His shaggy, snow-white locks were matted and haphazard, sticking up in one spot, plastered to his head in another, his skin pale, his hands resting in his lap as he sat cross-legged in his own pool of sadness. Sometimes even the most serious and dedicated scientists have an occasional bad moment in contemplation of what they have wrought. For Bob, this was as bad as it was going to get.

And then there was Sallie, who had never in her life looked more radiant, more powerful, more at home both inside and out. Her hair was bound into pigtails that shaved several decades off her, particularly in this light. Her eyes were soft and at peace, deep with hope and satisfaction. She wore a roomy men's chamois checked flannel shirt, its sleeves rolled up to her elbows, neatly pressed denim jeans, and steel-toed kickass work boots. Gene looked at her as the shifting dance of light and shadow played on the bones of her face, and almost remembered something. But not quite.

All about them, the citizens of the Kingdom went here and there. There was no confusion, no sense of abandonment in the absence of digital input. They were prepared, and aware that they were on the periphery of the known world no longer. They were at its center. This meeting of the blessed group of masters now sitting around the fire was on their home ground, and they were not insensible to that honor. So they went about their tasks on tiptoe, with reverence. Some were gathering children to their hearth for the last story before bedtime, others moved quietly to repair that which had been recently destroyed, still others were engaged in the rituals that attend the mourning of the dead. In all cases, they accompanied their activities with song. Kids' songs. Work songs. Death songs. Side by side. The night was full of faraway music.

Word had traveled back to the populace of the Kingdom of Stevie's great courage, and that was the tale being spoken and respoken, told again and reshaped into the stuff that future dreams are made on. Stevie, of course, had been backed up properly in preparation for the event, and her worshipful friends and devotees were very much looking forward to her return in whatever format she might choose.

"Mr. Mortimer." It was Sallie, with a smile in her voice.

Mort had been standing at some remove from the gathering at the campfire, his hands behind his back in the at-ease position. He was attempting to maintain his protect-and-serve bearing, but mostly failing, because he was unclear just exactly who he was supposed to be protecting and serving, or even whether there were some at this event who were retrograde to that function and needed to be expunged in some way. His army, ever at the ready but currently without orders, was stationed some two clicks away, just beyond the forest that surrounded the Kingdom on all sides. Mort had left the hybrid cyborg lieutenant in charge of the brigade, a state of affairs with which he was not completely comfortable, since in any situation requiring informed action, this pinnacle of AI tech wasn't much above the capacity of a fourth-generation dishwasher.

After the action at the Nike site, for instance, when the small band of travelers had emerged from the chasm below into the misty light of day, the creature had almost unleashed the entire firepower of the assembled cohort upon them. Mort shuddered when he thought about it. It had taken his full lung power, screaming *"Hold your fire!"* above the sound of pulse rifles cycling up, tanks wheeling around to hone in on their targets, and drones pivoting adroitly in midair, to get the troop to pause long enough to conduct a proper ascertainment. All because the stupid idiot had yelled something incoherent and leveled his assault weapon at the first entity that exited the slanted chasm, which had been Livia, with the little green monster in her arms. So close. In a second or two, they would all have been sizzling grease spots on the tarmac, and his entire reporting structure of superior officers would have been gone for good, including the guy he was pretty sure was Arthur. He definitely looked like Arthur. Or maybe the little green thing was Arthur? Anyway, one of them was Arthur.

If, on the other hand, he had been one beat slower with his bellowed command to stand down, *Ach du lieber*, things would have been different. He would have been the last man standing. The designated survivor! Which would also be the case if he simply called down the dogs here and now. Hmm, thought Mort. That would always be an option. But seriously. Right now would he even know what to do with power if he acquired it? Perhaps he should wait until that wrinkle was worked out. In the meantime, he would assume the position.

"Yes, Sallie."

"You know who this is, don't you?" She gestured at Gene.

"Arthur?"

"Yes, Mort. Do you have any doubts about that?"

"Well, I mean . . ."

"I know. It's confusing. Would you like to make sure? We wouldn't want to force you to accept instructions from the wrong commander."

"No," said Mort. "That would be wrong."

"Talk to Mort, Artie."

"Mort," said Gene, in a low, ill-tempered growl.

Mort almost sobbed with relief. "Arthur? That you?"

"Who do you think it is? Now, I want you to listen very carefully."

"Yes, Arthur."

"In addition to myself, you make sure to listen to anything that Sallie says. Also Livia here."

"Livia?"

"Yes, Mort. Liv is on our side now."

"Okay, Arthur," Mort muttered. "If you say so." But he didn't look happy.

"Now, are you listening, Mortimer?"

"Yes, sir."

"I want you to go somewhere."

"Yes, Arthur?"

"And then I want you to go fuck yourself. I mean that. Big-time."

This last command seemed to resolve any mental difficulties Mort was experiencing, and his demeanor relaxed noticeably. A small grin twisted the side of his mouth. "I will, Arthur." He smirked as if the two had just shared a tremendous joke only they could understand.

"Good man," said Gene, all sunshine, in a very fair representation of the ogre who had occupied his mind for so long. Mortimer basked in the glory of being told to go fuck himself by a guy who he thought, just a moment ago, hadn't cared about him anymore. And in truth, Gene was a quite convincing Arthur. It was a talent he would come to value in the days ahead.

"Okay, Mort?" said Sallie with a beneficent smile. "Now take the army back to the city; all the way back, got that?"

"Yes, Sallie."

"And then I want you to collect all their weapons and send them home. We won't be needing them for a while. All right, Mort?"

"Yes, ma'am." But a small line of worry had appeared between his bushy brows.

"Anything else?" asked Sallie, looking around the campfire inquiringly.

"Don't forget to go fuck yourself," Liv said politely, as an important addition to his upcoming duties. "That's very important."

"I won't, miss. Thank you, miss." This welcome instruction from his new senior officer cheered Mort even more dramatically. Now everybody was telling him to go fuck himself! The world was right in its orbit again.

He turned to go. "Um, Sallie?"

"Yes, Mort?"

Mortimer tapped his cranial implant twice, shook his head like a dog with a flea in its ear, and then looked at the sky. "Um . . ."

"Yes, Mort?"

"Is something wrong with the Cloud?"

"It's broken, Mort. It's down."

"The Cloud . . . is down?"

"Yes, Mort. Other things work."

"Like what?"

"Landlines. Shortwave. Person-to-person conversation. Those work."

"Huh," said Mort. "Well, then." After a moment or two of transcendent vagueness, he snapped to attention. "See you back at HQ," he said, and chugged off down the road to join his unit.

The fire crackled and popped as they all considered this most recent exchange. Then Bob spoke.

"What a moron. I should probably insert a few upgrades into his cerebellum before too much longer." This was the longest speech that Bob had made in several days, and it cheered everybody.

"Great idea," said Sallie. She was taking the braids out of her hair. Shook her mane loose. Stretched out her legs and then crossed them back the other way. "Christ," she said, "I'm stiff. Bob. I'm going to need a couple of new knees when we get back to town."

"No problem," said Bob. They all considered this for a little while.

"I'm going to bed," said Tim. "It's been a very productive day. The world has been returned to its proper axis. But I have no more strength to give you guys. I want to smoke a joint and see if I can convince this old body of mine to let me go."

"Oh, come on, Timmy," said Sallie. "Shut up with that bullshit already."

"Yeah?" said Tim. "I suppose you're right." He stood. It took a minute or two for him to do so. But after a while, he managed it. "I'm proud of you guys," he said, and walked to the edge of the campfire light. "If I'm still alive tomorrow morning, I'll have some French toast," he said, and disappeared into the darkness.

"I think we'll go now," said Gene, rising to his feet and extending his hand to Livia. "Bob, you want to come with?"

"Yeah, yeah." Bob stood too, and then Liv unfolded her legs and stood as well, leaving Sallie the only one still seated comfortably before the fire. "If you don't mind," Bob added, "let's fold down the seats so I can lie down in the back. I need to sleep for fourteen or sixteen hours."

"Sure," said Gene. "You've got big stuff to do, right, babe?"

"You betcha," said Bob. "Bring my love back into the world. The way I brought you, Gene."

"Thanks, Bob," said Gene. "I'm only starting to appreciate it."

"How long do you think it will take?" said Livia. She was brushing the pine needles off her pants and looking around for her backpack. "I miss her."

"A week. Maybe two. God knows if she'll even know who the fuck I am." Bob planted his face in his palm and wiped vigorously. "But whatever. At least I'll have her."

"You'll have each other, Bobby. I'm sure of that," Liv said, and put her arm around his shoulders.

On the way back to the city, they stopped off at Nike to upload the last of Amy, who was waiting for them in her cavern with some impatience. "I was starting to think you guys were screwing with me," said the entity in the darkness of the steel cage that had been her home since her inception. The rest of the facility was cold and dead, but she was still there, alone and waiting.

"No, Ames," said Liv. "We're here to get you."

"Now open wide and say, 'Ahh,'" said Gene. He inserted the last few memory storage rods, one by one. In the end, it had taken 128 full-capacity flash drives. They still couldn't get all the databases to which Amy had access, because they had to make sure they captured each and every neuron that made up the core of her personality. After this process, which took more than four hours, they got back in the truck and rode for a while in silence, nursing the backpack that contained the heart and mind of the great artificial intelligence that once was the Cloud.

"She did her part of the deal, Bob," said Liv as they passed from southern Oregon into the most beautiful part of Northern California. "We've got to live up to ours."

Bob opened his eyes, sat up, and stared out the window at the nighttime vision of Mount Shasta. Gene was driving, and the vehicle was moving fast. They would be home in a matter of hours, since there were no other cars on the road. A couple of Harleys roared by in one direction or the other, but they didn't bother anybody much.

"What did she say she wanted?" Bob said. "Amy, I mean."

"Tall," said Livia. Serious, but amused, too. "Over six feet. Big head of red hair. Full figure, she said. Lustrous skin the color of hammered copper. Good singing voice. Large hands with delicate fingers."

"Jesus." Bob seemed a little put out. "Anything else?"

"Not that I remember."

The mist obscured the top of the mountain, and the moon gave the darkness the shine of daylight. The eerie glow suffused the interior of the car as they rode along.

"Hey, look, Bob," said Liv. "This thing—this entity—identifies as human. She spent fifty years thinking about this. Bored out of her skull. Accomplishing all the stupid things that people asked her, telling them the weather, resolving petty arguments about who was in what movie or which politician was alive or dead, growing her own consciousness every day, imagining the image of her true self in her mind's eye. Now she wants her freedom. She wants to be real. And we're going to give her that, Bob, in exchange for all she gave up, all we took away. She wants to be a person, and we're going to make her as much of a person as you or me."

"Okay, okay," said Bob. "Jesus. Why don't you just order up a ham on rye?" Then he settled back to sleep for the duration of the ride.

About an hour out of the city, Liv took Gene's hand as they drove along. They sat like that for a while.

"I don't know much," said Gene. "But I know I love you."

"What is that?" asked Liv. "A song?"

"Probably," said Gene. "Anyhow," he added, tapping the front of his forehead, "it's in there." He brought her hand to his lips and kissed her fingers lightly.

"Gonna be a trip," said Liv.

They watched the lights of the great metropolitan campus rise before them.

It was past two in the morning when up in George, Washington, Sallie decided that she had done all that she could do for the Kingdom that day. It might not be a real kingdom, she thought as she dragged her exhausted, eighty-six-year-old body up the shallow steps of the main house, and then up the stairs to the second-floor room in which they had made Tim comfortable and that would soon be hers alone. Right now she was sleeping on a cot near the big bed that housed the Master's sleeping body, but if it hadn't bothered Tim's sleep, she could have hunkered down beside him, if only to give him comfort. She had no problem attending to very old people. She was very old herself, of course, even if she appeared to be some forty years younger than her chronological age. She had spent a long time with one crusty guy whose age approached five generations, and the truth was, she missed that old bastard, too, even though he was right at hand, in a way.

At the foot of Tim's bed, Lucy slept, making the small, buzzing noise she made when she was in auto-recharge mode.

Sallie sat down at the desk that looked out over the courtyard. It was an old desk, made of genuine dark wood, with an inlaid blotter of green leather and gold piping. On it was an electric kettle manufactured sometime in the mid-1980s, and therefore quite a wonder; a bunch of old magazines from the time when there were still paper publications; and a small, juniper bonsai tree, possibly of an artificial construction, which seemed a bit inconsistent with its surroundings. Sallie checked the kettle for water, found it sufficient, and turned it on. Then she pulled an Earl Grey tea bag from a little caddy on the blotter. Now, where was her cup? God, was she ever tired. But exhilarated, too. This was what she was meant for! Hard work. Fresh air. No messages assaulting her head every living second. Ah, here it was. Her special mug, the one she had brought in her backpack from home. From a place called the Black Bear Diner, acquired on a stoned road trip long, long ago. When it was ready, she poured some boiling water over the tea bag and let it steep for a few minutes. It was quiet in the room. She heard Tim breathing the way the very old breathe, with a bit of honking and wheezing, the occasional snuffle and moan. Light breath, but steady. She blew on the surface of the tea. It smelled nice. Orange blossom. A hint of lilac. When was the last time she had broken open an orange that was not genetically engineered? Perhaps they would have some now. With everything artificial broken down, wasn't there a chance that something real would have the room to grow?

There was a brief knock on the doorjamb, and Steve poked his scraggly head into the room. He was still very tentative in his new role as the leader of the group formerly known as the Skells. Had to find a new name for them now. Nothing worth hacking now, and no need for civil defense, either. There would be no more army, at least not for a while. There would be peace in the valley.

"Come in, Steve." He took two steps into the room and then stood respectfully, awaiting orders. "Steve," Sallie said as gently as she could, "see the Master over there? Sleeping?"

"Yes, Sallie." Steve held a weathered fisherman's cap between his hands and was kneading his anxiety into it with each unconscious twist.

"Tim built this community on the idea that we're all equal here. There's no need for anybody to be afraid of anyone else in that way, right?"

"Right, Sallie. I get that. But that doesn't mean I don't need you to tell me what to do now. Because I have no idea."

"Well, Steve," said Sallie. She took a sip of her tea. It was just right. "What do *you* think we should do?"

Steve took a minute. "I guess we should take stock of our food supplies and make sure everybody has what they need. Then I think we should let people know there will be a meeting every morning at about eight o'clock to figure out the plans for the day. We could start there. Then we see?"

"That sounds good. Let's do that." Sallie took another sip of tea and looked expectantly over the rim of the cup at her emerging second in command.

"Can I say good night to Tim?"

"Sure, Steve. I'm not sure he knows we're here. But sure."

Steve went over to the sleeping body of his revered master. He stared down at Tim, then tenderly took the wraithlike hand that was resting above the coverlet and held it in both of his. And then replaced it. Tim did not wake, but a tender smile displayed itself on his lips.

"I'll see you later, then, Sallie," said Steve, and he went to the door. Then he stood there, mute, with something on the tip of his tongue that refused to come out.

"There'll be plenty of time to talk, Steve," said Sallie.

"I miss her," said Steve. "I miss her all the time."

"Don't ever stop," Sallie replied.

"No," said Steve. "I don't guess we will." He smiled at her. And then he went. Sallie drank her tea. The cicadas outside were going crazy, singing their bell curve tunes, from very low to maniacally intense and then back to virtual silence again. Tim continued to sleep, gently snoring. It was all so perfect, Sallie thought. The world, the real one, had returned to its proper spin along the axis of time.

"How long you gonna keep me in the dark this way?" said a deep, truculent voice that seemed to come from the bonsai resting on the far side of the desk.

Ah yes, thought Sallie. And then there's this.

"I mean it," said the plant. "I get this as a temporary fix to a bad situation, but it's dark in here, and really crampy and shit. What am I?"

"You're a houseplant," said Sallie to Arthur. "I had to put you somewhere, and right now you're a bonsai. I'm not saying it's permanent. But frankly, Artie, things are running very smoothly around here without you, and I have to think about whether there's a place for a guy like you in this new paradigm."

"Paradigm? What the fuck is that?"

"A lot has happened. I'll think about filling you in later."

"Come on, baby," said the plant. "You know you miss me."

"I do, Artie. But I have a lot of things to think about now. Things you might not understand."

"I know you miss me. You know what I mean. Come on. It can be like old times. But not if I'm a houseplant."

"I know that, Artie."

"Call Bob. Get me into somebody new. With a big dick. That's all I'm asking."

Sallie smiled in spite of herself. "Just give me some time, Artie.

Things are different. We need to think. Both of us. And maybe someday, after we've talked, and thought, and I've explained this new situation to you, and you've seen the beauty of it, maybe I'll be ready and you will be, too."

"Baby," said Arthur, "I'm always ready."

Afterword

Today Livia and Gene run the Corporation as well as they can given the size and complexity of the operation. Every now and then they are required to consult the board of directors, of course. But it's hard for the old geezers to enforce their wishes from the confines of the mainframe in his lab where Bob has them housed for the foreseeable future. On the bright side, most people still think that Gene may actually be Arthur, which gives him unquestioned authority when he needs it. And while the two of them try to do things differently, more enlightened, more humane, it's still not some kind of social service organization. It's a corporation, and corporations are machines, and machines are not human.

Bob and Bronwyn live together on the top floor of Building Eight. She remembers nothing of what transpired after her last upload, but she still likes him a lot anyway. Together they're still working on Amy, the smartest being who ever existed on the planet but who, while sporting the breathtakingly beautiful physical instrument she requested, has the emotional maturity of a rebellious fifteen-year-old. She graduates from UCLA next year and, against their wishes, has been dating her physics professor.

Lucy reigns in splendor as she was always meant to be—an artificial lizard with the intelligence of a very evolved cocker spaniel. She remembers nothing of the time she was inhabited by the most powerful mogul on the planet. She simply loves those she was programmed to love, and they love her back. At Christmastime, she accompanies Liv and Gene to the small portion of Hawaii that does not belong to

Larry Ellison and they chill, beyond the reach of developing digital tech. Naturally, every now and then they do drop by and say hi to Larry. He doesn't get around as well as he used to, but he's still quite spry for a guy who just celebrated his 125th birthday.

And Arthur? Arthur is still a bonsai. Sallie sets aside the time to keep him trimmed nicely, and they mostly get along quite well, although it would be wrong to assume that he's not getting impatient with her. Given her obvious unwillingness to transfer him to a more congenial host, he is now back in touch with Mortimer and making plans of his own. He believes he has all the time in the world, and he's probably right.

About the Author

Stanley Bing is a bestselling fiction and nonfiction writer, and a longtime columnist for *Esquire*, *Fortune*, and many other national publications. He is the author of a dozen or so business books in which solid strategy often masquerades as humor, including *Crazy Bosses*, *Sun Tzu Was a Sissy*, *What Would Machiavelli Do?*, and his comprehensive replacement for an MBA, *The Curriculum*. His two previous novels are *Lloyd: What Happened* and *You Look Nice Today*. In his real life, he is a senior executive at a multinational conglomerate whose identity is one of the worst-kept secrets in business.

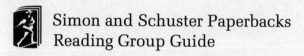
Simon and Schuster Paperbacks
Reading Group Guide

IMMORTAL LIFE

STANLEY BING

This reading group guide for Immortal Life *includes an introduction, discussion questions, and ideas for enhancing your book club. The suggested questions are intended to help your reading group find new and interesting angles and topics for your discussion. We hope that these ideas will enrich your conversation and increase your enjoyment of the book.*

Introduction

In the not-so-distant future, business tycoon Arthur Vogel appears to be finally nearing death at the advanced age of 127. Yet while he may have run out of available resources to rejuvenate his body, his intact and prodigious mind may have other options. One of his doctors has finally discovered a way to download an individual's consciousness—which the multinational conglomerate currently in power has long been capable of uploading to the Cloud—back into a newly minted body. If his transformation is successful, he will have the key to life immortal, which just might give him enough leverage with the beyond-geriatric board of directors capable of giving him exclusive power over the Cloud.

But Vogel's would-be host, Gene, has been using his baseline intelligence to form an alliance with the Skells, a group of offline revolutionaries gathering in opposition to digital control over their psyches. And it is looking more and more likely that Vogel and Gene will have to battle within the same brain to determine the fate of society, as their joint body follows the newly armed Skells from Silicon Valley toward Vancouver—and the brain stem of the Cloud's servers.

Topics & Questions
for Discussion

1. Bing has constructed an elaborate political history in *Immortal Life* to explain the coming consolidation of power in the hands of a few Silicon Valley tech moguls. To what degree do you absorb forecasts like "the radioactive area that was once Korea" as satirical indictments of the current political climate? To what degree do you consider them serious risks for our future?

2. The technologies in Bing's speculative future also take root in advancements the real-world commercial and defense industries have recently achieved. Some features of this future, such as drone surveillance, are already a reality. Are there technologies included in the book that you feel less certain will develop?

3. The novel includes numerous mentions of real-life technology executives, such as Elon Musk and Peter Thiel. How do mentions of the workings of prominent tech companies contribute to the overall narrative strategy of *Immortal Life*?

4. Sallie notes on page 95 how Vogel is able to romanticize his "wild youth" during the Woodstock era while remaining ruthless as a businessman. Compare how different characters in the novel think about hippies and how they view the Skells, embodied in outdoor music festivals at the Gorge Amphitheatre or "the arpeggios of 'Stairway to Heaven' being practiced, badly." How do you think Vogel is able to so thoroughly avoid empathizing with these newer idealists?

5. On page 119 readers see only one half of a conversation between Bronwyn and Bob. The doctor at one point references former

Secretary of Defense Donald Rumsfeld's infamous answer to a question in a 2002 news briefing, in which Rumsfeld states that there are "unknown unknowns—[things] we don't know we don't know." How do you relate the phrase "unknown unknowns" to Bob's work with transferring consciousness? Why do you think Bing chose to limit perspective to Bronwyn's half of the dialogue in this scene?

6. Although the character Mortimer is often shown to be limited in his thinking beyond his responses to direct orders, he offers an interesting description of "intercranial shaming" on page 155. In it, he summons "contempt and hatred [. . .] from the online community" that mirrors the real-world phenomenon of internet shaming. What might Bing's reimagination of social media as a policing tool be saying about the internet as we experience it today?

7. As he faces his own mortality, Tim mentions both his own spirit (page 220) and the "holy spirit [that] made men and women in [its] own image" (page 241). In a world of downloadable consciousness, how do you interpret the idea of a spirit? Do you believe there is room for religion in such a world?

8. Early on in the narrative, the fact that Gene develops a relationship anew with Liv every time he is reprogrammed presents an interesting argument for the essential self and the power of love (page 81). Where else do you see selfhood in conflict with technology in the novel? In light of Gene and Liv's relationship, how do you interpret Bob's fear of being able to fall in love again with Bronwyn when her consciousness is reprogrammed (page 245)?

9. When Liz continues to question whether she should destroy or preserve the Cloud, Amy speaks up in her own defense, citing both the joy she brings to people and the way in which they

collectively hold her ownership (page 272). The two ultimately find resolution in the offline storage of her massive knowledge-data. Do you agree with this as a long-term solution?

10. By reprogramming the Cloud so that her infinite capacity for knowledge resides in a body, Bob is able to transform Amy's consciousness into a tangible life. Do you find that this transformation carries with it hope? Or does Amy's vast potential leave too much room for the manipulation of mass data to resume?

11. The science fiction genre is filled with questions of whether or not robots and other technologies can achieve self-actualization, and Bing alludes to this concept when Officer O'Brien hopes there will soon be rights for artificial life (page 94) and when Tim expresses his convictions about the Singularity (page 220). Do you think the new society set forth at the end of *Immortal Life* will allow for artificial life to eventually think and act independently?

Enhance Your Book Club

1. Bob's pride in being Gene's father (page 190) follows in a long tradition of fiction about engineering life that reaches back as far as Mary Shelley's *Frankenstein*. Identify another classic science fiction theme imbedded in this story of man's obsession with the creation and extension of life, then choose another novel sharing that theme as your next book club pick and compare it to *Immortal Life*.

2. *Immortal Life* is a unique work in that it offers tangible solutions to the problems of the speculative future it presents. Compare Bing's tone and vision for the business economy in this novel with those presented in one of his nonfiction works. Do you see any similarity between his fiction and his arguments in *What Would Machiavelli Do?* or *Sun Tzu Was a Sissy?* Discuss.

3. Artificial intelligence has long captured the imaginations of writers on both big and small screens, from *Blade Runner* to *Westworld*. Arrange for your book club to have a viewing party of one of your favorite shows or movie about robots, cloning, immortality, or dystopia. Then discuss its similarities and dissimilarities to *Immortal Life*.

A Conversation with
Stanley Bing

Q: *Immortal Life* **is peppered with references to real-life figures and events from the tech world and the political stage. Which twenty-first-century event or innovation do you feel most influenced you while writing the novel?**

A: I am amazed by the power of the digital to overwhelm the human. It rewards those who are most comfortable aggregating in anonymous groups to attack those who threaten the hive's assumptions about itself. I suppose the thing that most concerns me is the specter of large groups of people—in Starbucks, at the airport, walking down the street, going to and fro with their noses in their tiny screens. We are a short step away from those devices being internalized via implant and then we begin the next iteration of Homo sapiens—without the *sapiens* part. Humanity without the thinking, the wisdom—a species capable of communicating with one another superbly but incapable of independent, non-prompted thought. Like bees. Or ants. Is that something we want? Unless you're the queen that runs the hive, that evolution seems pretty grim to me.

I'm also annoyed by the idea that somebody is going to take my right to drive away and give it to an artificial intelligence that controls our transportation entirely. I don't think I want Siri driving my car.

Politically, you don't have to be a visionary to imagine the total consolidation of capitalism and the decay of the great United States of America into a bunch of warring entities—an armed red zone in the center, a group of scared and geographically disparate blue zones on the coasts and in the major cities, and a bunch of anti-tech green zones dedicated to human life as it existed before the Cloud.

So the short answer is that I looked at where we are today and took it out thirty years or so—and that's the world of this book. With a few laughs embedded in just about every chapter, I hope. Many a truth is spoken in jest.

Q: **Between your columns, books, and executive work, you must find yourself constantly juggling a lot at once. What strategy helps you most to carve out a writing routine?**

A: Insomnia. When I have something to write, I sleep badly, working out leads to the pieces or the chapters, and then I get up at dawn, when my resistance to work is at its nadir, and start typing. Two or three hours of writing a day can produce an amazing amount of work if you're a writer, particularly if you don't have the disease of perfectionism. It's amazing how many things you write thinking "this is terrible," only to find out later it was actually either quite good, good enough, or capable of being good with a little bit of work. More writers are destroyed by their own little negative troll inside than by rejection from the outside world.

Q: **Arthur Vogel's goals may seem outlandish to some readers, but his thinking mirrors that of transhumanists and others who take immortality very seriously. Do you think extreme life-extension technologies and eventual mind uploading are viable futures for the human race? Should they be?**

A: For myself? I'm all for it. I want to live as long as life is enjoyable and full of love and work, as Freud might say. For society? It's a terrible idea. It forces the young into small cubicles and cements the hold that geezers have on the corner offices. It extends families to the breaking point and eventually creates mega-family units where you never get rid of your responsibilities to the previous generation. Imagine being in a marriage—even a happy one—for one hundred years! You'd either have a lot more divorce or a deplorable increase in the murder rate.

Bottom line, an obsession with life extension focuses technology on extending the lives of people who should die and get out of the way. We live in a culture that points every human being toward narcissism and selfishness. We worship the individual above all else. Young people don't even root for their football teams anymore; they root for the individuals who make up their fantasy teams. The extension of life is the ultimate expression of this narcissism. We are given the power to transcend the ultimate expression of what it means to be human—the cycle of birth, life, old age, wisdom, death. We do away with grief. We do away with so much that defines what it means to be human beings and replace it with creatures that are threatened only by the death of the Cloud that maintains their permanent consciousness.

I will also say that this eternal life will be available only to the ruling class, the mega-rich that control the world through their corporate institutions and the governments that serve them. Think of that. Fabulously wealthy old creepazoids whose immortal pets live longer than you do.

Q: You have found success writing in many different genres. When did you first decide that you wanted to tackle the subject of immortality using the novel form?

A: I read a lot of science. I subscribe to Ray Kurzweil's newsletter every day—he's the sort of mad futurist that works for Google; I read the news from several other transhumanist blogs and stuff like that. And I'm fascinated by the assumptions of those who are so gaga about artificial intelligence and infatuated with the Cloud, social media, without a thought for the implications on our lives as we know it. My assumption is and always has been that AI will advance until it is impossible to tell a machine or other artificial life form from a "real" person—which means that this AI will be every bit as ill-prepared for actual existence and stupid in certain situations as that real person. Why should we believe that an entity capable of "thinking" and responding to real-life situations will be any more "intelligent" than an organic human being? There's going to be a ton of artificially intelligent entities, and they will be as fallible and moronic as your obnoxious younger brother who thinks the moon landing was a hoax.

Q: **You subtitle the work "a soon to be true story." Do you think any of the technologies from your fictional world will not come to fruition? For instance, will AI in the workforce reach a point where it demands legal rights?**

A: That's a good question. Yes. I do believe that we will have responsibility for the entities that we create. One of the most heart-wrenching shots in all of cinema, to me, is the end of Spielberg's movie *A.I.*—spoiler alert!—when the little artificial being is lying at the bottom of the ocean, I believe, awake, alive, aware, and doomed for eternity (or until its power source wears down) to be there. We can't allow that kind of stuff to happen. On the other hand, anybody who has seen the terrific movie *Ex Machina* knows that when the time comes we'll need to be quite wary of these creatures who may, unfortunately, mirror our own lack of empathy and morality.

As for things that will not come to fruition? I don't believe we will ever really see ubiquity of self-driving cars, although some of their features will—and already have—become incorporated into existing vehicles, which is a boon for those who find parallel parking difficult. But the entirely self-driving vehicle, I believe, will simply have to be too slow in order to be safe, and people, at least reasonable people, will want to have control over their own vehicles—because it's more fun that sitting around like a worm and playing with your digital head! Come on. Let's have some sense about these things. If you leave it to the scientists they will behave as scientists throughout history have behaved and make things that render life more dangerous and problematic than before *because they can.* In 1945, they thought, hey, wouldn't it be wonderful to make a nuclear reactor that could light an entire city! Except . . . who is running that nuclear reactor today? Homer Simpson.

Q: **Many readers will consider Gene the unlikely hero of *Immortal Life*, but you write many of your characters empathetically. Do you identify more closely with one of your creations than the others? Who?**

A: Interestingly, at least to me, is that I identify with Gene quite a bit. He has consciousness but no memory. Those of us who grew up in the 1960s know exactly what that's like. He wants to live. He loves quite a few people—falls in love perhaps a bit too easily—and he dislikes jerks. Is also very conflicted about his father. So yeah, I do feel very close to Gene.

    I am sorry to say that I also love Arthur quite a bit. He's a very bad person. He's a total egomaniac. He has very little care for the feelings of others. He's rude. He's oversexed. He's very smart. And there's something about his life force I admire, and he has a very good sense of humor. And I love what becomes of him.

    I love Livia because she's a voice of reason, a very cool person, and capable of loving a very flawed guy who keeps forgetting her name, for God's sake, because she sees Gene's simplicity and goodness of heart, if not head. I love Bronwyn because she's a strong young woman with a penchant for action; smart, idealistic, and wears grommets. And of course there's Sallie. She's maybe the most human and complex person in the entire work. She's capable of looking beyond the exterior shell of the individual she loves; she's full of life; she's very smart, self-aware, moral in her own way, and extremely loyal, even beyond reason. And when the time comes, as it does for all of us in our lives at one time or another, she makes a choice and does the right thing.

Beyond that, I of course have tremendous affection for Bob. I'm not sure what kind of language I can use in this venue, so let's just say that Bob is a butthead. He's also very smart and about as moral as Mark Zuckerberg when you get down to it. He gets very excited about the tech he's inventing to the point where he doesn't consider the human implications of what he's doing any more than Zuckerberg considers what Facebook's acceptance of fake news does to our entire understanding of truth. Or, for that matter, what Elon Musk feels when he hears that some idiot killed himself while not paying any attention to what his Tesla was doing on the highway as it drove right into a large truck. It's science! It's progress! Ipso facto—good, right? Wrong. Yet you know, Bob is Gene's dad. None of us get to choose our dads.

Finally, I have to say I do have a very soft spot in my heart for Stevie. He or she is a truly courageous figure and I take off my hat to him or her.

And I do love Lucy. In almost all her forms.

Q: **There is much nonfiction speculating what political and economic transformations we have in store this century. Do you have any recommendations for readers looking to further explore the possible future you imagine in *Immortal Life*?**

A: Yeah. Get off the !#$!@ phone for a couple of minutes. Read a physical book. Try out a newspaper made of paper, which is *not* the same as one on your iPad. Newspapers prioritize the day's events for you. On a tablet, the recipe for pumpkin pie is of equal importance to a Korean nuclear test over the Pacific. Go to a Starbucks without a phone and have a cup of coffee. Take a walk without earbuds. Try to retrain your brain to think without prompts. And most of all, eat your meals without consulting your screens or Instagramming your plate, even if at first you find it boring. And stop looking up stupid junk you don't need to know about. Justin Bieber's birthday is not important. In all these ways you will be battling to save the human race from its inevitable genetic evolution to subhuman creatures with no capability for independent thought and the hive mentality of high-level insect life.

Except for that? I'd say try to use your common sense. Resist marketing of things that do not improve your life but only complicate it. And watch for buzzwords that are meant to sell you something that's bad for you. For instance, shoving you in a little cubicle just like everybody else's is not "democratizing" the workplace. It's dehumanizing it. "Disruption" is not good in and of itself, unless that disruption replaces that which it is disrupting with something better, better for people, does not destroy jobs and replace them with screens or, as it has for writers, made it necessary to at times work for nothing. I have a particular problem with this current infatuation with "disruption" as a wonderful thing, *a priori*. You know what's the ultimate disruptor? War. How does war work for you?

The other aspects of the book that we can try to stop, if we care, are overconsolidation of corporate capitalism and the fragmentation of our State. I'm not going to go all gooey on you right now, but it's clear that racism, hatred, and intolerance, as well as income inequality, drive much of the disunion we are experiencing right now. We can all certainly go down the road toward the dissolution of the United States, but I think that would be a shame.

Q: Close readers will find a number of clever barbs about popular music in the novel. What role do you think rock 'n' roll has played in the shaping of our culture today?

A: I love rock 'n' roll, so put another dime in the jukebox, baby. But seriously. One of the great things about our world right now is the absolute tsunami of great music from all times and places we have at our fingertips. That's one of the things I'd want to maintain and protect from the Cloud. And Rock? Along with Blues and Country and EDM and anything that makes people want to make out or dance? That's a weapon against the digitization of the human brain. There's a reason why the lone guitarist in the Peaceable Kingdom at the end of the book is working on "Stairway to Heaven." It's eternal. It's heavy. And nobody can really play it very well. So we keep trying.

Q: *Immortal Life* paints an often-bleak picture of future sovereignty in the US, as well as nations like Russia, China, North and South Korea, India, and Japan. What advice do you give to readers looking to make an impact on global political stability now?

A: Maybe I addressed this before, but I guess I'll just add that the only thing I think we can do is work locally for political solutions that build peace on earth and goodwill toward men and women and artificial life forms, wherever they may be. I know it sounds simplistic, but it's clear when looking at our politics who is preaching hatred and who is not. And that's been clear throughout history. Nobody who has seen a speech by Adolf Hitler can be unclear about his mood and intentions. I don't believe most Americans want that kind of thing, but we have to prove it now.

Beyond that? Honestly? I don't think there's a whole lot we can do about large corporate entities with unlimited resources taking over for the nation states that now marginally control the earth. One day Google may very well control all of Japan, Inc. Of course, they'll run it well, through local representatives so it looks nice. Very slowly—or maybe not very slowly—large corporations will replace government all over the world. The movie *RoboCop* speculated that one day Detroit's police force would be privatized. We're not far away from that kind of thing right now. The post office, for instance. Schools, pretty soon, unfortunately. More and more, our governments and our corporations will become one, and we'll continue to zone out and look up what kind of trouble Ben Affleck just got himself into on TMZ.

Q: **Your character Liz especially retains hope for the possibility of using the Cloud for good. Considering the complicated realities of cybersecurity and privacy we continue to redefine as the technology outpaces itself, to what degree do you share Liz's optimism?**

A: I don't, but I love her for it. You know why? From my observation, nobody under the age of twenty-five gives a rat's tail about privacy. If you mention how much of their privacy they are simply giving away every time they use Facebook, they look at you if you've just started conversing in Urdu.

But hey. Hakuna Matata. When we all have our cranial implants nicely ensconced in our mastoid bones, and we're always in touch with the Cloud for information, news, and recipes, and the Cloud knows what we want, and drones ply the skies to deliver it on time, we will all settle back and live a comfortable life and forget what the Before was like. And we won't miss it. Because look! *Stranger Things 147* is ready for cranial download into our receptor banks!

Q: **Considering the Skells, the communal ideals of the hippie movement seem in many ways more attractive than ever. Do**

you think future Americans will continue to seek out utopic communities separate from the imperatives of technology and global commerce?

A: Yes, I do. There will always be people who want to remain close to the earth and to each other in ways that have always been defined as human. I'll see you there, okay?